I0557501

CHASING
KANE

ANDREA RANDALL

www.andrearandall.com

Published by Cincinnatus Press
South Hadley, Massachusetts
United States of America

PRAISE FOR ANDREA RANDALL

"Intelligent, thought-provoking, heart-twisting. Andrea Randall proves once again that she is an eloquent writer and creator of characters who will stay with you long after you finish the book."
   —Melissa Brown, author of Wife Number Seven

"An inside look at life in a Christian university ... the good, bad, and the ugly. Andrea Randall tells a story that's not easy to tell with conviction and ease."
   — Willow Aster, Author of True Love Story

...the story of a girl trying to find out who she is and where she belongs in a much bigger picture than she could've ever imagined. This is a book for everyone, not just the Jesus Freaks
   —Maggi Myers, Author of The Final Piece and Lily Love

By far one of my favorite reads of the year. Put all your preconceived notions away and devour this book.
   —Lindsay Sparkes, Beauty, Brains, and Books Book Blog

"It is a beautifully written story ... this is a book you need to experience for yourself."
   —Pamela Carrion, The Book Avenue

BOOKS BY ANDREA RANDALL

In The Stillness

Nocturne (with Charles Sheehan-Miles)

Something's Come Up (with Michelle Pace)

Jesus Freaks
Sins of the Father
The Prodigal
The Broken Ones

November Blue
Ten Days of Perfect
Reckless Abandon
Sweet Forty-Two
Marrying Ember
Bo & Ember

DEDICATION

For Charles:

My Happily Ever After in the
beautiful chaos that is our lives.

Forever.

ACKNOWLEDGEMENTS

I want to thank Marla from Proofingtyle for helping make this book as polished as possible, given we're all humans on this boat, Randall's Bitchin Betas for bearing with me during the sometimes stop-and-go process that is my writing, Randall's Readers for supporting every project I undertake, and, of course, Charles—you make this life easy, even in the hard days.

CHAPTER ONE

REGAN

"YOU REALLY ARE a stupid ass, you know that?" Georgia rolled her fire-brimmed eyes, shoving a seagull-embroidered pillow into CJ's chest.

"Nice to see you to, G," CJ shot back with his annoyingly juvenile grin. The one *all* the girls fell over themselves to be on the receiving end of.

"Regan? Any comments for your trash heap of a cousin?" my blushing bride gestured to CJ, speaking in a perfectly normal tone, as if discussing the weather. She continued throwing things—blankets on the couch, fresh towels too. Her face grew redder by the second.

I shrugged. "I … I just don't … know," I admitted with a humored sigh. "Anyone want a beer?" My hand was already on the fridge, because I sure as hell needed one.

Georgia ignored my attempt at passivity, continuing her assault on CJ. Her Eastern Massachusetts accent was always particularly thick and rough when reading someone the riot act. She dropped R's left and right. "She's a good girl, you piece of shit. I thought you guys had something," Georgia said of CJ's girlfriend—ex-girlfriend—Frankie.

CJ tossed his backpack on the floor by the door, offering little more than a shrug against the onslaught of my wife's words. He stood at least a solid eight inches, at least, over Georgia, but that didn't stop her and, frankly, he's always seemed a bit intimidated by her. I like that in both of them.

"We did have something," he started, annoyed like maybe he and Georgia had had this conversation before. They probably had. "I can't pretend to be someone I'm not—you know that. This is just a break," he said rather unconvincingly, which surprised me given he's usually such a smooth talker.

"It's not just a break if she has half a brain in her head," Georgia mumbled under her breath before grabbing her keys. "I'm heading down to the shop to bake. Stop down when you guys are headed to the studio?'

I nodded. "Yep."

"Do something with him," she said with disgust, gesturing to CJ like he was week-old garbage.

I laughed. "He's your best friend, love."

She shot me a death stare. "He's your cousin, and was long before I came around."

There was never any good thing to say to her when she was in this mood, so I just shrugged, shaking my head.

Georgia stopped at the behemoth in the doorway long enough to assess him with a scrutinizing gaze. "What happened, CJ? I mean, honestly? Why are you throwing everything away?"

He didn't answer. For the first time in all the years I'd seen those two interact, CJ had no comeback to dish out to Georgia. She shook her head, and she was gone in a hurricane, leaving CJ and I in relative silence. He stared at me, pulling an amused grin.

All I could do was grin back, gesturing with an amber bottle. "Beer?"

"Please." He took the drink from me and walked to the huge window-wall on the far side of the apartment Georgia and I had lived in for years; even back when it was two apartments and we were just neighbors, before we fell in love and knocked down all kinds of walls.

CJ took a long swig. "What's up her ass?"

"You," I snorted.

He sighed, heavy and loud. "It's complicated."

"Clearly," I offered, toeing the line between wanting him to talk and not wanting to push him away.

He took another long sip. "Maybe I'll turn out to be like him after all."

"Dude." I put my hand on his shoulder briefly, shocked at his honesty, "No. It's not possible. You're a good guy."

"With a track record to the contrary." He looked out into the water, the weight of whatever he was holding in shone across his intense eyes.

"You and Frankie had a great record, right? Only, what? One major fight-break thing in the last three years?" I'd never seen CJ so happy, in fact, than when he was in that relationship.

He bit his bottom lip, shaking his head and letting out a small growl. Suddenly, like the previous few minutes hadn't even happened, his old frat-boy face was lit up and ready for action. "Welp, less baggage for the tour, I guess, huh?"

"You know, I'm thrilled we get to tour together, but you didn't have to break up with Frankie on my account."

CJ shot me a sideways glance, reaching for my face. "And you didn't have to grow a beard on mine, you scruffy bastard. What do the kids call that nowadays? A lumbersexual? You've got the man bun and everything, though you'd have to put on a little muscle to achieve full lumberjack status."

Without looking at him, I reached out and punched his side. "I was wearing this man bun before anyone gave it a name."

"Yeah," he replied, "whatever. You look like a girl with a beard."

I laughed, causing a few bubbles of carbonated hops to infiltrate my nose. "You're a class act, CJ Kane, you know that?"

We stared for a while in silence out at the calm Pacific Ocean beneath us. I never asked CJ many questions when he showed up on my doorstep, and this time was no different. It was the first time he'd mentioned his father in years, though. Even if it was just by pronoun. I was unprepared for the conversational atom-bomb, and half-hoped he'd bring it up again before another few years had passed. It was such a mess, though, I wouldn't blame him if he buried it down deep for another decade, or so.

CJ's trip to California was planned, but his showing up solo wasn't, which prompted Georgia's outburst. Frankie had seemed, by all accounts, to ground CJ's wandering ways for at least a little bit. And, I'll be damned, despite his stereotypical drummer, rocker-boy ways, CJ really seemed to settle a little with Frankie.

The summer they met he shared more about himself with her than he did with almost anyone else in his life. This I heard mostly second-hand from Georgia, who dissects relationships on a level of expert I could never reach. Also, she talks to CJ more about things that guys just don't with each other, and became friends with Frankie. Frankie assumed from the beginning that she couldn't change CJ's bad-boy lifestyle, and their relationship started out as fun. But CJ was the first one to want more, which shocked the hell out of G and I. Also, he opened up to Frankie about his extreme success and wealth in the computer industry, an area in which he's notoriously silent. His success with social media and various apps he'd sold off and basically rolled in the money from. Not only did he not normally talk with anyone about it, he never talked about it with the women he entertained. Georgia and I took all of that as excellent signs pointing in the right direction for a guy who used to go through women like beer.

Yet here he was, alone in my living room drinking said beer like none of it happened.

"All right you punk, ready to head over to GSE?" I took the empty bottle from his hand and tossed it into our overflowing recycling bin.

He stretched his arms overhead and walked to the door, rummaging through his bag for a minute before producing two beat-up drumsticks. "Yeah buddy!" he said with the enthusiasm of a toddler on Christmas morning.

Because CJ essentially was a toddler on Christmas morning, all the time.

***

Grounded Sound Entertainment, GSE, is the studio I'd been contracted under for the last several years. I met the manager, Yardley Honeywell, through two of my best friends who have been artists with them for just a hair longer than I, though they live and work primarily on the East Coast. I'd played with Bo and Ember off and on in Cape Cod, Massachusetts for a while before they came out here to play, secured a sick record deal, and I was granted one with a new group—Celtic Summer—to boot.

Celtic Summer included myself, a violinist, Shaughn—another violinist—and Chris, a drummer. We achieved formidable market success for a unique band such as ours, and were taking a year off to rest after what was basically a three-year, non-stop tour, and to pursue our individual interests. For me, my only interest ever was playing. I didn't care if I was by myself or with a professional orchestra, I just had to keep playing. My love was always with the violin.

CJ had slowly tired of the Cape Cod summer pub circuit he'd played for over a decade, and talked for a while about coming out here to find a new band to play with. It was hard to do what he wanted—to walk into an established group as a drummer, which is the position most relied upon by any group. But, he was determined.

I had a quick conversation a few months ago with Yardley about the possibility of setting up some tour dates with other bands signed under GSE, which would allow CJ and I to stand as our own act without having to carry a whole show—a tough act to sell with just one drummer and one violinist, but wicked when it worked.

Yardley, seemingly always eager to consider my input, complied. Georgia was certain Yardley had a thing for me, but I always liked to think she had a thing for my talent, and was willing to keep me loyal to the GSE label.

So, at the start of this summer, CJ and I were headed over to GSE to record a few numbers that the marketing department could use in promo materials as they put together a lineup that would take us across the country and back, over the course of the next six months. We would head east as summer heated up, and back west as it turned to fall and winter.

While I'd spent most of the last few years on the road, I was looking forward to this particular summer, as I was sure it would be my last set of long touring for a while, since Georgia and I had begun thinking about starting a family. She insisted nothing would have to change about our current lifestyle, but that was her way of being her borderline-martyr self. It was no use telling her my traveling days would be numbered once that pregnancy test was positive.

"That hottie manager of yours going to be here?" CJ asked as we pulled up to the sizable brick building that housed GSE.

I sighed, turning off the car and leaning my head back against the headrest. "Listen," I started, but CJ cut me off.

"I know, I know," he said, grumpily. "No screwing the staff."

"It's not just the staff, Casanova, she's my boss. And your boss for the next six months. You're going to have a contract and all kinds of big-boy, grownup stuff."

He flipped me the bird and exited the car.

"I'm serious," I said, falling into step with him across the parking lot.

"Me too, asshat. You don't have to talk to me like I'm a kid."

I took a deep breath. "Then, just for this afternoon, don't act like one, okay?"

I loved CJ like a brother, and that meant we fought like brothers sometimes. He's only a few years younger than I am, but maturity wise … Let's just say that even though we went to different high schools, I ended up nursing the broken hearts of one too many of his conquests to count. I was not signing up for that this summer, and I needed to make that clear.

I never took my talent as a means to an end with girls. My talent was the means and the end. With CJ, though? His motives had always been as cloudy as his morals, before he met Frankie, anyway, and I had no desire to clean up one single mess of his anymore.

He said nothing else as we walked into the studio and headed for the main recording room in the back, where we were to meet with Yardley and some members of the GSE staff who hadn't yet had the pleasure of meeting my 6-foot-one-million-inch cousin, whose shoulders are as wide as they were tall, despite his middle school maturity level. We are the same height, though CJ takes up nearly triple the space I do. He could have been one hell of a football player in high school if he'd bothered to keep his grades up and his dick in his pants as far as the coach's daughter was concerned.

Alas, it wasn't meant to be.

CJ and Yardley had met before. Years before, when I signed my first major recording contract. I was praying to God Yardley didn't remember any interaction she'd had with him then, because I couldn't remember, and honestly CJ could be one giant, walking liability.

"CJ," Yardley greeted as we entered. "It's good to see you again." Her genuine pleasure in his presence gave my anxiety a rest for the time being.

"You, too," CJ answered with mild provocation as he took her hand in his and kissed the top of her knuckles as if he was the Duke of anything except sleazy bars. Old CJ seemed to be back in full force, and I wasn't sure I liked it even a little bit.

Yardley blushed, though her eyes grew dark as if she were silently cursing herself for being so easily taken by the obvious player in the room. I wanted to offer my condolences, to tell her it really wasn't her fault— that I'd seen this play out for nearly twenty years and she really couldn't help whatever supernatural pheromones he released—but I kept my mouth shut and decided to let it ride. Yardley was one hell of a businesswoman, and I knew she'd have him wrapped around her finger in no time. CJ would never see it coming.

"So," she continued, gracefully shaking her hand free of CJ's grasp, "your cousin tells me you're something of a percussion prodigy?" She tilted her head, challenging him. I grinned.

CJ's tongue ran across his lips as he flashed a charming grin. "If he says ..." he challenged right back.

"All right then." She rolled up the sleeves of her bright-pink shirt and folded her arms across her chest. "Prove it."

I half expected Yardley to choose a song for the two of us to play together. Instead, she waved me into the sound booth with her. Normally a staunch boardroom type, Yardley had relaxed some over the previous couple of years. Working with a bunch of hippie musicians in California will do that to a girl, I guess.

She'd traded in pantyhose and heels and skirts for jeans and T-shirts most days, relaxed and flowy dresses for performances on others. She still donned her boardroom wear from time to time, and I just prayed CJ was never around when she walked in in that uniform, or we'd all be in trouble. She has legs for days, and a chest that renders most men speechless.

Most girls with boyfriends, or even recent ex-boyfriends, often found themselves nervous around Yardley. She's from Georgia—another point that annoyed my wife--and is traditionally stunning. Full, high cheekbones, a soft, rounded face, sunny blond hair, which she recently cut to just above her shoulders, and curves in all the right places. She's taller than I personally go after in girls, but I haven't gone after girls in years anyway.

So, maybe Georgia's concerns weren't invalid in a general sense, but they were as far as I was concerned. I was always a one-woman man, and it would take a hell of a lot more than a great set of stems and a nice rack to make me look twice.

Georgia used to lose her mind about Yardley, even for a while after we'd gotten married. Clearly her issue, and not mine, but as her wedded husband, I'd pledged to help her get over insecurities and bizarre, unreal fixations. I think those were in the vows, anyway. She was certain Yardley was hunting to get me in the bedroom, and I can't ever say if that was true or not, because I never paid her any attention in anything other than a professional context. I'd asked Ember if Georgia had justification to be paranoid. She was little help, casting Yardley a suspicious sideways glance and growling toward her own husband, Bo. That was all a few years in the past though, and we'd all moved on from those insecure people—I'd hoped.

So, maybe having CJ around as the token label playboy would give all the women a rest from their Yardley Hysteria. As far as I knew, she'd never taken advantage of her professional standing with any of her artists. Maybe CJ could be the exception, at least for a while.

"Whatchya gonna have him play?" I asked with masked amusement as we shut ourselves into the tight sound booth.

Without a word, and only a slight grin, Yardley clicked on the mic that allowed her to talk to CJ on the other side of the window.

"All right, hot stuff. Feel like some Travis Barker?" She said it like she had all the authority in the world which, at least at GSE, she did. I immediately dropped my head, shaking it as I braced myself for CJ's reaction.

Sure enough, it came. "That rusty son of a bitch, are you serious? Is Blink 182 the only damned band with an okay drummer anyone knows anymore?" He held his sticks out in epic offense. "People really have to stop comparing me to him."

"Well," Yardley grinned against the microphone, "guess you should stop getting tattoos like his and stop walking around like your shit doesn't stink … like he does then, huh?"

I chuckled and took a cleansing breath.

This was going to be a long summer.

CHAPTER TWO

REGAN

"**Y**OU'VE REALLY NEVER tapped that?" CJ asked as we saddled up to the dark, mahogany bar at Molly Molloy's tavern. Molly's by the locals, and Molly Molloy's by drunk men reporting their whereabouts to their wives and girlfriends.

"CJ! I was with Georgia before I even met Yardley. You'd better hope I answer no to that."

"Damn straight." He clinked his heavy mug into mine. "You'd better hope, you scrawny motherfucker." He'd always been protective of Georgia.

I rolled my eyes. "Your mouth. God. Care to clean it up?"

He shook his head unapologetically. "Not really. Why? You entering the priesthood?"

"Adulthood," I shot back. He, in turn, gave me the finger for the second time today.

"Anyway," he said, swallowing half the contents of his mug in a few sips, "I think today went pretty well."

"Me too. Don't get cocky," I preemptively cautioned. "You're not the only decent drummer to walk through those doors, and you won't be the first one escorted out by the tip of Yardley's shoe if you don't pull your weight."

His face turned serious. "Cut me some fucking slack, would you? God, you've been on my ass since I got here"

He was right, and I instantly felt bad. "I'm sorry, dude. Look, I just … ugh, it's hard having my cousin and wife being best friends. Especially when they're at war. And she likes

Frankie, to top it all off, so you breaking things off with her really set Georgia on a warpath yesterday."

"Why does she care so damn much?" He looked down, something he'd done a lot already today, and seemed like he was cursing himself. I don't know … he just wasn't truly himself. Not the self of the last few years, anyway.

"She cares about you," I answered honestly. "We both do. She knows Frankie was and is good for you." Finally, I was honest with him. "Why'd you really cut her loose? You've been on small tours while with her before and held it together with fidelity. Why break things off now?"

CJ held his hand up to the bartender, pointing to a front-and-center bottle of tequila before pointing back to us.

Great.

With shots in hand, CJ toasted our summer together, and didn't say another word until we swallowed the smooth liquor.

"I'm freaked out," he admitted, to my astonishment.

I kept my cool, pushing hopes of his impending growing-up down as far as they'd go. "About?"

"Settling down. All that."

I proceeded with extreme caution. Talking to CJ about commitment to anything beyond his drum set was a risky maneuver. I reminded myself to take it slow. "Frankie puttin' the pressure on for marriage, or something?"

He shrugged. "Maybe I'm putting the pressure on myself, I guess. Thirty isn't too far off. I've got plenty of money and tons of options in front of me in computers and music … what am I stalling on?"

"I …" I was so shocked by his apparent candor, I didn't know what I could possibly say to him. Luckily, I didn't have to waver for long. Because he burst into hysterical laughter.

"I'm just screwin' with you. I want to get laid, brother!" He stood and slapped me hard on the shoulder, a smile on his face that didn't quite reach his eyes. "I've gotta wiz. Where's the pisser in this joint?"

I pointed him in the right direction, and watched as my burly cousin hit on every girl in his path between the bar and the bathroom door.

Moments later, a sultry voice spread a grin across my face.

"Hey handsome," she said, wrapping her arms around my waist as her lips found my neck. "You waitin' for someone special?"

I swiveled my stool around to face the five-foot-two-inch powerhouse I was lucky as hell to call my wife. "Just you," I remarked, pulling her into a kiss. "Always you."

"Hmm," she purred, taking the seat next to me. "A few hours with the infidelity brigade and you're extra happy to see your wife, huh? Monogamy looks pretty good, doesn't it?"

At that, I pursed my lips. "Don't start. Just because CJ and his insatiable libido roll into town doesn't change my commitment to you or our marriage." I'd been dreading this conversation for weeks, and if I had my way about it, it wouldn't turn into a conversation. But, sometimes I can't help myself. "I've never once given you a reason not to trust me, Georgia. I don't know why you insist on playing the role of jealous wife. That's not who you are. That's not how we are."

I braced for a verbal backlash from my take-no-prisoners partner, but was met with a sigh instead. "You're right. I'm sorry."

I looked up from the foamy head of my beer. "What?"

She grinned, smacking me. "Don't look so surprised, Kane," she teased. "I can have humility, too."

"You can," I said slowly, egging her on.

She crinkled her nose and ran her hand over her shaggy-short blonde hair. Short in the back and long in the front, with a million layers in between. It was blonde today, anyway. No bets on what tomorrow would hold. But, as usual, she had a red bandana tying it back. A smudge of flour was evident on the side, from the bakery. I brushed it away with my thumb.

"Bringing your work out to play?" I teased.

"He just riles me up," she said of CJ, ignoring my attempt at lightness. "He has no self-respect, and less for women."

I tilted my head to the side. "I wasn't going to say anything …" I started, then thought better of it.

"What?" she demanded. "Tell me."

I sighed, blowing air out with puffed cheeks. "He mentioned his dad today."

Her mouth dropped open, eyes almost as wide as they'd go. "What? Did he hear from him or something?"

I shook my head. "God no, are you kidding? He … he said he thought he was just going to end up like him." I took another sip of beer.

Georgia's face went from angry to anxious in a second. "Oh, no … He hasn't been down this dark road in years. Like, high school years. Seriously? He said that?"

I nodded. "I swear to God if you tell him—"

She put up her hand. "I won't. Promise," she said as CJ emerged from the restroom and sauntered back to his seat on the other side of me.

"What are we talking about?" he asked after the bartender slid him his second frosty mug.

"Your treatment of women … as a whole," she answered, trying to suppress a grin.

He leaned to the side and eyed Georgia with playful malice. "Not this again. G, give it a rest. I love women, am an equal-opportunity provider, and am just having fun. Just because you went ahead and grew up, doesn't mean the rest of us have to."

"Whatever you say, Heff," she retorted, keeping it light and playful, like their usual selves.

"What, so you're not pissed at me anymore?" CJ asked, catching on to Georgia's drastic change in demeanor from earlier in the day.

She shrugged. "What do you want from me? I can't stay mad at your dumb ass for long."

"All right," I cut in. "I gotta get home." I reached for my keys and tossed them to CJ. "I'll ride home with her and allow you to get your bearings. I trust you'll drive sober, or call me if you're drunk?"

He made the sign of the cross over his chest. "Scouts honor," he answered half-convincingly.

Georgia leaned in and gave CJ a peck on the cheek. "Sorry for being a bitch earlier."

He kissed her back, flicking her shoulder at the same time. "I'm not sorry for being a dick."

She rolled her eyes, he grinned, and all seemed back on track with the two of them as Georgia and I left CJ on the loose and headed back home to enjoy some much needed quiet time.

***

With our work schedules, it was rare to be in the same bed for long. My late nights bled into her early mornings, and we often resorted to surprising each other at our places of employment to sneak kisses or the oh-so-sexy afternoon delight. So it's no surprise to me that the first place we sought out when we unlocked our door was straight for the king-sized bed that took up nearly three quarters of our bedroom.

"When do you guys head out on tour?" Georgia asked, breathless as she sank to her knees on the bed and unbuttoned my shirt while I stood before her.

My eyes rolled back into my head as I savored the feel of her fingertips across my chest. "Some day other than today."

Her nails dug playfully into my shoulders, begging for a real answer. "A month," I said, shaking my shirt to the ground and savoring her quick work on my belt.

"Six months?" she asked of how long we'd be gone.

I nodded, nudging her onto her back. "We'll have at least a couple long weekends in there, like always. And, as always, you can fly to meet us whenever you want."

Georgia's gorgeous blues widened, taking me in as if she wasn't entirely sure when she'd see me again, despite it being spelled out on the calendar. "June is prime wedding season, Regan. And the rest of the summer, for that matter. You know that. I'm booked nearly solid through early September."

"It's okay," I whispered between kisses over her ample breasts. "We'll make the most of tonight, tomorrow, and the next thirty days. And I'll be home in between, hon. I'm not gone for six months straight." My mouth worked its way down to her belly button, where I enjoyed the squirm of her hips before hooking my teeth around her lace panties.

She took a deep breath, the soft skin of her stomach heaving under me. "I can't sync my ovulation schedule to GSE's touring plans."

Her panties snapped back against her stomach as I pulled my head up. "What?"

Georgia propped herself on her elbows and held up her hands defensively. "No need to panic, sailor, I was just saying …"

I shook my head. "I'm not panicking, I just thought it was weird to throw medical talk into the bedroom is all. Are you … keeping track of all that? Ovulation and stuff?"

She shrugged, which was a yes, but she said, "No."

"Weren't we going to just stop using condoms or whatever for a while to see how things go? Just let nature take its course?"

"Sure, if you want to drag this out for another year or two." She rolled her eyes, sitting all the way up and against the headboard, drawing her knees in close.

Game over.

I sighed, heavily and frustrated, positioning myself next to her. "I don't have to do this tour, you know. It was just some fun idea CJ and I tossed around. We're not even headlining—we have no singer, for God's sake." I laughed, she merely smiled.

"CJ can sing, you know. You can, too, if you wanted."

I nodded. "I know. But that's not the point."

"You're scared about having a baby." Her gaze drifted out the window and into the ocean.

"Hell yes, I'm scared. That shit's scary!" She looked at me in horror, but I continued. "But that doesn't mean I don't want it. I've wanted all kinds of things that are scary. A career in music, a relationship with you—"

She jabbed me in the side with her elbow, giving me the opportunity to hook my arm around her waist and roll her underneath me.

"Why don't you pick on someone your own size," she giggled, panting.

I buried my face into the crook of her neck. "You're just the right size. Fun sized."

"So where are we?" she asked, turning the water cold for the second time in five minutes.

Sitting back on my heels, I took a deep breath. "We're right here." I playfully dug through my pockets. "No condoms."

"But no tracking ovulation," she stated with some reticence.

No. Not yet.

"I don't know … what do you think?" was what I came up with.

"I think you've talked me off the ledge. There's no rush," she said much to my deep, deep relief. "We can just let things happen, right?"

Grinning, I unzipped my jeans and kicked them off the bed behind me. "Now, if you would just let this happen …"

I grabbed her ankles and slid her body down until her head was on the pillow and Georgia was once again looking up at me with hopeful, loving eyes.

"I don't want you to leave in a month," she said, moving her hands across my hipbones and to all points south.

I swallowed a moan, pressing myself into her hand. "But the welcome home sex is oh, so fine."

She reached around and smacked my bare backside, letting out a small yelp when I again rolled her over so she was on top of me.

"Well," she half-slurred, drunk with lust, "I guess I better remind you what'll be waiting for you at home."

***

The good and bad news is that the month went by relatively fast. More bad news was always in saying goodbye to my wife. She's tough as nails, at least through her first few layers, so she never really did weepy, long goodbyes. But she's pure mush beneath the granite around her heart, so it never took more than a couple of days before I started getting a mixed bag of text messages ranging from I miss you to Don't do anything stupid.

The good news—great, really—was that all evidence pointed to CJ's ability to keep it together at work, thereby reducing his professional liability on tour, but I couldn't yet speak for his social risk. I knew he wasn't anywhere near being over Frankie, but that wasn't a conversation I was about to drag out of him.

He spent much of his non-studio time at Molly Molloy's, quickly referring to it as Molly's any chance he got, but the good news there is that there wasn't a single bar fight. And, if he spent much of his time hooking up, he didn't do it at our place.

Still, I hadn't seen him in much more than flirty conversation and ass-grabbing, which made me wonder how long it would take for him to admit his still-lingering feelings for Frankie. Or push him over the edge into complete regression to his old self.

With a smile on my face, I barged into Georgia's bakery, situated one floor below our sprawling apartment. Sweet Forty-Two was her pride and joy, in very much the same way music was mine. We learned more about art from each other in our different mediums than we ever could have if we stuck with our own kind. Though, we often argued which art was more satisfying to the soul—food, or music.

"What are you so happy about?" she spat out behind a wildly menacing grin. Sarcasm through her face at its finest.

Checking to be sure there were no customers, I hopped onto the counter and slid myself down until I was next to her. I simply beamed at her in silence.

"You're weird," she said. "And you're dirtying my counters. People eat on this, Regan, seriously." She shooed me away and I situated myself in the open kitchen.

"Our tour starts tomorrow," I started, my hands rubbing together.

"And?" She scrubbed at the counter, annoyed.

"Our first two weeks—two weeks—are through California. Starting here. So, really, we've got another couple of weeks before I'm too far for a booty call."

Georgia turned on her heels and cracked my hip with a fast whip of her towel. "Ass."

"Yours." I winked and grabbed her hips. "You're still gonna send me goodies on the road, right?" I eyed the display case filled with mouthwatering cupcakes, danish, muffins, and brownies.

"We'll see," she retorted. "Only good boys get cookies."

Just then, CJ came in through the back door. "You better get baking then, sweet thang, because I've been just this side of a saint."

Georgia shot him a look. "CJ, the only saintly thing you could do is sterilize."

He held his hands against his heart, playing hurt. "I'll have you know, I've been a good, good boy," he said with some measure of regret.

Crossing my arms, I leaned against the large, stainless steel prep table. "What's that been about?"

"What?" he and Georgia asked in unison.

I pointed at CJ. "Don't think I didn't notice your rather chaste behavior these last few weeks. It's freaked me out. What gives?"

"Don't trust me?"

I shook my head. "Nope."

His eyes lit up and he stuck out his tongue to reveal the silver barbell stuck straight through the center. The one that had been there for at least ten years. "Good, you shouldn't. I'm saving myself for the road." He produced a plastic grocery bag from the other side of the door and emptied its contents onto the table. "Always be prepared."

Georgia stared with tired resignation at the pile of boxes spilled before us. Extra large, Ribbed For Her Pleasure, Warming Sensation, Ultra Thin …

I picked up the box of extra large condoms. "Thinking mighty highly of yourself these days?"

He snatched them from me, stuffing his loot back into the bag. "You're just jealous you don't need them anymore." He couldn't stop himself, but knew he should have. I could tell the way his eyes flashed to Georgia and back to me in an instant.

"Yes," I said with hyperbolic awe, trying to defuse the tension "tell me the story about not remembering who you're waking up next to again? Oh! Or the one of getting chased down the stairs by an ex-boyfriend with a bat who returned home early? Yes," I said, wrapping my arm around Georgia's shoulders, "sign me right up for that life."

He waved his hand, staying in character, but knowing not to push it anymore. "Eh, you never made a good slut anyway."

CHAPTER THREE
REGAN

THE THING ABOUT Georgia is, she's not truly a jealous person deep down. She's insecure, with wounds that go a little deeper than even I know. It's a difference that took us a long while to sort out when we first got together. Her dad was … complicated. A successful business man in his own right, but a drunk who did the best he could to raise her until his best wasn't much, and she moved to California while still in high school to live with her mother.

And her mother … that's even more of a tangled web. Amanda Hall, while healthy and functioning now, and for the last couple of years, was a diagnosed schizophrenic. When I first met Georgia, her mother had just completed a lengthy stay in Breezy Pointe—a mental health facility—and had just begun receiving ECT, or shock treatment, for the first time.

While schizophrenia isn't all that common to begin with, and the risk of developing it is only mildly increased for those with it in their family DNA, this didn't help Georgia's outlook on life. She was terrified around every corner that she'd be struck with a diagnosis of her own—her very own worst-case scenario.

When our relationship began, Georgia hadn't had a loving relationship in years, aside from her friendship with my cousin, but they hadn't seen much of each other since high school. She was wary, and had every right to be. I was, too, which didn't help matters. At the time of our meeting I was still recovering from some emotional devastation of my own. Needless to say, we were quite the pair when we first met. Damaged, battered, but hopeful. While it happened less as time went on, I still had to coax Georgia out of the thickly wooded forest of her fears from time to time.

Boiled down to its simplest parts, it's not that she didn't trust me—she didn't trust that she was worthy of the love we have between us.

"Sorry 'bout that earlier," CJ finally said as we fooled around with our set at the studio that night, pulling me out of the silent psychoanalysis of my wife.

"With Georgia and your flaunting of condoms? Don't worry about it. Just … you know how she is."

He set his sticks down and crossed his arms over his chest. "I thought she'd gotten better about all that. You're married for Christ's sake."

It had gotten better, he was right. Until recently.

"And we thought you had gotten better," I shot back as lightly as I could.

He just rolled his eyes, ignoring me.

"We're talking about having a kid," I blurted out. "She's been more insecure since then. Like we've gone backward in the trust department."

CJ eyed me carefully. "Does it have to do with all her mom stuff? Worried that she'll end up like her?"

"I think so. Or that she'll pass it along to our child …"

"What are the actual odds of that?"

"Higher than zero," I admitted. "I don't know the numbers because I know it's quite small. At least for the schizophrenia."

CJ huffed. "Yeah but not alcoholism."

"That's the truth …" I didn't know the genetic likelihood of passing addiction down to our theoretical child, either. And, I wasn't sure of the best way to bring any of this up with Georgia in a way that wouldn't have her thinking I was accusing her of being a genetic liability. Because I didn't think that at all.

In truth, I often tired of having to play out our potential conversations in my head before having them. I know, relationally speaking, that wasn't the healthiest behavior to engage in, but it was a tough habit to break.

CJ lifted his eyebrows, smiling. "But a fucking kid? Really?" His face broke into a smile and, inexplicably, he rose to his feet and grabbed me into a brief, but tight, hug. "Me! An uncle!"

"Calm down." I chuckled, shuffling my sheets of music together and stuffing them into a folder. "We're talking about it. We're just going to see how it goes. Let nature do its thing."

"You better do your damn thing, Kane." He pounded on his chest like a caveman, talking like one, too. "We Kane men are strong. We bring the sperm."

I broke into laughter, realizing that despite his faults—and maybe because of them—CJ really would make one hell of an uncle. Someday.

***

Our first gig of the tour was at a local concert hall. Small compared to the ones we'd see later on tour, but a huge step up out of the bar scene CJ was used to. Sure, he'd played to bigger crowds before, but I'd be lying if I said I wasn't looking forward to him getting through a little stage fright here and there. No harm in knocking a cocky bastard down a few pegs.

Grounded Sound put together a fantastic lineup and tour, further proving Yardley's strength as a businesswoman in her own right. Her family is well-entrenched in the music industry, having started in Country before expanding into other territories. Yardley had a hunch that the independent and folk-rock scenes were on the rise, and got her claws into this division as soon as it became available. According to Yardley, her parents sent her off to California half-expecting that her "little project," as they called it, would end soon enough and she'd have to sell to the highest bidder.

Much to their surprise, Yardley's instincts were right on. Groups like Mumford & Sons, The Lumineers, and The Civil Wars—until they broke up, anyway—took off, leaving the local circuits hungry for artists that could provide that unique sound right in their back yards.

Our lineup was comprised of instrumental-only acts like me and CJ, solo artists with their guitars, and larger ensembles that rounded out the folk sound with banjos, tambourines, and the whole nine. One of the groups, The Brewers, actually asked me to step into some of their numbers to add in a violin solo— called a fiddle by most of the folks in the genre. It's the same instrument, which some people don't honestly know, but has alias' depending on the setting. I agreed to jump in wherever they needed me. Performing has always reinvigorated me in ways little else could.

"We're opening?" CJ asked when we arrived at the concert hall.

I nodded, handing him his cymbal stand. "Damn straight." I winked. "I'm a star."

He rolled his eyes. "Save your winks for the girls, Kane."

"You can have 'em. You know I'm spoken for. You were at the wedding."

"So you never flirt? A wink, that sideways grin of yours that gets everyone all hot and bothered?"

Taking a deep breath, I conceded. "A little," I admitted. "Just show. Georgia knows, sees it, all that. It's just a performance thing."

He held his hands up. "Dude, I didn't come out here to babysit you. I know you're Captain Fidelity, and I admire that. Especially when your wife is my best friend, and I'd really hate to kick your ass if you hurt her. As for me ..."

The fluidity of his morals wasn't shocking, but I did find some relief in it. Musicians, athletes, actors, anyone who is up for public consumption, is expected to maintain at least some level of availability for their fans. Despite knowledge of marriages, babies, girlfriends/boyfriends, whatever, part of the popularity of commercial artists is the ability of the fans to sink themselves into fantasies and daydreams, just enough that they come back for more. More songs, more shows, another interview, anything.

That was the hardest adjustment for me as a commercial musician—the showmanship of pretending. At the meager beginning of my career, flirtation was second nature. As familiar to me as the bow I drew across the strings. As mine and Georgia's relationship developed, though, I became increasingly uncomfortable with the idea. She knew how it had to be—she's no fool. In fact, she got to know me while I played at a bar she tended when we first met. She was on the receiving end of the inviting smiles and casual glances. But as our pasts revealed themselves to each other, and our futures became one, I grew weary of not only my part in the act, but the attention I received. But maybe having CJ around to remind me of the social part of my job would make things easier, which would be a huge relief to Yardley, who always held her breath during post-show mixers with fans, wondering how stand-offish I'd seem.

Reclusive is sexy, she'd always say. Unavailable is suicide.

"Who's that," CJ interrupted my thoughts, gesturing to a young woman testing sound equipment on stage. "Crew?"

"Nessa? Nah, she's in The Brewers. Lead vocals, sometimes keys."

"Keys?" he asked with a hint of mocking. "Keyboard or piano too good for you now that you're a superstar?"

"Whatever, just stay away from her, okay?"

"Yeah," he said inside a deep chuckle. "Whatever."

I gave Vanessa Crowley the once-over, instantly regretting the words I'd spoken—he'd taken them as a challenge. Her hair was black and pixie-short, save for one long chunky strand that was dyed blue and always hanging in front of her right eye. She said sardonically that it was there to make her eyes match. The left one was blue, but her right was green, which was enough to intrigue men up and down the California coast alone. She was of medium height—taller when she wore her signature combat boots—slender but strong, and had light, creamy skin that secured her position as a local folk music goddess.

The Brewers weren't signed with GSE, but were under contract with another local folk-focused label. I'd run into them several times at local festivals during my stint with Celtic Summer. Nessa was the first to ask me if our band was on break or a break-up when she heard the news that CJ and I were gunning for this tour.

I assured her it wasn't a breakup, but an indefinite break. Shaughn, Celtic Summer's lead singer, was originally from Ireland, and moved here in middle school. She had long hoped to earn enough money to go back to her homeland and sustain her while forging a solo career, and this summer it finally came together for her. Our drummer, Chris, had plenty of opportunities waiting for him, and had a deep, nomadic spirit that made three years just long enough for him to be with one group before exploring other ventures.

"Is she attached?" CJ asked, ignoring my request that he leave it alone.

I shook my head. "Not that I know of. I've never seen her with anyone in particular."

"Anything wrong with her? She a bitch? Or a lesbian?"

"No," I couldn't help but laugh. "I don't think she's either, but I'm certain she isn't a bitch."

"But she could be a lesbian," he stated with a whiff of defeat.

Arching an eyebrow at him, I gave him a challenging grin. "They could all be lesbians," I teased.

He held his arms out, tilting his chin to the sky. "I could never be so lucky. Why is she off-limits, though? D'you ever bang her?"

"No, I never banged her. I didn't even meet her until last year. But The Brewers are actually going to be with us for most of the next six months, and I'd rather you found someone else to fornicate with than risk them bailing on the tour because you're a pig."

He continued to gawk heavy lidded, at our tour mate as if he hadn't taken in anything I'd said. "She's been in the business a while, right?" he accurately assessed by her fluency on stage and with the equipment.

"Yeah, why?"

CJ turned to me with renewed hope springing across his face. "Then she'll know what to expect from a drummer."

At that, I had nothing left to say. CJ said he and Frankie were broken up. While I didn't buy his over it act, there was nothing to do. Or say. Except, "Good luck, and don't make too big of a mess of things."

***

The show was sold out and a great way to kick off our tour. After a relatively short meet-up with the crowd, the artists retreated to Molly Molloy's for some decompression time. Despite all the energy I received, in the moment from a show, they're immediately draining. I was revitalized by the next time I stepped on stage, sure, but giving it a hundred and twenty percent all the time left me weary, needing a beer and a good night's sleep before doing it all again.

"Good show, Kane," Nessa said, leaning against the bar where I was seated, tilting a brown, slim-necked bottle of beer to her lips.

"You'll have to be more specific these days, Ness. My cousin shares my last name, and I'd hate to have you waste a compliment on him," I teased.

Her mismatched eyes grew wide. "The drummer's your cousin?"

I nodded, stretching my arms over my head then my neck, side to side. "The rumors are true."

"What rumors?" she asked, poorly masking a grin as she fingered her signature pearl necklace.

"Whatever you've heard. It's all true."

She gave a slow nod. "Ditched a girlfriend to come on tour?"

"I guess," I said, though I had no idea where she got that information.

"Has played drunk while having a broken arm?"

"Most drummers have," I answered, unapologetically playing up the stereotypes.

"Womanizer?"

I laughed. "Where'd you hear all this from?"

"CJ," she answered, breaking into a full laugh.

"Of course." I joined her in laughter as we watched CJ work the crowd at Molly's. "Why aren't you off romping around with him when he gave you such a thorough and gleaming résumé?"

She threw her head back, the muscles in her long, slender neck contracting against laughter. "I figure I'll make him sweat it out a bit." Throwing me a quick wink, Nessa turned and linked arms with a female bandmate of hers—Clara, I think—and headed for the restrooms.

I'd never actually seen Nessa go off with any guy after a show—or girl for that matter—but I'd also never spent much time with her, knew nothing about her personal life, and there was the pesky little bit about it being none of my business. I stuck to my beer and enjoyed the comforting sights and sounds of the local bar, pulling out my cell phone.

Me: We're at Molly's, wanna come down?

It was a long three minutes before I got a response.

Georgia: Sleeping.

I sighed. Of course she was. It was two fifteen in the morning, according to my trusty cell phone, and she'd have to wake up in less than two hours to get the ovens roaring at Sweet Forty-Two for the Sunday morning brunch rush.

Me: I'll come home soon.

Georgia: Don't rush. You know where I'll be. I love you.

I didn't rush. I stayed, partying with my friends and acquainting CJ with everyone, and vice versa. We laughed and partied until closing time at three thirty when the designated drivers, myself included, poured our charges into our respective vehicles and deposited them at their desired locations. CJ didn't need a ride home, thanks to Mona, one of the waitresses at Molly's. So, when I'd dropped the last person off, I slid quietly into the back door of the bakery, which is at the bottom of the stairs leading to our apartment.

"Hey," I whispered, even though she'd peeked over her shoulder when the door opened.

Georgia turned with a tired, but gorgeous smile, her hands wrist-deep in pillowy dough. "Hey," she echoed. "Why are we whispering?"

I wrapped my arms around her waist as she continued to knead what would certainly become a heavenly creation. "It's early," I continued.

"Or late," she retorted, still soft. "You smell like a bar."

"You smell like brown sugar." I brought my nose to the crook of her neck and inhaled the thick molasses scent, letting a small moan escape in my exhale.

I let my hands run along the waistband of her worn jeans before bringing them over the sinful curve of her backside. Her grey T-shirt with the shop's logo on it was tied in the back, as usual, with a black elastic hair tie—while her trademark red bandana was tasked with keeping her hair out of her face.

Turning her face toward me slightly, Georgia allowed my lips to skim down her jawline where I planted a small kiss on the corner of her mouth. "You guys have another show today?" she asked

"Tonight." I nodded. "Later. Much, much later."

The mention of time weighed heavy on my eyelids as I stole one more kiss off the skin of my bride's cheek before giving her butt a firm squeeze.

"I'll come. Ride with you guys." I hadn't noticed she'd stopped kneading until she started again. Her narrow shoulders moving with the punching, stretching, folding, and turning. "Want me to wake you up later?"

Stepping back, I allowed the yawn I'd been holding back to roll through me. With a slow nod, I conceded. "Please."

Georgia looked at the clock hanging on the wall over her left shoulder. "Noon?"

I looked, too, as if I didn't already know it was approaching five in the morning. I didn't know how life-long rock n' rollers did it, I was sore.

"Noon's good," I agreed. It was a lie even Georgia chuckled at as she heaved the dough from the wide metal bowl onto the counter, rolling it out and sectioning it off into perfectly identical triangles.

Scones. Mmm.

"Well, it'll be good enough for today," I compromised.

"Don't burn yourself out right out of the gate, Mr. Kane," she teased, wiping her hands on the towel strung through a frayed belt loop on her jeans. "It'll be a long six months if you try to keep up this pace."

I sighed playfully. "You give me the same speech every tour, Mrs. Kane."

Her arms reached up and around my neck. She stood on her tiptoes and planted one small, soft kiss on my collarbone. "I always will, too. Now go get some sleep. Also, don't call me Mrs. Kane for right now. Someone might overhear and think I'm married to CJ." She chuckled to herself, throwing me a wink before waving me out of the kitchen, effectively sending me to bed.

I hesitated, hating that the tour schedule was already in place and we were back to two ships passing at the crack of dawn.

"Go," she encouraged, sensing my reluctance. "I'll come up and get you."

I left, and fell into bed with a relieved sigh, grateful for the blackout shades and sound machine that let me sleep while daylight ticked away.

***

"You were on fire tonight," Georgia remarked as CJ and I shut the back of the equipment truck. "On. Fire. Why didn't you tell me you were playing with The Brewers, too, Regan?"

I yanked on her hips, momentarily grateful for the short black shorts she wore over her netted black tights as I lifted her into a kiss and she wrapped her legs around my waist. "It was a last minute thing. I probably won't do it every show. Depends on the size of the crowd, length of the show, blah, blah, blah," I trailed off smothering her with kisses.

"Well, this is gross," CJ stated, bored. "I'm off to the bar. Coming?"

"Nah …" I started, but trailed off when I saw the look of question on Georgia's face. "What?"

She slid onto the ground and perched her hands on her hips. I was in fake trouble. "What? A superstar fiddler can't take his wife out for a good time?"

I rolled my eyes as CJ chuckled. "If you want me to show you a good time, I can think of ten thousand places other than Kinney's Pub to do so. I … kinda had plans for us," I added quietly.

Georgia blushed, looking down and trying her damnedest not to look at CJ who was making schoolboy teasing noises.

"Oooh," he cooed. "Georgia has a boyfriend."

She flipped him off. "A husband, you dolt. And a damn fine one at that."

"Whatever, you two go be boring. I've got skirts to chase." CJ fell into step with some of the band members from other groups and shuffled across the street and into Kinney's, where I was sure I'd have to return to later for at least one beer before carting half of them home.

"You think he's going to follow up all his talk with some walk?"

"CJ? With girls? I don't even know. It's been so long since he's … behaved like this. Have you talked to Frankie?"

Georgia's eyes widened. "Not about his current behavior. It'd kill her."

I made a noncommittal noise, toeing the line between wanting to know more, and not wanting to know too much, since I was the one that had to bunk with CJ for the next several months.

"What have you got planned?" Georgia asked, gracefully switching topics.

I laced my fingers with hers and gave her hand a tug. "Come." I nodded in the opposite direction of Kinney's. "Follow me."

Adjusting the strap of my violin case over my shoulder, I led Georgia across the street into an impossibly tiny restaurant called Live. It was new, not even open yet, but I knew the owner, Brian, and trusted his skills. He was a longtime cook at one of the pubs Celtic Summer frequented, eventually coming on the road with us as our main chef. He had a strong fluency in local and often unique ingredients, and I was dying to know what his menu looked like. Georgia was friends with him years before I came along, so he's family to us.

"There's no one here," Georgia noted when we entered the small space.

Tiny white twinkle lights bordered the ceiling, giving the dining room a soft glow. All the tables were set properly on black linen tablecloths, but only one had a small, flickering candle.

"There." I nodded to the table, bringing her with me.

"What are you doing?" she asked suspiciously as I pulled out her chair and slid her toward the table.

I didn't say another word until I was seated across from her and waved Brian over. He gave me a wink from behind the bar, and approached our table with two slender flutes of champagne.

"Glad you could make it," he said, setting the bubbly on the table.

"Brian?" Georgia stood, hugging the guy who she'd said was the only person allowed to feed me besides her. I don't think she was kidding, either. "You work here or something?"

Brian flashed me an appreciative glance for getting to tell her the news for himself. Georgia had often encouraged him to go out on his own.

"This is mine," he said proudly, with a grin to match.

"Shut. Up!" Georgia jumped up and down, still hugging him and nearly knocking the champagne bottle from his hand. She let go, smacking his chest once for good measure. "You didn't tell me?! I mean, I knew you had plans, but, God this is great!"

He shrugged. "Wanted to surprise you a little, so sue me. I want to talk to you later about maybe, I don't know, collaborating with me on a dessert menu?" He arched an eyebrow at her and now it was my turn to be surprised. Pleasantly so.

Georgia was speechless for a few moments. A rare sight. "Absolutely," she said almost breathlessly.

"Next week," Brian nodded, eyeing me. "Once your man is out there tearing up the road. For tonight, enjoy each other. I'll be back in a while with the appetizer."

Just like that, Brian disappeared into the kitchen, and Georgia turned to me with a bright, exasperated expression. "Did you know about this?"

"The restaurant?" I teased. "Yes." She shot me the look. "The dessert thing? No. I swear. That'd be killer, G."

She nodded. "It would certainly add a layer of depth to my business." Her eyes wandered out onto the sidewalk, silently considering.

Since the opening of her bakery a few years ago, Georgia constantly turned over new stones, bringing in fresh business and flexing her skills. She added new menu items all the time, expanded into catering fairly early on, is fluent in private orders big and small, and knows her niche—sweets. She never pretends to be something she's not. She never talked about adding lunch options or soups or any of that. Georgia knows what she wants and how to get it. On this night, she was thoughtfully weighing the benefits of branching into restaurants.

"It would be big," she finally said, taking a sip of her champagne. "Shoot! We need to toast."

"To us," I said simply. "To our dreams and successes individually, and as a couple. To the future."

Georgia swallowed hard. "How can you always do things like that on the fly?"

"Because I mean it. You should go after this. Who knows what else it will open up for you?"

"We're a pretty impressive couple, you know." She grinned, but it was stained with the grey shadow of melancholy.

Tilting my head to the side, I spoke softly. "What's wrong?"

"I love how successful we are. I do. I'm amazed every time I hear something of yours on the radio, or catch a mention of you on the Internet. When I come across press of the bakery?" She waved her hand and grinned. "I'm over the moon …"

"But," I picked up where she trailed off.

"Are we leaving room for a family?" she asked, lowering her eyes. "Or are we kind of self-sabotaging? How would a baby fit in here?"

I took a deep breath, reaching across the table for her hand, swallowing the lump of emotion that rose in my throat. "Listen, I'm sorry if I haven't seemed that enthusiastic …"

She waved her hand, cutting me off. "Oh it's not that. I know even if you panic you'll be on board. You're a man." She grinned, but it was cautious.

"Bo and Ember do it," I answered. "Quite perfectly, if you ask me."

Bo and Ember were not only my best friends and fellow GSE artists, but they were husband and wife at the head of a growing family. They'd met on stage and that truly set the tone for their relationship. Ember was the daughter of counterculture musicians, and Bo was a rather enigmatic entrepreneur who found his home in music. They married on tour, survived a miscarriage on the road, and got pregnant with their first son, Jackson, on the road. They spent most of their time at their New Hampshire residence, but maintained a solid touring and recording schedule. They slowed down a little after Jax was born, and again when Vivian Rae came along, but once she was toddling around the estate, they were back at it full swing.

"It's part of their lives, the music," I continue. "Part of their family, just like music and the bakery are part of ours. What kid wouldn't love to have music and sugar as the backbone of their childhood?"

This drew a smile from Georgia. "Are you sure? When I was growing up, my dad …"

"Don't," I whispered. "We're nothing like your dad. Sure, he owned his own business, but … his priorities …"

I hesitated to recount her childhood to her as if she hadn't been there. Her dad owned a great pub on Cape Cod, running it successfully for a long time, even as his alcoholism took a stronger hold on him year after year. Georgia was put in difficult situations at younger ages than appropriate. Tending bar before she was legally allowed to, breaking up bar fights when she should have been preparing for the SAT's, and nursing her father's hangovers when she should have been with friends.

"His priorities were shit," she said, finally. She finally took a deep breath, and with the exhale, I swear I saw the resolve return to her eyes. "And we're not shit."

I shook my head. "Nope. Not at all."

"So what do we do?"

I kissed her hand. "We take it a day at a time. We work hard and welcome a baby when it comes."

Georgia swallowed the rest of her champagne, setting her glass down with a challenging smile. "Awfully sure of yourself, huh Kane?"

I summoned more confidence than I actually possessed. "Naturally," I teased.

Georgia and I enjoyed the rest of our meal on cloud nine, eagerly anticipating the opportunities and plans before us.

CHAPTER FOUR

REGAN

THE HOTGRASS FESTIVAL, as Yardley coined the tour, wound leisurely down and back up the California coast over the span of two weeks. The gigs seemed to come and go in the blink of an eye, while the days in between stretched lazily on. Georgia made it to a couple of shows in Wine Country, but as expected, wedding season was dawning and her orders were piling up. She had some part time help from her mom and a couple of other employees she'd hired over the last two years—one of which was gaining experience toward her goal of becoming a professional pastry chef—but Georgia wasn't one to relinquish much control, making her a very busy woman.

Our goodbye was short and sweet, as Georgia always liked to keep it. A hug, a slightly longer kiss, and promises to call and text whenever we could. While she said she might meet us for our show in Oregon, I honestly didn't expect to see her until we were out on the east coast.

The tour was going to cover sixteen states in six months, mainly festivals that would have us performing two or three days at each site. We were to start in Nevada, wind up through Oregon and Washington, skimming the Northern US with Montana, Minnesota, a stretch in Chicago, then onto Ohio and New York City before anchoring in Massachusetts for a couple of weeks. Yardley had graciously put a two-week break at our Massachusetts stop, which would allow for a mild respite in the middle of a lengthy travel schedule.

Once we closed out summer with a second set of shows in Massachusetts, we were scheduled to head to D.C. and North Carolina before spending a few days in Georgia, another several in Tennessee, and two shows in Texas—one in Austin that I was really looking forward to. We'd finish with a set in Arizona, and a final show somewhere Yardley still hadn't disclosed. I couldn't tell if she hadn't nailed down the details yet, or was simply holding in a surprise. The second seemed against her personality, but I'd learned over the years to assume little about women.

"You ready for this, bro?" I asked CJ as we stretched out in a room second to the back of one of four tour busses in our caravan. Three held band members, and the last was mainly equipment and supplies.

CJ didn't look up from his phone. "Damn straight," he said without conviction.

"You all right? Tired already?" I teased.

He shook his head, not speaking, but by the way his thumbs raced across the screen and the tension in his jaw, I gathered it was either Frankie he was texting with, or some other ticked-off girl he'd come across. Though, he'd gotten pretty adept at not giving out his phone number over the last couple of years. He used to give out fake numbers, but he found his life freer of hassle if he left his personal contact information out of the equation.

Letting him be for the moment, I picked up my own phone.

Me: We're in the desert now. Nevada awaits.

Georgia: Don't have too much fun ;)

Me: You either. Is your mom staying with you at all?

While Georgia's mom had been able to live on her own again for the last two years, after spending a couple of years living with her sister, Sue, Georgia often thought of creative ways to ask her mom to stay with her while I was on the road. Even though she'd spent many years one hundred and ten percent on her own, Georgia had come to find comfort in the emotional connective tissue between humans. And, now that her mom was healthy, they could enjoy each other's company in a way that was less challenging than when Georgia was acting as Amanda's caregiver.

Georgia: In a couple days, crazy few weeks coming up.

Despite seeing my wife's newfound emotional vulnerability for what it was, I kept my mouth shut. She kept up the pretense with me about needing her mom's help as much as she did with her mom.

Me: Maybe someday I can help with the weddings.

Georgia: hahahah. Stick to music.

I knew it'd make her laugh. I could hand her items in the kitchen, and sometimes stir, but she rarely lets me measure or actually bake anything.

I'd planned to tuck my phone into my bag and close my eyes for a nap, since we had three hours left before we arrived at our destination for tonight's show, but my attention was soon turned to the animated text conversation CJ seemed engaged in. Turning onto my side and propping myself up on one elbow, I watched his facial expressions with increasing interest.

His cheeks puffed out, frustrated, and growling noises permeated our small bunk room from the back of his throat.

"What the fuck," he huffed, throwing his phone to the edge of the bed before laying back and rubbing his hands over his face.

I waited a few seconds before brightly asking, "Problem?"

"Screw you, Regan," he snipped.

I pursed my lips. "Don't be a dick. It'll be a long six months with that shit attitude."

"It's not a shit attitude," he said, still holding the gravel in his voice like he'd smoked a pack of cigarettes last night. Maybe he did. "It's a bullshit relationship I never should have gotten into in the first place. Relationships can blow me, for all I care."

Taking a few seconds before I spoke, I considered exactly how to respond. Despite CJ and Frankie having been together for the last few years, I didn't get emotionally involved in their relationship the way Georgia did. The way all women seem to do. From what I knew through Georgia, and sometimes Ember, who lived close to CJ and sometimes worked with him, Frankie was a one-man woman the whole time. And, to the shock of everyone around, CJ seemed to be a one-woman man. I could still only recall one major fight roughly a year into their relationship when he seemed to have cold feet of some sort, but I supposed it was entirely possible more went on behind the scenes than I was privy to. But, then again, if it were anything like him having cheated on her, I would have certainly heard about it from Georgia.

It was unclear through the piecing together of my estrogen-laden sources if CJ ever actually cheated on Frankie while on that one brief break a year into the relationship because, as I've come to learn, men and women have different definitions of cheating. And different rules around behavior when a couple is on a "break."

"Frankie?" I asked after about twenty seconds, as if he'd tell me anything. He was touchy with his personal life. Sometimes flagrantly, inappropriately open, and others … steel trap with barbed wire.

CJ planted his hands behind his head, elbows flayed to either side as he stared at the bunk above him. He shook his head as if he hadn't even heard me and punched the inside of his cheek with his tongue. His classic move when he wanted to actually punch someone, or something, but also wanted to avoid an arrest.

I took that as a resounding "yes," and decided to push no further, and text Georgia once more.

Me: Gonna grab a nap while it's quiet on this bus. I love you. So much.

Georgia: I love you, too. CJ's an ass, by the way. Tell him that for me. Wait. Don't. He probably knows.

At that I sat up, intrigued, but wanting to be discreet enough so I wouldn't alert CJ and his nosy ass.

Me: He's been quiet. What's going on?

Georgia: I just got a screen shot from Frankie. Texts he sent her all lusty and wanting to revisit things once you guys get out to Massachusetts.

My jaw dropped a little as I cast a sideways glance in CJ's direction. He was still staring rather intently at the wood above him.

Me: That's … out of character, I guess. Right?

Georgia: Have you seen him with anyone since he first came out to CA?

While I couldn't report detailed statistics, I hadn't seen CJ coming or going with anyone in particular, but we're guys—we don't talk about what we don't see, and even less about what we do. CJ was usually more than willing to offer up play-by-plays of his sexual encounters, but I also hadn't seen much of him until this week because I was cramming in quality time with Georgia before the tour.

Me: Not that I know of, and I usually know far more than I'd like.

Then, Georgia proved to me once again the glorious horror of technology advancement by sending me a screenshot of the screenshot Frankie had sent her.

My head hurt some days.

Georgia:
> CJ: Looks like we'll be in MA Aug/Sept.
> *CJ: Hello?*
> *Frankie: So?*
> *CJ: Just thought you might want to clear your calendar ;)*
> *Frankie: For …*
> *CJ: Come on …*
> *Frankie: Don't start your shit, CJ. You made it *really* clear how you felt about me when you left*
> *CJ: I'm sorry*

I took a break from reading his private texts to glance once more at my cousin—a man who, to my prior knowledge, had only ever apologized for anything under sarcastic circumstances. His back was turned to me. I couldn't tell if he was asleep, but his phone was still teetering at the foot of his bed, so I turned back to the text that wasn't meant for my eyes. See what happens when you get involved with women?

Frankie: For what? For being yourself? You spent a long time warning me about who you might become. Guess you finally proved us both right.

CJ: There's a lot here you don't understand, Frankie.

Frankie: Exactly. Three years in a committed relationship with you and there's shit under the surface I still don't know. Fuck me for being pissed about it. I deserve better. I deserve someone who's going to man-up when shit gets rough.

CJ: Don't start THIS SHIT with me, Frankie. You knew I was fucked up and that I changed when I was with you. Because I love you. Then I'm honest about how I'm feeling when YOU KNOW it's hard for me, and that's a problem? You told me you loved me as I am.

CJ using the word love? No wonder he looked homicidal during this exchange—poor kid had never been in love so far as I know.

Frankie: I do love you, CJ. Probably always will. Lucky for me, I don't believe that there's just one love for everyone, and I need to find someone who I love and who can give me what I want and need out of this life. It's too short to wait on a guy to be faithful to me between tours and until he gets bored.

CJ: I was faithful to you the whole time, Frankie! Why don't you trust me!

Frankie: Because when someone has to ask after three YEARS "where we stand," it makes me wonder where they thought we stood before.

CJ: Whatever. Fucking whatever.

I guessed this is where CJ discarded his phone, or close to it, because this is where the screenshot stopped.

Me: Well that was intense. And personal. Do you guys share everything?

I knew they did.

Georgia: Yes. When we want to have someone with some sense weigh in on something … :-p

Me: I love you. Napping now.

Georgia: Don't tell CJ I showed you.

Me: Wouldn't dream of it.

What I did dream of, though, was much better. Georgia, our bed, and a family in the works. I always loved the beginnings of tours when all I could think of was my wife and the future before us before it turned into desperate missing her and doing all I could to keep my mind off of it.

***

"Hot as balls out here," CJ droned as we finished setting up the stage for the night's show.

I nodded, scratching some sweat away from my chin as Yardley came up beside us with a devious grin on her face. Dressed in a tight denim mini skirt and a snug tank top that prominently displayed her breasts, I prayed CJ would keep his comments to himself, if not his eyes. This look was uncharacteristic for our manager, but not all together outlandish. She'd been relaxing more on tour with us, only slipping into her more professional attire for certain venues and crowds.

"You," she said, pointing to me.

"Yeah?" I pulled one of Georgia's bandanas from my back pocket to swipe across my forehead. She had a dozen, so I knew she wouldn't miss one while I was on the road. I needed her with me more than she needed the red fabric anyway.

Reaching behind her, Yardley produced a disposable razor from her back pocket, wielding it in front of my face.

I shrugged. "Don't know what you expect me to do with that."

"You've gotta clean up the facial situation. Just a little," she pleaded.

I laughed. "Says who?"

"Me."

"Why?" I challenged.

"Because you're one five o'clock shadow away from Hermit-ville, and that's not really the image we've got painted for you.

"Come on!" I stroked the edges of my jaw playfully. "It's hip, isn't it? CJ, what'd you call it? Lumbersexual?"

At this, Yardley laughed. "Nice try. You need about seventy-five pounds on you for lumberjack status. CJ? With a little facial hair he could pull off that label."

"You callin' me fat?" CJ asked, his accent thick as he feigned offense.

Yardley shot him a challenging glance. "Never. You're not. All brawn."

He flexed his arms, wriggling an eyebrow like it was a drunken caterpillar. "You know it."

"Anyway," I pulled the conversation back to the topic at hand. "I'm not using that. I'll get an electric razor and trim it. It's not all coming off."

She sighed. "Fine. But tight to the face, Regan. Please."

"Why does Ronnie get to keep his beard?" I asked of the lead guitarist of, and Nessa's co-lead singer in, The Brewers who had a beard he could probably tie an elastic around.

"Because that's just … Ronnie. It's all very him."

I nodded. "I see. Would you talk to a woman like this? Nip this, tuck that, dye this, have that?"

Yardley tossed her blond hair back, thick from the heat as she laughed, open mouthed and facing the sky before giving me any attention. "Oh, Regan," she started, recovering from laughter. "Sweet, sweet Regan. If you only knew half the things women were asked to do in the name of image and business deals. Bet you've never been asked to sleep with anyone to help close a deal," she said in dark seriousness.

CJ stood, suddenly interested, sliding between the two of us. "No one's fuckin' asked me that. What's a guy gotta do to get laid around here!" He held his hands out to his sides, half playing and half something I barely recognized before turning and marching up the stairs to our bus.

"Fine," I conceded, not wanting to get into a conversation with Yardley about who has ever been asked to sleep with whom. "I'll go right now."

"Thanks. You're good people, Regan. The label is lucky to have you." She walked by me and onto the stage, checking the work we'd all just completed. By far one of the most involved, hands-on managers I've ever read about or come across.

"What was that about?" Nessa's warm rasp of a voice came from behind me.

She sounded like she grew up singing in old-time jazz bars. The kind filled with cigarette smoke and martinis. It wasn't dry and unattractive, rather it was as unique as her style. I turned to face her, always surprised by her appearance. She donned a long, fitted black and white striped sleeveless dress, hot pink combat boots, and a light, flowery pink scarf around her neck that allowed just the shadow of her black pearl necklace to peek through. Her jet-black hair and as-striking blue streak in the front made her a complicated puzzle to figure out, especially when she got behind the mic and belted out the raw, bluegrass-come-pop sound her band executed with perfection.

I scratched at my face. "Hermit's gotta go."

She chuckled, playfully reaching up and twirling the hair at the end of my chin in her fingers. "Thank God."

I bit the inside of my cheek, feeling something like blush rising through my face. "Don't like it?"

"It's fine, but I prefer you with it a little ... less. The hair, though? Never cut that. Go down fighting for that!" Her hand shook over my head, messing up my already disastrous hair before she bounded the stairs to the stage.

"Good luck tonight," I said, turning for my bus.

She slung a guitar over her shoulder. "You too. You're playing with us, right?"

I nodded. "We're on before you, though, I think. So I'll be warmed up."

Nessa looked down at her guitar, which she'd only recently learned to play. "Regan," she said playfully, "I have a feeling you were born warmed up."

I blushed fully this time at her compliment. "I could say the same for you. Don't over think it up there. Rest that voice of yours until then."

Once on our bus, I shut the door behind me to keep the heat out since the AC was on for the time being. I waded through the front, where members of The Shakes were napping. They were a full-on bluegrass band, only recently signed to GSE. They were as wide-eyed on stage as the newbies they were, and they partied a little longer than the rest of us. Well, them and CJ. I trusted that by the time we hit Montana they'd settle into a routine and not party every night like it was their last. At least most of them would. Their own drummer and CJ were clearly cut from the same mold, and had only one operating level: On.

CHAPTER FIVE
CJ

MY EYES WORKED over the soft mounds of her succulent chest where I found her face and those startling mismatched eyes. Staring right back at me.

"You lost?" Nessa asked, pointing behind me as I leaned against her bus. "I think your bus is back there."

I shook my head. "I'm not lost," is all I said, creating a silence I've learned can be more inviting than uncomfortable under the right conditions.

I sensed she could handle the way I was looking at her—undressing her quite slowly with my eyes and enjoying every damn second of it.

She blinked a few times, crossing her arms and leaning against the bus, too, facing me. She swallowed once before speaking.

Come on. Almost there …

"You did a hell of a job tonight," she started, tucking the electric blue piece of hair behind her ear.

It looked like the energy from that ball at that museum we went to in fourth grade. The kind that sent electricity through the whole class as we held hands, causing our hair to frizz up with the residual static. I'd be lying if I said my hair wasn't standing a little on end as I stared, watching confidence flow off her. Nessa didn't fidget with her fingers or spend time studying her shoelaces. Eye contact was her game, and lucky for me, it was a game I'd mastered long ago.

"Thanks," I said, straddling the line between confident and cocky. Between being humble and a horse's ass, as my dad always said. Too bad he wouldn't know humility if it kicked him in the teeth.

Which I wish it would.

"What does CJ stand for, anyway?" her head leaned slightly to the side, eyes narrowing as she weaseled her way into my head.

"Not without a drink first, Vanessa," I teased, winging a guess at her given name.

A smirk slowly peeled one side of her mouth upward. "Not really a big challenge you overcame, there. I'm not weird about my name like you seem to be."

"Who's weird?" I took a deep breath, shrugging it off. Frankie and I had had a similar conversation three years ago when she first asked me what CJ stood for. So, I did now what I did then. I reached for my wallet, handing Nessa my license. "See? No periods. Just CJ," I assured before shoving it back in my jeans.

She nodded, skeptically, the way Frankie had off and on for the first few months of our relationship. I knew Nessa would eventually drop it. They all did. Even Frankie, though it took her longer than most.

You drop it, Kane. Frankie wants nothing to do with you ... just like you knew would happen.

"But, Nessa's a name all by itself, so I took a chance there," I continued.

"It is?"

I nodded. "It's a Gaelic name, actually. Nessa was the mother of the King of Ulster. His name was Conor. She was wildly powerful and beautiful, and really looked out for her son."

"Oh yeah?" Nessa eyed me with almost comical suspicion.

I put my hand to my chest. "I'm dead serious. She tricked her second husband, King Fergus, into giving up the throne and kingdom to his stepson for a year. But, during that year, Conor was such a wise and awesome ruler, that the people chose him to be their permanent king." I smiled proudly.

"Wow, you and Regan really dig into your Irish history, huh?"

"That," I admitted, "and I take a minute to Google interesting names when I hear them on the off chance that they fit into my culture. Got lucky with Nessa, I guess. Not a bad namesake. I've got nothing on Vanessa, though. Sorry." That earned me a hearty laugh from Nessa.

"So, does your C stand for Conor, by any chance?"

I laughed. "Hardly the king type."

Looking around, desperate to change the subject, I noticed the usual division amongst members of our tour. Some headed to their busses, phones in hand, talking to loved ones no doubt. The rest of us? We were just bored, itching for trouble. To my deep, bubbling pleasure, Nessa was still leaning against her bus, seemingly assessing the two different cultures. Deciding which she'd assimilate with for the night.

Taking my chances, I nodded my head to the crowd flowing away from our own RV-like park in the middle of the desert. "Come get a drink with us."

Me. I wanted to say me, but I'd learned a lot over the years, and was far ahead of the testosterone filled hook-up attempts of my earlier youth.

She sighed, heavy as if I'd asked how a dying relative was hanging in there. "I don't know …" Her eyes were cautious, no doubt scanning my face for signs of delinquency. Assessing her own ability to maintain whatever composure she thought she was maintaining around me.

I shrugged, dredging from the depths of the barrel the last of my tricks. "I heard some of the guys say they were going to some bar called Rocky Springs. Join us if you want, but ..." I paused, forcing her eyes up to mine. "Don't come alone, okay? New city, weirdos, all that."

She laughed, her face glowing with the creamy fluorescence of the last of the stage lights left lit. "How big brother of you."

I grinned, throwing a wink before turning on my heels. "Not any big brother your parents would want you hanging around." I walked away, my heart alive in my chest with the intoxicating sensation of fresh flirtation.

One, two, three, four ... shoot, five, six. Did I misjudge her? Seven, eight ...

Finally, it came.

"CJ, wait up." Her voice sounded nonchalant in the few seconds it took her to catch up to me.

I kept walking, saying nothing but allowing her to fall in step next to me, her long, muscular legs making easy work of keeping up. I'd been so entranced by her eyes, I'd failed to notice until now that she'd changed from her stage wear into shredded, tight-as-sin jean shorts with a white T-shirt stretched impossibly across a black-lace bra. She kept the pink combat boots, though. I liked that.

"Tough choice?" I teased. "A night out with fun people over staying in your bus reading, or sitting around the campfire singing Kumbaya with my cousin?"

Her mouth dropped and she punched my shoulder a little harder than a flirt. "What do you know about him? He can party as hard as we're about to."

The good news was, she affirmed we were in for one heck of a night.

"What do I know about him?" I half-scoffed. "We just grew up together, he's married to my best friend—"

"Georgia is your best friend?" She looked shocked for a moment, but it quickly faded. "I guess I can see that," she said with a shrug.

"Yeah?" I arched an eyebrow. "What makes you say that?"

"I suppose if someone the likes of you would have a girl as a best friend, it would have to be a take-no-shit girl like Georgia," she said with an approving smile, nodding her head. "And you never slept with her?"

"Why does everyone ask that?"

"Bet they don't ask her," Nessa challenged, accurately compartmentalizing mine and Georgia's personalities and lifestyles.

I clicked my tongue against my teeth. "If you must know, no. We've never slept together. Seen each other through too much shit for that nonsense."

"Yeah," Nessa replied wistfully.

Something in her voice made me slow and turn to look at her. Her head was tilted down slightly, just enough for the electric blue swath of hair to hang forward, masking the view of her face from the side.

"What?" I nudged her side, needing to break the cloudy mood looming in her posture if we were going to have any kind of night at all. "Missing a boyfriend back home?"

Her spine straightened and she shot me the most deliciously incredulous look. "Nah," she answered, waving her hand, "I dropped his ass long ago for feeding me the same lines you're serving up."

I laughed, glancing at the sky for a moment and shaking my head. Nessa was going to be some work, and I was willing to give myself one night to decide if it was worth the effort for what I'd hoped would be a couple-night fling at best. Maybe some more down the road if we got too pent up on tour—but nothing more.

***

"Come on, big boy, hit one!" Nessa cheered—jeered, really—over a shot of tequila that was a number I lost count of hours ago.

Standing—for certain interpretations of standing—a few paces back from the dartboard, I sloppily brought the feathers of the dart in front of my eye, squinting the other. Though that was an exercise in practice over principle, since I couldn't see straight anyway, no matter how many eyes I had open.

Squaring my shoulders to the board I tilted back slightly before lurching my weight forward, hurling the unassuming dart toward its target. It missed spectacularly, the dart bouncing off a stone column and landing right in the drink of some girl sitting off to the side of the board.

"Score!" Nessa hollered, raising her strong arms into the air, fists of glory above her head.

The girl, a petite brunette with shoulder-length hair in tight curls looked offended as she wiped what smelled like rum and Coke—probably Diet Coke—off her cheeks and chest. Her friends mimicked her look of disdain until I spoke.

"Sorry, honey." It rolled off my tongue as practiced as breathing, despite my thick inebriation. I pulled an empty chair next to her and turned it around, straddling it as I sat, facing her. "Let me get that for you." I took the napkin from her hand and wiped away the last carbonated droplets of my intentional miss off of her collarbone.

"It's okay," she managed, trying not to look too offended or embarrassed. Her eyes darted from my face to the table and back again.

I shook my head, taking her hand. "That won't do. Come, dance with me."

Curly Sue looked shocked, her face all roses as she stood, her hand tight in mine.

"Lucky bitch," one of her friends whispered not so quietly as I escorted her away from the table.

I winked at Nessa for the second time tonight as I scooted passed her and onto the tiny, crowded breeding ground of a dance floor.

"Oh, come on," she teased, loud. "Is that the consolation prize for being assaulted by your own drink? A dance with the tattooed wonder? Run, girl, run! It's all a trick!" She fell into a fit of laughter, signaling to the waitress walking by that she would, in fact, love another shot. She could really put them away—I'd have my work cut out for me if I decided to pursue her.

"Is she a friend of yours?" the girl asked as we secured our tightly bordered real estate on the dance floor.

I took hold of her wrists, placing her hands on my shoulders as mine girdled her tiny waist. "Sort of. Tour mate. What's your name?"

Her eyes widened as if seeing for the first time. "You are that drummer!" She quickly recovered her gaping stare, circling her hips a little deeper at her apparent recognition of me.

"What's your name?" I asked again, my lips an inch from her ear.

"Kayla." Her voice was fluttery.

"Hey Kayla, I'm CJ. That drummer."

The smell of sweat off her neck was intoxicating and new—far more than any libation offered by the bar. I spun her around, encouraging her to grind her round ass into me as I sucked in the sweet scent of pheromones from the back of her neck, a pleasure I'd missed over the last few weeks.

Frankie smelled better.

I growled the thought away, grazing the back of Kayla's ear with my lips. Not kissing, but so close I could taste her. I just needed a few dry runs to get back in the game. That was all. It would be like riding a bike, I told myself.

Kayla turned back around, a smoldering look standing in where her shock and adoration had been previously. "You are really good."

It didn't matter if she was talking about my music or my moves; she was right on both accounts. I nodded lifting her chin with my index finger and bringing my lips closer to her ear than before. The tiny, soft hairs brushed against my lips. "You have no idea."

Before she could respond, Nessa was at her side, eyeing me with bear trap intensity. "Can I cut in?"

Casting a glance to Kayla, I watched her bedroom eyes shift to indignant shock as I stepped back to allow Nessa into her dance space. Not wanting to be the total ass I risked portraying myself as, I leaned to Kayla once more, talking into her ear.

"I'll be here all night, hon."

This was enough, and Kayla bit her bottom lip, quickly falling into step with another intoxicated loner on the dance floor.

"She marched loyally right into your little trap there, didn't she?" Nessa remarked, placing one hand on my shoulder, using the thumb and forefinger of her other hand to pinch my chin.

"I feel bad." I chuckled. "It was so easy, like luring a baby deer away from its mother."

Nessa shook her head. "And the barbarian uses a hunting metaphor. Shocker."

I held the barbell on my tongue between my teeth, wiggling my eyebrows for a moment as I grabbed a firm hold of her hips, moving easily in time with her in the humid bar.

"Yes," she said in a bored sigh. "You have your tongue pierced. Is this two-thousand-one?"

I ignored her jab and just kept moving.

As the music blared on and Nessa and I fell into our own grinding beat, I let myself get lost in her own, unique scent. Tequila, sweet flowers, sweat, and the intoxicating aroma of a lead singer. Leads command any stage they grace, literal or social, and Nessa was no different in that way, but was worlds apart from many others I'd known over the years in her approach. She didn't showboat, and wasn't ironically standoffish like so many try to be when desperately wanting to appear hip.

She was a quiet storm, like a puppet master vaguely aware of the strings in her hands.

CHAPTER SIX

REGAN

"W HAT'S YOUR COUSIN'S deal?" Nessa asked the morning after our final performance in the desert. We were winding back into the Pacific Northwest and had stopped at a roadside diner. Only a few of us were wide awake that early, many of us placing extra orders to take back onto our busses to our sleeping and/or hungover friends. Nessa and I were settled into a quiet booth in the back, surrounded only by black coffee, eggs, and waffles.

"Deal?" I said with a shake of my head and a mouthful of syrup. "Dare I ask why you're asking?"

She leaned forward with a sly grin. "You seem nervous."

"He makes me nervous. Especially around women."

Nessa waved her hand. "Oh I know all that stuff, remember? His wrap sheet is standard. I just mean, I don't know … He seems like he's got more."

"He does seem that way," I conceded.

Of course there was more to CJ. More to all of us on this tour. But, CJ's road persona was carefully curated and closely guarded—nothing I was willing to dismantle for curious on-lookers.

"You know stuff," she guessed.

"Sure," I admitted. "He's my cousin. And not distant once-a-year at Christmas cousin, either. We grew up together."

"Skeletons?"

I shook my head. "Nothing dire. It's not like he's got a pregnant wife back home or a legal record containing more than a few bar fights. I believe those ever went on his record, come to think of it."

She laughed. "You take care of him."

"He stopped letting me do that long ago." I took a long sip of my coffee and sat back, waiting for my stomach to make more room for food. I can never get enough of diner breakfasts, no matter how old I get or how many I eat in.

"You look out for him then," Nessa conceded.

"You were out with him last night, can you blame me?" I chuckled, going in for my third waffle.

In all honesty I was extremely curious what had gone on last night, but given Nessa's calm demeanor, I guessed she was at least partly spared CJ's usual tricks.

"He got a girl?"

At this, I sputtered a little on my coffee. "Shouldn't you be having this conversation with a girl?"

Her eyes widened and she sat back, looking satisfied. "He does, then."

I shook my head slowly. "He does not," was as much as I'd let go.

Nessa pursed her lips. "There's somethin'."

I shrugged, diving back into the last waffle. "What about you? Boyfriend?"

"No one I'd write home about."

I looked up, catching a satirical glance that made her pass for far older than her late twenties. At least I figured she was in her late twenties—though I wasn't even going to get into all of that with a woman.

"Fair enough."

She eyed my plate. "Want some waffle with your syrup? Jesus."

"My wife trades in sugar, what do you expect from me?" I gave her a grin and a quick wink.

Her eyes lit up. "Ah, so that wink is a Kane family specialty then."

"Oh," I sighed deeply, giving her a look of pity, "if CJ gave you that then you're in big, big trouble."

"Why?" she asked, rabid for inside information. "What's it mean? You just gave it to me …"

"Touché."

"Come on," she pleaded, slapping her hand on the table. "Give me something to go with."

I sighed. "Fine. Wanna know my opinion? If you're looking for a good time, I can point you in the right direction." I gestured to CJ standing in the parking lot, smoking a cigarette. I hadn't seen him do that much so far, but it was none of my business. "But if you're looking for something, anything else …"

"Got it," she cut me off.

"Besides," I started, rising from the table and throwing enough money down to cover our breakfasts and tip, "do you even want to get into sleeping with people on the road? This is a long tour—wait."

She eyed me, curious. "What?"

"This is your first long tour, isn't it?"

She nodded.

"Consider the implications … that's all I'll say. The busses get smaller the longer we live in them, and if sex is involved—"

Claustrophobic.

"Sex?" she cut me off. "Oh hell no … I just wanted to play with him a little … like a cat with a mouse, or something."

The determination in her eyes calmed any hesitation I had about her getting mixed up with CJ. There was something going on with him, but it was up to him and anyone he came in contact with to figure out.

I wrapped my arm around her shoulders, giving a quick squeeze as we left the diner. "Just don't leave his mangled carcass on my doorstep, kay?"

***

"I miss you," I whispered into the phone when Georgia picked up.

"Already?" she teased. "You've just been gone a week."

I grinned, rolling onto my back, feeling the seductive pull to sleep by the road moving underneath the bus. "You going to come to Oregon?"

"I wouldn't miss it," she answered, which piqued my interest.

Typically Georgia teased me about any time she may or may not meet me on the road. She'd play like she was too busy or didn't want to travel a certain distance but, more often than not, she showed up, waiting for me when I arrived in whatever city. A conversation we had weeks and weeks ago lingered in the back of my head.

Ovulating ...

Not a word I'd ever thought I'd care too much about until Georgia uttered it in our bed a month before the tour began. A word that signaled the official start of our attempt to make a family.

But, after a week on the road, two performing, I needed her—badly. The good-looking women around me day after day on tour, never mind the ones in the crowd who call my name and flash their perfect breasts—it was driving me crazier earlier than it usually had. Maybe it was all the baby talk that was revving up my libido. Good to know some evolutionary things pan out.

I wanted my wife under me, over me, and every way I could get her. So profound was my instant desire that I had to shift, rolling onto my side, my back facing CJ, to avoid any comments about my swelling need. He'd likely never be in this position on the road—having to wait for the woman he loves in order to satisfy any longing he might have.

"Regan?" Her question pulled me back to the present, where I'm painfully aware of Georgia's absence.

"Sorry," I sighed, "I just miss you so much."

CJ got out of bed and tapped me on the shoulder. "I'm going to the back to play cards with some of the guys—wanna come?"

I shook my head, anxious for him to leave my personal space. "Talking with G."

He nodded and, without a word, disappeared to the back of the bus.

"Was that CJ?" Georgia asked.

"Yeah."

"He behaving?"

"Let's not talk about him. I can't think straight right now, I miss you so bad."

A low purr came from the back of her throat and in my head I could see the face she always made to accompany that delicious tone. "Real bad?" she asked.

My voice came out more breathless by the second as I slid a hand to my jeans. "Bad, G. You have no idea how badly I want you right now. Right here. Right now." I was so hard, my body was more than relieved when I undid my button and zipper, releasing myself from constraint.

She whispered. "You're all alone right now?"

I nodded, as if she could see. "Yeah."

"Me too. In our bed. The sheets still smell like you."

I swallowed, my throat dry as I wrapped my hand around my rock-hard cock. "Keep talking …"

Her voice was playfully seductive. Low, enticing, luring. She was a predator of the best kind, and I'd fall for her every time—

in person or not. "I'm in the blue silky panties you like … with the black polka dots."

"What bra are you wearing?" My pulse quickened at just the thought of her in those damn panties.

"I'm not," she answered, sending me into another level of ecstasy. "I'm running my hands over my breasts, wishing they were your hands." Her breath picked up the way it did when I put her nipple between my lips.

"Jesus …"

"Tell me what you'd do if you were here. I miss you, Regan …"

I groaned when she said my name, closing my eyes to bring her as close to me as possible, pretending for a little longer that she was actually here and not in a whole other state. "I'd run my lips from your nipples to your navel. Slow, making you squirm." The noises from the other end of the phone told me to continue as I stroked myself harder, faster.

"Then," I continued, barely able to form words the closer I got to climax, "I'd bring my mouth into you, swirling my tongue."

I could tell from the faint hum in the background that she had her vibrator in bed with her, and that just turned me on more, causing my orgasm to flood over and through me in a garbled mess of words and soft moans. I tried to be as quiet as possible, but there's only so much control one has …

A few seconds later, Georgia got hers and, for a few quiet seconds we sat on the phone, listening to each other breathe.

"I miss you," I said again, for what would be one of a million times over the next several months.

Panting, she answered back. "I miss you. I'll see you soon and give you the R-rated version of what we just did."

I groaned playfully, stripping from my jeans and boxers under the blanket, needing to wash those as soon as possible, and reminding myself of proper road etiquette for situations like this—be prepared. This took me off guard, though. Rookie move.

"See you in Oregon," I said. "Goodnight."

"Night, babe. I love you."

"I love you."

When the line went silent, I took another deep breath, savoring the temporary relief my own hand would provide before the desire swept up again, like waves on high tide—back in as fast as they leave.

A knock on the door separating our section from the back of the bus startled me—this wasn't really a knocking type of crew.

"Yeah?" I called.

"It's CJ, can I come in?"

I scrunched my eyebrows. "Yeah …"

A second later he burst into the "room," all grins and bravado. "Thank God. I was wondering how long it would take you to polish one off."

"The fuck you talking about?" My cheeks heated, and I hoped the dusky light of sunset would hide my embarrassment. I'm not the showman CJ is.

He waved his hand, giving my shoulder a hard clap before falling onto his own bed. "Come on, Regan. All low talking and whispers with Georgia? I know when to take a hint."

I grumbled, rolling over. "Then take one now and shut up."

He laughed. "All right, all right. But, just know this—"

"Do I have to?"

"Yes. I've got mad respect for you, man. Guys drop their girls left and right around here—wife or not. You don't. I mean, G's my best friend, so I'd hate to have to kick your ass if you started sniffing around—"

"You really are vile, you know that?" I cut in, peeking at him from over my shoulder.

He raised his hand. "Let me finish. I'm just saying, I'm happy for you and Georgia that you're relationship is as tight as it is."

"Thanks, man. I love her."

"I know. So, I'm willing to clear the deck whenever you need to shine your knob."

I flipped him the bird before slipping quickly into a satisfying sleep.

CHAPTER SEVEN

GEORGIA

"F OR THE CANNOLI," Brian asked, "do you make or purchase the shells?"

He looked up after my long silence, chuckling when he saw my face. I crinkled my nose like I smelled garbage.

"What?" he asked innocently, laughing.

I put my hand on my hip and arched an eyebrow. "I wouldn't sell them if I couldn't make them. You know me better than that."

A small grin took over the corner of his mouth. "Just checking," he murmured.

"Do you mean for people to call this place Live, as in 'I live here' or Live as in 'Live band'?" The question had been nagging at the back of my mind since Regan brought me there before he left on tour.

Brian looked up from the binder filled with pictures of my work and my many catering offerings, light in his eyes. "That's part of the art. I call it the first way, but it's about being open to expression and where we are in life. I'm an artist, like you, like Regan, but I'm not confined to just food." He lowered his head, continuing to pore over my portfolio.

"Hmm." I poured him coffee, thinking it over. "I think maybe you're playing off not thinking things through all the way."

His face was almost pale when he looked up again, his mouth open.

I swung at his shoulder with a towel from my apron. "I'm just screwing with you. I've known you too long to think you're careless."

Thankfully he laughed, his sense of humor seemingly fully in tact despite keeping up with the grueling schedule of a restaurant owner—a new one at that.

I used to waitress at bars he managed throughout the region. Sometimes I followed him outright when he left for another establishment, and other times we happened to end back up together and were a fierce crime-fighting duo with the after-midnight crowd.

In truth, I was now as exhausted as Brian. And my nerves were on edge, especially with Regan gone and me being left to my own devices. I'd been working a breakneck pace for years to get the bakery off the ground while working on my relationship with Regan, never mind dealing with the anxieties around my mother's health. It would be enough to send anyone insane. But the double-edged sword of it all was that work was the only thing that helped keep me grounded one hundred percent of the time. I was never into drugs or boozing as an escape—productivity was my high.

"Always a smart ass," Brian cut in, yawning. "Can you leave this place well enough alone to go hook up with your husband in Oregon?"

I walked back into the kitchen, double checking the contents of the refrigerator with the list in my hand to assure things would run as smoothly as possible while I was out of town. "What's that supposed to mean?"

"You're more balls-to-the-wall than I've ever been." He left his booth and joined me in the kitchen, swiping my list and leaning against the counter. "It's been a hell of a successful few years for you, and I don't want you to get burned out."

I huffed, irritated to be having this conversation. There were far more men in the culinary business than women—at least here in San Diego, and conversations always veered down this path. "Do guys talk to each other like this, or is it my tits that subjects me to the 'take it easy' talk?"

Brian pursed his lips.

I pursed mine back in his silence. "I don't tell you to take it easy. Wanna know why? Because you're a grown-ass man who can handle himself."

He shook his head. "Look. You and Regan both have a wicked work ethic. I just want to make sure you leave time for an actual relationship."

I held out my hands. "When did this turn into couple's counseling? Regan and I support each other in everything we do."

"Friends can do that, too, G. Just nurture the love between the two of you, kay? The connection that first drew you to each other. Friends can't do that the way lovers can." A pall of sadness washed over his face. Distant, but visible—like a lighthouse in the fog.

Suddenly, I realized this wasn't all about me.

"What's going on with Randy?" I asked Brian of his long-time partner.

"Don't turn this around—"

"Don't be vague with me," I cut in. "We've been through too much."

He sighed, finally setting my list on the counter behind him and rubbing his hands over his face a few times. "He's staying with his mom for a while ..." His voice clipped off at the end of his sentence and I flew in to hug him as hard as I could.

"No," I whispered. "What happened?"

"Life." He shrugged. "He supported me, I supported his teaching career, all the way through his doctorate ..."

"I know. So what happened?"

I let go and he leaned back, looking war-torn all of a sudden where his bright and affable face had been only minutes before.

"At the end of the day," he sighed, "we realized we'd basically been support staff for each other for too long, and the love … it was on life support and the plug was hanging loose."

"No." I shook my head, panicked heat rising through my chest. "Love doesn't just go away. You guys have been together for, what? Fifteen years? That's not lust—it's love. And love lasts." I knew it took a lot more than love to keep two people together, but the other stuff seemed even more intangible, and volatile—if it was possible to find something more volatile than love.

"Maybe," he conceded. "But I wonder if maybe we're different people than we were a decade-and-a-half ago. Too different, I mean. Two people who might say hi in a coffee shop, but that's it. Talking about dreams is a lot different than the realization of those dreams. The day-to-day."

My eyes scanned his face, rapidly moving back and forth as I tried to make sense of his words. So, I paced. Around the stainless steel island that had been the focal point of my existence over the past few years. Where all the "magic" happened, as the food critics stated in their write-ups. The write-ups that made me, thankfully, busier each time. Causing me to spend more time around this steel rectangle.

"That's not me and Regan," I blurted out, stopping long enough to grip the edge of the island. "He was a professional musician before I even met him. Teaching, playing live on the side … and my bakery was underway, too, for that matter."

Brian was roughly five foot ten, but his grand personality typically made him seem taller. On this day, though, he looked every bit his height standing in my bakery as I stared at him, and not an inch more. His Italian-olive skin was washed out, his dark eyes hopeless as he crossed his arms around his soft middle. Never trust a skinny chef, he always said.

"Georgia ... look," he started tiredly.

Then, it dawned on me.

"Did Regan say something to you?" I questioned.

Brian's a terrible liar, looking down and to the right every single time.

"Brian ..." I prodded when his eyes shifted.

"We're friends," he started. "Me and Regan. We were just ... shooting the breeze before the tour and he was clearly anxious about having another tour—a long one even if it is relaxed—coming off the heels of nearly three years of nonstop touring. He was worried about you."

"Bullshit." Regan may very well have been worried about me, but he always told me that—there was something more there.

Great. This is just great.

Here I was, planning to spend a whole weekend away with Regan—a busy weekend for the bakery at that, and he was running around panicking to his friend. A mutual friend who I knew first, thank you very much—because we started talking seriously about having a baby. Total. Bullshit.

"Look, I'm just going to go back to the table and finish my order, okay? We can talk about all this more later ... or not. I didn't mean to dump my personal shit on you—or to have you turn it into your shit ... again."

That pushed me over the edge on which I built my camp. "What?" I snapped.

"It's always that way. Yeah, part of having friends is the back-and-forth of shared experience, but, fuck, G. You always find a way to make it about you and sometimes ... once in a fucking while I'm the one who needs an ear."

The thing about Brian was he was different than almost all of my other friends. He'd go toe-to-toe with me in a way almost no one else did, except Regan, maybe. That's what I loved and hated about him. I didn't mind being challenged—but I would have rather had the challenge come about my opinions and not my behavior. I am human after all.

"But," I challenged, "didn't you make this about you in order to throw a parable my way? Is Randy even at his mom's?"

That was the wrong thing to say.

Brian's eyes misted over and he did that thing guys do where he sniffed, swallowed, and coughed at the same time in order to prevent something that might pass for a tear.

"Yes," he finally answered through gritted teeth, pacing back to the booth in the front window of the store.

"Then why didn't you tell me until now?" I followed him, sitting across from him in the booth while he tried to avoid my gaze.

Brian shrugged, flipping fast enough through the pages of my portfolio that I knew he wasn't actually looking at anything. "Because we've been busy, Georgia. Isn't that what we do, me and you? Busy?"

"Jesus," I grumbled, slight panic rising in my chest. "Are you having a nervous breakdown now? People don't usually come here for the breakdown. It's usually to prevent or recover from …"

Thankfully, my humor in tone and timing was enough to crack Brian's tough exterior. He growled, folding his arms across the book and resting his head on top of them, "Why is life so hard?" he roared into the table.

I sank back in to the booth, a sober realization dawning on me. "It is, isn't it …" I trailed off.

This is a problem.

"What?" Brian looked up, reaching across the table to put a warm hand on my flour-covered arm.

I shook my head. "Nothing. And, no, I'm not trying to fish for anything … to make it about me. It's … nothing."

"That was a dick thing for me to say. We all pull that shit sometimes, and it wasn't fair for me to take my bullshit out on you."

I swallowed hard. "Be honest with me?"

He nodded. "Overly so, most of the time. Shoot."

"Is Regan just freaking about trying to have a baby?" The words came out in a near-whisper, as if I was more afraid of the question than the answer. Because asking it revealed more about me than Regan.

Because I was freaking out.

Brian's eyes bugged out. "A what?"

Shit.

Regan and I had said we weren't going to broadcast our journey to family-hood because we'd seen struggles and heart-break in friends of ours, and we wanted to protect ourselves from the expectations of others, since we certainly couldn't help ourselves with ours. But, I guess I'd just screwed that up a little.

"G?" he questioned, a broad grin lighting up his entire face. "Seriously?"

I shrugged. Nodded. "But he's worried about me now … he doesn't think I can handle it."

Brian shook his head. "He was worried about you resenting him, Georgia. That's what that was about. Not what he said, but what he meant. I know these things."

"I wouldn't resent him. Not ever. And for what?"

Brian took a long deep sigh and I knew the totality of the truth was upon us. "He didn't tell me you guys were starting a family. But he did say that he was worried that taking on this tour was going to signal to you that work was more important than anything else. And that's not what it is. He was concerned you guys would … you know …"

"End up like you and Randy?" Brian had clearly told Regan of his situation.

Brian nodded. "Yeah."

"But this is part of his work. Just like weddings and shit are a part of mine. He doesn't resent the month of June," I said of the busiest wedding month of the year.

"Now I have more information about his statement, what with this whole baby business. I know guys pretty well," he said with a chuckle. "And if Regan is the kind of guy I think he is, I bet he's worried about you taking this tour as a sign that he's not on board with starting a family. It certainly makes more sense in that context."

I threw up my hands, rocking my head back against the booth. "Well isn't this all just assumptions and hurt feelings over nothing! Ugh."

"Pack your bags," Brian said calmly. "And get your ass to Oregon, show your man a fine time, and communicate. If you can do that now …" he trailed off as an obvious warning.

Leaning forward, I look him directly in the eye. "You do the same. Let your manager run the show for a night and go woo your husband back."

He laughed. "You know, we never had these problems until we actually got married. I'm starting to wonder what the whole Prop-eight fuss was about," he joked about his constitutional right to wedded bliss.

"It's all a scam," I joked back. "But, seriously … fight for him. Everyone needs to be fought for once in a while."

I had to swallow a huge lump in my throat after I said it, remembering the tireless way Regan fought for me—for us—when I wanted nothing to do with him or anyone else. At least that was the lie I had been living in before he blew into town and taught me I was worth it all—fighting for, loving others, and being loved. That last one was the hardest, and one that I battled daily.

Brian held up the binder. "Can I take this to pore over while you're away? Is there another one here in the store?"

I nodded, waving my hand. "Keep it. I expect you to be a frequent customer."

He stood from the booth, kissing me on top of the head before he headed for the door. "Get that fiddler of yours, Georgia. Before we try to woo him to our side. He'd make a great addition to our team."

I flipped him off, only causing him to blow me a kiss. And, as soon as he left, I locked up the bakery—closing it early for the first time since the doors of Sweet Forty-Two first opened—and packed my things for Oregon.

CHAPTER EIGHT

REGAN

"**D**O YOU EVER notice that all drummers look the tiniest bit resentful? Like … all the time?" Nessa pointed to CJ, who was practicing with Moniker. They would be without their drummer for the next few shows due to a bar-fight induced broken wrist.

I laughed. CJ was perched behind the set—his favorite place in the entire universe—and he looked like he would sooner hang himself. His eyes were glazed over as he lightly thumped a steady beat on the base drum. Moniker was on the folksier end of the groups on the tour, as opposed to some of the bluegrass and fringe rock offered by the other acts. Alas, they didn't have a ton of need for a drum set, so to speak, just someone to keep a beat and offer a cymbal roll once in a while.

"This … isn't really his speed," I admitted.

"Well at least he's being a good sport?" Nessa suggested.

I shrugged, peering at my phone for the tenth time in what, unfortunately, had only been twenty minutes.

Nessa nudged my side. "She'll be here soon."

My cheeks heated.

"Come on," she teased. "I see that grin on your face. I think you two are cute."

I rolled my eyes. "Never use that word around Georgia."

Nessa laughed. "I wouldn't dream of it."

She'd only met Georgia a couple of times, I think, but one thing about Georgia is she gave everyone all of her personality right away. Despite being cute, Georgia would rather cut someone than have that nickname applied to her. She was five foot two, with mouth-watering curves that could easily confuse onlookers into thinking she belonged on a 1950s pinup calendar. She switched her hair color from bleach-blonde to jet-black from time to time, but always had on bright red lipstick, which worked wonders against her milky skin.

Just thinking about her made my neck sweat.

This was just a practice session before our three-concert set this weekend in a revived opera house in Portland. Most of the members not practicing were scattered around the city sight-seeing, or sleeping on the busses, I liked to watch. Nessa did, too, and we often found ourselves commenting—constructive or in appreciation—about each band during their practice, sometimes making notes to take back to our own bands. And, since I was a few years removed from the hardcore partying scene, I found myself with a lot of time on my hands while on the road. I didn't know Nessa's "story," per se, so I didn't know why she wasn't out with the rest of the small handful of women on the tour, but I was just as happy to not be alone—or with CJ—the entire time.

"Well," Nessa yawned and stretched at the end of Moniker's set, "I'm gonna go take a nap. See ya." She gave me a quick slap on the shoulder and disappeared onto the streets as CJ leaped off the stage.

"Where's she going?" he asked, sounding irritated.

I shrugged. "Not my turn to watch her. Why do you look like you want to slit your wrists up there? I know you're doing them a favor, but don't be a dick."

He rolled his eyes. "Sorry, Mom, I'll do better at the show tonight. But, seriously, where was she going?"

"I don't fucking know … she said she was going to take a nap—"

"Ha!" CJ wrapped his sticks together before shoving them in his back pocket. "Thanks," was all he said before he disappeared out the same door Nessa had, moving faster than I'd seen him move in a long while.

Whatever …

"Mind if I sit?" Yardley Honeywell's voice swooped in from behind me.

I looked over my shoulder and nodded, gesturing to the seat. She climbed over the back, plunking herself down next to me, pointing to the stage.

"What do you think of them?" she asked of Moniker.

I nodded slowly, forming my answer.

"Come on," she prodded. "You spend more time watching these bands than anyone else on this tour … including me. What do you think?"

I grinned, folding my arms across my chest as Yardley and I sat in the middle of the empty opera house, well out of hearing range of the group dismantling their set on stage. "They're good."

"Bummer. Just good?" She twisted her lips, rubbing her hand under her chin as if studying a medical chart.

"They're like … hmm … how do I say this …"

"I don't know," Yardley said as she chuckled. "With words? What is it about them? There's something …"

"Missing."

"Yes."

I took a deep breath, gesturing with my hands as if explaining a complicated math problem which, to be honest, music was. "Their girl—"

"Cheryl?"

I shrugged. "See? I didn't even know. Anyway, yes. She's got a good voice but she plays it safe. I've heard her just kicking around off-hours … even at karaoke. She can really let it fly. Like Christina Aguilera fly."

"Really?"

I nodded. "Yes. And I'm not saying she should do that, because I believe she likes the music her group does and that would totally blow their sound, but she needs to open up. They need to write more of that into their music. Their guitar guy … Luke? He can bring it up a bit, too. All that to say, their vocals are weak, and not for lack of talent."

Yardley nodded, still looking pensively at a now-empty stage. "You're absolutely right."

"I feel like they could use something more … instrumentally. Like a fiddle, because I'm partial—or some more keys. I just feel like the two guitars and occasional percussion is a little too Peter, Paul, and Mary … or something. And their drummer, too—before he broke his wrist—he's good. CJ hates him, so I know he's good. I think they're just trying to be someone they're not, if you want my fully-disclosed opinion. They need to let their hair down a bit."

A wide, pearly-white smile broke Yardley's tight-lipped stare onto the stage. "Let their hair down … you're good."

"Who writes for them?"

She shook her head. "No one at the moment. They wrote all the stuff they're singing now, but new stuff is kind of up in the air. You wanna do it?"

I threw my head back and laughed, loud. "Yeah, I have no time for that."

"On this tour you do," she challenged.

"Holy shit," I looked at her wide-eyed, "you're serious."

She arched an eyebrow at me, the smile fading slightly. "I'm trying to decide if I want to renew their contract. They were with some tiny label, Blue Mountain, that we swallowed a couple of months ago."

The casual way Yardley talks business was always fascinating. "I didn't know GSE swallowed anyone."

She offered a shrug. "It just became final, and some of their artists we took with the deal. These guys ... this is kind of an audition for them ... sort of."

I puffed out my cheeks with a long exhale, stretching my arms overhead. "Do they know this?"

"They're not dumb," was how she answered that it hadn't been explicitly discussed, rather implied.

"Doesn't GSE have some people who could throw original music their way?"

"No one as classically trained as you." She faced me now, crossing her legs. "No one with your ear. I agree with everything you said about them, and I want to give them a good shot. It doesn't have to be a lot—two or three pieces maybe."

I laughed, shrugging exaggeratedly. "Just two or three original pieces, that's all. On instruments I don't even play."

She waved her hand, unfazed by my anxiety. "You can play the piano, first of all. I've heard you. Secondly, your education is top notch. You know how to score music. Teach, too, if my research and your resume line up correctly."

"Stalker," I muttered.

"How'd you get two master's degrees at the same time?"

"I was intense. Lived, breathed, ate, slept music. And, mostly didn't sleep. The first break I'd had since high school was the summer I met Bo and Ember."

I leaned forward, pressing my elbows into my knees as I bowed my head. She was right, of course. I was at that time the only classically trained musician under contract at GSE. That did not make me a better musician by any stretch of the imagination. GSE had some talented artists, not the least of which were Bo and Ember, who were representing the label on the east coast. But what it did mean was exactly what Yardley had said—I could score music in my sleep. My undergraduate degree was in classical studies, but my master's was in composition, and I got another in education. All that was fancy talk for me being a workaholic whose passion and paycheck happened to align.

After a long pause, during which Yardley didn't flinch once, I sighed. "I'll do two songs. One slow, one fast. If you like them, you pay someone to write you more."

She cheered, giving me a quick hug. "Regan you'll be compensated handsomely for all of this. Don't worry about that part."

I waved my hand. "I'll do this as a favor."

She shook her head. "I'd rather not. I might need another favor from you at some point."

"What's the deadline? I need one." I grinned, feeling like this was more mafia than music.

"Sunday?"

My face fell. I could feel it. I knew I'd never have the all-the-time poker face like Yardley had, and I didn't care. "Georgia's coming today for the weekend."

"Oh …" Yardley's face stayed still as her eyes wandered widely around the room as she tried to work out the problem.

"You know what?" I cut in. "It'll be good. Sunday will be fine. I've got some mostly-finished stuff I've been toying with that I can shuffle around and add some other instruments to anyway."

"No, no. I don't want to impose on your personal life. You know we really try—"

I cut her off again, standing. "I know you do. And you guys do a great job of treating us like family and not just saying it. You take care of all of us. But I want to do this. It'll be great brain work, and if it'll help the label that really helps all of us in the end, doesn't it?"

Almost certainly despite herself, Yardley grinned. "You've always been one hell of a team player, Regan. I don't know what we did to deserve to get you or keep you."

"I had to be a team player to spend three years solid with Chris and Shaughn," I joked of my Celtic Summer bandmates.

She laughed. "I think it worked out to just under two years when we factor in the breaks you had."

I staggered back comically, as if I'd been shot. "Breaks? Breaks!?"

Yardley and I fell into laughter about the insane tour schedule we'd been on. Celtic Summer headlined some shows, simply participated in others, and all told it did do great things to promote the label, and us as artists, so the breakneck pace was well worth it.

"You're a good sport, Regan. Anyway, I think that was the last practice of the day. I'm heading to the hotel." When we didn't have to stay on the buses, we didn't. It gave all of us—the busses and drivers included—a much needed break. And a chance to be cleaned.

I eyed the stage, picking my case up from the floor. "Mind if I stick around for a few minutes?"

"Not at all," she said with something bright in her eyes. "Enjoy your time with Georgia. And, Regan?"

"Yeah?"

"Don't work too hard, okay? Early next week is fine for the score."

She turned on her heels and marched toward the exit without a look back. Once the door was closed, I bounded onto the stage and tuned my violin.

Finally, I took a deep breath, closed my eyes, and brought bow and string together. The fingers of my left hand glided their way up and down the neck of the instrument as my right worked the strings with the bow in the opposite direction. I paced the stage, my steps far slower than the notes I was play-ing, but the playing in itself relaxed me, regardless of the tempo I was turning out.

The violin was always a talisman for me. I remember the very first time I held one, when I was five at a music festival on Cape Cod. Most bands there that weekend had set up booths with information, tour dates, meet-the-band, etc. Some bands even let people—mostly children—try their hand at an instru-ment. My parents and CJ's parents brought us—our moms are sisters—and it's so vivid in my memory because he was only three then, but picked up drum sticks and never set them back down. It was "cute" at the time, but had quickly turned into a loud, sometimes maddening, obsession.

When I'd wandered into the booth of an old-time bluegrass band, I remember staring, mesmerized by the old man with the impossibly long, grey and white beard swaying to and fro as he lazily played his violin. His eyes were closed and he looked like he was meditating. To my five-year-old self it looked like he was playing in his sleep. Despite being a pretty hyper kid, I remem-ber standing so still my mom was certainly afraid to talk to me or anyone else in the booth out of fear that she might snap me out of my trance and I'd be off and running like the lunatic I usually was.

Before long, the man finished, and when he opened the twinkling eyes set in his wrinkled and leathered face, he smiled at me. Really smiled. Then, he handed me his instrument. Just dangled it in front of me like it wasn't his heart beating outside his chest. I know now that it's because it was such a part of him that he was able to set it in the hands of a gawking kid.

"Go ahead," he'd said.

My mom had interrupted, politely horrified. "Oh no. No, we couldn't possibly …"

He waved his hand. "If we don't share music, it becomes extinct. Passing it down through the generations is the only way it survives. It's the birth and death of the arts—the willingness to pass it down or forget about it."

He really said that. I don't remember it from that day, but my mom repeated the lines so often that it became part of my reconstructed memory. Before I took hold of the instrument, I remember my mom getting down at eye-level with me and speaking softly, with a growl between clenched teeth and a smile.

"Be gentle," she'd said, before doling out her threat. "If you break this instrument I'm never taking you out in public again."

I remember nodding, taking it, and trying to hold it the way I'd seen him doing it. It was a full-sized violin, not designed for the short arms and stubby hands of a five-year-old, but I made it work, somehow. I closed my eyes, the way I'd seen him do it, took a breath, and slid the bow across the strings.

It sounded terrible.

Kind of like cats in a blender is the only way I can describe it, but I didn't care. I'd just made music on my own for the first time. I moved my hands haphazardly up and down the neck of the old violin for a few seconds, producing one God-awful note after another, a huge smile forming on my face with each note. I wasn't embarrassed in the least, because I'd had no idea how bad I'd sounded--I was just making music. When I finished and opened my eyes, the old man nodded at me with a wink, held out his hand, and when he took his instrument back he'd said, "Well done."

That was it for me. After several minutes of him talking with my mom, he became my first teacher.

It was more than a decade before I could play "Flight of the Bumblebee" like I was today, on an empty stage in Oregon, but every single day of my life between the day I first held a violin until now felt the same. Awe. Wonder. Creation. I made a vow to myself somewhere in high school, when I transferred to a private performing arts school to prep me for the Boston Conservatory, that if I ever stopped feeling that way, I'd lock the instrument away and never look back.

So far, so good I'd say.

Throughout my career, I taught little kids all the way through adults, performed with orchestras, small ensembles, and out here in the rock-n-roll world. I've taught at conservatory workshops and privately. I was always asked in interviews what my "favorite" thing to do is with music. The answer was always the same—play. It didn't matter how, when, or where. I just had to play.

Taking a deep breath at the end of just over a minute of exhausting playing—"Flight of the Bumblebee" is as much of a workout as going for a run—I set my arms down and rolled my neck side to side, ready to play again. Before I could raise my instrument back up to my shoulder, however, a soft clap came from the far back of the old opera house, commanding my attention.

Because the stage lights were still on, I had to duck and squint to make out the figure now walking toward me.

"Georgia?" I asked softly, not wanting to get my hopes up since she told me she was running late.

"Regan Kane?" she answered back, putting on her best fan-girl impression.

Carefully, I set the violin on the stage, then leapt the four feet down, grinning like the love-struck fool I was as I jogged toward her.

"The one and only," I finally answered, wrapping my arms around her waist.

She squealed for a split second as I lifted her off the ground, circling once with her pressed close to my body before setting her down and planting one hell of a road-weary kiss on her full, painted red lips. Cadillac red, as always.

"Miss me?" she questioned, trying to sound sarcastic, but I could hear slight relief in her voice. It didn't startle me—she always sounded that way. Surprised that I might actually miss the love of my life.

She still wasn't used to being loved unconditionally. Not all the time, though are any of us ever prepared to receive that?

I surprised her again, lifting her up and setting her on the stage in front of me before I lowered my forehead, resting it on the warm, soft tops of her thighs.

"You have no idea," I sighed through my answer.

Her hands touched the top of my head, soft as she gently raked her short, black-painted fingernails down my scalp a few times, as if coaxing a feral cat. There's a bit of stray in every road musician, and Georgia always recognized when mine needed to be nurtured.

CHAPTER NINE
REGAN

G EORGIA AND I only swung by the hotel for a minute so I could deposit my violin and Georgia could change before meeting CJ for dinner. We'd have plenty of time to catch up physically later—which killed me to convince myself—but it was important to me that I didn't turn into one of those guys that went MIA when his girlfriend or wife showed up. Life on the road is always about maintaining balance when able.

"How'd you manage to con your way into getting your own room?" Georgia asked as we entered the hibachi grill restaurant.

While it was fairly common for me to have my own room when on longer tours with Celtic Summer, because our budget was nearly bottomless, it was much less common on smaller tours, regardless of our label's income. Yardley was smart with money, and while she didn't cut unnecessary corners, wasting money gave her anxiety.

"I paid the difference," I admitted. "Yardley said she didn't mind, but I don't want to turn into that guy, either," I said of the prima donna's that reveal themselves on every tour, no matter how big or small.

"Regan," Georgia chuckled, "I don't think it's possible for you to ever become that guy."

I stared down at my wife, looking succulent in a black, 50s-style dress that highlighted her ample cleavage and flared out over her incredible hips.

Perhaps going to dinner before doing anything else was a short-sighted decision on my part.

"What?" she playfully snapped. "Stop looking at me like I'm on the menu."

I leaned in close to her ear as we worked our way to the private area reserved for us. "Oh," I whispered against her earlobe, "but you are." I grinned in satisfaction as goose bumps popped up along the slope of her neck.

"There you guys are!" CJ announced as we entered the tucked-away area with its own, private grill. "We got worried you decided to hammer it out before dinner, and we're starving."

He grinned like a sixteen-year-old as he stood and walked to Georgia, lifting her off the ground in a bear hug that nearly swallowed her inside his broad body.

"How you doin', kid?" he asked when he set her down.

She smiled at him like he was her big brother, which in some ways, was quite true. "Fine. You? Behaving yourself on this tour?"

"Never," he teased, returning to his seat.

I took a few seconds to introduce Georgia to a couple of the guys from the other bands she didn't know yet. There were eight of us in all—myself, Georgia, CJ, then five members of The Brewers, including Nessa, who Georgia had met on a few occasions before.

As we settled into our seats and placed our drink orders, Georgia leaned in, whispering. "What's up over there?" she asked of CJ sitting next to Nessa, engaged in what appeared to be normal, pleasant conversation.

"I hope nothing," I answered back, keeping my tone low. "But, I'm not anyone's caretaker, so ..."

"Oy," answered Georgia. "Frankie's a mess."

"What?" I said of CJ's sort-of ex-girlfriend back in Massachusetts, a little louder than intended.

Georgia rolled her eyes. "She didn't break up with him because she wanted to."

I paused, waiting for Georgia to explain it.

"Well, she wanted to, but she didn't want to want to, you know?"

"Barely."

Georgia leaned in closer. "Look. CJ didn't tell us all the details. And Frankie hasn't been explicit except to say that she was done hoping for more. She thought he'd really bought into their relationship."

"I think we all did," I admitted.

"But what fucking choice did he leave her? He manages to be faithful on home turf but needs to run around like a cock in heat when he's on the road? What shit is that? Anyway, she's a crying mess."

"Did she say that? Has he cheated on her before?"

Georgia shrugged. "He can't keep secrets for shit, so I doubt it."

"Yikes," I replied, not even knowing where to go with this conversation.

"What?" CJ broke in. "Telling secrets?"

Georgia silenced him with a wry grin. "Nah, I was just telling Regan I'd chatted with Frankie today," she said casually, perusing the menu.

CJ's jaw tightened and damn if he didn't do his best to unclench. But it didn't work.

"So," he replied.

"Ohh," Nessa entered, interested with devilish eyes. "Who's Frankie?"

"No one," CJ answered, clipped.

"Someone," Nessa concluded with raised eyebrows.

Georgia waved her hand. "Yes, someone. But no one you have to worry about, Nessa. She's out on a date tonight three-thousand miles away."

At this, CJ pushed back his chair and stood. "I'm grabbing a smoke. If the waiter comes, I'll have the number eight. And ten."

The waiter did come, shortly after CJ left, rescuing us from awkward silence. While the rest of the group placed their orders, I whispered to Georgia once more.

"You didn't tell me about Frankie."

Georgia smiled, looking quite pleased with herself. "That's because it's bullshit," she whispered back. "Guess we found out how he really feels about being free from Frankie, huh?"

"You're evil," I replied, only half kidding. She didn't meddle much anymore, but when she did, Georgia could go to the mat with the best of them.

CJ soon returned to the table, looking a little less homicidal than when he'd left, but only slightly so. The group eased into conversation about our upcoming shows, set lists, and our favorite foods, leaving all conversation of CJ and Frankie in the dust.

"Don't tell CJ," was the last thing Georgia whispered to me before our drinks arrived and we carried on with dinner with our friends.

***

Inevitably, dinner led to a discussion of where we'd go drinking and dancing next. At that point, I was itching to get my girl back to the hotel room, but she seemed to be enjoying the night out, so when she went along with plans for "part 2" of our evening, I did, too.

Soon, we found ourselves at a club that looked like an old movie theater from the front—it very well may have been once—but was wide open on the inside, and packed wall-to-wall with hot, grinding bodies. And, because luck in these places is rarely on my side, the bar was smack dab in the middle of it all.

"Well," Georgia sighed, sounding playfully resigned as we scanned the crowd, "let's go get sweaty."

She took my hand and led me through the writhing crowd that was twerking along to PitBull and Jennifer Lopez. Despite her generally loathsome attitude toward club life, Georgia was able to make herself at home fast. Balancing on fairly high shiny red heels, she swayed her hips back and forth in time with the music, weaving us masterfully through the crowd. Not only did I have the best view in the house from behind her, but I got to watch as nearly every man in the crowd, some probably ten years younger than us, gawked at her as she walked by. Almost every one of them. Some for a second, some for far longer—enough to earn swift elbows to the side from their girlfriends.

It would bother the hell out of some guys to have a wife that garnered this much attention—and it does bother G when the roles are reversed and I'm ever the center of lewd glances—but it doesn't upset me one bit. She's stunning. Beautiful, sexy, and masterfully in control of it all. She knows it and works it, even if she doesn't always believe it deep down. And, she's mine.

"Two vodka sodas," she called across the bar, up on her toes and leaning dangerously close to the bartender. Certainly using her breasts to our advantage in an effort to be served before the dozen or so people who were there first.

He gave her a swift once-over and got straight to business as if the other customers didn't exist. He handed her our drinks, and when she turned to hand me mine, the bartender caught sight of me and his face lit up.

"You're Regan Kane!" he shouted over the crowd, inevitably drawing attention from some people around us. Ones who didn't know me quickly took out their phones and, undoubtedly, Googled me.

I nodded, air-toasting him. "I am. Thanks for the drink, man."

He extended his hand across the bar, and I leaned in to complete the handshake. "My girlfriend is a huge fan of yours. I'm texting her to get her down here. Bet she won't complain about this job after tonight."

Georgia opened her mouth wide and let out a full-bellied laugh. "Well when she gets here, we'll be out there." She gestured to the dance floor and led me away.

I never had to actually do much when Georgia and I went dancing, since she had enough moves for the both of us. Tonight would have been no different, but I put some effort in. If I couldn't be making love to my wife in the hotel room, I'd do a PG-13 version on the dance floor.

"Brought your moves tonight, Kane?" she breathed heavily, those high heels of her not tripping her up one bit.

I pulled her close. "I want you, Mrs. Kane. Badly.

She let out a low moan I could only feel with my lips against her throat. "I asked you not to call me that."

My lips grazed across her neck. "But that's who you are."

"Is CJ chasing Nessa?" she asked into my ear.

"How romantic," I teased.

Georgia rolled her eyes, grinning. "I'm serious."

I shrugged. "I don't know. I don't think so, but I'm not … in charge of anyone. Why? You're really shaken up about Frankie, huh?"

She nodded, looking lost for a moment. "They'd been doing so well. He'd been doing so well. Do you think he got scared? Cold feet?"

"It's hard to say with CJ. Frankie was the longest I'd ever seen him with anyone. I didn't think he did relationships." Despite our semi-serious conversation, we never lost beat with the music. Georgia turned her back to me, grinding against me and speaking over her shoulder.

"He didn't. Until her. After they'd been together six months I thought maybe she was a stepping-stone to his budding adulthood, which would have been progress. After two years I figured they were as good as betrothed. I think she did, too." She faced me again, worry still in her eyes. "Is life on the road that good? To risk an entire relationship?"

I sighed, feeling the weight of her question. Her real question. Would you ever do to me what he's done to her?

"It's horrible," I admitted, half-serious. "The road or you? I'd choose you every time."

Half her mouth flicked up into a grin. "I'd never make you choose."

Playfully biting her shoulder, I answered, "And I love you for it."

With conversation seemingly transitioning away from Frankie, CJ, and his many potential conquests, Georgia and I found ourselves lost in the music for several songs. The DJ was working it hard tonight, a statement I wouldn't have said before meeting real-life professional DJ's a few years ago. Willow Shaw, signed under GSE as well, is the half-sister to Ember. She mainly works between San Diego and Napa Valley, and she works hard. Mixes insane sets designed to do just what Georgia and I were doing—connect, forget, get lost.

A sheen of sweet sweat laced Georgia's chest. I was going to lose it right here in the club if I didn't move soon.

"We have to go," I growled into her ear. "Now."

Georgia pinched her bottom lip between her teeth, arching an eyebrow. "Let's go."

As we wandered off the dance floor, the bartender called after us, distressed that his girlfriend hadn't showed up yet to meet me. I told him to have her come to our show tomorrow and give them my name. He promised she would, and told me her name was Amy and she had long, red hair in case anyone asked.

Out of the corner of my eye on the way out of the club, I caught sight of CJ and Nessa in conversation near the bathrooms. Her back was against the wall and he was in front of her, one hand on the wall to the side of her shoulder propping himself up.

"We're out," I called to them, only eliciting slight waves from both of them.

"Looks like he was selling her hard," Georgia remarked rather glumly as we walked down the sidewalk. "Does she like know about Frankie? Other than what I said at the restaurant?"

I shook my head. "Not unless he told her. She asked me if he had a girlfriend and I didn't really answer."

This earned me a smack to the side of my arm.

"God! What?" I laughed, rubbing the sore spot.

"You could have told her about Frankie."

My eyes widened and I laughed. "Tell her about his ex-girlfriend? What sense does that make?"

"Like five-seconds ex," she grumbled.

"What difference does that make? Ex is ex, isn't it?"

She looked at me like I had two heads, stopping in her tracks. "Seriously?"

I mimicked her look. "Seriously. What the hell business is it of hers when he broke up with anyone? If two adults break up, and stay broken up for more than a day or two it's probably a real breakup right?" My pre-Georgia life wouldn't have included the two-day window, but she "enlightened" me—as she likes to call it.

Georgia crossed her arms in front of her and huffed.

"Look," I said, soft as I took her hand and resumed our walk. "I know we're all protective of CJ on one level or another. But he's an adult, God help us, and so is Nessa. And ... wait ... wait ..."

"What?" Georgia slowed down to stay in step with me.

"At dinner ... did you say Frankie broke up with CJ? I thought ..." I shook my head, trying to arrange the details I thought I knew. "Didn't he dump her before he came out to California?"

Georgia nodded. "That's what he told us. I didn't talk to Frankie until a few days later, and she set me straight. Our boy got canned."

"But I don't ... understand why."

She put her hands on her hips. "Because he ... he questioned their relationship. He was basically asking for six months of free passes from her so she kicked his ass out."

"Is that what he said?"

"No, it's what he meant," Georgia answered definitively.

"Out? Were they living together?"

Georgia rolled her eyes and started walking toward the hotel again. "It's just an expression. And, basically. He'd been staying at her house almost every night."

"So ... how does this change things as far as CJ's wild oats-sewing goes this summer?

"Because they still love each other."

"This makes my head hurt. Maybe they love each other, but CJ appears to be going through something right now. And if Frankie wants—"

"What? If Frankie wants what, fidelity?"

I growled. "This isn't even our business!" I exclaimed with as much humor as I could, because I didn't want to ruin my plans for the hotel. And, because it really was none of our business.

"I'm just saying," Georgia stated, regaining composure, "Frankie's devastated and CJ's acting out. With all kinds of women."

"I haven't even seen him go off with anyone," I mentioned in passing.

Which was enough to stop Georgia in her tracks.

"Come on." I tugged her hand. "We'll never get back to the room at this rate."

She followed, but worked out her theory as we walked. "He still loves her."

"I'm sure he does. They were together for a long time, and you don't just fall out of love with people, regardless of the circumstances."

"I mean he's still actually in love with her. You haven't seen him with anyone?" she questioned, brightly.

"Don't," I pleaded. "Don't go telling Frankie all this. I know how you women are."

A sheepish grin spread across her mouth, but her eyes stayed dangerous as always. "I won't."

I squeezed her hand. "Seriously. G. Their relationship is none of our business."

Finally, she sighed. "Fine."

I didn't believe her. Still, I let it go. We were standing in front of the hotel room and I only had one thing left on my mind.

**

"Mmm," Georgia purred, her legs wrapped around me while I was still inside her. "I missed you."

Kissing her collarbone I inhaled deeply, savoring her scent. "You feel good."

She slid her hands to my bare backside. Pulling me into her a little deeper even though we were finished. It felt like being home, there on the bed on top of her and inside her at the same time. Maybe I wasn't quite finished, after all.

I moved my hips, picking up steam as I nipped and kissed at her breasts, loving the way her back arched, pushing her breasts toward me as her head tilted back.

"I love you," I half-moaned.

"I love you." She was breathless in an instant. "I need you."

Maybe this baby-making thing wouldn't be so bad.

And, I should have kept that thought to myself. I learned quickly that some jokes are not for the bedroom.

"You just need me for my potent sperm," I joked.

Joked.

Idiot.

This stopped Georgia cold. She pressed her hands against my shoulders, eyeing me seriously. "What?"

I chuckled. "Come on, G. I was just playing."

"You think I came up here for that?"

"No." I shook my head. "You came up here because we're married and I'm on tour and you missed me. We're making love because we love each other."

I bent down to kiss her, but she turned her head, pushing my shoulders back slightly. "Then why would you say that?"

"I was kidding." And, I was panicking that this was turning into a whole thing.

She shifted her hips to the side, silently telling me to get out and off. I complied, rolling over and pulling her to me. She'd already turned her back, so I was forced to talk to her shoulder.

"What's this really about?" I asked.

"Why can't you ever take what I say at face value? I don't always speak in code, you know. I'm not trying to trick you into anything."

I sighed, heavy. "Georgia, I was just teasing. What the hell?"

She sat up, facing me with betrayal in her eyes. "It's not funny Regan. I know we only started officially trying like two months ago, but we stopped being careful months before that."

"And?"

"And I'm not pregnant yet. Something's wrong with me." She threw the covers off her, picking my button-down shirt off the floor and draping it across her back.

Shit.

Sliding to the edge of the bed, I failed to reach her before she stepped away and paced to the window, pulling the curtains open slightly to stare at the sparse nightlife going on six-stories below us.

Before going after her, I watched her for a moment. Dim moonlight mixed with yellow streetlights reflecting from below highlighted her pale face. Her sad eyes.

"I'm sorry," I said, taking the sheet with me and wrapping it around the both of us when I reached her at the window.

Just beyond the borders of the city was a small strip of green forest with the thick tall shadows of trees. On the other side of that forest was the icy shore of the northern Pacific Ocean. An ocean where Georgia had always centered herself. Her bakery was so close to the shore in San Diego that it was nearly in it. She knew she was always half of a natural disaster away from commercial devastation, but the freedom of the waves was too great a benefit to pass up, she always said.

"Why?" she asked, unmoving as if talking to the window.

I sighed. "I don't think I realized how … how much this was affecting you."

"Because it's not your body," she said calmly, without a hint of cynicism.

"I guess," I admitted. "But you're my wife, and when you get pregnant—"

"If," she cut off.

"When you get pregnant," I continued, "it will be our baby. And while you are busy growing it, I'll be busy pampering you. So, no, your body isn't my body," I gave her shoulders a squeeze, "but it kind of is. You're my wife. The soon-to-be mother of our child."

With that, her shoulders sank and she let out a long, cleansing sigh that showed me she was backing down from what could have been a spectacular fight.

"I'm sorry," she said, finally facing me, tilting her head far back to look me in the eyes. "God," she said with a chuckle, "if I'm this emotional now, imagine what I'll be like with pregnancy hormones?"

I feigned a horror-movie gasp, which made her laugh.

"You're too good to me," she said, giving me a playful pinch on the side.

"Get over here." I grinned, pulling her head close to my chest, kissing the top of it before leading her back to bed.

Given I only hung out with road-musicians most of the time, I didn't have very many friends with children. At least not wives and children. A lot of guys had a couple of kids from different wives, stereotypically scattered from coast to coast, but there weren't a lot of families in this part of the business. I tried not to focus on those facts as Georgia drifted off to sleep with her cheek on my chest.

As my eyelids gave way to the ticking of the clock, I realized one thing for sure; if this family life was one I wanted—and I did, badly—then it was time to call the people who seemed to be winning at family life and the music industry.

CHAPTER TEN

REGAN

"I WAS WONDERING WHEN I'd hear from you," Ember answered brightly when I called.

I lowered my head as if I were in her presence and wanted to appear as bashful as I felt. "Sorry, love. You know how it is."

She laughed. "Road life. I do. You guys are doing well, I hear. And, I trust when you mosey on into Massachusetts and have your break, you'll stay with us even for a few days?"

"Of course," I answered with a smile.

My sister, Darcy, was five years older than me and wrapped up with her corporate job in Boston and family life. I didn't resent this, as we enjoyed each other's company when we were around each other, but we'd never been particularly close. Ember Cavanaugh was like the chummy sister I never had.

I met her at a beachfront bar in Barnstable, MA, when her last name was still Harris, and I'd just finished a long teaching stint in Ireland. I was looking for my next project. She and Bo were just dating then, and barely at that time—they'd just met, or were on a break … it was still confusing. But, I met and became completely enamored with Bo's younger sister, Rae.

It was kind of a head-over-heels, fast-paced summer romance that swallowed us until a freak horseback riding accident took her away. And I'd been the only one to witness it. We were trail riding and a bees' nest put the period at the end of our brief, intense affair.

It was really after that that Ember and I grew a lot closer. We were certainly brother and sister-like before that, but in the days, weeks, and months after Rae's death, we formed a sort of haphazard family between all of us, Bo included. Ember's parents lived out in San Diego at the time, but traveled most of the year, the life-long hippies they were, and Bo and Rae had been orphaned years earlier when their parents were in a car accident, so even though I had family in Cape Cod, Bo, Ember, and I kind of became each other's home.

"So what's up, buttercup?" Ember's sentence was highlighted by toddler sounds in the background.

"How's the crew?"

She sighed. "Loud. Messy."

"And how are you, like, feeling?" Her second pregnancy—with Vivian Rae—had been a doozy. She even had to spend time in the hospital early on because she was sick so much.

"Loads better than last time," she admitted, sensing the origins of my question. "But I'm sure you didn't call to talk to me about the finer points of pregnancy … did you?"

"Actually …"

She gasped, then said, "Shh! Just shh. I'm. On. The. Phone. Sorry, Regan, what was that? Is Georgia pregnant?" Her voice rose expectantly at the end of her sentence.

"No, but—"

"Jackson! Shut it! Seriously! Do you see me on the ph—oh, great, now you made your sister cry. Sorry," Ember returned to our conversation, sounding a little out of breath, "give me a second?"

"Take your time," I answered, peeking over my shoulder at a still-sleeping Georgia. It was only six in the morning here, so Ember's day had been underway for hours already.

"Bo?" I heard her call. Her voice sounded like she'd stepped outside. "Bo! Can you, like, take Jax for a minute? Regan's on the phone, Viv needs to eat … yeah, I'll tell him. He says hi," she said to me, sounding all of a sudden like she was in a tunnel of silence.

"Tell him hi. Later," I said, laughing. "You all set? Want me to call back?"

"God no. I just locked myself in the bedroom to feed Viv. She's distractible enough now that she can walk and never wants to sit down, but having an almost four-year-old boy in both of our faces at feeding time really doesn't help things. Sorry, talking to me on the phone must sometimes feel like talking to someone with Tourette's."

I let out a laugh a bit louder than intended, causing Georgia to stir a little. Once she settled back into sleep I thanked God that she's usually a heavy sleeper, then snuck out of our room, down the stairs, and into the fresh Pacific Northwest air.

I decided to just let it out. "So … Georgia and I are talking about having a baby."

"Nice," she answered brightly, if not a bit cautiously.

"But we only have been, like, trying for a month or two … but we stopped, like…"

"You can say words to me, Regan."

I laughed, instantly relaxed. "We stopped using any birth control stuff a few months ago. Not really trying but not preventing. Georgia's freaked out that she's not pregnant yet. She melted down last night a little. She was fine by the time we went to bed, but I know her … this insecurity won't go away until she's pregnant."

"Then it will be replaced by pregnancy insecurities and parenting insecurities," Ember said flatly.

"Helpful."

"Truthful. Look, Georgia mentioned to me a while ago that you guys were trying. She asked for advice, or whatever, and I told her the biggest thing was to relax and surrender. That's it. Even if there was a medical issue preventing her from getting pregnant, doctors wouldn't even take her concerns seriously until you guys have tried for, like, a year."

My throat went dry. "Could it take that long?"

"It did with Viv," Ember admitted.

"I didn't realize ..."

"It wasn't a big thing ... but once we decided to have kids we kind of wanted them close together. I mean, look, I'm breastfeeding my 14-month-old while five-months pregnant with baby number three. It seems crazy but we just didn't want to spend like ten years having kids. Jax was just over one when we decided we were ready to try for baby two. They're almost three years apart if that tells you anything. Part of it was an ovulation thing—some women ovulate when they're nursing, some don't. I didn't with Jax ... apparently I do now," she laughed, giving a contented sigh and I heard the soft babble of Vivian Rae, apparently through with her breakfast, or whatever.

"So what'd you do? What'd Bo do?"

"It wasn't such a struggle emotionally because we already had one baby. But, with Georgia ... you know she's sensitive and insecure—even more sensitive than I am. Just be patient. Love on her. Listen."

There was a long silence between us before Ember spoke again.

"And," she added, "make sure this is something you both want and are both ready for."

"What's that supposed to mean?" I didn't say it with any sort of tone, but that sentence is hard to interpret with anything but.

Ember took a deep breath. "It doesn't necessarily mean anything. But ... look ... take me, for instance. I was pretty certain for most of my life that I didn't want kids. Or, if I did, that I'd want to settle all the way down and not travel the way my parents did."

"Well," I interrupted, "they didn't really travel in the conventional sense. They were more … nomadic."

"You get my drift," she answered with a chuckle. "All I mean is, who knows what they actually want ever, anyway? It wasn't until Bo and I were married and kind of stretching out our limbs in our combined lives that we reevaluated where we were at with everything. And we keep reevaluating. Who wants to live the same marriage year after year and call that a life?"

"So what changed?" I asked, shifting my weight from foot to foot.

"I don't know," she admitted. "I guess I kind of grew up and let my assumptions go, and so did Bo. We're having more kids than I thought I wanted, and traveling more than either of us thought we would. And I certainly never thought I'd be a professional musician. But we just kind of … take life as it comes."

"You gonna keep traveling once this baby comes?" I admired the pace they were able to keep, but it was so different from Georgia and me because Bo and Ember worked together.

"Probably. I'm due in the winter, which is actually nice, because by the time spring and summer come and festivals start up, I'll be out of my post-birth haze that usually lasts three or four months. I'm sure we'll stay local for a while, like we usually do, but we also haven't figured out what will happen when it's time for Jackson to go to Kindergarten."

"Guess that's more of the reevaluating stuff, huh?"

She chuckled. "Guess so. Well, that's enough talk of my breasts and ovaries. How's everything else? CJ seems to be doing well from what we hear."

I nodded instinctively. "He's right in his element and is getting even better if you can believe it."

"You think Yardley will offer him something?" she asked of our manager.

"Hard to say, but it wouldn't surprise me. He's filling in for another band's drummer. Guy got in a bar fight and broke his arm."

"He still on the outs with Frankie?" Ember asked as if I were one of the girls.

I sighed, then laughed a little. "I guess. I'm trying really hard to stay out of it, but you girls are making that damn near impossible."

"That's because we can't talk to him like a normal human being, so we gotta go through you. I like Frankie. This breakup hasn't been easy on her."

I huffed and laughed at the same time. "That's what Georgia said. I didn't realize you and Frankie had gotten that close."

Ember sighed. "Well when you took off to Cali-friggen-for-nia, I had to befriend CJ." She paused, chuckling. "Just kidding. He's actually not terrible, and was far more palatable when he was with her. And I like her a lot. She's smart and not in the industry, which is good for him. Maybe it's good for all of us to have someone around who's not steeped in our world."

"I guess, though it must also be nice to share your complete passion with Bo, huh?"

"Sure, but we also each have our own things. He doesn't bother me with yoga, and I've taken on a more supportive role at DROP." DROP was the name of Bo's drug prevention organization started while Rae was still alive. She'd struggled with drug abuse in her teens, and their parents used some of their millions to fund the program. When they died, the program was in Bo and Rae's hands. Now everything was on his shoulders.

I should call him more.

"Regan? Where'd you go?"

"Is Bo doing okay?"

"He's fine," she answered almost dreamily. It warmed my heart to hear the love they had for each other, even when I was three thousand miles away. "So. To recap. Don't panic about the baby thing. Be patient, loving, and listen."

"Got it. Thanks."

"Love you, Regan."

I smiled, in need of a hug. "Love you too, Ember."

When I returned to the room, Georgia was sitting up in bed, looking around, confused.

"Did I wake you?" I asked.

She shook her head. "No, but where'd you go?"

I nodded to the door. "I was talking with Ember and didn't want to wake you." I slid off my T-shirt and removed my jeans, sliding into bed next to her.

She nuzzled into my chest as soon as we got settled, and breathed deeply, already half asleep.

"They doing okay?"

"Yeah," I whispered, kissing the top of her head. I didn't want to draw too many questions from my conversation with Ember, since I'm a terrible liar. "She said Frankie's a mess. Like you said."

Georgia clicked her tongue against her teeth and shook her head. "Well," she yawned, "maybe it will be good for both of them to be apart for a while and decide if being together makes them better people, or worse. Brian and Randy are separated," she added, sounding further and further into sleep.

"What?" My tone was a little loud for the quiet, darkened room, but Georgia didn't startle. She just nodded, and yawned again.

"Big dreams, all coming true ... you know ... where was their relationship in all that? Hey ... you were out of bed around midnight with the light on at the desk. Everything okay?"

I nodded, preparing a non-lie. "You know me. I can't sleep sometimes when I've got music in my head. I was just jotting it down for later."

Until I got more information on Brian and Randy's separation, and Georgia's state of mind, there was no way I was going to worry her with an insignificant, non-project I was working on for Yardley in my spare time. Because I don't know how, in her emotional state, I could make Georgia believe that it wasn't me being a workaholic and avoiding starting a family or, at the very least, delaying it.

Because that wasn't it.

It wasn't it at all.

This was just something my boss was asking me to do to help her out. And I'd be getting paid—well. And, since I had a lot of non-partying time on my hands while on the road, why shouldn't I take on some side work?

I was tired, but couldn't fall back to sleep.

Be sure it's something you both want.

Ember's words bounced off the walls of my mind as I tossed and turned. At some point, I looked over at a sleeping Georgia, and a swelling feeling of contentment filled my chest. Our marriage was solid and we loved each other deeply and uniquely. I felt a sense of completeness with her that I didn't think I'd been missing before we got together.

Maybe that's what this whiff of anxiety was all about for me. Maybe I just didn't know how wonderful it would be to have kids until we had one. I never dreamed of having kids. Hell, I'd never sat around and dreamt about being married either, but here I was, madly in love with a fantastic woman who I got to spend the rest of my life with.

And, Georgia and I never really talked about kids before we got married. Nothing negative or positive to say about it—it just didn't come up.

How did it not come up?

Taking a deep breath, I rolled to my side, draped my arm over Georgia, and kissed her shoulder. I couldn't fool myself into thinking that I'd figure out the parenting thing once I was a parent. I knew too many screwed up families to take this as anything less than seriously. But I needed to figure out exactly what the hell I was feeling before it was too late.

My tongue felt like it was swelling as the anxiety worked its way into my throat. People divorced over this—miscommunication of life goals and dreams. If I got to a place where I was certain I didn't want kids, would that non-desire be strong enough to risk losing Georgia over? The last thing I wanted for either of us was to end up in a resentment-filled relationship around a child who didn't ask to be born in the first place.

I couldn't think about this now, and Georgia wasn't in town for long enough to justify me bringing this up in the next several hours. Instead, I let the rhythm of her soft breath lull me back to sleep.

CHAPTER ELEVEN

CJ

"WHAT?" I ASKED a fired up looking Georgia as she stood in the doorway of my hotel room.

Truth be told, that was an unfair assessment of her look. She always looked fired up in one way or another. This morning, though, the comic gleam in her eye relaxed me.

"Anyone in here?" she exaggerated craning her neck to try to peer around the door.

"For your information, no," I answered, rather proudly. Which was odd.

"Good. Dress yourself and come with me. Unless you want to walk the streets in your boxer briefs?" Her eyes didn't move from my face as she talked, which was rare for women in my half-naked presence. Georgia and I almost dated for like half a second in high school before settling into the friendship roles we were much more comfortable in.

Still, I gestured to my body for good measure. "What? You don't want a piece of this?"

She snorted with her trademark genuine and berating amusement. "As if."

"My cousin may be your husband, but I could bench-press four of him without breaking a sweat."

She rolled her eyes. "And he could out-romance four of you before breakfast. Get dressed and meet me in the lobby."

I playfully smacked her round bottom with the back of my hand as she turned to walk away. This earned me both a yelp and the middle finger.

We were marching toward the coffee shop in the damp morning fog when Georgia killed my decent mood. "I've been thinking about you and Frankie."

I growled, rolling my eyes and my head back. "Why," I said, long and exaggerated.

"About how it's none of my damn business."

I nearly tripped over my Doc Martins. This was a startling and suspicious development—interfering was Georgia's thing.

I furrowed my brow at her, and resumed my pace. "What tricks are you up to?"

Georgia adjusted the red bandana around her almost white blonde hair and eyed me cautiously. "It's not," she repeated. "We've known each other for so long that I forget we're not two banged-up hooligans hanging at my dad's bar in Provincetown anymore. We're adults, God help us, and you deserve to be treated like one. So, if you say your relationship with Frankie is over, then that's it. I can't decide otherwise for you, as much as I like her and what she used to bring out in you."

My stomach dropped a little. "Okay …" I finally said.

"But know this," Georgia continued, waving her index finger in front of my face. "Frankie and I have developed a nice little relationship apart from you that I want to maintain if she wants to."

"Of course," I answered quickly. "Why wouldn't she want to?"

"Maybe it would keep the wound a little too fresh, having me around. She might just want a fresh start, away from the hurt."

It felt like the sidewalk slid away from underneath me as we reached the door of Grind, a small coffee shop recommended by the locals. I'd told Georgia and them that I'd let Frankie go—giving the illusion that I'd dumped her. Letting her go wasn't a total lie. She drove me to the airport the day I left for

San Diego, which was decent of her all things considered. I was sorry at that point for everything that'd happened the week before, but she didn't want to talk anymore. Frankly, neither did I. So, I did let her go, once she asked me through tears to stop staring at her that way before I got out of the car and onto the plane.

I'd become someone—something—I never thought I'd wanted to be. I still managed to hurt someone even after working hard to make sure I didn't. I thought I'd given my all over the last three years, but she wanted more and I panicked. And, in turn acted like the ass she didn't deserve.

I was never good at long-term relationships because I'm not a long-term kind of guy.

Frankie didn't stand a chance when it came to my uncanny ability to self-destruct.

So why do I feel like shit?

"Hello?" Georgia snapped her fingers in front of my face. "Anything to say for yourself, player?"

But she dumped me …

I shrugged, plastering on the most apathetic face I could. "What do you want me to say, G?"

Her bright blue eyes stared into mine curiously, as if in disbelief. "Nothing, I guess," she finally said. "I just … I thought she was going to be, like, the one for you." Easily, Georgia slid back into pure friend mode. One where she was less girly and more tolerant of my "bullshit ways," as she always put it.

"Can we just get some fuckin' coffee? I'd also like a cigarette, so can we sit outside?"

She rolled her eyes, nodding. "I'll get your usual. Large, three creams, six sugars, and some insulin." She winked after reciting my guilty pleasure order and turned for the counter.

Once alone on the sidewalk, I put the end of the cigarette in my mouth, clicked the lighter, and took one deep, long, slow drag. And forced myself not to cough. I hadn't smoked regularly in over two years, save for a few now and again on weekends. Frankie hated the taste; said she didn't like feeling like she was licking an ashtray.

Well, screw her ...

When I blinked I saw Frankie in her bed—one I'd stayed in almost every night for two years. And I saw her. To-die-for curves I grabbed onto every chance I got, delicious nipples, and that mouth ...

I quickly shook the thoughts from my mind. She's the one who ended it. Not that I begged her not to. I wasn't equipped with begging skills or desire, which let Frankie slip right through my fingers.

As soon as Georgia returned, rolling her eyes at my nicotine habit, I took a swig of hot, sweet coffee and stared into the tree line in the distance.

I took one more long drag before saying anything as I exhaled. "You know she dumped me, don't you ..."

She was quiet for a second, then sighed. "Yes."

"Why aren't you consoling me then?" I asked, only half-kidding.

"Because I don't blame her," Georgia answered, flatly if not a little reluctant. "It was a long time coming."

"Fuck you?" I said it like a question to lessen the sting.

She shrugged, unaffected by my crassness. "What the hell, CJ? You wanted a six-month free pass, for fuck's sake. This isn't high school, or even college, anymore. She's ready for the next phase. One that, at one point, probably included a life with you. And you didn't give a damn."

Now I was angry. "Didn't give a damn?" I snapped. "Didn't give a damn. Interesting. I sure as hell gave a damn when I entered into the relationship, didn't I? And gave a damn when I brought up to her us moving in together, too, I'd say. You might be interested to know she shot down that idea."

Unaffected, still, by my tantrum, Georgia looked up at me. "When did you ask her to move in together?"

"A year or more ago, I guess. What? Your new BFF didn't tell you that?"

"Grow up." Georgia's face turned sour. "You didn't tell me that."

"She said she wasn't ready then. What else did she need? We'd been together for more than a year by then." I shook my head, taking the last drag of my cigarette, stomping it out, and lighting another one.

"Easy there, Marlboro Man. Don't you think she wanted something a little more than a roommate with benefits who probably wouldn't sleep around?"

"And, to set the fucking record straight, I never asked for a pass on anything. I just wanted to talk about where we were before I left."

Georgia leaned forward, holding her head between her hands. "Do you have any idea how heartbreaking that had to be for her to hear? Her boyfriend of three years asking where are we?"

I sucked hard on the cigarette. "For the last three years I've done nothing but be a better person for her. I didn't sleep around with other girls. Not once. And don't do much more than a wink or a flirt here and there—and even that's when I'm performing. You know, persona." She nodded, understanding, and I continued. "I spent less time smoking and more time eating right and working out. I focused on computer stuff for a while; taking an interest in the companies I have stock in. For fuck's sake, Georgia, she was like the only person besides you and Regan to know about that social media app, and all the money that went with it. I gave her everything I had in me."

"For her sake or yours? And, don't assume sex is the only rotten thing anyone can do. She's not an idiot. You had a bumpy first year."

"But it got better," I countered.

Georgia shrugged. "Sure, but what did you do to repair the trust? It's not enough to just not cut any fresh wounds if you don't treat the old ones. Were you behaving like a grownup or trying to get by on your charm? Also, would you have done all that self-improvement stuff if she wasn't around? Or is it not you? Do you think it was an improvement? Or did you just lead a girl on for almost three years, giving her what you thought she wanted until you pulled the rug out from under her?" Georgia snatched the cigarette from my lips and took a drag.

"What the fuck are you talking about? I was growing as a person, Georgia. Isn't that what adults are supposed to do? Who cares why or how I started." I leaned down, getting eye to eye with her. "I loved her. And she dumped me."

Standing on her tiptoes, Georgia wasn't about to be intimidated by me—not that I wanted her to be. "I bet it made you feel good to get all that attention from Frankie. A woman who put you first above all other men so easily. That work you did wasn't for you. It was just for her, which is why you felt like a caged animal and got the taste of excitement when this tour came up. She didn't get the real you, one who could have made changes because he wanted to, when he was ready."

"I loved her," I repeated, turning back for the hotel.

"I just think you're scared to grow up, CJ." Georgia chased after me. Breaking into a jog as my long legs covered more ground than her short ones could. "A life long Lost Boy who escaped Neverland, got his tongue pierced, and found himself a pair of sticks. I think you did love her. Maybe some of those changes were genuine, but after a while you got hot under the collar and instead of running to the woman who's stood by you for three years, working it out with her, you bailed. A man doesn't bail CJ."

I stopped, catching her surprised face as I turned around. "It's that easy, huh? Ask my mom, Georgia, because that's the example I've got. My dad was a good guy. She thought. Then he up and left overfuckingnight and started a new family in Long Island without so much as a look backward. Out of nowhere!"

Georgia and I hadn't talked about my dad in years. I hardly talked about him with anyone—even Frankie got the barest bones of the story. There was no risk of having my mom or anyone else in my family bring him up because he torched every bridge he could on his way out of town and the wounds never stopped seeping. No one talked about him with anything but their eyes in a passing glance here or there.

"CJ," Georgia said, dropping her arms and sinking her shoulders. "You're not him. You know that."

"Do I?" I hissed, turning to punch the wall of the closest storefront. It was brick, so I thought better of it and put my hand down.

Georgia put her hand over my forearm. "CJ …"

"They were high school sweethearts, Georgia. And overnight, when I was too young to know what the fuck was going on … he was gone. That's what love and commitment got my mom. Abandonment."

"He didn't love her," she said, taking a step back when my head whipped toward her. "Because real love doesn't allow for that. She tried to love him enough for the both of them, and it didn't work. But she did love you enough for the both of them."

I was pissed after listening to her assault my character for the last several minutes. Accusing me of still being the boy she met in her dad's bar more than fifteen years ago when she knew better. She'd seen me go through more shit than I'd let anyone else see. She watched me changed. She was hitting below the belt and I'd had it.

"Let's talk about you for a minute. We both come from broken-ass backgrounds and trusted no one for years."

She shrugged. "Until Regan. He's it for me.

"Hmm," I started, intentionally sounding like the biggest ass I could. "Seems interesting, then, that you're already popping up on this tour more than you ever have before. Before we even left California you were at like every show. Is it because you're afraid that now I'm a free man, I'll rub off on him, and you're worried he'll notice Yardley's tits for once? Or are you just ovulating?"

Georgia's mouth dropped, her eyes wide, but I cut her off. "Yeah, Regan told me you guys want kids. But, answer me this? Do you honestly think a baby will make things easier? Yeah, kids are known for smoothing out rough patches in relationships."

She ground her teeth together, sneering at me. "That's not why we want a family, asshole. You know that. We're not even in a rough patch, you douchebag."

"How does it feel to be judged?" was all I said before storming into the hotel lobby and back to my room.

Alone.

Better off alone.

I didn't need a sidewalk psychology discussion from Georgia or anyone else about my "daddy issues." I was there—I knew the facts. I saw how my mom suffered after doing nothing but loving the one man she'd loved since she was in braces.

What I needed was to do my job on this tour and have my kind of fun when I wasn't on stage. Risk free, strings free.

And fuck anyone else who wanted to tell me otherwise.

CHAPTER TWELVE

REGAN

"WHAT'D YOU DO to CJ?" I questioned Georgia as we stood in the airport. She had a few minutes before she needed to go through security.

She shrugged, pressing her tongue into the side of her cheek with an unamused frown. "I didn't do anything. He figured out I knew Frankie canned him. Then he made it her fault—"

"What?" I asked when she stopped short.

Georgia huffed. "He brought up his dad."

I winced, knowing that couldn't have ended up anywhere pleasant since he almost never mentioned him. "Again?"

She nodded. "He … he thinks the risk is being in love, not being a playboy. Like … his mom got screwed even though she loved his dad, while his dad just got to run off like nothing happened."

"Ah," I nodded, "he thinks he's just turning into him right out of the gate. Damned if he does and damned if he doesn't, huh?"

She nodded back as she looked down, biting her lip for a second before settling her mouth into a frown.

I kissed the top of her head, savoring the inhale of her fruity body spray.

"Look at me," I whispered, lifting her chin with my index finger. "That's their life. It's not us, you know that right?" The tortured look on her eyes, highlighted by the crease between her eyebrows made me wonder if this tour brought back all the fears and insecurities Georgia had had before my first.

"I know," she spoke into my chest, squeezing me harder.

I'll never forget her complete breakdown before I left on my first tour. A breakdown that masqueraded as a fight until she sank facedown on our bed and sobbed so hard all I could make out was she was afraid I'd find somebody better on tour. Saner. More put together. Helpless and unprepared, all I could do was kiss the top of her head then, too. I did all I could to assure her, gently, how wrong she was. That no groupie could ever take her place. And, if it was musicians she was worried about, I told her sanity wasn't a strong suit in that bunch.

My humor was enough, then. For the moment.

It took a couple of years and a lot of tours before Georgia and I settled into our own rhythm of trust and security. Her dad chose booze over her, and while her mom was committed to her as much as she could be, the schizophrenia stood in the way of a truly deep connection most of the time. Georgia had only ever had her self to rely on. Letting me in was like a new birth for her, and setting me free on each tour opened old wounds. I didn't take her trust for granted.

Eyeing a digital clock on the wall across from me, I knew we were on borrowed time. The airport was small and not busy, but Georgia had a full week coming up, and missing a flight would set her back more than half a day. Unacceptable in the world of fondant and gluten-free bridezillas.

"Come on." I grabbed her hand and tugged her along half a step behind me. "I'll walk with you as far as I can."

"Tell CJ I'm sorry. Wait. Don't … I don't know. The way he stormed off …"

I moved my hand to her lower back, bare from her midriff top, and savored the smooth, warm feel of her skin. "He'll cool off."

She sighed. "I know. But I love him and hate to watch him fuck up his life. And Frankie … it all just sucks."

"Yep," I agreed. "This adult thing can really be the pits."

While I was relieved our conversation during her stay hadn't veered into ovulation and menstrual cycles, it struck me as odd. For the last couple of months, while not becoming over-the-top about it, Georgia hasn't been shy about either of those topics. This past weekend? Nothing. It occurred to me, albeit briefly, that maybe Georgia's intense focus on CJ and Frankie had something to do with this baby stuff. Maybe she picked up on some of my anxiety and was trying to deflect. Though, that seemed unlikely since it had been mere hours since I'd admitted the anxiety to myself.

"You did amazing this weekend, Regan. Really. I can't even believe that you get better every time I hear you play. Will you ever max out?" she teased.

I smiled pulling her in for another hug, letting out a forced chuckle under the heavy circumstances. "Never."

She smiled. Her tired eyes from what little sleep we'd managed through the weekend looked bright and misty on the horizon of our goodbye.

"Don't cry, okay?" I asked, more of myself than her. I didn't want her to leave. I wished things were different. That she could join me on every tour, even if she never went on a stage in all her life.

I couldn't wish away her bakery, though. And I'd never wish away the music. So, it was what it was as I kissed my wife goodbye, and watched her navigate the maze of metal detectors and loud, pushy travelers throwing their shoes into plastic bins.

I was relieved the maid service hadn't come through yet when I returned to my room. It always stressed me out to leave my violin unattended anywhere except the tour bus, actually. I'd never had an instrument stolen, but knew enough people who'd had them stolen or damaged to give me a healthy protectiveness.

As I stuffed my clothes into my duffel bag, something red caught my attention out of the corner of my eye. I grinned, reaching for the pillow Georgia had used last night. She always slept with half her face smushed into the pillow, mouth gaping open. On the crisp white linen pillowcase there was the bright red proof that my wife had slept deeply next to me the night before. A perfect half-kiss stain left in her absence.

I missed her already. I knew the longing would only last a couple of days at most, and at least I had the project from Yardley to help distract me. Still, it didn't make the days of missing her any easier. I sighed, stripping the pillowcase from its host, and shoved it in my bag.

***

"Here," I said to Yardley, handing her some torn-out pieces from my music composition notebook. "Have them try this, and if you and they like it, I can do more."

We were loading the busses, preparing for our short stop in Washington before the twelve-hour trek to Billings, Montana. Our shortest drive, for the first half of the tour anyway, was the ride from Reno to Portland, Oregon. It would have been just over nine hours with no stops, but we're typically a hungry bunch.

Yardley took the papers, arching her eyebrow as she gave me the once-over. "I tell him no rush," she says to no one, "and he gives it to me early."

I playfully shrugged. "What can I say? This kind of stuff is fun for me."

"Wasn't Georgia here? Didn't I see her at both shows?"

"Yeah, she had a great time. Thanks for the good seats for her."

Yardley rolled her eyes. "She's as much royalty as you are, Regan. If I could sit her right on the stage I would. I'm grateful she shares you so openly with us." She scanned through the pages, nodding as if trying to understand them. I knew Yardley didn't have a strong knowledge of composition, but she was learning enough to at least offer suggestions and opinions.

"Shares?" I questioned.

"You know," she said, making eye contact with me. "This life isn't for everyone. And, in my experience it's the spouse that tires of it long before the musician. Take care of that woman of yours, Regan. She deserves it. Though," Yardley blushed a bit as she spoke, which was a rare break in her business armor, "I'm sure you're a great husband. You're quite the romantic."

Now it was my turn to blush. "God. Stop."

"I mean it," she replied, insistently. "The way you work the crowd with your eyes and body? It's inviting without being perverse. Sure, some of our audience likes the more overt sexuality provided by your cousin and other ... lively ... members of our tour. But you're safe. You bring something out of people that's already deep inside them, rather than trying to shove something down their throats. You're a true artist, Regan. A true performer."

I swallowed hard. While I wasn't overly bashful in discussions regarding my playing ability, when it came to my personality—my self—it was a different story. Ember had a way of crawling right inside my head from the moment she met me, and it disarmed me. It seemed that Yardley was her West Coast counterpart.

"Thanks ... I guess?" I finally responded.

"I'll take a look at this and run it by Cheryl and Luke. CJ too, I guess, since he'll play with them at least through Billings, if not longer."

I nodded. "Sounds good. Oh, you'll notice," I moved next to her, pointing at the sheet music, "I did add a fiddle part, just to see. I know they don't have one, and that's fine. We could also substitute it with a second guitar, and I made that suggestion on the back of this sheet. It's easy enough that any guitarist from any of the bands could probably sight-read it, but important enough to the sound that they should give it a try."

"I'd offer to play the fiddle part," I continued. "But I don't know if I'd want to commit to that for the rest of the tour. CJ and I have a pretty aggressive set, and we add to it by the minute. It'll be a relief for both of us when their drummer is healed, though I think CJ would just play twenty-four seven until he bled out."

Yardley grinned. "He is kind of a workhorse isn't he?"

"Limitless. Until he hits a wall, that is. He's gotta learn some self regulation. Maybe he doesn't. I don't know …"

She waved her hand. "Anyway, don't stress about the fiddle part. Maybe I'll have you play it in rehearsal just so we can see how it sounds? We'll do a guitar, too. Then we can make a collective decision about how we want to proceed and deal with it from there."

"And if they like the fiddle?" I asked, hesitantly. I almost regretted scoring a part for violin, but couldn't help myself. I truly thought that, along with vocal work, could really push Moniker to front and center on the tour. Or at least even with Nessa's group, The Brewers.

"I'll smoke one out of somewhere," Yardley answered slyly. "I'll prod Nessa. She could use a little shakeup now and then."

My ears perked up. "Nessa? What about her?"

"I think she brought her violin with her, anyway. I'm sure she did," she said, waving her hand again. "She's hardly without it."

I pushed my head forward a bit, my eyes widening. "She plays?" I asked, trying to remember the last time I'd been this pleasantly surprised.

Yardley seemed to ignore my shock. "Yeah," she answered as if it were yesterday's news, still poring over the score. "I'm sure she wouldn't mind standing in for a while. She's hardcore, too. Doesn't mind pushing herself."

I felt a long-lost vibration of excitement rolling through my body as Yardley asked a few questions about the arrangement, and requested my opinion in other places. Once she headed for her bus, still studying the pieces I'd written, I raced to find Nessa.

"Hey!" I called, spotting her closing the large door underneath the black bus.

"Hey yourself." Nessa wore black yoga pants and a grey long-sleeved shirt. A far more comfortable look than she usually paraded in on stage. A decidedly intriguing relaxed contrast to her black and blue hair and last night's smudged mascara.

"I've gotta dump my stuff onto my bus, but I need to talk to you. Don't ... go anywhere." I was nearly giddy.

"Okay!" she answered with mocking excitement.

I left my violin slung over my shoulder as I bounded up the steps to the tour bus I shared with CJ and The Shakes. Entering the section where CJ and I slept, I was oblivious until I heard the muffled profanity coming from CJ's bed.

"Shit!" I exclaimed without looking, tossing my duffel bag on my bed while two bodies—one definitely CJ's—scrambled for cover under his tousled blankets. "Sorry."

"... the fuck out," CJ mumbled, seeming to not miss a beat as his mouth remained mostly connected with his guest's.

I huffed, leaving as quickly as I came, pissed that he'd pull this right before we were leaving. I just wanted to hit my bed and sleep. But, renewed energy surged through me when I realized I wanted to talk to Nessa, anyway. Amazing how the sight of your naked cousin can really derail a person.

"What's with you?" Nessa asked, meeting me halfway between our two busses.

I held out my hands. "I'm temporarily homeless. CJ's … busy. I don't know who with, but we're rolling out in like two minutes, so unless he's bringing a guest—"

"Guys!" Nessa called over her shoulder to a couple of her bandmates loading the last of their wares under the bus. "I found Clara!"

She turned to me with a mischievous grin. "They were circling each other all weekend. Sounds like one of them finally went in for the kill."

"Charming," I mumbled, shaking my head. "Can I ride with you guys till dinner? By the split-second looks of things I had, it didn't seem like they were going to wrap it up any time soon, and while I like the bus driver well enough, I've got shit I need to talk about with you."

Nessa looked startled. Amusingly so. "Yeah? What the hell did I do?"

I shrugged. "Play the violin without telling me, maybe?"

She turned bring red, looking down before taking a deep breath. "I dabble."

"Bull," I said, heading toward her bus. "March it, Lady. You've got some 'splaining to do."

CHAPTER THIRTEEN

CJ

ME: HEY ...

Frankie: Hey ...

Smartass.

I grinned. Carefully rolling to my side so as not to wake Clara, I tapped away on my phone.

Me: I miss you.

Frankie: I miss you, too.

Me: Can I call you?

Frankie: I don't know ...

Me: Please? *Please?*

She took a long time to respond. Then, hope.

Frankie: You know it's like midnight here, right?

Me: Is that a yes?

Frankie: I guess.

I slipped out of bed as quietly as possible, snatching my cigarettes and lighter from the floor before ducking out of the bus. After lighting the cigarette, I dialed Frankie's number.

She took three rings to answer.

"Hello?"

I sighed. Relief, maybe. "Have second thoughts about answering?"

"Yes," she admitted without further explanation. "What's up?"

I took a long drag, sitting on the loose gravel beneath me, leaning against the large tire of the bus. "I … I don't know Frankie, shit …"

"You're smoking again, huh?" She could always tell, even over the phone. Said I talked through my nose more when I had smoke in my lungs. Which was true, I suppose.

"Yeah," I answered, hanging my head. "Just don't lectur—"

"I'm not going to. You're a big boy." Her voice was clipped, and I couldn't tell if she was bordering on tears or annoyance. Maybe both.

"Frankie … I screwed up." I let the words spill out as messy as I felt, rocking my head back against the bus. "I screwed the fuck up."

"I don't want to hear this, CJ," she said, her voice sounding shaky now. "Your life just isn't my business anymore."

I cleared my throat, whispering as loud as I could with it still being a whisper. "You broke up with me, Frankie. You did."

"Not because I didn't love you," she whispered back, tears evident in her voice.

"Then why—"

"Because I do love you! Because I love me, too, and I deserved better. I deserve better."

"I know. I know," I cut in, unable to bear hearing her cry. It was almost as bad as seeing it in person. At least I was spared by three thousand miles. In some ways, though, that broke my heart more. "I disrespected you, and I'm sorry. I didn't even have a plan in my head when I asked about what your expectations were when I left for the tour. I don't know what I was thinking. I wasn't thinking," I added, hoping that would help.

It didn't.

Frankie sniffed, and I imagined her running her sleeve over her face before she spoke, the way I'd unfortunately seen her do too many times before. "That's it, CJ. That's the crux of it. You weren't thinking. About anyone else."

"I'm sorry. I never cheated on you though, Frankie."

"You came close enough," she answered without much emotion. And, that was true. I had toed the line early on. Maybe seeing what I could get away with … like a little kid.

It wasn't more than a kiss on the cheek here or an ass grab there, and it did stop. But it was clear I'd done too much damage to her trust, like Georgia said. Maybe permanently. And, maybe when I came to her asking what her expectations were of me on this tour, that was all she could take anymore.

During the long silence I had to swallow an uncomfortable feeling down my throat. When I felt moisture at the corners of my eyes, I got up and paced around the bus, breathing deeply. I really fucking blew it this time. Frankie and I hadn't ever been in a perfect relationship, but that was partially because neither of us had had a serious relationship in a while. Well, her in a while. Me … ever. We had a lot of bumpy patches at the beginning, but it smoothed out after a few months and we were in a comfortable pattern. Then, I guess, I got itchy. I don't know. She was understanding the first time I brought up my commitment issues, and even gave me the benefit of the doubt when it came up last year after she thought we should wait to move in together and I got pissed because I had opened myself up and she turned me down. Though there were a few days of tension-thick dinners and phone calls. This last time though? The proverbial straw. The last one. The one that broke the camel's back. All of it.

"CJ?"

It was my turn to sniff. I didn't mean to, and hoped she didn't notice. "Yeah." I coughed, clearing my throat again. "Yeah, I'm here."

Her voice softened in a second. "Are you … are you okay?"

I stopped pacing, facing the bus and resting my forehead against the cold steel. "No. No I'm not. I miss you, Frankie. I love you. So much it physically hurts me when I realize what I put you through."

"I know you love me," she whispered. "I love you, too."

"Then what the fuck are we doing?" I shook my head, looking up at the stars.

"This is kind of an intense conversation to have over the phone, you know?"

"Come see me," I blurted out.

"Ha! What?" Frankie's voice was less guarded now, more conversational. More like it used to be.

I knew I told myself that I didn't care what anyone thought about my love life. And that was mostly true. But I did care, a fucking lot, what the gorgeous, kindhearted woman on the other end of the phone thought. She was the only love life I'd ever had. Still, there was a woman in my bed on that bus who wasn't Frankie. And for that, I had no excuse.

"I'm serious," I answered, a smile finally forming. "Just … pick a date and come. See me. I miss you, and I won't be in Massachusetts till you're back in school. Do high school kids really need an English teacher?" I teased.

"We don't start until after Labor Day."

My mouth held a full smile now. "Oh, so you've checked it out ..."

"I like to know where you are. Where your shows are ... old habits die hard."

"I don't want to be an old habit, Frankie." She was right; this was too much to do over the phone. As much as I hated emotional crap, if I wanted to get her back, it wasn't going to be like this. "Just ... think about it? Visiting me."

After a few seconds, Frankie sighed. "I'll think about it."

And, just when hope had finally balanced on the tiny point it found in my chest, the wind blew.

"There you are!" Clara squealed, jumping up onto my back and wrapping her arms around my neck. "I thought you'd disappeared, you sneaky boy ..."

"Who is that?" Frankie asked, alarmed.

"I ... it's just—" I tried to answer, but Clara kissed my neck and my ear and made enough noise that it seemed to be all the answer Frankie needed.

Just like that, the venom returned to her voice. "Are you fucking kidding me right now? Like, honestly, is there a fucking camera somewhere?"

I shrugged Clara off. Not gently, but I didn't want to toss her to the ground, either. Well, I did, but... "Listen, Frankie. Please. Please. I told you I fucked up, and—"

"And I told you your life was none of my fucking business." She was talking through her teeth, I could hear it. "And then you told me you loved me—"

"I do!" I cut in. "Frankie, please. You said you love me, too." I paced again, my voice growing hoarse as my heart raced. Clara watched me closely, probably still drunk from earlier because she wasn't grasping the intensity of the conversation I was having. Either that, or she was a complete moron.

"Did you even bother to remove the condom first? Presuming you had the brains for one."

There was nothing I could say. I could do what I normally did, and try to talk my way out of it by saying Clara wasn't here the whole time—but I knew that would only make things worse. Words weren't going to help me tonight.

"Why'd you even call me?" Frankie demanded, her voice filled with angry tears. Why can't you just leave me alone?!" she asked again when I didn't answer.

"I don't know," I finally said, feeling more defeated than I had in my whole life. Even more than the day my mom told me my dad was never coming back. "Just … I'm sorry." I didn't mean to say it, but I had to. I meant it. With every fiber of my being, I meant it.

"Take that song someplace else, CJ. It's been overplayed in this house." And just like that, she ended the call.

Rage washed over and through me as I turned to Clara, but I breathed it away. This was far from her fault. I told her I was single. Because in practice, I was. But not in principle. Frankie would never get over this. I wouldn't, if I were her. I had no tricks left up my sleeve, no cards left to play. Just the sorry excuse of a human being I'd become. Just like him.

Mom will be so proud …

"Did I interrupt something?" Clara slurred.

I took out another cigarette, lit it, and inhaled for a long, long time. "I think you should go," I said on my exhale. "I need you to go."

"Are you serious? Did I do—"

I shook my head. "No. It's not you." I chuckled blackly to myself. "And for once, I mean that. This isn't about you at all."

Looking at me with a mixture of disgust and confusion, Clara stormed past me and up into the bus, no doubt to get her things. When she returned twenty seconds later with her purse, she faced me angrily.

"When anyone asks," she started, but I held up my hand.

"Tell them whatever you want. I don't care. But I don't plan on mentioning it."

Clara's shoulders sank a little, like she was relieved. Like my reputation had certainly preceded me and she was setting up to protect herself. "Okay," she said, sounding caught off-guard. "Thank you."

Once Clara was safely back on her bus, I sank to the ground again, thumbing through my phone. To the only girl on planet Earth who could help me out of this. Maybe.

Me: Sorry for being a dick earlier. When you were here.

Georgia: Give me a sec.

A few seconds later, my phone rang. I didn't get to say hello before she dove in.

"What in the fuck did you do?"

"What?"

"I just got off the phone with Frankie. Sobbing. I ended the call to talk to your dumb ass. And I don't know why the hell I'm even telling you that."

"To hurt me," I said quickly. "And I deserve it."

"What the hell CJ?"

I sighed. "I know, Georgia. I know. I do. I just … I need your help."

"You're helpless, you fuck. But I'll do what I can," she said to my surprise.

"Really?"

"Yes. By staying out of it."

My mouth hung open. "Are you kidding me? I need your help."

"Listen, babycakes," she said, rather brightly considering the circumstances. "I'm going to do it by not talking to Frankie about you and your pining. She's hurting. I'll help you by telling you what you need to hear. You need to get your thick head out of your ass and grow up. If you want her then you get her. I'm not getting her for you. I'm starting to think maybe she does deserve better than you. I like her. And as much as I love you, I sure as fuck don't like you right now."

I thumped my head against the bus, sighing loudly.

"I know," Georgia answered my non-response. "Buckle up. Adulthood is a damn toilet show."

Our conversation ended as quickly as it started, and I pulled myself off the ground, shuffling back onto the bus and into bed, where I stared at the ceiling as the busses pulled onto the highway. I didn't know if I had it in me, deep in me, to get a girl back. I'd never tried. I'd never bothered.

But I never loved anyone like Frankie before. It hurt like hell and just overall sucked. I couldn't decide if the chase was worth the pain in my chest.

CHAPTER FOURTEEN

REGAN

"**H**OW LONG HAVE you been playing and why for the love of God didn't I know?" I asked Nessa as we settled into the "kitchen" area of her bus.

A far nicer bus than the one we were on, but that's a detail I was willing to overlook for the time being because I felt like a sailor must when they spot land for the first time in months.

"Just ... whatever," was how she answered, setting two cups of coffee on the table between us. She sat across from me at the booth-style table and leaned to her left, just far enough to reach the mini fridge for cream.

"Got any half and half?" I asked out of habit.

She arched an eyebrow. "I'm sure you're man enough to handle full strength." She chuckled, sliding the glass pint of cream my way. "We bought it at the farmer's market this morning. It's like heaven. Trust me."

Stirring the thick, sweet cream in, I grinned. "Trust you? A tall order from someone who lied to me."

"No one told any lies!" she shrieked, holding out her hands. "And, anyway, who told you? Did Clara run her mouth before using it on CJ?"

"Classy," I responded. "But, no. It was Yardley, and in passing, so she didn't seem to think it was a secret. Come on, throw me a bone?"

She rolled her eyes. "I heard through the grapevine you were asked to compose on the fly for Moniker. Can't they write themselves?"

"Not everyone can write music. And, they can, but they're stuck in a rut."

Nessa's broad, but slightly bony shoulders rose and fell with a deep sigh. "I was four," she admitted. "I was four when my parents dragged me and my brother to a classical performance in Phoenix. I fell in love and never looked back."

The dreamy look in her eyes proved her story on its own, without words. It brought me back to the bluegrass festival where I first fell in love.

"Tell me. Everything. Did you take lessons? Play in ensembles? High school, college, all of it. Tell me." I was near-jittery with anticipation, but did my best not to seem like a stalker.

GSE didn't have a single other violinist on their rap sheet now that my former bandmate, Shaughn, was back in Ireland. And it wasn't until Yardley mentioned Nessa's ability that I realized how much I missed Shaughn and her brassy attitude. I wanted to play every song, right now, with Nessa. It was like the feeling I had when I travelled briefly through Indonesia during college and ran into groups of people who could speak English. It was exciting and a respite all at once to be among my people, even if they weren't American. We could speak the same language. And to know that I was sitting across from a musician who could speak my violin language? It was perfection. I didn't know how often she played, but I knew it must be enough that Yardley knew and was fine with suggesting that she take the stage with Moniker for an original song.

"Go," I implored. Impatient.

Nessa shook her head, pulling her hair away from her face with a wide stretchy headband that had been slouched around her neck. Bright pink.

"Well, yeah, I took lessons. I went to a public high school and played in ensembles there, but they had a regular concert band, not an orchestra. No other violinist. One bassist but, what can you do?" She shrugged.

"No private schools around?"

She huffed through her nose. "My parents couldn't even afford lessons all the way through high school, let alone a private school on top of it." She looked down just briefly. Enough for me to feel the weight of the unspoken. Whatever it was.

"What about college?" I swallowed, hoping to slide past the lesson misstep.

Nessa grinned, taking a sip of her coffee. "No money for lessons, no money for college."

My stomach sank. I was failing this conversation wonderfully. And, worse, there was no way out now that the busses were merging onto the highway. I was stuck in this seat for at least the next couple of hours.

"But you kept playing," I encouraged the conversation in yet another direction.

"Hell yeah I played. I shouldn't have been so depressing. I did get to take lessons through high school. By junior year my parents couldn't pay anymore, but the instructor I'd had since age six took pity on me. I helped out teaching some of the little kids in exchange for lessons myself."

I shook my head. "That wasn't pity. He saw talent."

She shrugged, opening her mouth, but I cut her off. "No, listen to me. I've taught private lessons. In poor countries and rich neighborhoods in the US. It's not the most lucrative way to earn money as a musician, and pity isn't worth its weight in dollars when you're trying to feed yourself. Whoever your teacher was knew it was a greater risk to the world to lose you as a musician than to skip the organic chicken on their next grocery trip."

"Jeez." She blushed, swallowing hard. "You're awfully sure of yourself for not ever hearing me play."

"Show me," I asked softly. "I know Yardley doesn't settle. Especially on something new. If she thought you could handle what I scored from a sight-read, I'd say it's worth it to her. And," I reached my hand across the table, offering hers a gentle squeeze, "if you travel with your violin after all these years …" I took a deep breath. "It's your passion."

Her eyes met mine and held onto them for what seemed like years. One blue, one green, both desperately vulnerable. Pleading, almost, but I didn't know for what.

"Come on," I encouraged with one last squeeze of her hand before pulling it away.

Nessa stared a few seconds more, then cleared her throat, looking around as if she just dropped back to earth. I didn't know what she was holding back, but I bet if I watched her play for long enough I could get some idea.

"Fine," she spoke, sounding more like herself and less lost as she had before. "But you can't look at me."

I screwed up my face incredulously. "What?! That's half the story. Watching someone perform."

"You didn't ask to watch me," she corrected, reaching into a storage cabinet above her, pulling down a worn nylon-covered hard case. "You asked to hear."

"Ah," I corrected, smiling. "You said I'd never heard you. I said show me." I crossed my arms in front of my chest, leaning back quite proud of myself.

She shrugged, reaching to put the violin back into storage. "Fine," she said flatly.

I lunged forward, my hands waving in surrender. "No, no! Fine. Sorry. I'll … I'll turn around."

"Relax, legs. I'll just move to behind you. Your beanpoles won't fit backward at that table."

I sighed a breath of relief that I'd get to hear something that was clearly closer to her than she let on.

"Guys!" she called to the rest of her band through a cheap pocket door between the kitchen and the rest of the bus. "I'm playing for a few minutes. Deal."

Muffled sounds of consent sprang from the back of the bus.

"I'm just going to warm up a sec."

Lacing my fingers behind my head, I splayed my elbows out and leaned back. "Take your time."

After a brief pause, she struck her bow against the strings and drew out long, low notes. Each one two-seconds long, or more, before changing to another. After ten seconds she picked up the pace, offering one note per second, still a slow pace, but fine for warming up. Every ten or fifteen seconds, though, she upped the tempo, and the notes became more familiar. She wasn't warming up with scales, as is traditional—though I sometimes skipped those too.

She was using Bach's "Partita" number... two—no—three. In E major. She was using a lovely Bach sonata as her warm up. At a moderate tempo, she hit all the notes and held on lovingly to some at the ends of measures or lines. I closed my eyes. If they were open, I'd be searching for her. Before long she held onto a high note, and it was clear to me that she was changing songs, or warm-ups, or whatever it was she was doing.

She started slow again, but closer on pace with the "Sonata No. 1 in G minor" I easily identified. Bach sonatas are lovely and intricate, whether playing for a crowd or using as a warm up. Within ten seconds, Nessa was working the sonata at its presto tempo, flawlessly fingering the complicated collections of notes. Keeping my eyes closed, I leaned forward and placed my elbows on the table and rested my head on my hands. I took a deep breath. I wanted to turn around. I wanted to join her. But, she asked that I listen. So, listen I would.

"Okay," she finally said as if she hadn't already played marvelously for four minutes. "Here goes. No looking."

I put up my hands. "Not gonna."

She chuckled softly before taking a deep breath, and striking her strings once more.

Immediately, I wanted to cry.

Chopin's "Nocturne" never did anything less than put a lump in my throat. A mournful love song. A goodbye. A plea at best, but a gut-wrenching tale of broken lovers nonetheless. Chopin dedicated the song to his dear friend, and his friend's wife—who had a messy situation of their own. Regardless of the original intentions of the piece, it had always been one I played on a rainy day when I needed some self-inflicted brooding.

But on this occasion, I knew I was hearing something more than notes she'd memorized. As the strings wailed under the gentle touch of her bow, I could wait no longer—I turned around. Before me stood a tall and swaying Nessa. Her eyes closed, squeezed so tightly shut I could barely see her eyelashes. Whatever tension she was holding in her face, she released through the instrument.

I didn't know her story, and didn't know if I ever would. She came from far less money than I did, and had what seemed to be much fewer opportunities and less professional experience, but you couldn't tell. It didn't matter. It never did with those born with an instrument sewn to their soul.

Despite my own desires, I forced myself to turn back around. I didn't want to blow Nessa's trust if she saw me staring at her when she'd asked me not to.

Not if I hoped for a shot in hell to get her to play like that for me again. Or in public. She was far too good to leave her violin on the bus when she stepped on any stage. I didn't need to hear her play any more to be assured of that.

At the close of the piece my eyes were full with tears. I missed Georgia just as badly as I did when I dropped her off at the airport this morning. I breathed. It would be a few days until my road equilibrium returned and I wasn't looking for her every time I turned around. "Nocturne" always made me think of Georgia. It made me miss her and love her and need her. Also, even though I didn't know the details, it made me feel for Nessa. For the reasons behind her emotion in that song.

"Okay. Done," she said without much fanfare. "Happy?"

Speechless, I turned around and tried to hide the emotion in my eyes with a smile. She caught me in my act, meeting my eyes and immediately looking down.

"Yeah," I said, exhaling. "Hell. Yes."

Standing, I faced her and put my hands on her shoulders. "Why? Why don't you play this? Like on stage?"

She rolled her eyes. "And be compared to you for the whole tour? Please. I've followed your career since you were in college, Regan. It's a tough act to follow."

My eyes bulged out. "Excuse me?"

She waved her hand is if this was run-of-the-mill. "Everyone who has a clue about the classical music scene for the under-forty crowd knows you."

I shook my head. "Maybe people in the scene ..."

"No," she cut me off. "You turned out that little album your senior year in college—Dublin Nights or some cliché-as-shit title. Right before you left to teach around the world." She winked, then continued. "People passed that hand to hand, and all of us in or around the scene made sure it got to any bar with a whiff of Irish—even if they were only Irish on St. Paddy's Day."

I swallowed hard, feeling heat spread across my face. "I knew bars on the cape played it ... But then I was out of the country for nearly two years."

She grinned. "It went a lot further than your precious peninsula."

"Stalker issues aside," I shook my head, wholly uncomfortable with this kind of attention, "you're amazing. And," I caught her wrist as she turned away, facing her back to me, "if you've followed me for as long as you say, then you'd know I don't dole out compliments that easily."

She laughed and I dropped my hand. "Yeah, you are kind of a snob, aren't you?"

I shrugged, crossing my arms in front of my chest. "Music will never survive if we all settle for mediocrity."

Nessa swallowed hard, sliding by me in the narrow space to place her violin in its case and tuck it safely away in the cargo hold above the table. She bent down, reaching into the mini fridge, and came up with a bottle of Bailey's Irish Cream in her hand and a comical grin on her mouth.

"You're Irish, right?"

I slid back into my seat, sliding my mug toward her. "Even if I wasn't …"

CHAPTER FIFTEEN
REGAN

OUR DINNER STOP consisted of a roadside diner in one of the most middle-of-nowhere places I'd ever seen besides the back roads of New Hampshire. There was something in the parking lot that claimed to be a food truck, chucking burritos, but I stayed with steak and eggs. And a couple of waffles.

As soon as we'd gotten off the busses, Nessa nabbed Clara when she departed Moniker's bus, which was weird since she'd started this leg of the trip on my bus. In CJ's bed. She didn't look as pissed as I'd have thought for someone in her apparent position, but I tried not to think much more about it. Nessa escorted her into the diner and into a booth far in the corner for what I assumed would be CJ-related girl talk.

Mine and Nessa's conversation on the bus in the hours before stopping for dinner stayed far away from the violin or this tour. She asked me about teaching music from Indonesia and Ireland, and I was brutally honest in an effort to get some information from her, too. And, I had nothing to hide. But, no dice. When the questioning shifted to her, and I asked how she got hooked up with The Brewers, she wasn't rude, but she kind of breezed through the whole story.

She'd been singing with a band at a local bar in Phoenix, where she's from, and an old friend from high school swept her away to San Francisco to be starving artists in the music community. She did, however, speak with wild light in her eyes about her time in San Francisco, and promised stories in more detail over drinks. I could only imagine.

By the time we had arrived at the diner, I knew conversation about or around Nessa and her violin was to cease. For the time being, anyway.

Halfway through my steak that actually wasn't half bad for the looks of the diner, CJ plunked down in the seat across from me.

Without really looking at him, I started with, "Just … one of the other band members? Seriously? You could have your choice of any woman at any concert—married or not, unfortunately—and you choose one who we'll be shacking up with for the next several months?"

He was silent. So silent, I lifted my eyes from my plate to see him staring into space, and his hands in fists under his chin as his nostrils flared.

"Ceej?"

His empty eyes met mine for a second before he stood and barged out of the diner and into the parking lot. Instinctively, I followed him, asking a passing waitress to box up my food and hold it at the counter. Nessa caught my eyes as I left, and all I could do was shrug.

"CJ," I called after him.

"Not now Regan," he answered with his back to me, holding up his hand. He made his way to a set of benches that sat on the edge of a thick, dark forest.

"What's wrong?" I asked, unaffected by his attitude.

"I said drop it," he snapped.

"No you didn't." I plunked down next to him. "What the hell?"

"Georgia get home okay?" He changed the conversation one hundred eighty degrees. "Not that I even care," he added. This was his roundabout way of asking me if she was still pissed at him, or to tell me his side of their fight.

"Obviously you care, fucker. And, yes, she's home. I got a text from her a while ago that she was back at work."

She was probably up to her eyeballs in hysterical mother's-of-the-bride by now, trying to change the filling choices for the cakes or cupcakes at the last minute. I don't know how Georgia had the patience for that. No one came up on stage in the middle of my performances and told me to adjust a note.

"Did she tell you about our fight?" he asked, almost accusingly.

"Does it matter?" I sighed, shaking my head. "If she didn't, you would have."

He shrugged.

I added, "She didn't tell me any details, though."

CJ looked out into the twilight, clearing his throat. "Frankie's not stupid. She knew I had a girl on the side when we first got together." It was a jarring change of subject, but I walked through the conversation with him, anyway.

I winced. "You did?"

He looked down, shaking his head. "I wasn't fucking her. We barely hung out. I made out with her a few times, but that didn't last long."

I shrugged. "So what was it?"

"I just … kept her in my contacts, you know? We'd text once in a while …"

A heavy sigh was the only response I could muster.

"It almost broke me and Frankie up before we had a chance to get off the ground. We were looking at pictures on my phone one day from a show I'd done, and a text came in from that girl. Only the first line came up but, like I said, Frankie's no fool."

"But you said that's when you first got together?"

CJ leaned forward pressing his elbows into his knees. "I didn't go out of my way to be a good guy to her."

"What do you mean?" I was uncomfortable hearing the strain in his voice. Not quite on the edge of tears, but certainly circling regret.

He shrugged. "I never sent her flowers at work. I only offered to make dinner once in a while, but we went out a lot …" He lifted his head, looking into the vacant space a few feet in front of his face. "I didn't search old bookstores for her favorite authors or take her to poetry readings. I just kind of said, 'This is my life, come along if you want in.' I didn't try to make a life with her."

"Because your dad did all those things with your mom and it was a lie." It was harsh, but factual.

He only stared.

"You know your parents loved each other in high school, right? And even after? When they had you—"

"I know," he cut in sharply. "But he just fucking romanced my mom nonstop so she wouldn't see that he was starting a whole new life outside her peripheral vision. She had no reason to think he was doing anything wrong. He showed up everywhere he was supposed to, showered her with attention and gifts, was hands on with me …"

"I remember," I admitted, feeling a lump in the back of my throat.

I knew this story all too well. I'd loved my uncle almost as much as my dad. CJ and I had the best early childhood. Our parents lived on the same street in a picturesque seaside town. A model American childhood for both of us. Loving families, involved dads, everything was perfect.

Until it wasn't. Almost overnight. It would be years before we realized the extent of CJ's dad's damage, and the second family that technically gave CJ step siblings and half siblings that he's never met. Knowing the manipulation his dad laid on, I doubt if those kids even know CJ exists.

My dad dove right in, sweeping up his brother's mess and never treated CJ like anything less than a son. When we told people how we were related, we always just said our mom's are sisters, because that was true. In law, sure, but also in heart, and then we didn't ever have to talk about CJ's dad unless he wanted to. Which was basically never. Until now, it seemed.

"Frankie knows about Clara."

I leaned forward and buried my face in my hands. "That's … bad."

"Georgia's not gonna help me. She says she's tired of my shit and it's time I grow up."

"You talked to her already?" I was relieved and curious that she hadn't roped me into the conversation already.

"A lot of good it did," CJ answered. "She's staying out of it."

I nodded approvingly. "Seems appropriate."

"Maybe it'll be good for me to be alone for a while."

"Have you talked to anyone besides Georgia about this?"

CJ cracked a laugh. "No. Except you, but you're not much help."

I huffed through my nose. "I don't really know what you want from me, Ceej. I … I think you've gotta kind of cut the shit about your dad."

His head whipped toward me, rage in his eyes. "What the fuck did you just say?"

I sighed, grinding my back teeth together. "My dad did a hell of a job taking care of you and your mom after your dad left, CJ. I was there, remember? Jesus Christ, just … focus on the positive examples you do have and stop wallowing in what you lost."

I stood, his ungrateful, victim attitude really started getting under my skin.

"Oh it's just so easy for you, isn't it, Regan. From your perfect little family—"

"You're part of that family!" I snapped holding my hands out as he stood. "Jesus, you were so worried about pulling the wool over girls' eyes that you just became a wandering dick and a womanizer. Honestly, I fail to see how that's any better than what your dad did."

"Fuck you, Regan." He had murder written across his face, but apparently decided not to get into it with me right there. Instead, he pushed past me and stormed toward the bus.

"Hey!" I shouted, jogging after him.

He turned around, his shoulders heaving under angry breaths. "What?"

"Don't be a dick just because you screwed up." I pressed my index finger into his shoulder, leaning in close and lowering my voice. "Every fucking time I turn around you're either moping, pissed off, or feeling up some girls ass in a bar. Feeling sorry for yourself? Change it." I pressed harder before dropping my hand, my adrenaline starting to kick in.

CJ ran his tongue across his teeth as he took a deep breath. "Don't touch me again, Regan."

I lifted my chin. "Is that a threat?"

"A warning," he growled as a few members of the tour switched their attention to the scene in front of our bus. "My life is none of your fucking business."

"Then," I spoke sharply, "leave me and my wife out of it." I turned away, betting he wasn't likely to hit me from behind— that wasn't his style—and headed into the diner to retrieve my food.

Apparently, we'd caused a minor scene, as all eyes were on me when I grabbed the loaded Styrofoam container off the counter and walked back to the bus.

"So …" Nessa stepped in front of me just before I reached the bus door. "Anyone gonna die tonight?"

"Not now, Nessa," I snapped

"Hey." She touched my shoulder, her eyebrows pulled in as her look morphed from sarcasm to concern. "Chill, okay? If you need to crash somewhere else, you're welcome on our bus."

"I'm not packing up just because he's an asshole."

She dropped her hand. "The offer stands. Will you guys be okay to play when we reach Seattle?"

I laughed dismissively. "I did a concert a month after my girlfriend died. I'm pretty sure I can handle my shit."

She pulled her head back, pursing her lips. "You don't have to be a dick."

I sighed, my shoulders sinking. "Shit. I'm sorry. I just ..."

Nessa touched my shoulder once more, and this time, it grounded me somehow.

"I know," she said. "Later." She shot me a quick, almost reassuring smile before boarding her bus.

Once finally on mine, I tossed my food in the fridge and entered our "bedroom." The curtain on CJ's bed was pulled. Just as well. I changed and got under my covers as quickly as possible in order to sleep, but it was in vain. I ended up staring at the ceiling for an hour before rolling over and pulling out my phone.

Me: He's just such a thickheaded dick sometimes. It's enraging.

I stared at the three dots in anticipation of an incoming text.

Nessa: I know. We all are. Sleep with one eye open ;)

I smiled, switching my phone into airplane mode before putting in my earbuds and falling asleep with the sounds of Chopin's "Nocturne" playing in the background.

***

Seattle was fantastic and, as I predicted, CJ and I carried out our professional responsibilities as professionals. Neither one of us are big on drawn out apologies and make-up scenes, so it seemed for the time being that what happened at that roadside diner was swept under the rug.

The tour was really picking up steam, selling out left and right. Since we had a week before we had to be in Billings, Montana, Yardley added in a fourth Seattle show for us. Moniker was pleased with their new songs, and it seemed to reinvigorate them. Through the Seattle shows, though, they stuck with the guitar over the violin option.

I didn't really understand why, since when I practiced with them using the violin it really brought the sound together, but maybe that was my bias. Despite not being a musician herself, Yardley did have a great ear for the ensemble. Still, the idea of setting the violin aside just didn't sit right with me.

At an overnight road stop somewhere in the western part of Montana, I pressed Yardley.

"Give the fiddle another shot with Moniker. If I have to take it on for a while, I will. I think it sounded right on."

She looked up from her iPhone, situated next to her sparse salad, in surprise. "What are you talking about?"

I winced a little, not wanting to sound snobby. "The guitar's fine. I don't mean the player—she's great—I just … the sound …"

"We're going to put the violin in, Regan. Chill. I'd like it for Minneapolis, but I talked to Nessa, and she says she'll need longer—maybe till Chicago. She sight-read it just fine, but she hasn't performed on stage in a while, and wants more time to polish it."

A wave of relief washed over me. "Oh good. Okay. Well in the meantime, if you want me to step in …"

She grinned as I did, shaking her head. "Workaholic. I'm not in the business of burning out musicians so, for now, stick with CJ. You guys are one hell of a team together. Did you play around like this in high school?"

I laughed. "No, I was way too much of a prick, then. High and mighty with my classical instrument to slum it with the likes of him while he banged away on steel barrels. That's what I used to say to tease him."

Her right eyebrow flicked up. "Did he … kick your ass?"

I winked. "Nah. I could always run faster. Thank God. And, he wasn't the sweet human he plays now, either. Used to say the violin was gay." I rolled my eyes, thankful that at least we'd moved past those days.

"I really can't see you as the prick type, Regan. I gotta say. You're one of the most down-to-earth genuine guys I've met in the business. I held my breath the whole time Celtic Summer was touring. I was worried you'd get sick of it and leave us all in the dust."

It wasn't the first time Yardley had mentioned her apprehension over losing me as an artist.

"Down-to-earth and faithful," I remind her. "Our business relationship is important to me. I love my job and the life I get to have because of it."

She nodded, the rosy apples of her cheeks swelling as she smiled. "I know."

"But, about the prick thing? Yeah. Some of it was general self-centered adolescent stuff, and some of it was environmental. Private performing arts high school, the Boston Conservatory … it was a ripe environment for intellectual and musical superiority to reign." I chuckled, thinking about the high horse I'd long since retired. "It was the work abroad in Indonesia,

Ireland, and South America that helped knock me down a few pegs. Watching kids with ripe, fertile, feral passion but with literally no opportunities brought me back to the first time I held a violin. When I got back to the states I was courted by Boston again for their Tanglewood summer program, but I just couldn't do it. I weaved through the inner-cities and rural towns of Massachusetts, hosting workshops and holding fundraisers … the bitch of it is it's the public schools that suffer most. Cost-cutting there happens in arts and physical education first. It's not something you see in private schools that cost as much as some colleges … I'm rambling …" I chuckled, taking the deep breath I so desperately needed.

Yardley blinked a few times as if she'd been in a trance. "No—God, no—it's fascinating. I mean, I've seen your resume, obviously, but that? What you just said? Not on there. That's good. Where'd you learn your tricks? I can't picture you in an orchestra setting, but that's where you've spent more than half your life so far."

"The guy who became my first teacher held me back from trick-playing for a while. He saw I had the wild streak in me—as he called it—but insisted I learn the rules first. Can't break 'em right until you understand them, he'd always say."

She laughed, silencing her phone when it rang once. "I like it."

"Anyway, he let me loose a bit in high school. Even though I was receiving instruction at that point through my school, I still went to him on weekends. He was my friend, above all else. But it wasn't really until I was out in the world that I let it fly completely. The kids in Indonesia and South America, especially … they were poor enough that they might never actually see the volumes of classical sheet music I'd already played from in their lives. I worked with them on the barest of basics—identifying each note on the staff and corresponding that to the fingers on the instrument. After that it was all free-play. Some of these kids came up with things that I can still hear in my head. It's two sides of the same coin really—tricks and classical instruction. And I don't think you need one before the other, anymore. Not if you've got it in here." I pointed to my chest and took another deep breath.

"We've gotta hold workshops," Yardley said, not blinking for several seconds.

A surge of electric feeling whizzed though my chest. "Yes! Let's do it! There are some lags on this tour where we have several days between shows. We can set something up in one city, then the next."

She held out her hand. "I was thinking more at home, in San Diego, but way to take on yet another project on the road, Regan."

"Sorry … I just. Outreach is so important. Music is handed down through generations like language. If no one is around to hand it down because we're all locked away playing in our ivory towers … we've got nothing. We're hoarding it away from our great-grandchildren."

Yardley shook her head again, a look of disbelief crossing her face. "You make it hard for me to not parade you around like the amazingness you are. But we've all got to keep a vial of humility in our pockets, huh?"

I grinned. "I guess. So, when do we get started?"

CHAPTER SIXTEEN
GEORGIA

BRIAN STOOD AT the counter of Sweet Forty-Two with his weekly dessert order for Live in hand.

"Are we still friends?" he asked, biting his lip and grinning at the same time he handed me a mile-long list.

"Depends." I arched an eyebrow, snatching the order sheet from him and giving it the once over. "I guess," I said in a sigh. "You're lucky Regan's not around or this shit would be hard to fill. I'm ovulating and he's in fucking Minneapolis."

It had been over a month since Regan last held me, and the warmth of his arms and the scent that always sat in the nook of his neck and shoulder was only just starting to fade. Still, staring at the ovulation calendar taped to my bathroom mirror drove me nearly mad. It was like a visual biological clock. A loud one, at that.

Brian's eyes creased at the sides as he winced. "Seattle wasn't a winner, huh?"

I shook my head. "No, and thank God you're gay. I can barely talk about ovulation with Regan, let alone any other straight male in my life."

He held out his arms. "We all have a cross to bear. Your cycle is mine."

I threw a rag at him, which he caught and threw back, smacking me in the face with a cloud of powdered sugar.

"Anyway, I know we only had two days last month, but I was hoping my body would be as efficient as it is in the kitchen. You know ... all the analogies of buns in the oven ..."

Brian laughed, walking around the counter to join me and put his arm around my shoulder. "If nothing else, your sarcasm will save us all."

I rolled my eyes. "Or be the death of me when spewed at the wrong time."

"How's the tour going, by the way?"

"Good, I guess. They're getting great crowds. I think the diversity of the acts helps. And summer is always prime demand for those kinds of shows. Oh, and they're going to do some clinics for kids, and stuff. Workshop sort of things, like the ones Regan remembers from when he was little."

There was a nagging piece of a recent call with Regan that was tugging at the back of my brain, but I was letting it go for now.

It was nothing.

Brian jumped up, sitting on the pay counter. "Is Celtic Summer going to record more together? I mean, they had a few albums that were massive hits ... even the Grammy nom."

Ah, yes. The Grammy's. Regan never talked about it, but Celtic Summer did get a nomination after the release of their first album for Best New Artist. It had been a while since a group had won in that category, and that year a solo artist won again, but the nomination was a huge leap for Regan, the members of Celtic Summer, and their genre as a whole. Well, their non-genre as Regan liked to call it. He confided shortly before the awards that he never wanted to win a Grammy because he was afraid of what it would do to his head.

"The humility in that man ..." I said out loud.

"What?" Brian asked, alerting me to my slip.

I sighed. "He told me he hopes he never wins a Grammy because he's afraid he'll become an egomaniac. Isn't that insane? I'd gun for a Nobel Peace Prize if bakeries could enter."

"They should," Brian encouraged, lifting up a cupcake from my discard pile before shoving it in his mouth. "Who's not peaceful with a brain full of sugar?"

"This is what I'm saying. Don't eat all of those, I crumble them up to make cake pops."

"In all honesty, though?" Brian continued. "It doesn't surprise me. He's more an under-the-radar kind of guy. Odd for someone who spends half the year on a stage, but I get it."

I cocked my head to the side. "How? How is he so good at that?"

"The stage is a boundary, you know? He's on it, then he's off it. Doing music twenty-four-seven, yeah, but he's available to the fans through albums and on stage. Period. A Grammy would tear those walls down in a heartbeat. It's good he knows himself as well as he does. He is who he is."

"Yeah …" I trailed off.

It was nothing.

"What's that look?"

"It's nothing," I said out loud, shaking my head at myself and checking on the dough, rising in four different steel bowls across one of my prep surfaces.

"Clearly." Brian didn't buy it, crossing his arms in front of him, still sitting on the counter.

I put my hands on my hips, huffing petulantly. "It's just … there's this member of another band he told me about. One on tour with them. I mean, I know them, but … he found out a few weeks ago that they also play the violin, though not on this tour, I guess. But they might, or something, I don't know—it was hard for me to pay attention."

"Is that because the they you're so eloquently referring to is a she, perhaps?"

I twisted my lips. "He told you?"

He pulled his head back. "Fuck no. Regan and I don't talk about girls."

My mouth dropped open, but he cut me off.

"Not because of you, weirdo. Not like that, anyway. Because he's married and I'm gay. What's there to talk about? And, we don't communicate a ton while he's on the road, anyway. You know how he is. Brood City. "

I grinned. Regan's hermit-like nature was often mislabeled as broodiness, but he didn't mind and neither did I. There was a fine line between the two, anyway, and he was just as likely to fall on one side as the other. He was quiet, but fierce and passionate. Sure of himself in a way I admired and aspired to.

"Anyway, yes. It's a girl. The lead singer of The Brewers."

"Nessa Crowley?" he asked, sliding off the counter to pour himself some coffee.

"Ah, it has a last name."

Brian's eyes were wide as he turned, but he relaxed his face when he saw I was smiling.

"Yes," I continued. "Nessa. I know her last name. She's lovely. Quiet, but lovely."

"So ... what's the problem?"

I fumbled for an answer because, really, there wasn't one. Not one I could put my finger on, anyway. I trusted what I knew of her. And that didn't even matter. I trusted my husband above all else. There was something else, though.

"Is it because she plays the same instrument Regan does?"

I shook my head. "That can't be it. He spent years with Shaughn and that didn't bother me."

"True. So ... What is it, then? What has you all tongue-tied and paranoid—shit ... sorry." Brian winced.

I sighed, waving my hand dismissively.

It's common American vernacular to tell people to calm down and not be paranoid when things were bugging them.

When anxieties surfaced. But for me, the word paranoid was always attached to my mother's diagnosis of paranoid schizophrenia, which caused storms far greater than any sized panic attack ever could.

"Don't worry about it." I threw him a wink, but he still looked reserved.

"Anyway," I continued through the awkwardness, "I don't know what it is. I just miss him, I think. It's been a month since we've seen each other, for fuck's sake. And, while sexting is all fine and dandy, it doesn't give mind-blowing orgasms."

"And it won't get you knocked up, either," he added with a laugh.

I twisted my lips. "True. Then Regan would have no mini-him musical protégé to usher through the world."

I hadn't thought much about having kids while I was growing up, but hearing Regan tell stories of his time teaching impoverished children warmed my heart, and showed me without him having to tell me how great a dad he hoped to be someday.

"Go to Minneapolis," Brian said out of nowhere.

My eyes bugged nearly all the way out of my head. "Excuse me?"

He rolled his yes, waving his arms around dramatically. "Whatever will San Diego do without you for one night? Look," he pointed to my calendar. "You've got the next two days free. Get on a flight today, shag his rocker brains out, and you can be back the morning before I need my cannoli's."

"He's planning to come out here between Ohio and New York for a couple days, and then he's got a few weeks in Massachusetts, and I was going to go out there—"

"Blah, blah, blah," Brian cut me off, handing me my cell from the basket by the bakery's phone. "Call the airline. Get you some."

My pulse pounded in my neck and my throat ran dry. "I can't … I've never left the shop on such short notice."

"Can't or won't?" Brian lifted his eyebrows, then his look shifted. Slightly pleading.

"Neither," I said before I had time to think about it. "I'll go. Can you—"

He held up his hands. "Yes. I'm a chef, and I know your OCD ways with this kitchen."

An energy I'd never felt before swirled through me. "Am I crazy for doing this?"

Brian smiled, all the way to his eyes. "Not at all. This is your husband. And you miss him. And have you ever surprised him like this?"

I thought for a second. "No. I mean, once or twice very early on." My face fell. "While his band was on tour, we were taking off business-wise here. So all my trips were well calculated and planned.

He reached for my shoulders, his warm hands giving me a playful squeeze. "Then this will do both of you some good, don't you think?"

"Spontaneity is really Regan's department. Relationally, I mean. Like, I have all these tattoos, and he has … none. But he swoops in and does the flowers and brings me lunch even though I work in a kitchen and am twenty feet from my home kitchen …" I trailed off, untying my apron, grabbing my phone, and moving toward the door. "Holy shit, am I doing this?"

Brian nodded, grinning like a love-struck fool. I wondered how he and Randy were doing, but thought better of asking right at that moment. "You're doing this, Kid. Go, now. Make it a first-class ticket if you can!"

"Let's not get carried away," I teased before bounding up the stairs.

Within a half hour I did my makeup, packed two carefully chosen outfits, and was out the door without looking back. My pulse raced and I was jittery like the one time I drank three-too-many espressos during a long wedding week two years ago. But this was better. This adrenaline rush wasn't from work at all.

It was from my husband.

As the plane took off, miraculously on time and a direct flight to Minneapolis, I stared at the twinkling landscapes below me. I wondered, pressing my head against the window, if there were two people down there even a fraction as happy as Regan and I were. Settling back into my seat, I took some cleansing breaths. Yes, I was ovulating. But I was going to try to keep that way in the back of my mind as I seduced my husband. Normally our sex life is fantastic, but since this baby thing it's all seemed a little forced and calculated.

I just wanted to show him a good time, and love on the man who has loved me when I couldn't or wouldn't love myself.

***

If my calculations were correct, I'd actually beat the tour buses to the hotel in Minneapolis. They had been lumbering their way from Billings to Minnesota, swinging through random towns here and there for R&R. A break from the tour grind.

Regan left me a detailed itinerary before he left on this tour, and any time it changed he would always call or text. My short-term memory was filled with brides and first birthday parties and gender reveal cakes—that's a thing now. I couldn't fill it with trying to remember where he was at any given minute.

I'll never forget the first time he forgot what city he was in. It was hilarious. He was well into his first long tour with Celtic Summer, and he wandered on the streets for a minute until he figured it out because he didn't want to ask anyone. Men. It was Richmond, VA, by the way. We joked we should name a child Richmond, though we couldn't decide if it would be applied to a boy or girl.

Still energized despite the long, uneventful flight, and the fact I hadn't slept since the night before, I took a cab to the hotel that was next on the travel docket. I decided not to rent a car, since once I arrived at the hotel I didn't plan on going anywhere—or wearing clothes—until my return flight late tomorrow morning.

It was late. Ten o'clock, meaning I had less than an hour before Regan was scheduled to check in.

"Hi," I greeted the bored-looking twenty-something, male receptionist at the check-in desk. "I'm Georgia Kane, checking in early to Regan Kane's room. It might be under Grounded Sound Entertainment."

He nodded once—not rude, but he could have certainly used a little coffee—and began clacking away on the keyboard in front of him.

"Hmm," he said, squinting as if that would change the information before him. "I don't have you—"

I put up my hand. "Let me stop you right there. I'm aware that my name isn't on the reservation. Regan is my husband. He's on tour. Kind of a big deal," I started, checking the time on my phone. "So, I'll show you my license, passport, almost whatever you need to prove to you he's my husband so you can hand me a key to his room. Because, one way or another, I'll get in that room." I shot him a wink and a slightly flirtatious smile, keeping my voice light and airy throughout.

I'd been through this multiple times in the last few years. Then, it donned on me.

"Click on special requests."

"Huh?" He looked at me like this was his first day on the job.

I sighed. "The special requests tab for Regan Kane. My name will likely be there."

He arched an eyebrow, but did as I asked. A few seconds later, he eyed me. Georgia, you said?"

I nodded, smiling. "That's me."

"Says here to add you to the room."

I nodded once, gesturing to the keyboard. "If you will …"

Yardley's good. We started that system halfway through Regan's first tour, when I encountered a difficult front desk manager—no doubt concerned with keeping their job, and the band's safety a close second. The surprise was ruined when I called Regan, blubbering that they wouldn't tell me where his room was. I hadn't thought of calling Yardley then. Still, after that incident, she put my name on every room Regan stayed in. I hadn't talked with her about it for this tour, but it seemed she really did take care of her label family.

"Here you are, Mrs. Kane. Sorry for the delay," the young man said with renewed enthusiasm for his job. "Your husband's amazing, by the way."

I blushed. "He is," I agreed. "Here. For your trouble." I reached into my oversized tote bag that served as my carry on, and handed him a baked and decorated this morning Sweet Forty-Two cupcake in a plastic container. Iced sky blue with a deep red cherry on top.

"Seriously?" He smiled at the confection.

I nodded. "Enjoy."

With a quick wave, I sauntered to the elevator, reveling in the sound the plastic box made as it popped open, and the front desk boy took his first bite. And moaned. It helped to travel with currency such as mine. I couldn't remember anything I wasn't able to talk my way out of as long as I had a bag full of sugar over my shoulder. Regan often doubted sugar's power, even over money, until he saw it in action. The boy at the front desk was one more satisfying data point in my favor.

I paused for a minute in front of room 825, pressing my ear to the door to be sure Regan wasn't in there. I didn't hear anything, but didn't want to scare him if he was sleeping. So I texted him, making sure to turn off my location first, of course. Some mistakes I only made once.

Me: Hey babe. You guys in Minneapolis yet?

Regan: Yeah we're on our way to the hotel finally. I'll be passed out within the hour for sure.

Me: Goodnight. I love you.

Regan: I love you.

I grinned like a fool, sliding my room card into the slot on the door. Turning on a hot shower, I began the process of washing the travel off me, and slipping into a little number that would most certainly have landed me on a no-fly list had I worn it through security.

Spaghetti straps, silk covering only the top half my backside, black and red lace, and really very little to the imagination. I paired it with red, very high heels—Regan's favorite. I was still shorter than him with them on, but he didn't have to lean so far forward to lift me up so I could wrap my legs around his waist.

Practical and provocative. Multitasking sex-wear.

Almost exactly a half hour later, I heard the familiar ruck-us of a band tumbling down the hallway and into their rooms for the night. Back slapping, tired grumbles of plans for food in the morning, and requests by some to others to not get too drunk.

Settling myself onto the bed, I rested on my elbows with one knee bent and the other leg straight out. I wanted to run to the door, fling it open, and drag him to the bed without so much as a hello, but decided on seduction as the barest of foreplay.

I heard Regan's voice through the others. Making plans for the morning and the next afternoon. Talk of measures, chord progressions, and vocals. Always wheeling and dealing. Push-ing himself and everyone around him to do more and be better.

My heart thumped with the click of the door unlocking. Regan was still talking as he opened the door, and I had a slight moment of panic that he might tear in with CJ or some other band member. But, my fears were assuaged when I reminded myself that Regan values his private time on tour above almost all else, and almost always takes a room by himself when he can.

Almost.

His duffel bag thumped down just out of view, and he was going to round the corner any second.

"So," he said. Still talking through the door, I thought. "I'm glad I convinced you to come up here with me."

"You're a hell of a salesman." A light giggle followed him into the room. "It's hard to say no to you."

It was a woman.

My pulse worked wildly in my neck as I scrambled, trying to get under the sheets as quickly as possible, but my fucking heels kept catching on the fabric.

No. This isn't happening. Not Regan.

Whoever this bitch is has another thing coming.
I can't fight her half-naked, though.
Fuck yes I can.

With one shoe off, I was able to gain traction. Sliding from the bed I was on my feet, though quite unbalanced with one heel on. No matter, I grabbed the other one as a weapon. Adrenaline would steady me. But, my planned element of surprise was in vain, as Regan spotted me a split second later.

"Georgia?!" Regan shouted, looking as confused as I'm sure I did horrified.

That horror shifted to darkness, and my mind clouded with shouting rage as I sized up the tall, flawless woman next to him.

Nessa.

CHAPTER SEVENTEEN

GEORGIA

"GEORGIA! SORRY!" NESSA shrieked, turning around and covering her face as she walked toward the door.

I was dizzy from rage and embarrassment. "What the hell are you doing here?"

She faced me, but looked up to the ceiling. "I ..." she started.

"Oh Jesus Christ, Nessa, it's lingerie. Get over yourself and answer my question." My voice was a dark version of itself—one I hadn't heard in a long time. Years maybe.

Nessa swallowed hard, looking to Regan, whose eyes wisely stayed on me.

"I'm over here," I snapped. "I trusted you—and I don't trust other women—and you show up in my husband's hotel room?"

"It's not like that," she answered quickly. Panicked.

"Georgia?" Regan said again, reining in my attention. His face was still, highlighting his shock.

I shrugged, certain my face was rage-red. "Surprised?"

"Nessa and I were going to go over set stuff ... new songs ..." He wasn't pleading so much as informing.

"I'm gonna go," Nessa whispered.

I dismissed her with a wave, not wanting to waste time on the person I wasn't in a relationship with. She slunk away with a tail-between-her-legs sort of slink.

Regan stared at the closed door for a moment before refocusing on me. "When ... when did you get here?"

I took a deep breath. "A half hour ago ... well. A half hour plus five naked minutes ago. When I texted you ..."

"You looked pissed when—"

"Well, yeah. I mean ... I heard a girl say you were a sweet talker and—"

He pulled his head back, his eyebrows scrunching to the midline of his forehead. "Seriously, Georgia?"

"Yes. Seriously. I was laying here half naked waiting for you and ... wait ... are you mad at me? You're mad at me?"

Regan backed over to a chair next to a pointless table and sat with his elbows on his knees, his head in his hands. He took a long, deep breath before looking up at me, his chin resting on his interlaced fingers.

He stared at me for a long few seconds before speaking. "You thought I brought another woman to my hotel room."

"To be fair ... you did."

"You know what I mean, Georgia." He sighed. He seemed to be doing that a lot these days. "You didn't have to be such a—"

"A bitch?" I filled in the blank. "I kind of did. You showed up late at night with another woman."

"You wouldn't let me explain. We're working on a whole new fucking set and it takes time. A lot of time." His tone was growly. Tired and ragged.

Also, Regan hardly swore in a serious context. This conversation was headed in an uglier direction than I could have imagined given what the situation originally appeared to be.

"Yes," I snapped. "You told me. But it was still another woman—"

"A fellow musician, Georgia. A coworker." His voice was as annoyed as I'd ever heard it.

I backed up, kneeling in front of him so he could see me, eye to eye. "Understand where I'm coming from. She thanked you for inviting her up, you said you were glad you could convince her … I had no other context, Reg—"

"The context is our marriage," he nearly growled again, keeping his tone low as he stood, and walked around the far side of the bed.

"You keep walking away from me." My nostrils flared as I spoke. "As if I've done something wrong."

He held out his hands, his tired eyes staring right at me. "When will it ever be enough for you? My word. When will that hold up, Georgia? I gave you my word when we were dating, on our wedding day, and have kept it every single day since. When is that enough?"

I scrunched my eyebrows, confused at the direction this conversation had headed.

"It is enough. It's not you I don't trust. It's others."

He shook his head. "We've been down that road, too. It's not about the others. If you trust me enough, whatever anyone else does shouldn't matter." He stood with his hands on his hips, head hanging low as if weighed down by his feelings.

"I was startled, Regan." I knelt on the bed. "It was just a gut reaction."

He looked at me, and I wished he hadn't. His eyes were stained with hurt. Heartbroken. "A gut reaction to not trust me."

I swallowed hard, the fight leaving me quickly. Regan was never an instigator—he never started a fight for the exercise of it, so I believed the pained expression and defeated words. They weren't show.

He shrugged, sitting on the bed next to me, folding his hands in front of him. "I'm just … disappointed."

I wanted to cry so immediately and hard that it knocked me off balance. Sure, Regan and I had had fights before and been pissy with each other here and there, but nothing that a good night's sleep couldn't fix. He'd never verbalized disappointment, though. At least not in me or us.

"I'm tired and excited to be here and … I don't want to waste the next twelve hours fighting …" My eyes welled with tears, but I looked to the ceiling to dry them, not wanting to fall all the way apart in that moment.

"Let's get some sleep?" He leaned over, placing a soft kiss on my temple before rising to discard his clothing, save for his boxer briefs. "I'm going to hop in the shower quick."

I nodded, whispering, "Kay."

Once the shower was on, I took a minute to assess the situation. The blankets on the bed were swirled like a disheveled bird's nest, the comforter lay on the floor with the heel of my shoe peeking out underneath it. Regan's duffel bag and violin case were a few feet from the door, where he'd dropped them. I kicked off the shoe I was still wearing and slid under the covers, trying to figure out my next move.

How had things gone so wrong? Had I truly overreacted? Was he the one being too sensitive?

A few minutes later, the shower turned off and Regan came naked into the room, stopping at his bag to retrieve a fresh pair of boxers. The space filled with the tropical scent of his favorite shampoo, and it brought me some comfort to have scents from home in this foreign, cold place.

I had only a split second to decide if I was going to pretend to be asleep already, a tactic I was familiar with, but chose the adult move instead. As Regan situated himself under the covers, I turned to face him. Operating on autopilot, it seemed by the half-vacant expression on his face, Regan opened his left arm, allowing me entrance to his warm, soft skin. Settling into the dip of his shoulder, I tilted my chin up to kiss his jaw.

"Regan," I whispered, trying to keep the tears away, "I'm sorry."

He kissed the top of my head and gave my shoulders a squeeze. "I know. I love you."

No I'm sorry too, no I forgive you, just I know.

"I love you," I said.

Then, I just went for it. We weren't some new couple tip-toeing around each other's feelings, this was my husband, dammit, and I'd come a long way to make love to him. I slid my hand from the center of his chest, down to his boxers, and slid my thumb under the band, tracing an imaginary line from hip to hip. He shifted, and I thought things were finally going in my favor—the evening I'd previously planned.

"Georgia," he said, almost regrettably, which really should have been my first hint. But, with Regan, I was always an optimist. "I'm exhausted."

He gave me another kiss, this time on the forehead, and rolled over, snoring once, the way he did when he first falls asleep. Then, his shoulders rose in fell in the dreamy rhythm of deep sleep.

Just like that.

I rolled onto my back, whiplashed from the wild turn this evening had taken. Hadn't Regan come into the hotel room prepared to work for however many hours with Nessa on tour stuff? Now he was snoring less than twenty minutes after entering the room.

I drained him with my accusations and suspicions. Regan had never once—not once—turned me down for sex. Not even when he had pneumonia last year, but I took pity on him then and let him sleep. Yet in the spacious hotel room in the middle of Minneapolis, my husband, who I hadn't seen or touched for a whole month, was too tired to touch me. Or for me to touch him.

I stayed awake for another hour, or so, mulling over all the orders at the bakery left to the hands of people who weren't me, while I was busy not making love to my husband.

So much for spontaneity.

***

I rose early, scoring coffee and croissants from the hotel's five-star kitchen while Regan's clothes were being laundered. I took out a small notebook dotted with hand-drawn cupcakes on the cover, and made a note to really give croissants a go this year. I knew they were hard—I made them at home for Regan and I from time to time—but I needed more practice if I was going to produce something worthy enough to sell.

"Georgia?" CJ's early-morning grumbly voice startled my attention away from the window where I sat, staring out onto a busy Minneapolis street.

"Hey," I offered with a smile.

He looked around, hands out, asking for more.

"Surprise," I mused. "Got a cigarette?"

He crinkled his nose. "You came all the way to Minnesota to bum a cigarette off me?"

I arched an eyebrow, sighing.

He put his hands up in defense. "Fine, fine. Come on."

Once out on the street, CJ handed me a cigarette and a lighter, and I inhaled long and deep before exhaling slowly.

"So you, like, smoke again? I thought you left that behind when you were twenty." CJ snatched his lighter back, filling his lungs with smoke before sliding the cancer starter pack in his back pocket.

I gave him the once over. "And since when are you more than just a casual smoker?"

"Don't start," he said, rolling his eyes. "Why aren't you upstairs making babies with Regan? And, I don't think those things will help the process," he said, gesturing to the cigarette hanging from my lips.

"We had a thing last night."

"A thing?" CJ leaned against the cement of the side of the building, bending his knee to put his foot flat against the wall behind him. I mimicked his position, welcoming the cool of the concrete against my bare shoulder blades.

"I guess it was a fight, but it wasn't like … normal." I took a minute to fill CJ in, not skipping a detail.

"Ouch," he said when I finished.

"To who?"

CJ stomped out his cigarette, tossing the butt in a nearby receptacle before answering. "Both of you, I guess. I can see both sides."

"You can see his?"

CJ sighed, sliding down the wall until he reached the ground, knees bent and looking tired. I realized he probably intended on going back to bed after his early morning smoke, so I knew I was on borrowed time.

"Yeah," he said, rubbing his eyes. "I mean, you're married. He loves you more than all the guys in those stupid fucking romance novels you read. And those get you all fired up, don't they?"

I grinned, smacking his shoulder, sitting next to him with the cigarette burning away between my fingers. "Yeah."

"He loves you more than any of those guys could."

I arched an eyebrow. "You're an expert now?"

"Frankie read those books, too. I thumbed through them a bit. Impressive dudes, no doubt, but Regan's got them beat by a long shot." He stared out into the delivery-truck traffic on the street in front of us. It was only six in the morning, but the sun was rising and life had to go on.

I took CJ's hand, interlacing our fingers and leaning my head against his shoulder. "You miss her?"

He was silent, but gave my hand a tight squeeze. He didn't need to say anything.

"I'm sorry," I whispered. "That you guys broke up and that I gave you such a hard time about it."

CJ was quiet, and for a few seconds it felt like we were in high school, sitting on the deck of my father's Provincetown bar in the wee hours of a Sunday morning, savoring the quiet before he would help me nurse my dad's hangover. Which honestly consisted of helping him sleep as long as possible while we cleaned up what he couldn't from the night before.

"Anyway," CJ said as if he'd slipped back there with me, too. But he said nothing more.

Looking up, I found his tired eyes. I could have easily mistaken them for the ones I saw on Regan last night. They don't generally look alike, those Kane boys, but their eyes are deep and dangerous.

"CJ ..." I started, then started to trail off. I needed to tell someone.

Why did my best friend have to be my husband's cousin?

"Yeah?"

I swallowed hard, then chickened out. "He was really mad last night."

"He won't stay mad for long, you know him."

"Maybe ..." I was about to find out what kind of good a full night's sleep did for him. For us. "He was going to work with her for who knows how long last night. But as soon as it was just me and him, he passed right out." I choked the last words out, trying not to well up with tears, but it was futile.

CJ slid his index finger under my chin. "Chin up, Kid. You know how Regan is. Stress wipes him out. And he holds it all in, to boot—wouldn't kill him to punch something once in a while."

I laughed, holding up my hands and wiggling my fingers. "He can't damage his goods," I said of the fickle bones in the hands.

CJ waved me off. "I wouldn't read too much into it. If he was really harping on something he'd have been up all night, right?"

"Sounds like him." I thought back to the time we met in Seattle, a month ago, and he was working at the hotel room desk well beyond midnight.

"I get that it looked bad. If I had been in your shoes, I'd have flipped, too."

"I don't think Regan would have," I admitted. "He trusts me."

CJ shrugged. "Not just you. He just trusts. People are all made up differently, right? Listen," he implored, giving my forehead a quick kiss, "you've got your happily ever after upstairs. Nothing to be sad about."

His face broke my heart into pieces. My best friend; the raucous, mouthy, sexually deviant drummer looked like he wanted to go home. He wasn't weary from travel, but emotionally drained. I was willing to bet he'd give anything to talk to Frankie, but I also knew he was hurting probably as much as she was at this point. He looked like a man bearing the weight of all his mistakes at once.

And, I told him I was staying out of it.

"Can you promise me you won't completely self-destruct on this tour?" I begged. "Please? I've seen that look on your face. Remember the summer you came to stay with me after Tonya?"

I delicately, with much held breath, brought up the only girl who'd ever made his face look the way it did now. Tonya Ryan, a punchy, foul-mouthed looker, from South Boston of all places, who held CJ's heart for almost nine months before she dropped him out of nowhere. That was a brutal two months while he got over her. It was a few years before he met Frankie, but I could still feel the weight of that breakup, and see it on CJ's face.

"Can I tell you something?" CJ asked, standing and holding the door for me.

I nodded. "Obviously."

Once inside the lobby, CJ stuffed his hands in his pockets, lowering his head and voice. "Frankie was so much more than Tonya."

It was so rare for CJ to be honest about anything regarding actual emotions that I forgot how to handle him for a moment. I didn't have time to say anything before a tiny redhead with a bubble butt came out of nowhere and slid her arm around CJ's back.

"There you are," she said, yawning, eyeing me up and down like I was the enemy.

Oh, sweetie. You have no idea …

In a split second, CJ's demeanor shifted and he looked wildly between me and her, his mouth hanging open.

She was still staring at me, so I decided to take matters into my own hands.

"Hi," I started, extending my hand. "I'm Georgia. Regan Kane's wife. So, you know, no need to be scoping out your next kill."

"This is Jennifer," CJ cut in. "She lost track of her friends last night and crashed in the other bed in my room. I came down to call her a cab." He turned to her. "It should be here in a minute. Why don't you go get your stuff?" He unraveled her arms from his waist and nudged her barely playfully toward the elevator.

The girl disappeared reluctantly, with a sour look on her face, and I refocused my attention on CJ, grinding my teeth in an effort to keep my mouth shut.

He put his hands up in defense. "I did nothing, I swear. That girl was blackout drunk last night, anyway. Even if I was a free man, that's not how I roll."

"Aren't you?" I asked. "A free man?"

He twisted his lips, a move I don't think I'd ever seen him make. "Nah. Even if Frankie never takes me back—which is probably how it's gonna go—I need to get my shit together. And that's hard to do if I'm chasing ass."

Despite the crass delivery, I was encouraged by this mature development.

"I love you," I said, still wanting to stay as out of it as possible, but letting him know I supported him. I wanted to tell him maybe he shouldn't have girls staying in his room, no matter how innocent, because temptation is an evil bitch. But, I kept my mouth shut.

The art of staying out of it.

He pulled me in for a bear hug that only he could give. "I love you, too. You coming up?" He gestured to the elevator.

"No, I've gotta pick up Regan's clothes. Get back to sleep, huh? You look like shit."

He laughed, then turned for the elevator. Before entering it, CJ looked over his shoulder at me, his eyes as sad as before. With one look he proved that Frankie was levels above anything Tonya had ever meant to him. Whatever heartache Frankie was going through, CJ was above and beyond anything I could have imagined for him. All I could do was hope he wouldn't dive headfirst into the self-destructive behaviors he'd mastered through high school.

I took the stairs after fetching two fresh croissants and coffees. One each for Regan and me. The two croissants I'd eaten earlier didn't count. Mood food has no calories. The matted, ashy feeling in my mouth reminded me I really shouldn't smoke anymore, even if it was only five or six a year at most. It tasted horrible, Regan agreed, and if I was going to get pregnant anytime soon, I should really keep bad habits at bay.

But, as far as bad habits, they could pry the butter and sugar from my cold, dead hands as far as I was concerned.

Just before entering the hotel room, I got a text from CJ.

CJ: I didn't sleep with her, promise. I've never even kissed her. She was too drunk to find her way home last night.

Me: Why are you telling me this?

CJ: I'm miserable and want to fly back to Mass.

I chewed the inside of my cheek, searching for an answer.

Me: Don't bail on the tour just yet, okay? And, maybe for practice, don't take strays into your room. Have a girl help them out, okay?

CJ: I miss her, Georgia. I want her back.

Me: I know you do. Give it some time.

CJ: Do you think she'd even take me back?

I didn't know, honestly.

Me: Don't push her, okay?

CJ: Not an answer.

Me: I know … sorry. I love you.

CJ: Love you.

I sighed, my heart breaking for my best friend who was going through the growing pains of becoming a man. A decent man, unlike either of our fathers.

CHAPTER EIGHTEEN

REGAN

THE SOFT CLICK of the hotel door unlocking pulled me fully away from the hazy just-waking up stage I'd been hanging out in for the last several minutes. It took my eyes a while to adjust, but I saw Georgia's curvy form set some things down on the table near the door before draping garment bags over the chair.

A few blinks later, the previous night came flooding back to me. I'd slept so hard that I wasn't up tossing around about it all night long. Instead, I was granted with the delightful thud of a flashback.

She didn't trust me. It was as simple as that.

It is so much more complicated than that, and you know it, you dolt.

Sigh.

I stretched my arms overhead, groaning in ecstasy. "Morning," I called softy to her.

"Hey," she whispered back. "I got coffee and croissants. And your laundry done. The duffel bag is out on the balcony airing out the best it can." She stood awkwardly in the middle of the room, working her fingers over each other.

"Come here." I opened the sheets and my arms, but she hesitated. "Georgia?" I sat up on one elbow.

"I'm sorry," she said, lowering her head.

I sat all the way up, hating to see her look so defeated. "Come here. Please."

Still staring at the ugly carpet, Georgia shuffled her way to the bed and took a deep breath before kicking off her sandals and sliding under the sheets with me. She leaned her head against my shoulder.

"I'm sorry," I said.

"For what?"

I kissed the top of her head. "Last night. I just …"

"Don't," she started, but I cut her off.

"No, you don't. Listen. Look at me." I shrugged so her head would lift off my skin and she'd face me. Her mascara was freshly applied, and her lips as bright as ever. I caressed the side of her face with the back of my hand and kissed her square on the lips. Full and long. "I'm sorry, Georgia. You did an amazing thing last night by surprising me all the way out here. Leaving work behind and dressing like you did and waiting for me … it was hot."

"But …" she led.

I swallowed hard. I couldn't say what I wanted to. I couldn't tell her that, yes, our marriage was the context, as I'd said, but it was the context of so much more. Including Georgia's healing. She hadn't been able to trust that anyone would stick around for the long haul, whether through fault of their own or not. Our marriage was the salve for more than two decades of hurt and insecurity. Strong, yes. Magical? Probably not.

I didn't want to bring this up to Georgia, because she would get defensive. That was only part of it, really. I knew she trusted my fidelity. I knew it was her worth she didn't trust. I knew that, but dammit if it didn't make things hard some days. Still, was I willing to live up to the vows I made to her? That I'd take care of her for as long as I lived?

Her rich blue eyes filled with tears—a rare sight for Mrs. Georgia Kane. "I just wanted to surprise you." Her shoulders fell and she pressed her forehead into my shoulder, letting out a deep sob. By the sounds of things, one she'd been holding in for quite some time.

"Sorry," she said, pulling back as quickly as she landed. She pressed the edges of both index fingers under her eyes, catching mascara-stained tears before they rolled down her cheeks.

She always apologized when she cried. I used to think she was telling me she was sorry for ruining a shirt with her blackest mascara, but it always washed out. It took me about eight months to realize she was apologizing for the crying itself. And another four for her to admit she'd never really been allowed to cry when she was young. Sometimes it made her dad uncomfortable and he'd leave the room, other times he'd accuse her of using her tears to make him feel bad or to get what she wanted. Then her tears made her mom feel bad. Guilty for a mental illness she could control no more than she could the weather. I knew her mom, Amanda, well enough to know that the tears Georgia shed didn't make her feel like a bad person, they made her hurt for her daughter.

Whatever the reason, by the time I'd met her, Georgia hadn't allowed herself to cry freely in years. But in this hotel room was the first time in many, many months that she'd apologized for it.

Had last night set her back that far?

"Georgia," I started. "Don't apologize for crying …"

"Don't tell me what I get to be sorry for," she replied flatly. Point.

That's the rock and a hard place we found ourselves in through counseling, sometimes. Calling each other out on our old, harmful behaviors is the rock, and validating one another's feelings is the hard place. Come to think of it, we hadn't seen our counselor in quite a few months. Perhaps that was shortsighted on our parts, thinking we'd somehow graduated …

"Okay," I answered in a sigh, ready to employ another tactic. Honesty. "I admit it. I was frustrated with your reaction last night. I felt like all of a sudden we were back at E's bar a million years ago when we first met and you couldn't even trust that the sun would rise the next morning."

"But—"

I put up my hand, grinning so she knew I wasn't upset, but intended to finish what I was saying. "But I also admit that if the roles were reversed, I'd probably have been the one to lose my mind. If I came downstairs and stood outside the door of the bakery and heard some guy saying all kinds of sweet stuff, even if it was about your food, I'd go mad."

She snorted. "No you wouldn't have. Even if you did, you wouldn't have made a scene."

I sighed.

"See," she continued. "I'm right. You trust. Period."

Rolling my eyes, I opened my mouth to speak. "What do you want me to say?" I felt the tension between us build again. "I know you mean to trust me …"

"I do. I mean, I trust you and I have to practice it," she cut in. "Last night didn't help."

I sat up, leaning against the headboard, holding out my hands. "I don't know how to help here. There's always going to be fans, and female musicians, and … I … do you want me to stop touring? Change careers?"

She scrunched her eyebrows, twisting up her face. "Um, no. Did I say that?"

I huffed. "I don't know how else to fix it. I've done nothing to prove untrustworthy, and I feel like I'm running into a brick wall, and the only thing that would make you happy is to have me in the bakery with you, or something."

Georgia gasped. "That's not true. I'm not something to be fixed."

I grumbled, thumping my head against the wall behind me. "I didn't say that." We weren't yelling, but our volume increased by the minute. I decided to keep my tone as level as I could.

She sighed pinching the bridge of her nose. "Can we back up?"

"Please."

"I feel like this trip has just been a total nightmare."

"I …" I trailed off for a second. "What do you want me to say?"

She brought her knees to her chest. "So you're saying it has been a nightmare."

"You did!" I laughed incredulously. "Don't put words in my mouth. I hate it when you do that. I didn't say that," I reiterated. "You did."

"But you agreed."

"So that was entrapment? Look around, Georgia, this isn't exactly a honeymoon state of affairs. I'm trying to work through this. Join me."

She was quiet for a long time, taking deep, loud breaths. My eyes traced the intricate tattoos up and down her arms. Many themed from Alice in Wonderland, reminding me what a complicated puzzle she really was. A comical doorknob with a keyhole for a mouth, Alice falling butt-first down one of her forearms, and We're all mad here etched on the underside of one of her wrists.

Ain't that the truth.

"This is what I get for planning a trip around my ovulation," she finally said.

Heat filled my neck and tightened my jaw. "What?"

She looked up at me, "What?"

I ground my teeth together as hard as I could. I did not want to talk about this now. "I think we're too tired for this conversation."

She crossed her arms over her chest. "I don't think we are."

My eyes felt scratchy from exhaustion and hotel room air conditioning. "Georgia," I took a deep breath, "I just thought you did this for me. For us. I … I'm too upset to talk about this right now," I finally said out loud. "Can we table it?"

"For when?" she demanded. "Texting later? A late-night phone call?"

I leaned forward, rubbing my hands over my face. If she pushed much more, I wouldn't be able to hold it in.

"And," she interrupted my screaming thoughts, "I figured a baby was kind of for both of us." She misinterpreted my angry silence.

"It is," I said, exhaling in defeat. "I'm just … I can't force myself to be in the mood every time the calendar says I should be. I'm tired and upset. What do you want me to do?"

She turned her head slowly to me, sucking in her top lip. "Nothing. I don't want to make you do anything you don't want to do—like sleeping with your wife."

I pressed my lips together. "Georgia, don't start. This isn't about not desiring you." I threw the covers off me and slid out of bed. "I'm going to take a shower."

"Yeah, you go do that," she snapped back.

Grabbing the large coffee off the table, I took it with me into the bathroom. "Thanks for the coffee," I mumbled before shutting the door behind me.

Georgia wasn't able to stay for a show, since our first one wasn't until tomorrow night, and I didn't have enough room on my watch to bring her to the airport this time, so we had to say our goodbyes in front of the hotel.

"I love you, so much," I said, breathing in her scent before she entered the cab. "I do."

Her response was a cold silence.

"Georgia, I don't want to leave things like this."

She shrugged, looking up at me sympathetically. "We might have to."

I frowned, gripping the tip of her chin between my thumb and index finger as she slipped into the white taxicab and rolled away.

For now, Georgia and I were treading through normal, post-storm waters, but I couldn't fully shake the feeling of uneasiness. The familiarity of the uncertainty. Absolutely an oxymoron, but one that matched the complexity of my wife.

I knew she loved me the way I loved her, but I was some-times holding myself back from shouting, show me! Maybe I needed to call my therapist for a little Skype session. We'd been over this, my therapist and I, that couples don't always show each other love the way the other needs, but rather the way they need to be loved. It's like a malfunctioning closed-loop circuit. Not manipulative, because it lacked intent, but destructive in its own right if left unchecked. Dr. Weeber assured me that the only way to make progress in that area was to bring all of this up with Georgia in our couple's counseling session.

I was nervous. I knew Georgia well enough to know that she'd emotionally self-harm, beating up on herself if she felt she was failing with me. But, Weeber was quick to remind me whenever I argued this point with her, wasn't that self-inflicting emotional harm on myself? Putting on the martyr's cloak? Or, as I countered back, was this really what marriage and love was about down at the core? Love and sacrifice? Linda Weeber liked to toss back that self-sacrifice only serves the greater good until the one doing the sacrificing starts to whither inside.

Taking a deep breath as the taxi drifted out of sight, I won-dered if my reaction last night was a sign of the dry soil inside me. I'd been running for a long time on loving her enough for the both of us. Preaching to myself that the fact that she let me in was all the love she needed to show me. That her trust in me was love enough.

The problem was, I didn't think it was anymore.

CHAPTER NINETEEN
REGAN

WITHIN AN HOUR of Georgia's departure, I was at River Junction Studios with CJ and members of The Brewers, and Moniker, too, to make things extra cozy. Our performances in Minneapolis were at two different venues over several days, but they were both outdoor spaces. Since a lot of the groups were working on new material, we all needed a little extra practice time than would typically fit in the hour or so warm-up time we were afforded before shows.

Luckily, Yardley had amicable business ties with River Junction, and they afforded us full use of their studio for a couple hours each day we were in town. Most large, national labels have several studios scattered across the country. In our section of the industry, it was far more common for the label and studio to be one entity, making their offerings as unique as they were grand. River Junction had a lot of artists under them, and sacrificed a significant chunk of space for us. Three whole studio spaces. I was baffled by the graciousness of the deal until I saw the way their president and Yardley looked at each other.

As soon as she blushed in his presence, that was the only answer I needed.

"Yo," CJ whispered into my ear as Yardley and RJ's president, Norio Vincent, decided where we'd each practice. "Do you think they … you know?"

Impressed by his seemingly accurate social assessment of Yardley and Norio's apparent flirtation, I wanted to tease him a little. "You know? No … can't say as I do."

He didn't let me have fun for long. CJ got a wicked grin on his face and arched his eyebrow, slowly gyrating his hips in his seat. "Oh," he said, "you know."

I laughed despite myself. "Who knows. Or cares."

Still, I took a second look at their interaction unfolding ten feet away from us. Norio was Japanese-American, about as young as Yardley—early thirties, if that. He was tall and lean with shaggy, jet-black hair. He looked tired, but a lot of the managers looked as such for most of the year.

Large record companies have many more layers of bureaucracy than smaller, independent labels do. There's typically a president and executive vice president, with legal departments and business affairs at the top. Just below them is a host of jobs like promotion, artist development, marketing (with sales and art departments beneath them), publicity, new media, and A&R (artists and repertoire). Each of these jobs is a full time plus job in their own right, but with Grounded Sound, for example, there are far fewer people than that to fill the roles.

GSE did have legal and business departments, though Yardley was heavily involved on the business side of things, given her MBA education. But Yardley was the president, acting manager of most groups under the small, but growing label, publicity, and A&R. A&R is a tough job, but it was Yardley's passion. She loved seeking out new talent, developing set lists for albums, and all that goes along with it. Still, if the label was going to continue growing the way she'd designed it to and gunned for, she'd have to give up some of her hats at some point.

River Junction was run very similarly, from what I understood, and Norio had acted as a mentor to Yardley when she first took over GSE. Norio's talents, according to Google, centered around A&R, of course, but also in new media. He coached Yardley on how to maximize artist exposure and brand recognition through social media. Truly independent labels aren't as numerous as many people think. In the US, anyway, a shitload of them are actually funded by Sony. So, social media was the best chance indie outfits had to combat the thick wallets of the major labels—to get our music into the hands of those who loved it, and coax them out on tour. Most labels couldn't afford a tour like this, but Yardley seemed to know what she was doing. Kicking ass and taking names, as CJ might say.

I'd never seen, or heard discussed, Yardley dating anyone, but who would have the time with a schedule like hers? Maybe Norio was up her alley. Maybe I needed to stop thinking like a girl.

"Okay, guys …" Yardley was bright as she returned from her pow-wow with Norio. "Brewers, you guys are in the large studio. Run through some of your instrumental stuff with no lyrics first. Moniker, the same goes for you in Studio B. Nessa and Regan, I want you two in Studio C, running through those numbers for Moniker forward and back. I'd like to push those out to the listeners by the end of the week."

CJ moved into Studio B with Moniker, and The Brewers walked down the long hall to A. Meanwhile, Nessa's chest and neck turned red as she stood to address Yardley.

"This week?" she questioned, her voice sounding dry. "Chicago. Not Minneapolis. Chicago."

Yardley's eyes didn't move from her iPad, where she was scrolling through lists and schedules. "Yes, but things have changed. There are some high-profile music bloggers who are coming to the shows all week. They've kept their eye on Moniker, it seems, since we took them over. For the label's sake, and the bands, we need to put their best face forward." Yardley took a deep breath and eyed Nessa carefully. "I don't think I need to explain to you how big of a deal this could be for Moniker if they get a good write-up from any one of those bloggers. And, of course, that will help the label and those signed to it, but that's just icing on the cake."

Nessa swallowed, placing her hands on her hips and taking in a heaping serving of humility with her breath.

"Understood," was all Nessa said before gathering her things and heading into Studio C.

I lifted my eyebrows, nodding once to Yardley in reverential appreciation of her skill, before following Nessa into the tiny studio.

Well played, Yardley.

It was a San Diego music blogger who had followed The Brewers on the California music circuit for years and opened doors for Nessa and The Brewers they'd have almost certainly missed otherwise. The independent music scene is a real bear.

This blogger, though, was ruthless. Tough Critic Band Blogger struck curiosity and fear into the hearts of many small bands if the bands knew the blogger was in the house for the night. Which they never did because Tough Critic—TC—was an expert at keeping their identity hidden for just that reason. So, it was all rumors whether or not TC was in the audience during any given show.

Anyway, this blogger had taken on bigger and bigger shows over the years, and criticized and praised acts big and small. What caught the attention of those who ran labels was the no-holds barred attitude the blogger took to their reviewing. They didn't seem interested in blowing smoke up anyone's ass or giving credit anywhere other than where it was due. Tough Critic took on indie bands that had already made household names of themselves. Their purpose wasn't to get or prevent bands from getting record deals. The purpose of the blog seemed to give true, honest reviews and critiques of the songs, music, and ensemble make-ups.

A three-note rating on a five-note rating system became equated with success and cheers around the bar. Four and five-note ratings gave bands hope that a call from a record company might be around the corner. If not, at least a visit by one at their next show.

Such was the case with The Brewers. Yardley approached me with a TC post published solely about them two years ago, while Celtic Summer was still on tour. I read it, liked what I saw, then scrolled through the archives where it was revealed that Tough Critic had followed The Brewers for at least three years before that. There were small mentions of them in the scheme of larger articles, even if it was just including them in the line-up list of a festival. Further on there were profiles of each of their musicians as Tough Critic took a keen interest in them. When Nessa joined the band that year, TC went nuts in the best possible way.

TC admitted that the band had started to fall flat, needing something new and refreshing in their lineup. Even TC was shocked when the all-male ensemble—as they had been for years—chose this shocking beauty as their new lead singer. The blogger vowed to keep a close eye on the group and held up their end of the deal. The Brewers received mentions every few days, it seemed. The blogger was impressed with Nessa's vocal range, command of the stage, and instrumental knowledge. Nessa played the keyboard and sometimes guitar—though there didn't seem to be mention of a violin in any of those articles now that I think about it.

That aside, Yardley was unsure about pulling the trigger on signing them, as they were a much larger band than she felt equipped to handle at the time, so she called up Toni, her friend at Wound Sound, and asked her to take a listen. Toni liked what she heard and made quick work of putting together an offer.

An offer that at this moment in River Junction's studio, was thrown graciously in front of Nessa as a reminder of her responsibilities as a contracted musician. Yardley didn't use the word contract. She didn't have to. All she needed to do was remind Nessa that despite the flexibility and creative authority afforded by indie labels to their artists, Nessa was still under someone. Wound Sound at home, and GSE on this tour.

"Well, that was tense," I attempted humor as I pulled out my violin and shuffled through some sheet music.

"Fuck her," Nessa spit out.

My jaw dropped. "Um ... okay. So ... uh ... what?"

I tried not to ask her what, but it was nearly unheard of for any of the musicians working with Yardley to speak poorly of her in any context. She treated her charges like family, not because she had to, but because she wanted to.

Nessa sighed, her shoulders dropping in what seemed like defeat, but I hadn't a clue what she was fighting. "Nothing. Let's just play?"

I fought my curiosity. Hard. I picked up my violin, nodding to Nessa that I'd honor her request that we get down to business. I even struck my bow against the instrument and spewed out a few notes on a scale, but I couldn't follow through.

"Nope," I said, setting the violin down, and closing the case. "Nope ..."

Nessa, halfway through a chromatic scale, held her hands out, still holding the violin and bow. "What the fuck? What are you doing?"

I extended my hands, taking her instrument from her, and locked it away in its case before setting my hands on my hips. "I'm taking you to dinner. And drinks. Let's go. Yardley?" I shouted, causing Nessa to jump and swear under her breath. "Someone lock down this studio. Nessa and I have a non-instrument practice thing to do."

Yardley poked her head inside the studio, her south Georgia accent like syrup. "What's that now?" she asked with a nervous smile.

I put my hand up. "No one steals the violins. We'll be back. Trust me?" I asked with a firm pat on her shoulder.

"Do … I have a choice?" she responded, sounding confused, but conservatively trusting.

I shook my head, grinning. "Nope. Come on, Ness," I extended my hand, which she accepted easily, "let's go."

***

"So … gonna tell me why we're here?" Nessa handed the waitress her menu after placing her order, keeping her eyes on me.

I quickly ordered my sushi dish and another one—ramen—before looking back at Nessa. "Dinner."

"Cute," she mused. "By the way, where do you put all the food you eat? Honestly …"

I laughed, raising my glass of water to her, since our ordered drinks hadn't arrived yet. "A toast. To relaxation."

She crinkled her nose, an adorable look of disgust and confusion before saying, "Cheers … I guess."

I took a sip of the ice cold water and leaned back in my seat.

"What?" Nessa asked, after a long minute of my silence. "You're freaking me out."

Sitting forward, I offered a non-committal shrug. "It's just been a hell of a month. We've been playing and practicing a new set for a whole month without a break."

She winked. "You got a break last night. By the way, please, please tell Georgia I'm so sorry for that."

I waved my hand, forcing a grin. "It was nothing. We made up for it this morning," I lied. "Anyway. It's been a lot. And, you had an … interesting reaction to what Yardley said back there."

"Are you saying I overreacted?"

"I'd never dream of telling a woman how she acted."

Nessa laughed, relaxing a little. "I know Yardley's not a bitch. But that was a nasty move, wasn't it?"

"Reminding you of how you started? Hardly. Look, whatever stall tactics you're employing to avoid getting up on that stage with the violin … fine. But, even if you use them all up, you'll never be able to play the way I've heard you play if you carry around that nasty attitude."

Her jaw dropped. "Do you presume to know what emotions I can play through on stage?"

I arched an eyebrow. "Well done. But, I have no proof, since you refuse, for whatever reason, to do it. Play your violin in front of anyone but me."

"Consider yourself lucky," she mumbled.

Reaching my hand across the table, I made contact with her arm and gave it a gentle squeeze. "I do," I said, my voice near a whisper. "I do consider myself lucky. And, I can't keep what I've heard from you all to myself. You've gotta share it."

Nessa rolled her head back and let out a groan. Facing me, she looked rather indignant as I sat back. "Let me ask you this, Regan. Have you ever lost someone that you love so deeply that you walk around with a gaping hole in your chest? Certain that it's visible to the outside world? That you're just see-through."

Rae.

Closing my eyes, I thought of my former girlfriend and the horseback ride we took that day.

"Yes," was all I could say.

I didn't know if she remembered me mouthing off about Rae a month ago at that truck-stop diner when CJ and I almost got into it, but she didn't seem to.

Why didn't we choose a different activity?

Nessa leaned close to the center of the table, and I did, too, while she whispered. "Then let me ask you this. Has that ever happened while the other person was still alive?"

Her eyes misted over and the tip of her nose turned red. It became clear in seconds that she was holding back more than just tears, but something too heavy to discuss over dinner, or maybe ever.

"No," I finally answered. "Not while they were still alive."

She cleared her throat, her eyes drying almost instantly. "Well, then. It seems like we have a lot of ground to cover."

Our drinks arrived just then, and I unabashedly took a large swig of the beer.

"Guess so," I said. "Guess. So."

***

"So, who died? The girlfriend?" The music around us was blaring, a driving bass thumping through my chest, but her question silenced almost all background noise.

Nessa and I had enjoyed a civil dinner with general tour conversation at the sushi restaurant before making our way to a nearby pub that morphed into something of a nightclub with a DJ on Thursday nights, it seemed. It wasn't often we found many exciting things to do on Thursday nights while on tour, so it was a solid score for Minneapolis in my book.

We were a few drinks in when she tossed the question. She was just loose enough to ask it while maintaining eye contact. And, I was just loose enough to answer. With questionable eye contact.

"I figure it was a long time ago," she shouted. "Since you and Georgia have been together forever."

"Rae," I started. Then stopped.

We were tucked away in a small part of the bar that remained a seating area while the rest of the place turned into a dance floor. It was loud and private at the same time.

"Rae ..." She sounded out, looking for more information.

I ran my tongue across my teeth, setting down my pint glass. "One for one?"

"Excuse me?"

I nodded toward the pool table. "We'll shoot. Whenever we make one, we ask the other person a question and they have to answer."

Nessa shook her head. "Pool's not my game."

My eyes widened. "Seriously? With arms and legs that long you could glide right across the table."

She laughed. "Darts?"

"Nah, that's all CJ."

"Oh, right. I remember ..." she trailed off, and I didn't ask for more. "Cards then."

I patted myself down, comically buzzed after a few beers, but nothing serious. "Fresh out."

Inexplicably, Nessa reached behind her and produced a pack from her back pocket. "Here."

Nodding in approval, I said, "I thought those were a pack of cigarettes, which I thought was weird since I've never seen you smoke. Who carries cards with them?"

She grinned, opening the pack. "Someone who's picked up some tricks on her first tour. Always be prepared."

"Fair enough. What do you want to do?"

"Keep it simple." She split the deck in half, gesturing for me to choose one pile. "We turn over the top card at the same time, person with the higher card asks the question. We go until we're out of questions."

"Or cards?" I suggested.

She laughed. "Oh, I have way more questions than cards."

I shot her a challenging glance, then ordered a pitcher of beer for myself, prepared to settle in for the long haul.

"Can I order a pitcher of vodka?" Nessa asked the waitress. I thought she was serious. The waitress seemed to think so, too, judging by her shocked expression. "Whatever," Nessa continued with a wave of her hand, "I'll have a pitcher of whatever he's drinking."

Okay then …

"Flip 'em, Kane."

To my dismay, my three was trampled by her ten.

"Shoot," I said, leaning forward on my elbows.

"Rae," she said. "This was the girlfriend?"

I nodded. "Yep."

"Long time?"

I waved my index finger in the space between us. "Uh uh. That would be another question …"

She didn't look amused, but turned over another card. A seven. I turned over a nine and raised my hands in victory. Still, I decided to start easy.

"How many brothers and sisters do you have?"

Her eyes pinched at the sides for a split second. "One. One brother."

It was her turn next.

"Were you and Rae serious?"

I allowed a soft smile. "I guess …"

Nessa won the next flip, too, and I chugged half my beer down, prepared for more Rae questioning.

"What is Rae's last name?" she asked.

Was. What was her last name …

"Cavanaugh."

Nessa looked confused for a moment, then her eyes widened and focused back on my face. "Rae Cavanaugh. Like Bo Cavanaugh's little sister? Shit," she cut off my start to answer, "different question."

I put my hand over hers as she started to flip another card. Her eyes met mine again. "I'll give you this one. Spare you the agony of the fate of a deck of cards." I swallowed the rest of the pint and filled it up again, setting it to the side. "Yes, Rae Cavanaugh, Bo Cavanaugh's little sister. We dated but didn't really break up."

Nessa swallowed hard. "Horseback riding accident?"

"Yeah …"

"Sorry," she said, shaking her head and looking down. I moved my hand off hers. "Can we flip? This is heavy."

I beat her four with a king.

"Did you find out about Rae on the Internet searching for me? Or for Bo?" I let the beer ask the question that had been tumbling around my subconscious mind.

"Bo. He's dreamy." She fluttered her eyelashes and rested her chin in her hands like she was a Disney princess at a window.

"Real nice," I mused, rolling my eyes.

Nessa burst into laughter. "It's true. He's a total dreamboat. So sue me, it was like three years ago and I was new to the business. All you guys were like my idols."

I shifted in my seat, and she caught me.

"Ohh," she goaded. "Someone suddenly uncomfortable with attention?"

"Suddenly? Always."

She huffs through her nose. "Doesn't seem it up on stage."

I clinked my glass against hers. "Same to you. Seriously, do I seem self-centered in any way?"

She grinned. "Is that a question? We didn't flip."

I rolled my eyes. "Throw me a bone."

"Fine. No. You don't seem self-centered. Which is a bit annoying. Though, most people on this tour seem pretty down to earth …"

"Kind of the indie stereotype, huh?"

She laughed. "Yeah." Then she chugged the rest of her beer down that long, slim throat. "Fine," she said, slamming the pint down.

"Fine," I repeated, finishing off my pint and feeling quite cloudy. "Fine what?"

Probably from the vodka she'd consumed before downing half a pitcher of beer, Nessa's eyes were glassy and her speech wasn't fully slurred, but slippery.

"I'lltellyou," she said, as kind of one word.

I looked side to side, leaning in. "What?"

She patted the space next to her, sliding over. "Here. I don't want to yell it across the table."

I did as she commanded, joining her on her side of the table; loud, club sex music pulsating around us. Nessa leaned close, the sticky heat from her arms connecting with mine as her lips settled millimeters away from my ear. "I don't want to play that fucking violin on stage, because of my brother."

I swallowed hard, the sharp edge of her voice calling me to drop it. "We don't have to talk about it," I spit out quickly.

She waved her hand dismissively. "I'm not going to make you wait around for the next few months to find out why. And I might as well be honest with someone about it. It's not really a secret. It just … fucking sucks."

I nodded slowly, resting my elbow on the table and wrapping my hand around my chin. "Okay."

"But first," she said. "Tell me something about Rae. Something real that no one else knows."

Squeezing my eyes shut, I wanted to unhear the question. But I couldn't. Our one-for-one game had just become raw. I could have gone with something obvious like Rae's incredible laugh—but everyone heard that. Or her gigantic heart—also a no-brainer. I could have talked about the million little things she loved about the people around her, and ways that she practiced loving them. She always called love a practice, like it was a muscle that would atrophy if you didn't practice. Like the heart, she'd always say.

Instead, looking at Nessa, I went for the real, like she asked.

"She was afraid she'd never be good enough," I admitted out loud for the first time in my life. I sighed. "She'd gone through a lot of shit. Drug addiction in high school and early college, coming back swinging each time. She helped run an amazing nonprofit that Bo and Ember still run today. She smiled constantly, was insufferably happy," I laughed at my own assessment, "but she thought she was irreparably damaged. She wasn't manic about it, or anything. She didn't put up all kinds of smoke and mirrors—it was the most curious thing. She just ... kind of accepted the untruth about herself and went about trying to prove herself wrong, in a way. I don't know ..." I shook my head. "But she did cry a lot, when no one was looking. She had this weird strength, I mean, like I said, she just ... she had those negative thoughts about herself but also had these crazy-wonderful positive ones and just sort of, I don't know, decided to believe those. Live those ..."

"She sounds amazing," Nessa said softly, barely audible in the loud bar. Her eyes never moved from mine.

I smiled. "She was. I was an optimist before we dated, but she challenged me to be more. Be more of myself, really."

"Do you think you would have married her if she hadn't died?" Nessa's hand flew over her mouth before she even finished asking the question, her eyes wide. "Sorry. Shit. Sorry.

Thanks, beer. Wait. No. I'm not sorry. Do you think so? We're getting real with each other, right?" she rambled.

"I don't know," I answered honestly. "In the weeks and months following her death, yeah, I'd have answered yes. But the truth? We dated for like half a summer. Who knows where that relationship would have gone. I can't imagine my life without Georgia, honestly."

"You don't seem so mopey this time around," Nessa said. "Last time Georgia left for home you looked like a kid who just lost their balloon."

I laughed, pouring myself another drink. "It gets a little easier as the tour goes on," I half lied. In truth I was still processing the events of her visit. Definitely not planning on getting into any of that over drinks with Nessa. "Anyway … your brother?" I prompted.

"We're twins," she started without any hesitation. "And we were best friends and played the violin together, for fuck's sake. We even played local bars and other small venues until halfway through high school."

I remembered from one of Nessa's previous stories, the night I first heard her play, that her parents stopped being able to pay for private lessons at that time—halfway though high school.

"What happened?"

She looked to the table, continuing her story like she hadn't heard my question. Her eyes flitted wildly back and forth. "Vinny was just so good. Like you good. He was doing all kinds of tricks early on. Don't get me wrong, I'm good, I get that. But I was always in awe of how comfortable he was. He'd have no problem just strolling down the street playing if someone asked him to. Fuck, he may have done it if no one asked. He just … had to play. All the time."

"I can appreciate that," I said with a smile, remembering when my family and CJ's family each put in sound proofing in the basements of our houses to help deal with our loud hobbies.

Nessa groaned, her lips curling up as she bared her teeth a bit. "He was too good, sometimes. Just … as a person. Didn't think enough," she said, tapping at her forehead.

"What happened?" I asked again.

She faced me, finally, an indignant but heartbroken look on her face. "Joyriding through the desert with his friends on ATV's," she said. "If they brought helmets with them, they sat in the truck, and in one split fucking second, my larger-than-life brother misjudged a jump and his cervical vertebrae cushioned his fall. His C-4 to be exact." She blindly reached for her glass, filled it, and began to chug again.

I put my hand on her wrist, not wanting her to throw up all over the table, which is what was bound to happen if she didn't slow down.

"C-4?" I questioned, shaking my head. "Fill me in."

With a huff she said, "he's lucky he can breathe on his own, and talk. Everything else?" she moved her hand up and down the front of her. "Dead. Well," she corrected herself in a sarcastically bright voice, "he can kind of move his arms, and it's cause for a big fucking celebration since he wasn't ever supposed to be able to do even that. But he can't open or close his hands, and doesn't have great control over the arms—can you move?" she asked, nudging my shoulders. "I need some fucking air."

CHAPTER TWENTY
REGAN

I SWAYED INTO THE cool Midwestern night outside the bar, trailing Nessa.

"Can we bum two cigarettes off you?" I asked a pair of gawking girls a few feet away. "And a lighter?"

I smiled, they giggled, but a few seconds later I held the light to the cigarette dangling from Nessa's lips.

"Thanks," she said as she exhaled. "These are awful."

I grinned. "I know."

"Light up. Don't make me do this alone," she begged, half grinning.

In truth, the weight of her story made me want a cigarette without her prompting, and I couldn't remember the last time I'd had one. I was never a professional smoker, but sometimes life on the road operated under skewed rules.

I lit mine and tossed the lighter back to the barely legal girls flaunting their cleavage in my direction. Once the lighter was back in their hands, I shit you not, they began taking pictures of themselves with it—even kissing it.

Great, they know who we are.

"So," Nessa started again a few drags into the space she'd asked for, "overnight everything was different. My dad stayed home to do hands-on care of Vinny with the nurses since my mom's job as a pediatrician, of all fucking things, held the health insurance and paid a fuck of a lot more. I wouldn't say either of them adjusted well, but they made it—are making—it work. They still smile at each other, if that says anything. And the last time I was home for Christmas, they were cuddled on the couch and I saw them kiss." She bit her lip and looked down, a tear rolling down her cheek.

I leaned next to her, rocking my shoulder into her. "What about you?"

She shook her head, her cheeks turning redder as tears fell freely. "What about me? I … my violin instructor didn't just think I had talent. He allowed me to teach with him and get lessons for free so I wouldn't kill myself."

My jaw dropped. "Are you … serious?"

Staring forward and sniffing the tears away, Nessa held up one of her arms close to my face. Faint, shiny scars worked their way from her wrist to elbow.

"I wasn't serious," she said, interrupting my thoughts. "I was grieving and needed attention, I guess. Who the fuck knows what sixteen-year-old girls think."

"Yeah …"

She quickly elbowed my side. "Don't look so serious about it, Regan. God. It was negative attention-seeking behavior."

"Ah, yes." I laughed, exhaling some smoke. "A tantrum, but for the over-five set."

"Someone's been to a therapist," Nessa mumbled in amusement.

"Many," I answered back. "But that's another story for another card game."

"Anyway," Nessa started again, as if I hadn't said a word, "I kept playing, but never at home. And never in public. Basically just at my teacher's studio. I felt … guilty, I guess. That Vinny had the talent but not the ability anymore."

I stopped her with my hand. "Nessa, you have the talent."

She shook her head. "I know… but … he really was like you, you know. You remind me so much of him when you play. You play with your whole being. He was like that when he was

… able to move at all. He says he wants me to play, but I know it kills him that he can't."

"So … you don't want to play on this tour because it will somehow hurt him?"

"And me," she admitted, not trying to dress anything up. "I played for a long while after the accident to just see me through the darkness. But after that? I just wanted him next to me, playing."

"Nessa," I said, putting out my cigarette under my foot. "If I lost both my arms right this instant, I wouldn't want a single violinist to stop playing on my account. In fact, I'd want someone new to start to take my place."

Her eyes darted to me, almost hurt. "Now you sound like him."

She turned on her heels and walked inside. I followed behind, catching up to her as she tried to escape me by weaving through the dance floor.

"Hey," I shouted over the crowd.

She turned, looking drunkenly pissed. "What?"

It was all too heavy. Rae, her brother, actually talking about it. Not to mention the shit I wasn't talking about.

My wife might not ever be able to fully trust me. And we want to have a baby. Is that even a thing? Can that work?

Looking into Nessa's intriguing eyes, I felt relief. Someone who understood this life, even when everything around it was tangled and messy. Maybe especially because of that. A life where art is both torture and release. I felt safe in the camaraderie we shared. Safe from judgment and inquisition.

"What?" she asked again, taking a step toward me. "You gonna puke, or something?"

"Nothing." I shook my head, trying to sober up even a little. "Let's get back to the studio.

CHAPTER TWENTY-ONE
REGAN

HE GROUPS HAD pretty much finished up formal practice by the time Nessa and I got a cab and found our way back to River Junction's studio. My intoxication had downgraded from "borderline drunk" to "buzzed," and Nessa seemed to be in the same camp—quiet, but not swaying on her feet or looking sick.

After paying the cabbie, we noticed a small group of musicians in the back corner of the parking lot, and the tapping, cracking of snare drums mixed in with hoots and hollers.

"The hell?" Nessa asked, squinting.

"Oh, joy," I chuckled. "A drum-off."

Moniker's drummer was back in action after his broken wrist had sidelined him, and he, CJ, and The Brewer's drummer, Marco, were lined up with snare drums around their necks, marching band style. I hadn't seen CJ in a snare "competition" in a long time, but was looking forward to it. Despite being only one drum, these kinds of drum-offs are sometimes harder than using a set, because there's less noise-making, frankly, and technical missteps are noticed immediately.

"There you guys are." Yardley approached with a distressed expression, carrying both our violins over her shoulder. "I don't have kids for a reason—watching these was enough to give me palpitations. Here." She shoved them in our direction with a sigh of relief.

I bowed toward her. "Thank you, ma'am."

She arched an eyebrow. "You guys drunk?"

"Not anymore," I replied with a smile, only slightly unsure of myself.

"So your practice thing …" she questioned.

Nessa grinned. "Therapy. Emotional tweaking."

Yardley's eyes moved curiously between Nessa and me. Finally, she threw up her hands. "I don't know why it surprises me when you guys are weird as hell. I'm going to the hotel." She gestured to the drummers behind us. "Maybe do your best to make sure there's no bloodshed? No one gets impaled with a stick."

Nessa gave a mock salute. "Aye, aye, captain."

"So weird," Yardley mumbled to herself with a laugh as she ducked into Norio's waiting car.

"They're probably fucking," Nessa said rather matter-of-factly as the car pulled out of the parking lot.

I laughed. "That's what CJ said."

"Don't you think so?"

"I think men and women can be friends without nudity," I admitted. "One of my best friends is a girl and I've never seen her naked, nor do I wish to."

"Liar," Nessa teased. "Even if you don't wish to now, I bet you wished to at least once."

I rolled my eyes. "Whatever."

Stuffing my hands into my pockets, I walked over to the edge of the parking lot where the drummers were nestled, sparring away. Nessa followed, posting up next to me as we situated ourselves into the group of spectators. CJ was watching Marco intently. Out of the corner of my eye, I watched a wry grin pore over Nessa's mouth.

"Oh," she whispered, "he's intimidated."

"He should be," I whispered back. "Macro's wicked good."

"Wicked?" Nessa teased, laughing. "Is he? Is he wicked good?"

I moved to cross my arms in front of me and elbowed her side playfully. "Yes. Wicked."

Marco was engaged in a long drum roll, punctuating it with clicks to the rim of the drum, but never losing the roll in the process. All three guys were damp with sweat—they'd obviously been at this a while before we showed up. When Marco finished, CJ's eyes lit up.

"Alrighty then," he said, rolling his head from side to side, stretching out his neck.

He struck the drum, starting where Marco had left off. Same tempo, same stance—he was mocking him and I laughed. In a few seconds, CJ clacked on the rim of the drum, moving the sound of the roll from the head of the drum to the rim and back again, arching an eyebrow in the process. The crowed cheered him on, and then he pulled one of his tricks—spinning one stick in his hand like a tiny baton while maintaining an even roll.

"Wooo!" Nessa hooted between cupped hands, egging them on.

Soon, all three drummers were playing at once, each doing their own thing. It may have sounded like noise to someone outside our tight circle in the parking lot, but for us, it was fun.

"Regan!" CJ shouted to me. "Bring it in."

"What?" I grumbled. "Why?"

"Come on, fucker! Bring it."

Nessa nudged my side. "I'd do what he said if I were you," she teased.

I looked at her, narrowing my eyes. "Oh, is that how it is? We'll see …"

Amidst claps and hoots, I took out my violin, quickly ran through a couple of notes, then joined the drummers.

"All right, gentlemen, follow my lead." I laughed to myself, thankful I was buzzed enough to start this song.

Within a few beats, our tour mates were laughing, and the three snare drummers behind me were doing the best they could to keep a straight face while I glided through "Turkey in the Straw." They kept a beat though, cranking it faster as the song went on. I hadn't had a chance to play much bluegrass in the past few years, and I missed it. The sound produced in that style of playing is often what differentiates a fiddle from a violin in people's minds, even though they're the same instrument. In his heyday, you'd have never heard anyone ask Charlie Daniels to whip out his violin if you were at the Grand Ole Opry. Fiddle, they'd call.

I glided right into the next song, "Swallow Tail Jig." A change of tone from bluegrass to Celtic undertones, jigs have always been my favorite thing to play. Despite being English in origin, almost everyone I'd ever come in contact with associated the jig with the Irish—one connection I could stand behind.

"Swallow Tail" is easily recognized, even by people who claim they don't know any jigs. It's like the unofficial anthem of Ireland and all things Irish music. It's only three minutes long, but can easily loop over itself again and again. The drummers pushed me in tempo, added their own tricks to the mix, and soon the small crowd of road-worn musicians around us were dancing.

Glancing up, I caught Nessa's eye as she stared at me with a complicated look on her face. Happiness, maybe. But it was mixed with anxiety and unmistakable desire. Longing. I pulled the instrument away from my shoulder, dropping my arms to my sides, and turned to CJ.

"Just take my lead, okay?" I asked, quiet. Moving my eyes to the other two, I spoke a little louder. "Firm and steady, boys. Got it?" They just shrugged and nodded, looking to CJ for direction. The small crowd grew quiet, waiting for our next move.

Tucking the violin back between my shoulder and chin, I raised the bow, then gripped it under my left fingers, leaving it dangling awkwardly from the neck of the instrument while I brought my right hand to the strings. I paused, shot Nessa a wink and a grin, then brought the violin down in banjo-like position in front of my body. I knew it looked ridiculous, highlighted by the laughs stuttering through the crowd, but it was worth it to see the horror fall over Nessa's face.

"Don't," she begged with a nervous laugh, the beer clearly wearing off but still present. "Regan," she cautioned, "don't." She laughed again.

I teased her, raising and lowering my eyebrows several times before I plucked the strings with my right fingers and thumb. Pizzicato is the technical term for this, but almost no one outside of musicians knows that. Plucked. It's just a fancy, classical-uppity word for plucked.

I plucked the notes slow at first, one at a painfully-slow time. I was betting on Nessa being the only one to recognize them until I sped them up, and it seemed I was right. She pressed her tongue into the side of her cheek and shook her head.

"No," she spit out flatly.

"Come on," I egged her on, picking up the tempo slightly, then again until at least a few people recognized the melody.

"Dueling Banjos" wasn't written for violins, but it's a hell of a good time, anyway. It can be played solely plucking away, like I had started, but I was about to transition to using my bow once I lured Nessa and her violin out of hiding.

"Oh hell yeah, girl," Marco shouted to Nessa from behind me. "Come on."

"I hate you," she called to him before eyeing me. "And you."

I paced toward her, playing slightly louder and faster with each step I took. "Come on," I echoed Marco's peer pressure. "It'll be fun."

"Bet you can outplay him," CJ egged on.

I turned and faced him with mock betrayal. "Et tu?"

He just shrugged. "Seems like she doesn't want to embarrass you."

"Oooo," came the calls from the group, now forming a circle around us.

"Is that true?" I faced Nessa once more, teasing. "You're afraid to beat me?"

A small glint of fire sparked in her eyes, and I figured I'd won her over, but just in case, I leaned in close, so only she could hear.

"Your band's heard you play, I've heard you play, and at least half of these other people have heard you play. Come on," I encouraged close to her ear. "Fall in love with performance again. Chicago will love you for it." I pulled back and resumed plucking, carrying with me the scent of saltwater and grass that drifted off her neck

Shaking her head and taking a deep breath, Nessa slid her case from her shoulder and set it on the ground, finally bringing out her violin. Walking toward me she shot me a playfully evil look.

"You're lucky I'm just buzzed enough to engage in your little torture."

"But can you handle this?" I teased, bringing the violin back to my shoulder and playing a verse at moderate speed.

I wanted to get her playing, and keep it fun. Therefore, I had to do as little talking as possible, letting the music persuade her all on its own.

Often there are no drums in this song, but CJ and I had played this one together often enough that it was no big deal.

Traditional jigs often have some percussion for measure, so over time CJ and I adapted a duet of sorts, stripping the jig band down to their barest parts—melody and beat.

Cheers and claps sprung up as Nessa brought up her instrument into the ready position.

"All right hot shot," she started, refreshingly confident. "Whaddaya got?"

I bit my lip. "Uh uh. Ladies first."

And with that, Nessa eyed Marco and gave him a swift nod, and we were off to the races.

CHAPTER TWENTY-TWO

CJ

REGAN HAD ONLY mentioned in passing that Nessa could play—really play—the violin. I knew he'd written some songs for Moniker that Yardley intended for Nessa to play, as I'd been sitting in for Moniker's drummer for a couple weeks, but that was as much as I knew until she opened the challenge with Regan in "Dueling Banjos." I kept my eyes on Regan as Nessa marched moderately through several runs of notes, kicking off their little head-to-head.

The two of them had bailed on the formal practice session, which wasn't all that strange since Regan's methods could be weird as shit, but something didn't sit right with me when I saw them tumble out of that cab. They looked, I don't know, too chummy, or something. I figured it was just brewing jealousy since Nessa had turned me down in several creative ways at the beginning of the tour, and it stung to see her giving anyone that kind of attention—friendly or otherwise. I was more grateful than jealous at this point, though, so I let all those old feelings go.

Watching Regan watching her play, though? The feeling was coming back. An uneasy drop in my stomach, like I got while driving through Boston, attempting multiple lane changes at once. I knew Georgia had concerns about Nessa and Regan's relationship, but even she was trying to shake them off. Because this was Regan, and he was monogamous and professional. I couldn't tell right away if my discomfort would have surfaced without that talk with Georgia this morning, so I decided to drop it. Besides, it pissed me off to no extent when either of them butted into my business.

Nessa played her bars, and Regan shot back with his. It was fun kicking around like this. So far, most of the off-stage hours with the group had been spent partying or sleeping, but it was nice to goof off once in a while to remember what the fuck we were all doing in the first place—sharing music. Or, as my mom used to say, providing a healthy outlet for my ADHD. The tapping on everything around the house only got worse as the years went on. Drove Frankie nuts, too.

I swallowed hard, trying to push thoughts of my tall, curves-from-heaven ex-girlfriend out of my mind. I refrained from texting her since the night with Clara, but that didn't mean I didn't hover over her contact information in my phone more than a dozen times since the tour started. But after starting and stopping a dozen texts over the last several days, I knew I'd have to try something new. Something she deserved. Space, for one. And something more personal. A card, maybe? Flowers, definitely.

You know what you have to do. What she wants. What you need to do.

I sighed, knowing the level of commitment Frankie explicitly requested of me, that went above and beyond moving in together, and was even more intense than marriage. She wanted a piece of me that I wasn't ready to give to her. To anyone. Regan never even addressed me by my birth name. That was orchestrated. It took a few years for Georgia to learn it and, even though I really loved—love—Frankie, I just ... wasn't ready. I didn't know why, or if I'd ever be, but it was always important to her.

"CJ, take it," Marco cued me, which was a godsend. I couldn't remember if I'd missed a cue since high school, and that was embarrassing enough. A mistake at a competition I worked for years not to repeat. Woodwinds can be an uptight bunch.

By the time I refocused on the scene in front of me, the tour members circling Regan and Nessa were dancing to the rapid pace of the song. Regan was in the lead, this time, his full body working through the notes as he walked around Nessa. Her eyes never left him, challenging and inviting. I'd seen her in clubs before—the looks she gave "hot guys" around her. This wasn't quite the same, but it was almost there.

She dove right in when he finished, building on what he'd played, adding in more complicated chord progressions and picking up the tempo. Their back and forth was fun as hell to watch. It was fast, light, and full of life. It almost made me want to dance along. Almost. Nessa was certainly in Regan's league as far as strings go—I'd have to rub that in soon. It's supposed to be good to be reminded that the sun doesn't shine out of your ass. I wouldn't know.

Regan watched her, tapping his foot with her beat and moving his shoulders at the same time. He had a look I'd seen before—one he'd watched Georgia with the first week he met her. His eyes had lit up watching Georgia bust her ass around the bar she tended. Curious and intentional. Just like they were now.

The song ended with applause and black-slapping, Nessa and Regan laughing and out of breath from their performance porn. I knew jack shit about Nessa's personal life or her "game," but I knew Regan—which is why I fought the bitter taste of watching them have music sex with each other right out in the open.

Did he even realize what he was doing?

If he did, we were about to have a huge fucking problem.

***

We had a decent opening night in Minneapolis. Not our best, but it's hard to say why. There weren't huge errors or missteps. Maybe it was all in my head. I'd been a bit of a dick the last couple weeks—turns out I didn't know what to do with myself if I wasn't with a woman or chasing one.

I'd kind of gotten into the habit of being holed up in my hotel room after shows. At first it was because I didn't trust myself at a club, then, inexplicably, I just didn't want to go anymore. But, at Regan's urging after tonight's show, I found myself at kind of a trendy club. He said he didn't want to go "alone," meaning he wanted me to suffer, too. I tried to get him to stay back with me, but he was on some kind of high. It was weird, having the roles reversed—I used to have to drag him out by his ponytail to go anywhere.

"Nice job tonight," Regan shouted above the noise, clinking his beer bottle against mine.

"Same." I took a swig, eyeing the dance floor. I'd spent a lot of time on those, and I can't dance for shit. Turns out, it doesn't matter much as long as you move your hips along with the hot girl, and prop your hands on her ass. They kind of take care of the rest while you brew a killer erection for later.

"You okay?" Regan nudged my side.

"Yeah ... are you?"

His eyebrows pulled together for a second. "Yeah, why?"

I shrugged, taking another sip of my beer. "Nothin'."

I kept an eye on Nessa. She was at the far end of the bar with Clara, ordering and pounding shots. Clara didn't seem in the mood to spend much time around me. Can't blame her, really—I needed shots to hang out with me sometimes, too.

I was beginning to think maybe I'd made the whole music sex thing between Regan and Nessa up. Nessa seemed focused on Clara and whoever else they were standing with, talking and laughing as if she wasn't pulling my cousin down a dark hole. Maybe she wasn't.

I eyed Regan again, and followed his gaze. Straight to the end of the bar.

"That was fun earlier, with Nessa and the guys," I tried, casually.

Regan lit up like a Christmas tree. "Right?! She's good, huh? Good."

I nodded. "Yep. Have you guys been practicing a lot together?"

He shook his head. "Nah—that was actually the first time we performed together. But we shared some intense shit at dinner and kind of needed to cut loose."

"Intense shit?"

Regan finally looked at me. "Rae," he said. Casually, but with a visible swallow.

"And her?"

"Her brother."

"The paralyzed one?"

His eyes widened. "She told you about that?"

I shrugged. "Drunk conversation a few weeks ago. I don't know any details."

He seemed to relax a little when I said that. "Yeah, it screwed her up. He played violin too—don't … don't tell anyone, okay? I don't know who knows that."

"Jesus," I mumbled. "So she, like, plays for you now?"

He scrunched his face. "Not like that, pervert. We've practiced and I've coached her on some things in a few numbers. That's it. Why are you looking at me like that?"

"I think it might be like that," I mumbled.

"What the hell is that supposed to mean?"

I looked away, squaring my shoulders to the bar and staring straight ahead. "I think you're treading dangerous ground, is what I think."

Regan was silent for a few seconds. "You've got to be kidding me."

I shot him a sideways glance, sighing. "Look, I just think …"

"What?" he cut in, a sort of angry anxiety in his voice. "What do you think?"

Facing him, I shrugged. "Just be careful. I know how these things start."

"What things?"

"If you'd let me talk …"

Regan folded his arms across his chest and tilted his head to the side slightly. "Be my guest."

I rolled my eyes, not particularly in the mood for his smug attitude. "Nessa's a nice girl. Hot, too. Beyond all that she's a hell of a violin player. She's a road and festival musician, like you are, she's a little weird, like you are—a bit of a loner."

Regan's neck turned red. "Your point."

I held up my hands. "Look, I'm a believer that guys and girls can be friends. You and I have enough girlfriends to prove that theory. But I think as far as Nessa's concerned … the deck is kind of stacked against friendship here and more toward … affair territory."

"Affair?" His eyes bugged out.

"Chill out," I responded, trying to keep my cool while I really wanted to punch some sense into him. "I'm not saying I think you're sleeping with her—or would—"

"Damn straight I wouldn't. I'm—"

"Committed to Georgia," I cut back in. "I know. I just think you need to be on your guard emotionally. Emotional affairs are a thing, Regan."

He snorted. "Yeah, guess you'd be the one to know all about emotional affairs."

It stung, but wasn't out of the ordinary for zinger comments. Typically Regan isn't so quick-tongued but, unfortunately, he was right. While I spent a lot of time untethered to any particular woman, I'd been party to many emotional affairs women entered into behind the backs of their boyfriends or, once in a while, husbands. It's real easy for women to get lost in the fantasy of a young, horny musician. They were always way more invested than I was, but I saw how quickly it happened. They'd come to one or two shows the first month, graduating to full groupie status within weeks, not missing a show all summer. Living a different life from Friday night to Sunday morning.

"Look, dude, I was just trying to offer some help. I know Georgia was freaked out when Nessa came to your room—"

"She told you about that? Figures." Regan pressed his tongue against his cheek, shaking his head.

Now I was getting angry. "I'm her friend, you fool. Of course she told me. She was worried her reaction was going to put you over the edge with her. She said things have been tense for a while."

Regan pushed back his stool and slid to his feet, grabbing his beer from the bar. "You know what, CJ? I'm not even going to have this conversation with you. You haven't a clue what it's like to be in a marriage, let alone a long-term committed relationship, save for Frankie. And we see how that turned out. You have no idea what tension is. It's not worrying that a boyfriend or husband will come home before you've left his side of the bed. It's about supporting someone for years, talking about starting a family, and wondering where the fuck that leaves your relationship, never mind your career."

His jaw was tense, and I just begged my temper to stay back long enough for him to get this off his chest.

He stepped closer. "So," he said quietly. "Before you run around and point out your observations about everyone else's relationships and marriages, why don't you try getting your fucking act together for once."

We stared at each other for a long few seconds. It was like he was almost daring me to do something. Say something, maybe. I wasn't about to. Regan might joke around with me about my former lifestyle, or snap at me in a constructive way when he genuinely wanted to change, but he had never once in our lives dumped that kind of shit on me.

He huffed through his nose, a pretentious chuckle. "Whatever," was all he said before walking away.

And to the end of the bar, where Nessa still stood.

Even if I was unsure about what was going on with Regan before our conversation, I wasn't anymore. His defensiveness was hiding something. I didn't believe he'd fool around on Georgia, he wasn't that kind of guy. At least he didn't used to be. But the way he relaxed around Nessa—standing next to her as he leaned his elbows on the bar and laughed as if he hadn't just been a dick was enough to raise my suspicions.

Sure, he was my cousin and Georgia was my best friend, which made things almost impossibly complicated. But, if the roles were reversed and she was behaving like a brainless bag of hormones, I'd try to set her straight before going to Regan.

In this case, it sure seemed like Regan wasn't interested in being set straight. And I couldn't sit by and do nothing.

I stood to leave, tossing money on the bar and making my way for the exit, when an unexpected phone call vibrated my cell.

Frankie.

CHAPTER TWENTY-THREE

CJ

PUSHED MY WAY outside while the phone buzzed, wanting to be able to give her my full attention, without the music or Regan's attitude in the background.

"Hello?" I tried not to sound too hopeful, or anxious.

"CJ?" she asked as if she hadn't dialed my phone number.

God, what if she meant to call someone else? Stupid touchscreen phones.

"Yeah," I answered, slow. She was quiet. "Frankie?"

"I'm here." She sounded nervous. "Look … um …"

The hair on the back of my neck stood on end. "Frankie, are you okay? What's going on?"

She cleared her throat. "Oh, no. I'm fine. Someone … um … someone just came over looking for you."

Guy or girl would have been my response if this conversation happened three years ago, but we were far from there. At least I was, despite my behavior sometimes to the contrary. Still, it was strange for someone random to look for me there, since I never officially lived with Frankie.

"Who was it?"

"They didn't tell me their name." She was nervous. Her voice was shaky, but not angry.

"Look, Frankie, I never gave out your address, so I don't know how—"

"He said he was your dad."

I nearly blacked out for a second. My vision definitely clouded at the mention of his title. I steadied myself on the side of the building.

"What?" I growled.

"Yeah … I don't … um I don't know how …"

"Me either." Maybe it was someone fucking with me, and her. "What'd he look like?"

I didn't know anyone who would play a fucked up prank like that, but it was worth a shot.

Frankie cleared her throat, but when she spoke, her voice was heavy like she was trying not to cry. "Exactly like you, but older and in a suit."

It was him. That fucking bastard.

"Fuck," I growled. "What'd he say to you?"

"Nothing," she answered quickly. "He asked if you were here, and he asked if I knew where I could find you when I told him you didn't live here."

"What'd you tell him?"

"I told him that I wasn't in the habit of handing out personal addresses to strangers, and you were on tour anyway."

I sighed. Relieved and angry at the same time as I ran my hand over my face. Forming a fist, I pressed my knuckles into the wall next to me, but decided not to ruin my hands on his account. "Then what'd he do?"

"He smiled, all charm and charisma, and told me to tell you his dad stopped by and he'd try to see you soon."

The fuck did that mean?

"When's the last time you saw him, CJ?" Frankie continued. "I thought—"

"Years," I reiterated the truth I'd told her at the beginning of our relationship. "I mean, more than just years now, I guess. Ten? He claimed he was at my high school graduation, but I never saw him …" I paced down a seedy looking alley, needing a way to work out the adrenaline and rage surging through me that didn't involve potential jail time for vandalism or assault. "He smiled at you?"

"Mhmm," she answered. "It didn't seem creepy, or anything."

"Nah don't worry about ... that. He's not like, dangerous, or anything."

"Except to you," Frankie said, her voice full of the girl I dated, made love to. Before everything fell apart. "Like you," she reiterated in the way she used to when we sat on her couch and she'd press her index finger into my chest over my heart."

"Yeah," I whispered, then cleared my throat. "I have no fucking idea how he even knew about you, let alone where to find you. I'm sorry, Frankie."

"Hey," she responded gently. "It's okay. I know it's not your fault."

I cleared my throat, trying to hold back uncomfortable tears. I wanted to be with Frankie right now. In her living room or even in my hotel room. I just wanted to talk to her. To see her face and have her remind me in a way that no one else could that I wasn't like that. Like him. But, wasn't I? To her anyway.

Despite his dick behavior earlier, Regan did manage to serve me a dose of reality about my dad back a few weeks ago.

Cut the shit about your dad.

So, what was I supposed to do when dad dropped in unexpectedly and sliced right in the middle of a life that wasn't even mine anymore by showing up at my ex-girlfriend's house?

"Frankie I'm sorry," I blurted out in something that sounded like a sob, but there were no tears. It was all in my chest, tearing me apart. I sat on the dingy sidewalk at the end of the alley, next to a Starbucks and a pizza joint, and rested my forehead in my hand.

"For what?" she sounded alarmed, her voice high and anxious.

"Everything. You're right, you deserved better. But not better than me," I took a risk. "Better than what I gave you. I can do better, I promise. I am better."

She sighed. "Oh, CJ ... Look, I know this is heavy, but I don't think—"

"It's Callum!" I shouted into the phone, startling a fat pigeon and a young couple walking by.

For three years I'd managed to avoid this talk with her. Now, it was happening with more than a thousand miles between us.

Frankie gasped. "What did you just say?"

"My name is Callum." I was almost out of breath. "Callum James. No one's called me that since I was five because Callum is his name. And when he took off no one wanted to be reminded of it, anyway. They all just kept calling me CJ, even when I got in trouble it was CJ Kane, no first and middle name like everyone else got. I changed it when I was eighteen. That's why everything says CJ, except my birth certificate ..." My eyes finally watered, but the pain stayed anchored in my chest.

"I didn't know," she said, sounding like she was crying. "I suspected something like that, but you never gave me much to go by."

"And I pushed you far away from that part of my life," I admitted. "You deserved all of me, and I wouldn't let you in. He left when I was little. Had a private bank account he threw money in for a few years before he had enough to pay off the house my mom and I lived in and buy one for him and his side chick in Long Island. I saw him a couple times when I was young, but after he married her and they had kids ... I just ... phased out, I guess." I'd only told Frankie pieces of that story.

She knew my dad left in a flash, and had a whole new family now, but that's as much as I'd allowed her to see.

Frankie took a deep breath, followed by a long exhale. "You didn't tell me all that stuff," she reiterated my thoughts.

"Yeah," I huffed, "there you have it."

"Why?" she questioned. "Why didn't you tell me this before?"

"I didn't want you to know that I was just like him, because I was hoping I wasn't."

She made a small clicking noise with her mouth. "Like him how, CJ?"

"A flight risk," I answered flatly. "It's just so complicated, Frankie. He and my mom … they were high school sweethearts. They had the romance everyone wanted, but it was all a fucking lie."

"Oh," she said like she had a hundred lightbulbs going off over her head.

"But that doesn't excuse my behavior," I cut in quickly. "You deserved someone who would love you just like that, and have it be real. Genuine. That's how I loved you, you know. Well, love you. It scares me." I stood, needing to move again, uncomfortable stewing in these emotions.

I hadn't meant to tell her any of this, as she'd made it quite clear she wasn't interested in me any longer. But just the thought of my dad showing up, standing in front of the person I love most in my life … it cracked something inside me. I wanted to protect her, and from things beyond me.

"You still love me," she said as a half-question, half-statement.

"I do," I admitted before I could chicken out. "And I could never tell you enough times how sorry I am for acting like … like … myself. My old self. Being with you made me better. I wanted to be better, for both of us."

"Wow," she said inside a breath.

I wanted her to tell me she loved me, too, but I knew better than to ask. I'd done plenty of damage to our relationship before Clara ever came into the picture.

"Say something," I said after a few seconds of silence.

"We have to stop having these heavy conversations over the phone." She chuckled and sniffed—laughing through tears. There might be hope yet, I thought.

"I'm sorry I was so weird about my name, Frankie. I just … it was this thing. And, it's not anymore." I had no idea why, but it truly wasn't.

"Look," she said, sounding like she'd regained some composure, "I want to talk about this. And, I know that you're on the road forever right now, but I do want to talk about this."

Goose bumps covered the back of my neck. She wanted to talk to me, more. That had to be a good sign."

"Come to Chicago," I blurted out, my courage fueled by adrenaline. "I know you said no before, but—"

"Okay," she cut me off.

"Seriously?"

She laughed. God I'd missed that sound. "Yes. I'll see you in Chicago."

"We'll talk then." I nodded my head once, steeling myself for a grownup conversation we both deserved. I wanted to tell her I loved her again, but didn't want to overplay my hand. Instead, I went for casual and friendly. "I'll text you the itinerary."

"I have it," she said. "Unless it's changed?"

The searing pain in my chest turned warm, and didn't hurt so much anymore. "No," I grinned, "it hasn't changed. But if it does, I'll let you know."

"Kay."

"Okay, bye Frankie."

"Bye CJ."

I walked the twenty-minute walk back to the hotel, grinning like an asshole the whole way. I had a chance to get my girl back, and I wasn't about to blow it.

CHAPTER TWENTY-FOUR

REGAN

APPARENTLY, MINNEAPOLIS BROUGHT out the drinker in me. I barely remembered a single thing from the night before when I rolled over in my hotel bed to reach for Georgia. My arm falling flat onto empty sheets reminded me I was still on tour, and she was still far away.

I was groggy, a little dizzy, and a bit nauseated when I reached for my phone to call her. I owed it to her to be honest about how I'd been feeling the last few days and weeks, even if it was inconveniently this way. This couldn't wait until Massachusetts when Georgia was planning to fly out. With a job like this, sometimes discussions, decisions, and plans had to be made by phone.

I don't normally sleep through a ringing phone, but I saw I'd missed five calls from Georgia. Five. Not a single text message, but five calls. One on the hour, every hour, from three in the morning until just now. Eight. That must have been what woke me up, because five hours of sleep after a night like last night would not be enough. In a bit of a panic, I called her back as fast as my phone would let me tap over to her number.

She picked up on the second ring, but didn't say anything. I thought I'd lost the connection.

"Georgia? Georgia, are you okay? I saw I missed a bunch of calls from you. Hello?"

There was a long pause, followed by a still, ice-cold response. "How do you think … it makes me feel … when I'm woken up in the middle of the night by a text message about my husband dancing with another woman?"

"I … I … what? What are you talking about?" I couldn't remember a fucking thing about last night.

I rubbed sleep away from my eyes, hoping it would bring with it some clarity about what the hell happened last night. It didn't.

"Georgia, you've got to give me more to go on … I don't … I don't remember much about last night."

A sharp, horrible laugh pierced my ear. "Oh, that just puts the icing on the cake, doesn't it? I can't talk to you right now. I'll send you the picture and you can take a few minutes or days or whatever it is you need to figure out just what the fuck you have to say for yourself. Bye."

"Georgia—" It was too late. She disconnected before I could say anything else.

A second later, my phone buzzed with a new text. A picture from Georgia. Praying like I hadn't in years that I'd come out of this alive, I clicked. It wasn't a picture. Worse. It was a video. I didn't want to press play, but I did it anyway.

Immediately, the silence of my hotel room was filled with the garbled noise of chatter and music. I stared at the screen. Baffled. Nessa and I were there, dancing. It wasn't dirty, or anything. But, I gotta say, it didn't look good.

Our hands were clasped as we moved around one another, the rest of our bodies touching intermittently. It was clear we were drunk by the inability either one of us had to stay on any sort of beat, but it looked fun. Funny, even. I was relieved, confident in my ability to have a rational conversation about this with Georgia. It wasn't until the phone rang as I called her back that I started thinking about who sent it to her.

"That was fast," she answered, bitchy-like.

"Can I explain?" I responded, keeping my tone calm.

"I'd like to hear you give it a whirl."

"Georgia …" I started going in with a flustered attitude, but trailed off, taking a deep breath instead.

"What? Explain yourself."

"Seriously? It was Nessa. We were all goofing off, it wasn't just us dancing. Everyone from the tour was dancing with everyone. I watched the video, G. I saw what you saw, and I don't understand why you're mad."

"It was Nessa," she echoed me. "The same Nessa who just a couple days ago was traipsing into your hotel with you while you were wide-awake ready to rehearse, but when she left you basically passed out before the door closed."

"That's not tru—"

"It doesn't matter. We're trying to start a family and you can't even stay awake long enough to impregnate your wife."

"I'm fucking tired of that conversation, Georgia. You're just going to jet into town and leave when you got what you came for?" My words were sharp as I sat up quickly. Too quick, pointed out by the pounding in my head.

Georgia gasped on the other end. "You're fucking kidding me. Using you?! We're married, Regan. Though, I see you must need a reminder of that."

"Fuck off, Georgia. You know what? Fuck off. You would have a camera attached to me every second I was away if you could. I'm committed to you, but you refuse to believe that. I used to think it was because you were so wounded from your childhood that you didn't think you deserved love. But," I let a rough chuckle escape my chest, "you know what? I think you like the drama. I think you like all the theatrics that can go along with having a husband gone half the time. You think the only way for me to treat you right is to make me think you're mad at me all the fucking time!" I yelled, hurting my own ears.

"Well let me tell you something, wife," I continued. "I have loved you every second since two months before I told you for the first time. It took me that long to get the courage to say it because we were both scared and unsure. I have loved the piss out of you every damn second."

"Regan!" she screamed back into the phone, trying to get my attention, but I wasn't done.

"Don't!" I yelled back, getting out of bed and unsteadily pacing the room. Our first fight like this in easily two years. "You don't get to treat me like this anymore!"

"Like what?! Like you have it so bad," she spat back.

"Like I'm on probation for someone else's crimes! I've done nothing but take care of you and this is what I get in return? Suspicion? Judgment? If you can't trust me, Georgia, then what the fuck are we even doing in this relationship?"

"I do trust you—"

"Funny fucking way of showing it. And," I started, out of breath "is that what you want a baby for? To use as another weapon against me when I'm out on the road working?! A tool to use to make me feel guilty or to pit against me when you think I'm out interacting with someone instead of locked in my hotel room on the phone with you?"

"You fucking prick," she said, malice in place of her voice.

"Yeah, me fucking prick. That's right. Staying up when I get home early in the morning to help you get things done at your shop before getting a few hours sleep then waking up to bring you lunch. Me fucking prick. Also making sure I clean the house and get you dinner since you'd never stop to feed yourself, and leave you notes all around the house before I leave for the night. What a fucking prick I am, huh?" My voice was rough, raw from yelling. "How I make sure that favorite pink fluffy blanket of yours is always clean and on the bed with the damn dryer sheets you like because you say they smell like me.

All the texts I send you, notes and flowers while I'm on the road, and the fucking love songs I write for other bands to use that are about you in every note, every pause, and every lyric. Meanwhile, all I get from you is the occasional cupcake and accusatory text. I'm such a fucking bastard."

"I …" She seemed speechless.

"Every goddamn new song that I wrote and Nessa sings and plays? They're about you. You."

Met with more silence, I met the end of my patience.

Fine.

But then, her voice morphed into the tone she'd taken earlier in the conversation, even though she was a bit shaky. "CJ wouldn't have sent me that text if he didn't think it was any of my business."

"Brilliant," I snapped before ending the call and throwing my phone against the wall, speaking then to an empty room. "Just. Brilliant."

***

With my anger seething and heart racing, I lunged down the hall toward CJ's room, pounding unceasingly until a gravelly voice emerged from the other side.

"Who is it?"

"Me," I snapped.

"Regan?"

"Get the fuck out here."

He opened the door, standing in front of me in his T-shirt and boxers, looking like I pulled him out of a deep sleep. Good.

"I thought you left the fucking bar early last night?"

"I did," he answered, still holding the door open.

"Then how the hell did Georgia get a video from you of me and Nessa dancing at the club?"

Finally catching up to the purpose of my visit, CJ rubbed his eyes. He shrugged rather unapologetically. "Someone sent it to me."

I pressed my head forward, my eyes wide as I tried to breathe away my rage. "So you fucking forwarded it to Georgia?"

"Watch your fucking tone. You know what, Regan? I tried. I tried to talk to you about getting wrapped up with that girl. I didn't think you meant to get in that deep with her, but I saw it happening and thought I'd give you a heads up."

I took a firm step forward, grinding my teeth together and speaking low and threatening. "Get to the part where you dropped a grenade into the middle of my marriage."

He squinted at me. "Get over yourself. I had a fuck of a night last night. Then, on top of that, someone sent me the video saying isn't this your married cousin? And, you know what? Fuck me. When I opened it, there was my married cousin, grinding with the girl he isn't having an affair with." He said isn't with air quotes, the bastard

"I wasn't grinding with her." I brought my hands up and pushed CJ's shoulders. Enough to make him stagger back, but not fall. His hand stayed on the door.

"Watch yourself, Regan. I gave you a chance to see what the fuck you were doing, and you didn't take it. Georgia deserved to know what was going on before you and Nessa ended up in bed together—if you haven't already."

It was too much. I let out a low growl, brewing toward a yell. "I never thought the first punch I threw would be at you."

Before he had time to respond or react, I swung, making instant, hard, contact."

He let out a shocked, pissed yell as bright red blood sprayed from his nose. He brought his hand to his face, catching blood as it pooled in his hand and ran down his arm. "You fucker!"

It took a second for him to react, but I didn't step back. I wasn't scared. I wasn't angry. I wasn't feeling anything at all, which was proving to be a problem, since I didn't seem to care that I was going up against not only my cousin, but someone far bigger and more experienced in fights than I was. The only advantage I had was anger over my marriage being screwed with.

"Walk away Regan," CJ said, sounding like he was forcing the words out. "Now. I don't want to fight you." He started closing the door, but I stuck my foot in the space, preventing it from closing all the way.

"I don't give a fuck what you want. You went over the line this time, man."

"I think you broke my fucking nose," he mumbled under his breath. "What line, dude? I wasn't the one flirting with another woman. For once."

With a surge of rage, I elbowed the door open, ignoring the throbbing in my hand, and I sent a right hook to the side of his face. CJ reacted in time, backing up so my knuckles only grazed the side of his jaw.

He dropped his hand, blood still trickling out of his nose, but the bulk of it soaking into his shirt. With his eyes boring into me, he pulled the door open and took two steps toward me, the second one forcing me to step back into the hallway.

"That's the last shot you'll get on me," he stated with purpose before pulling his hand back and clocking me in the side of my face.

I'd already started pulling back out of the way, so my cheekbone wasn't hit with his full force, but it was bad enough. It felt like my cheek exploded. There was ringing in my ears and I had to blink several times to see straight. By this time, doors started opening around us, tour members and vacationing strangers unexpectedly with a front-row seat to our fight.

"That enough?" CJ asked, cocky with an eyebrow arch and a grin on his bloodied face.

"Hardly." I lunged forward, needing to get him off his feet. I succeeded quickly when I gave a swift kick to his ankle, knocking him onto the ground.

As I came down on top of him, planting knees on either side of him, he started swinging in defense. I was numb with rage and anger, at him, Georgia, and myself. I didn't care what I felt or didn't feel; I just needed to punch someone. CJ was that someone. The someone who played on my wife's insecurities and fucked everything up.

"You knew exactly what you were doing when you texted her, you bastard. You knew it would fuck her right up."

"You shouldn't do anything you want hidden from your wife."

I grabbed the sleeves of his T-shirt, trying to lift him up and slam him down, but the force of his back worked against me, so I only succeeded in tearing the fabric.

"You had enough of fucking up your own life you wanted to mess with mine."

CJ gained leverage, rolling me off him. I braced for impact, but he stood, backing up as if challenging me to stand. I did, though it was difficult given how dizzy I was both from my hangover and his punch.

He strode toward me and I couldn't help but to back up—my body's involuntary survival strategies kicking in, overriding my desire for revenge. CJ pressed his index finger into my shoulder so hard it made me wince.

"At least I don't deny fucking up. But I didn't try to beat you up over my mistakes, Regan." His breath was ragged from exertion and adrenaline, echoing mine.

Dodging his punches was an exercise in itself, but I wanted to get one more swing in. CJ ducked, launching his shoulder into my gut like I was some prop on the football field.

"I could knock you out on your ass right now, Regan," he said as a few guys from other bands—Moniker and The Brewers among others—walked toward us with obvious intent of breaking us up. "But I'm not going to. You deserve to sit in your mistake last night. It wasn't one I made."

"All right, guys, come on." Our tour mates approached us with caution. Wanting to separate us while maintaining their physical safety.

CJ pressed his shoulder into my diaphragm once more, forcing air from my lungs, before backing away with his hands up. "I'm done," he claimed. "He's not worth it."

My left eye must have caught hell from the punch CJ landed, I figured, because vision was getting questionable on that side. CJ didn't bother keeping his eyes on me as he walked defiantly back to his hotel room and slammed the door.

Alone in the hallway with some of the guys, as bystanders closed their own doors, I glanced tiredly at all of them.

"I should probably get this checked out," I said, holding up my hand. Then, pointing to my face, I said, "And this."

"I'll go with you," Marco said, waving everyone else off.

"Thanks," I mumbled, lowering my head.

As we walked down the hallway, I caught sight of Nessa as she moved toward the elevator.

"'What the hell happened?" she asked, staring open-mouthed as Marco and I entered the elevator.

He held up his hand. "Not now, Ness."

She looked confused, maybe even a little hurt. As the elevator doors closed, I shrugged, looking at her.

"Guess you and I had some fun last night …"

The doors closed, and I felt a little bad for leaving her with that, but figured she could piece the rest together herself. I had more pressing matters on my mind, like the possibility of at least one broken bone in my hand, a busted-up face, and then, the clincher. Memories from last night slowly swirled into my memory.

Of me asking Nessa to dance, her initial refusal, and my persuasive insistence. The smell of sweat and the feel of her hands on my lower back. And mine on her waist as we rocked away to the music ...

The elevator doors opened just in time.

"I'm gonna puke," I said to Marco before diving toward the nearest trashcan.

CHAPTER TWENTY-FIVE

REGAN

UNFORTUNATELY, THE NAUSEA wasn't from a concussion. My vitals were fine, and so was my hand, it turns out, but my conscience wasn't. Marco stayed with me in the ER while I got my hand and face x-rayed, and went back to the hotel via cab when I convinced him I was fine to—and needed to—walk back. There was only a few hours until the show and I needed all the time and space I could steal until then to think.

Exiting the sliding emergency room doors, I stepped into muggy, late-morning heat. It was approaching noon as I stood on the sidewalk, formulating my next move. Seemingly out of nowhere, Yardley emerged from a cab looking stressed. Make-up free, which was rare, and her hair pulled back in a loose ponytail, she approached me with her arms across her chest.

"Heard I might find you here," she started.

I tilted my head back, taking a deep breath as I stared at the clouds. "Yeah," I said rather passively. "Here I am."

"Well, I came to assess the damage, but it looks like you're in one piece ..." she trailed off, keeping a curious eye on me.

"What?" I asked, shrugging.

"CJ? Really? You two? What the fuck, Regan?" I could probably count on one hand the number of times I'd heard Yardley swear, so even in her syrupy accent, the words stung.

I waved her off, walking in a direction I hoped led toward food. "It's nothing."

"It's something," she challenged, following a few paces behind me.

"Don't panic," I assured her. "I'm sure we'll be fine to play tonight." While I'd never played this mad at CJ, it was hardly ever a struggle when we were mildly pissed at each other. I assumed we'd both be able to hold our professional shit together, if nothing else.

Yardley caught up to me, grabbing hold of my elbow, tugging it so I'd turn around. I did, and was met with a look of deep concern on her face.

"I don't give a damn about tonight's show. I'm more concerned with you." She pressed her finger into the same spot CJ had a couple hours earlier. It was still tender. "It seems like you've been running on empty lately."

I put up my hand. "Can I have a minute? I've had a lot of fucking input since I woke up this morning."

"Sure," she answered casually, walking next to me as quietly as if she wasn't there.

Two blocks of silent walking later, I spotted a hole-in-the-wall burrito joint that smelled palatable. I needed carbs to soak up the still-lingering hangover.

"I've gotta eat," I mumbled, opening the door, holding it for Yardley since I knew she'd friggen follow me anyway.

She smiled as she crossed the threshold. "Don't mind if I do."

Once we were settled at an outdoor table with fat burritos and soda, I waited until I'd taken a few bites before I spoke.

"What do you know?" I asked.

Yardley chewed, formulating her answer. "Probably too much and not enough. I'm not even concerned with the side bullshit, honestly. That's all par for the course and you're all adults. What I am concerned with is your mental health."

"I'm fine," I cut in without thinking.

"No." She shook her head. "You're not. Again, I'm not concerned with what did or did not happen at the club last night. But fighting CJ? That's not good. For me, that's a sign that things have gone very, very poorly for you. That's not your style."

"I was pushed," I stated flatly, talking through a mouth full of burrito and hot sauce.

"Regan, cut the shit." Yardley swore for like the second time this year—both times on the same day. "What do you need right now?"

"I need to get on stage tonight and fulfill my contract and obligations. I need to play."

"The second part of your sentence I buy," she said. "But, put the tour aside, put the label aside, and put whatever the hell happened last night aside. What do you need right now."

I needed to talk to Georgia. I needed to find out what went so wrong with CJ's night last night. I needed to apologize, even though I was mad. It wasn't him I was mad at, after all. I didn't need a therapy session to piece that one together. I needed to be a goddamn adult, own my shit, and figure out what I wanted, for me and for my marriage.

Yardley eyed me with an arched eyebrow as I formulated my answer. Finally, after a few more bites of food and a swig of Dr. Pepper, I was able to articulate myself.

"What I need," I started, "is to go home for a few days."

She nodded once, sage as if she was simply waiting for me to say what she already knew.

"Go," she nearly commanded.

My shoulders fell, disappointment that I'd let my marriage spiral out of control and, in doing so, I'd have to bail on work commitments. Turns out, having it all wasn't turning out to be all it was cracked up to be.

Especially if I couldn't have what actually mattered—my wife.

"I'll give CJ stuff to do for the next few shows, don't worry about him."

"I'll have to talk to him when I come back. I'll be back by Chicago, okay?"

Yardley leaned forward. "Even if you aren't, Regan, don't worry. We'll figure it out. There are eight billion musicians on this tour, so we can work something out. But keep me in the loop, okay?"

I nodded. Okay.

Yardley wrapped up her burrito and stood from the table. "I gotta get back and rearrange the set for tonight. Let me know when you're taking off."

I opened my mouth, probably to apologize, as was my habit, but Yardley held up her hand. "Not another word. Just go take care of yourself and come back as whole as possible."

"Thank you," was all I said before she gave me a polite smile and walked to the end of the block to hail a cab.

I finished my lunch within twenty minutes and decided to walk back to the hotel, which I figured would take a half hour, or so, and make my travel arrangements for tonight. Of course a last minute flight out of Minneapolis was going to cost a fortune but, really, it was both priceless and worth every penny. I knew Georgia and I could likely talk through everything that happened last night and today, and the past several weeks, but I didn't know if too much damage had been done. Or what I would do in that case.

Anything.

I would do absolutely anything to make my marriage work, I realized halfway back to the hotel. I thought I was going to vomit again when I replayed the awful things I'd said to her. Not awful in fact—everything I said was true—but wretched in intent and tone. I'd said everything in a way to hurt her. Because I was defensive. I'd pulled the same shit with CJ last night, too. A few hours ago I'd have even justified my defensiveness, insisting that everyone else was wrong and paranoid because my character was as spotless as my conscience.

The only problem was, now neither were clean. No, Nessa and I never had any physical contact outside of that dance floor, but that doesn't mean lines weren't crossed. I didn't know what exactly happened, or when it shifted into something that everyone else could see except for me, but I'd have a few hours flight to think on that before I faced my wife.

Once back at the hotel, I decided to avoid CJ's room, both because I was embarrassed and because I valued my safety. Walking out of that ER with a prescription for Tylenol 3 was about as easy as anyone had ever gotten off after a fight with CJ. After packing my bags, though, I did text Nessa and ask her to meet me in the lobby of the hotel.

My throat was dry with anxiety as she exited the elevator and headed to where I was sitting by the window. Her eyes stayed on me as she walked, but they were red as if she'd been crying. Her face wasn't puffy, or any of the other telltale cry signs I was accustomed to, but I knew cried out eyes when I saw them.

"Hey," I started, gesturing to the open seat next to me.

She winced, reaching up to touch my cheek. "Your face …"

I pulled back, avoiding contact. "Yeah."

"Sorry." She dropped her hand to her lap, as if she'd just touched a hot burner. "I didn't mean to do that."

At least it was obvious that someone filled her in on what the fight was about.

"CJ and I had a thing …"

She nodded. "Because of me."

I shook my head. "Because of me. Look, Nessa …"

She held up her hand in an attempt to cut me off, but I continued.

"Let me talk. I had fun last night, from what I remember. And, I mean, I don't know where the lines were crossed, but they were. And I'm sorry. Either way, I need to go home and make things right with Georgia."

She shook her head, her eyes wide. "Don't leave the tour on my account. I should be the one to leave. This is your label and you're headliner."

"Just one of the headliners," I replied honestly. "And it's not about the tour. It's about my marriage. My life. The rest of my life that goes on when the tour ends, and before the next one starts. You stay. You deserve the practice and exposure. I hope I won't be gone long—everything else aside, this has been a really fun tour, and I want to see it through." I took a deep breath because, if I was being honest with myself, I wasn't sure when my next tour would be, regardless of what GSE had planned.

"I wish I could be more help about what went on last night, but I don't remember much, either. I do remember laughing my ass off as you tried to rap along with Pitbull." She laughed, weakly, but it cracked me up.

"What is it with that guy?" I laughed at a fuzzy memory from last night. "Is he like the American club soundtrack? I can't get away from him!"

She gasped comically as if she were offended. "You don't loooove him?"

"I don't even know what he's saying half the time, and the other half I feel like I should be wearing a condom just to listen to it."

Nessa threw her head back and laughed a long, high pitched laugh that made me ache for Georgia's deep, throaty voice.

"Anyway," I continued, suddenly discomforted by our easy banter, "I didn't want to leave without at least letting you know that I hold no ill will toward you. And I intend to be back for Chicago to see you rock it. Promise?"

Nessa's face stilled as she recovered from her laugh and took a deep breath. "I promise to try," she said honestly. Vulnerably.

I bit my lip, nodding as I stood and threw my duffel bag over my shoulder. "I think that's really the best any of us can do."

***

Once I was thirty thousand feet in the air and the pilot gave the okay to use our electronic and cellular devices—what a marvelous development in air travel over the last few years—I took my phone out of airplane mode. That I hadn't received a single text message from Georgia was unsurprising, but mildly concerning. I could only remember one or two times in the entirety of our relationship where we were locked in silent treatment mode for more than a full day. One of those days was spent almost exclusively in our house, which made things extra fun. I was wishing for that now, though, because at least I'd know where she was. Or if she was angry, or crying, or, worse, withdrawn.

So, no texts from Georgia, but I had a couple from some of the guys who saw the fight earlier in the morning just checking in, and two more from other tour members asking if the rumors that I'd left the tour were true. Just after those texts was one from Yardley saying she'd filled everyone in on the new game plan to finish out the Minneapolis stint, and they all seemed on board. The Brewers apparently had a few numbers from an old playlist that included two drum sets, so she tucked CJ in there and said a bunch of the drummers got together and devised a several minute drumline number to perform on their own.

Part of me wished I could see that, since I'd always been fond of drumlines, but I was just relieved CJ wasn't left high and dry for the next few shows. We didn't need any more conflict or resentment between us right now. But, I'd have to deal with that later, too.

There were lots of laters because, even though I'd get to San Diego with plenty of daylight left, I planned to use every minute to my advantage. To salvage my character for the only person that mattered.

CHAPTER TWENTY-SIX

GEORGIA

"**Y**OU SHOULD GO up to bed, honey." Mom tried to act like it was a modest suggestion as she sifted flour, but there was telltale tension in her shoulders.

"It's three in the afternoon," I blurted out. "And, what I have ... sleep won't fix."

Rage, depression, confusion, giving-up-ness ...

"You'd be surprised. You didn't go to bed last night. In fact, you didn't even leave the bakery."

Sometimes, having my mom as a houseguest was like having Big Brother around. She's a light sleeper—always has been. So, when I was younger, sneaking in or out was out of the question. As for last night, she didn't hear me come into the apartment because I didn't. I couldn't.

I'd been wrapping up a relatively late night filling orders for a baptismal brunch and a bar mitzvah when I got the text from CJ. All he prefaced it with was, I'm in the hotel, but someone sent this to me. I don't know anything more than this.

Of course I called CJ right away, in a rage that I didn't want to dump on Regan without more information. CJ was pretty tight-lipped, and I sensed he was holding back something. At that point, though, it hardly mattered. Pictures don't lie, and videos are even more truthful.

It was Regan, dancing with Nessa on a crowded dance floor. By all accounts, he appeared drunk, but that wasn't even what bothered me the most. He was dancing with her like he always did with me. Hands in the same position, and I almost threw up when he leaned forward and touched his forehead to hers. It was only for a second, but for that second I hated both of them. I hated that she didn't have to wear heels to make that move a remote possibility—she had to be nearly five foot eleven. Vanity may have been my knee-jerk reaction; jealous of her height, her beauty, and the way she moved so easily with my husband, but that was just the tip of the iceberg.

Regan had been working extra hours on this tour, beyond his normally insane practice regimen. His texts were shorter and shorter as the weeks went on, and we hadn't sent dirty texts to each other for nearly two weeks before I showed up in Minneapolis. He'd been slipping away slowly, and I realized it too late. It wasn't until he rejected me in that bed in Minnesota that I knew something had gone horribly wrong. I wasn't naïve enough anymore to put this all on Nessa—I was sure she had little to do with Regan's initial pulling away—but she sure as shit didn't fuckin' help things.

"Georgia," Mom snipped as if she'd called my name several times already.

I took a quick breath, blinking myself back to the present. "Yeah?"

She nodded to the stand mixer whipping in front of me. "You've got enough volume there, I think."

Readjusting my attention, I saw that the egg whites I'd been beating for a meringue were nearly overflowing the bowl with their pillowy foam. I shut off the mixer and hung my head, taking a deep breath.

"Maybe I should shower." I conceded that I needed to change something about my appearance from yesterday morning, but I wasn't ready for sleep, or the dreams it would bring. "Put this in the fridge for me?"

Mom's smile was considerate and concerned, a sadness in her eyes as she reached for the bowl and stuck it in the fridge while I untied my apron. I studied her petite frame while her back was to me. Narrow shoulders and tiny hips. I got my va-va-voom, as Regan called it, from my grandmother. She was all butt by the time she was sixty. I tried to eat a little better than she did to hold off the butt-takeover but, honestly, I owned a bakery. It was only a matter of time. Mom's hair had shifted from salt-and-pepper to a soft grey over the last couple of years. She insisted she had more important things to worry about than her appearance and I assured her she had nothing to worry about. She was one of those women who looked as natural and beautiful with grey hair as she did when she was younger with jet-black locks.

"How easy was it for you to walk away from Dad and me?" I blurted out, too tired to dress it up in social niceties.

She froze for a second, closing the door slowly, turning around with a cautious look on her face.

"Sorry," I added, when I saw the startled look in her eyes. "I didn't mean—"

She held up her hand. "It's the truth," she admitted. "Harsh, but honest. Are you thinking of leaving Regan?"

Her question was like a punch in the gut. I felt like dry heaving, since there wasn't any food in my stomach to actually throw up. "No."

Well that was good news.

"So you think he wants to leave you."

I swallowed hard, my cheeks heating as I fought tears. "It sure seems that way, doesn't it?"

She sighed, approaching me with outstretched arms as her hands touched my shoulders. She was my height, but for some reason whenever she talked to me like a mom, she seemed several inches taller. "I think you need to get some sleep."

"You think he wants to leave me?" I choked out, taking a step back.

She shook her head. "I didn't say that. But if you really want to have that conversation, you need to be as clearheaded as possible, which is hard to do when you've been awake for, what, thirty-six hours?"

I spoke, but the brewing breakdown forced my voice out in a whisper. "Tell me what happened with you and Dad," I asked again.

"Before I got sick we were like any other married couple. There were ups and downs. Even before he got sick." It took her a few years to acknowledge his alcoholism as an illness, now it was just part of the oral history of their life together.

"I remember you guys fighting a lot."

She nodded. "We did. When you were real little, though, and even before we had you, we were a lot like you and Regan."

"That's ... hardly reassuring." My eyes grew wide as panic swam through my chest.

"It wasn't meant to be," she replied flatly. "It's the truth. Most couples start out like that—normal, young, carefree, dreams, hard-working ..."

"When did things change?"

"When we stopped talking to each other." She nodded firmly, eyeing me with careful intention. "It was slow, like how freezing rain builds up on roads. Slick at first, but eventually it's a free-for-all of chaos. I don't think couples need to be up each others asses all the time, but marriage is the most important business anyone ever oversees." She arched an eyebrow, casting a quick glance around the physical business I'd owned and nurtured for years.

"And with the changes you guys are talking about bringing into the marriage, like a baby ... that's ... that's not a passive fly-by-night decision, Georgia. How much talking about this have you two done?"

I shrugged. "I mean, we're both family-oriented, and have been married for a few years ... I guess we just figured this was the next step. Isn't it?"

Mom poured two cups of coffee. "Here. Go sit. If you're not going to sleep, you might as well focus for this conversation."

As I slid into a booth in the front corner of the bakery, Mom flipped the "Open" sign to "Closed" and sat across from me.

"Um, what are you doing? These are hours of operation." I pointed to the bakery's hours stuck on the window next to us.

She took a deep breath. "What are the hours of operation for your marriage?"

I opened my mouth, but she cut me off.

"That was a trick question. It's twenty-four-seven."

"Whatever." I sighed. "I knew what you meant."

"I never remarried after your father for a reason. It wasn't just the schizophrenia. Sure, that was a huge part of it—I didn't want to burden anyone with that, not even you," she said sternly. She was growing fussy around my constant checking-in with her. We both knew, underneath, that's how it had to be, but she didn't have to like it.

"Why didn't you remarry, then?"

She shrugged. "Marriage just isn't for me. Sure, I've dated and will continue to date, and I enjoy relationships, but I also enjoy my space, and I really don't have the mental or emotional space to take on caring for another human being for the long haul right now. I've got you and I've got me, and that's where I'm at. Could that change? Maybe, but I've learned that my life works better when I force less of what I think I should be doing, and focus on what works and brings me peace."

I curled my lip and rolled my eyes. "You're sounding like Ember. All new-agey and surrender and peace."

"Georgia," Mom said in with a frustrated sigh, "how many things that you beat into the ground have turned out the way you wanted to?"

I stared at her, feeling my attitude morph into that of pre-adolescence. I wanted to tell her I wasn't in the mood for a character analysis from a woman who abandoned her family, but I wasn't a pre-teen and knew there was far more to the story than that. There always is.

"None," I answered honestly.

"You took your time opening this place." She gestured to our surroundings. My realized dream. "Yes, you worked hard, but you didn't force it. You searched for the right place, saved money for years working hard jobs, and you've carefully and thoughtfully built your brand. If something doesn't work, you try a different angle …"

I pressed two fingers against my temple, squinting at her. "How … what does this have to do with me and Regan?"

I felt like I was losing my mind. Exhaustion is a slow brain death.

Mom reached across the table and gently patted my wrist with a sweetly condescending smile. "You need some sleep. But I'll spoon-feed you this: organize your business priorities, and always communicate with the board regarding big changes. Make sure everyone is on the same page. And that you're being honest."

My chin quivered as the unspoken weaseled its way through my throat.

"I'm afraid being honest will push him away. If he's not gone already." I was a desperate mess of emotions. Fear and sadness about the things I'd been pushing deep down, and rage over his behavior, mixed with more sadness. "We're a mess right now, Mom." Finally, a tear forced its way from my eye down my cheek.

She sighed. "I know. It happens sometimes. You either work through it or walk away from it, but don't sit in it. And don't do the second until you've exhausted the first. Trust me."

"I have to go shower," I whispered in an effort to avoid a full-on breakdown.

"I'll make the meringues," she replied as if we were in the most casual conversation in the world.

I dragged my sorry butt out of the bakery and trudged up the stairs to our apartment. I used to enter the door on the left, back when the place was two apartments. Back before Regan, before Sweet Forty-Two, and before I gave a damn what anyone thought. But that door was sealed shut now. The contractor put a wall in front of it on the inside. You couldn't even tell a door had been there.

I blinked, pulling myself back slightly from rambling door metaphors as I entered the one on the right. The one where I was an adult in a struggling marriage, needing to know if it was worth fighting for.

Moving more sloth-like with each step I took, I kicked off my shoes and discarded my clothes piece by piece on my labored march to the bathroom. I thought about how nice a bath would feel for my throbbing lower body after being on my feet for most of the last thirty-six hours, but that would be too quiet, too Zen-like for how I was feeling now. Instead, I reached for the shower lever, turning the temperature knob to as hot as I knew I could stand it. I needed the roaring noise, and the pain of the scalding water pelting my skin.

Once my skin was drenched and red, I started feeling other things again. I saw Regan again on the dance floor with Nessa. I felt the abandonment of him turning his back to me in bed after I'd flown to Minnesota wanting to make love to him. I wailed above the static noise of the shower, sinking to my knees when I admitted to myself for the first time that I didn't know if I wanted children—and how above everything else, that was likely to be the final blow to a marriage that was already on life support.

How could I possibly look Regan in the eyes, bullshit from the last few weeks aside, and break his heart with the news that I didn't think I was cut out for motherhood? How could I do that to the best man I'd ever known—one who'd make a better father than I could ever imagine?

CHAPTER TWENTY-SEVEN
REGAN

I'D STOOD AT the door of Sweet Forty-Two, peeking in as Amanda worked in the kitchen and a couple with toddler twins binged on cupcakes in the front window. After a couple of minutes it was obvious Georgia wasn't there. It was just as well, since I didn't want to do any of this in her place of business.

I ascended the stairs and heard water rushing through the pipes. She was in the shower. Unlocking our door, I planned to set my bags in the bedroom, and use the rest of the time to think about what I was going to say to her—and figure out how not to scare the shit out of her when she got out of the shower. She hated being startled almost more than anything.

Before walking into our bedroom, I decided to set my duffel bag in the hallway so she'd see it on her way back from the bathroom. The rest of my plan went out of the window, though, as I heard a sharp cry come from the bathroom. I paused, my feet cemented in place as my heart raced. It didn't sound like she'd hurt herself from a fall, or anything like that. It was a different kind of cry. A broken scream of complete heartsickness.

Within a couple strides I was at the bathroom door with a sweaty, shaking hand on the knob. My chest was still pounding with anxiety. I argued with myself about how comforting I could actually be for her in this moment, since I was the one that caused the horrible sounds spilling from her chest.

After a few seconds of her coughing, sobbing, and more coughing from crying so hard, I knocked on the door, still wanting to minimize scaring her. "Georgia? Georgia it's Regan. Can I come in?"

The crying stopped for a second. So did the shower.

"No!" she wailed.

I fought wanting to turn the knob. She never locked the bathroom door, and I couldn't bear the pain in her voice, but I knew that violating her requested privacy at the moment wasn't likely to help my case any.

"Please?" I tried again.

"No Regan. Don't come in. Please. What are you doing here, anyway?"

I swallowed hard, but it hardly helped the shaking in my voice. "I need to talk to you. I ... I'm, uh ... I'll be in the living room when you're, uh, ready, okay? Unless ... unless you want me to leave."

I was dizzy with anxiety while waiting for her response. I wanted so badly to fix this, but I didn't know how. I barely even knew the totality of what was wrong. I had a feeling that, for both of us, Nessa was just the catalyst of a whole bag of shit we'd been ignoring, but I was too strung out on worry and anger and maybe a touch of depression to begin to tease it all apart.

Finally, her voice came from the other side of the door again. Flat and exhausted. "You don't have to leave."

I exhaled. She didn't ask me to stay, and she didn't tell me not to leave, but she didn't kick me out, either. That was something.

I planted myself on the couch, which overlooked the ocean. The day was sunny, and white caps from the wind speckled the top of the water. I sat and leaned forward, my elbows digging into my knees as I cradled my forehead in my hands. I was exhausted and scared.

This position left my back to the rest of the apartment, only allowing me to hear the bathroom door open; soft, slow footsteps that seemed to pause for a moment before heading to the bedroom. It was all I could do not to turn around. But I didn't want to invade the privacy she'd requested, and I sure as hell didn't want her to see the mess I'd become over the last twelve hours. Not yet, anyway.

It was torture waiting for her to emerge from the bedroom, but once she did, I wanted to crawl into a hole. She walked around the large couch, bypassing the available cushion next to me in order to sit cross-legged on the oversized footrest facing me. She was wearing short pink cotton shorts dotted with a cupcake and ice cream sundae pattern. A long, snug white tank top hugged her breasts and waist. Her hair was wet and disheveled, the short pieces in the back scattered every which way, and the long pieces in front tucked behind her ears. I wanted to touch her, feel her skin and hug her and tell her I was sorry. But, I couldn't. Her face was pale, eyes grey underneath from lack of sleep and crying, I knew I had to give her her space while we talked.

Or sat in awkward silence.

"Look at me," I finally pleaded when she'd stared at her fingernails for two whole minutes. I know because the Cheshire Cat clock ticked away on the wall behind her.

When she did, I wanted to take it back. Her usually bright blue eyes were bloodshot and dull. She moved them around my face, her lips parting a couple of times as if she wanted to say something, but couldn't bring herself to.

Sliding off the couch and onto my knees, I inched my way to her. Her pouty lips were downturned, hopelessly frowning at the mess that lay before us. It was my mess, and I had to clean it up.

"Georgia," I started softly as I sat back on my heels, keeping my eyes in line with hers.

She looked at me out of the corner of her eye before shifting her gaze out the window while she spoke. "Did you kiss her?" she whispered, her voice hoarse.

I shook my head. "No. Never."

"Did you want to?"

"No," I answered quickly, then I sighed. "I don't think so."

Her wet eyes, brimming with tears, finally focused on mine. "You don't think so?"

I eyed her, helpless. "I don't know why I would have danced with her like that, Georgia. But, I don't want to start there."

She curled her lip. "Where do you want to start?"

I cleared my throat, not wanting to lose it before I really said much of anything. "With the awful things I said to you on the phone this morning."

Seemingly caught off guard, Georgia's face turned pink as her chin quivered and her mouth opened in a silent cry. She pulled her knees up to her chest and let her head fall to them, her back heaving, wracked with not-so silent anymore sobs.

She didn't flinch from my touch as I rested my head against her on her knees, wrapping my arms as far around her as I could in this awkward position. "I'm sorry for the things I said."'

"They're all true!" she shouted into the cave formed by her body folding over itself. "I know they are and you know they are. I just didn't know how bad I'd been fucking up, or how resentful you were about it."

"I … it's not … I'm not resentful," I started to say, then caught myself. We'd get nowhere, today or ever, if I wasn't brazenly honest. "Okay," I admitted. "I'd been getting resentful. But that just tipped things over. Or it was brewing in the background, I don't know …"

Georgia lifted her head, her tearstained and swollen face looking empty and angry. She fought her emotions as she spoke, her voice stuttering through persistent tears. "Y—you do all those things for me. All the th-things you sa-said. I know that. I thought you were just supporting me."

"I was," I cut in, pleading. "I do support you."

Her eyes pinched at the sides as her head collapsed again against her knees. "But I don't support you like that."

I was silent. I didn't know what to say. I didn't want her to feel like this, not in a million years. But there were shards of truth in the words she spoke that couldn't go unsaid. There were more times in the last few months that I'd felt alone in my marriage than I cared to count or remember.

"I mean to," she started again, lifting her head and wiping under her eyes. "But I fucked up, and I'm sorry. I just … supporting you has to go beyond me not giving you shit whenever you're on the road. It's just … you are the only person I've ever trusted completely in my entire life, Regan."

My jaw flexed as I took in the words, ones she's repeated since the early days of our relationship. Back when we were both treading carefully. Both wounded. Both needing security. I stood up, unable to keep it in any longer.

"That's too much pressure for me, Georgia!" I hadn't meant to shout, but I did. She jumped, looking at me, betrayed. "I can't be the guy with all the gold stars next to his name. I'm not perfect, Georgia. I never was, and never will be. I'm human and can't think that if I make a mistake that will be the end of us." As nice as the pedestal had been, it was time to tear it down.

Georgia's tears seemed to dry on the spot. She stood in a flash, gesturing her hands wildly. "That's a hell of a leap, Regan. From being so-called perfect to dancing with another woman in a club. You're suggesting this is my fault—that my expectations of you, or preconceptions, or whatever, drove you to another woman?"

I huffed, setting my hands on my hips. "That's not fair."

"You're fucking right it's not." Gone were the tears, replaced by rage as she cursed through her raw voice.

I ran my hands through my hair, tugging tight in frustration as I took a deep breath. "I think we need to back up."

She gestured to me before folding her arms under her breasts. "Be my guest."

I looked up to the ceiling. "This isn't even about Nessa."

Georgia shocked me with her flat response. "I didn't think it was." She stepped closer to me, speaking quietly as if trying to hold it together. From yelling or crying, I couldn't tell. "But what I want to know is what happened to get there. To her."

Looking down, I found my wife waiting expectantly for my answer. I collapsed into the chair behind me, biting the inside corner of my lip as I spoke. "I'm not happy," I admitted for the first time out loud.

"Neither am I," she echoed, sounding startled at her own voice.

CHAPTER TWENTY-EIGHT

REGAN

WE'RE NOT HAPPY.

Flailing in the aftershocks of our dual confessions, we stared at each other like deer in headlights. That stupid fucking cat clock ticked away, highlighting all the moments we said nothing, staring at each other like strangers and heartbroken lovers at the same time. She was hurt, so was I, and I didn't know how much fight I had in me. I'd spent a long time fighting for the both of us. Loving for the both of us. In that moment, however, I barely had enough energy to stand.

I sank deeper into the chair with a sigh.

"I'm no martyr," I started, though I wasn't sure if this was a martyr's final act, or not. "You love me. I know you do. You just show it differently than I do. Aren't there, like, five love languages, or something?" I stared into space, mentally scanning our therapist's bookshelf.

A therapist we desperately needed an appointment with if we made it out of this conversation alive.

"How do you know I love you?" She dragged the footstool two feet in front of the chair, sitting cross-legged on it once more.

I looked up at her. "What?"

She shrugged, speaking plainly like we were discussing the weather. "How do you know I love you?"

I looked down, blinking long and slow before answering. "You're kind. You're enthusiastic about my music, you're the loudest at all the shows and you're interested in the projects I'm working on. You send me stuff when I'm out on the road."

"That's all stuff," she replied flatly. "Just stuff. How do you feel it? How do you really know that I love you? Anyone can do all the things you just said I do."

Swallowing hard, I continued. "It's just a feeling that I have, Georgia. It's so intangible, like the wind. The way you stroke my face when we make love. The noise you make when I kiss your neck, all of it …"

"Then tell me why you aren't happy, Regan."

She was begging me for truth. Honesty.

I let it fly. "Because I feel like the biggest way you show me you love me is by letting me love you. And while that's huge, and I'm honored that you chose me, I need more, Georgia. I need—"

"You need someone to fight for you, too." Her voice rose to a high pitch at the end of her sentence as tears started to fall again.

It felt like my chest had been cracked open as her words, my deeply-hidden truth, were spilled out before us. I couldn't help the few tears that escaped my yes.

I nodded. "And you deserve someone who is honest about more than their whereabouts. You deserve someone who isn't just focused on protecting your feelings if it means hiding theirs. Why aren't you happy?" I asked quickly.

Her chin quivered as she considered her answer. "Because, in the end, I fear you'll choose music over me. And I don't know what that even means. It's your passion and runs through your blood, just like the bakery does for me … I … my insecurity isn't your problem."

"Until I proved your fears right with Nessa …"

She tilted her head to the side. "What is that about?" she asked quietly.

I shrugged. "I got carried away. It wasn't even attraction. I just … got swept up with the tour and her story and the violin … I …"

"She was new."

Looking at Georgia, I found her pokerfaced, impossible to read.

I shook my head, slowing down before offering a sigh. "I guess. There were no complications. NO questions about where we were or who we were with, because we were with each other. There was little to explain or worry about. No family drama, and she wasn't pressuring me to have a baby."

Georgia's head recoiled as if I'd slapped her. "You think I'm pressuring you to have a baby? We talked about that together."

"What was I supposed to say, Georgia? I figured as time went on … I figured as time went on I'd get fully behind the idea, but the truth is—"

"You're scared," she cut in.

"No." I felt pain deep in my bones as I prepared my next sentence. One delivered with rough tears. "The truth is I don't know if I want to have kids. At all. And I'm sorry." I pressed my face down into my hands as I cried through the rest of my words, unable to look at what they might be doing to her. "I'm sorry, Georgia. I just don't know if I'm ready, or if I'll ever be. I felt like our life was already revolving around a baby we didn't have yet and I wasn't … I'm not ready. And no matter what fun I thought I could have with someone else and, I promise you, it never went there, I was stuck."

"Stuck?" she asked, and I could hear the tears in her voice.

"I didn't want to lose you. I don't want to lose you. And I was afraid. Tired and afraid. Tired of you not trusting me, even before this whole Nessa shit, and afraid of what would happen to us if we had a baby we both weren't ready for."

Georgia sniffed, but I still wasn't looking at her. "Is that why you turned me down three days ago?"

God, has it only been that long?

I nodded, lifting my head and dragging the heels of my hands under my eyes. "And I'm sorry. I knew it would fuck with you, but I didn't know what else to do. I was scared to tell you. I didn't want the fight."

Georgia stared at me for a long time, her tongue working against the inside of her cheek. Licking her lips, she rolled her eyes up to the ceiling before she spoke. "I was scared, too."

"Everyone gets scared, I guess. But this is diff—"

She held up her hand. "No, Regan. I was scared that you'd leave if I didn't or couldn't give you a baby. I thought you'd be such a good dad, but ..."

"But what?"

"I don't think I'm ready for a baby right now. Or if I'll ever be. Or if we'll ever be ..."

I was confused by the fresh sobs overtaking her body. Hadn't I just said the same thing? Why did she seem like she was mourning something?

"Hey ..." I reached forward and tugged the footstool toward me. Once it reached my legs, I lifted her chin with my index finger. The first intimate touch we'd had in weeks. "Why are you crying?"

She took a deep breath, swallowing a few times before she was able to speak. "Be ... because what if I want kids in the future and you don't? What if you do? What if one of us does and the other one doesn't? I don't feel like I don't want kids ever, just not right now. But you ..."

I nodded. "I know ..."

What more could I say? The what-ifs hung over us like a thick raincloud, and there were no solid answers to be had in our stormy corner of the living room. Finally, I said the only thing I could think of. The only way to put this on hold until we had some time to clear our heads and organize our thoughts.

"Let me put you to bed."

She nodded, not fighting me when I cradled her in my arms and walked her to our bedroom. She looked worn out as I pulled the sheets up over her and sat on the edge of the bed next to her. I smiled when I stroked my hand along her jawline, uncertain of a lot of things, but not how much I loved her. I still didn't know if that was enough, but it had to be for tonight.

"Regan," she called to me, opening her eyes.

"Yeah?" I whispered back.

She reached for my hand. "Get in bed with me?"

A lump formed in my throat as she slid over and moved the covers so I could join her. Settling into her coveted side of the bed I pulled her close, reveling in the feel of her breath against my neck.

Suddenly, her body shook with tears she produced from deep in her chest. She pulled back, reaching for my face with her hands.

"I'm not leaving you, Regan. Not ever. I don't care how we have to work through this, but we have to. We have to. You're it for me."

I choked out a small sob, reaching for her face with one hand as she held mine. "I love you, Georgia."

"But if this is too much for you and you need to walk away when we've done all we can …"

"Don't," I cut her off. "Don't say that."

"If this doesn't turn out the way we hoped it would," she continued. "I just want to remember right now. And me holding you. Will you let me hold you tonight? You've held me for a long time …"

I had no words left as my wife shifted up on the bed to allow my head to rest on her shoulder, where I let tears fall onto her chest, and her tears streaked down her cheeks and neck to land on my forehead. I don't know how long we stayed like that, but when we finally fell into a deep sleep, I didn't wake till morning.

Swollen eyed, war-torn, and with more questions left than I had when I first showed up. I was sure the same held true for her, too.

Georgia slept, snoring softly next to me while I reached for my phone and sent a quick text to Yardley.

Me: I'm going to miss Chicago. I'll call as soon as I know more.

Yardley: Got it. Are things okay?

Me: Not yet.

Professional as always, Yardley didn't respond to my last text. I sighed, letting my phone slide to the floor as I shifted into a more comfortable position and brought Georgia's head onto my chest, kissing the top of her head.

Even though she was usually a deep sleeper, my kiss woke her, and she looked around for a second before tilting her head to look into my eyes.

"Hey, I thought I was holding you?" she said of how we fell asleep.

I kissed her forehead, stroking her lower back with my thumb. "You were. Now I'm holding you."

A small smile formed on her lips, right along with fresh tears in her eyes. "I think that's how this is supposed to work …"

I swallowed hard. "I think you're right."

"It's not going to ever be perfect, you know."

I nodded. "I know. I won't be, either."

"I know," she answered definitively. "And we have a lot of stuff to talk through."

"Yeah."

"But we should keep holding each other," she said, snuggling into my chest, kissing my shoulder.

I sighed, feeling the first twinge of hope I'd felt in months. "Yeah. Yeah, we should."

***

I fell back asleep at some point, with Georgia's head on my chest, but when I woke up, I was alone in our California-king sized bed that took up a third of our room. Rubbing sleep from my eyes, I realized I smelled bacon. The clock read twelve o'clock, which had to mean noon given I knew we'd slept all last night, and it was bright as hell outside, but I was so disoriented, I wasn't sure if I was waking up in the right day anymore.

Staggering into the kitchen, still rubbing my eyes, trying to make sense of time and space, I caught a glimpse of Georgia at the stove, flipping eggs and pulling a baking sheet lined with bacon from the oven. She wore the same tank and shorts from yesterday, but had a comical "French maid" apron tied around her waist. She'd bought it as part of a costume used to seduce me one night a few years ago, and she nearly died from laughter a few days later when she came home from work for dinner one night and saw me moving around the kitchen with it tied around me like a loin cloth.

"Hey," I half-whispered, knowing she most hated being startled in the kitchen.

She jumped a little, but turned with a soft smile on her face. By the way my eyes felt as I continued rubbing at them,

I was guessing they looked like hers—swollen and pink from tears and interrupted sleep.

"Morning." She grabbed two mugs from the hooks underneath one of our cabinets and poured us cups of coffee, sliding them in front of two stools positioned at the counter. We had a more formal dining table, but we ate most of our meals together at this counter.

"Thanks."

"Welcome," she answered softly.

I couldn't remember the last meal she'd cooked for me. Pastries, sure. And, to be fair, she served people food every single day as her job. She didn't ask me to play the violin for her on a daily basis. I did sometimes, but … that's different. Still, I just sort of took over cooking early in our relationship and neither of us questioned it, but it sure felt nice to be served in my own home.

Despite all the words passed between us last night, and even after sleeping in each other's arms off and on, there was a suffocating uneasiness left hanging over us. So much left to say.

I stared at my wife like she was a sort of stranger. Or someone I once knew. Or who once knew me. And, not totally in a bad way, either. Last night she held me. Tight. Last night she admitted that our marriage might not turn out "the way we'd hoped," but that she would do her best to make it work. She was scared, sure, evidenced by the entirety of our discussions last night, but she was angry, too. And had every right to be. She listened to me admit to pulling away from her, reveal I wasn't sold on the idea of kids, and had images of me dancing with another woman in her mind.

And still, she wanted to make it work.

She didn't want to run. Or, if she did, she wanted to make it work more than she wanted to run.

"What?" she asked, sliding a bacon and eggs-filled plate in front of me. "Are you okay? What's wrong?"

I shook my head, grinding my teeth together as if that was ever useful in stopping tears. "Come here."

Without a word, Georgia walked around the counter and stood in front of me. I extended my hands, figuring things couldn't get much more hopeless than they had been in our living room last night, and she walked into my arms. I hooked my legs around the back of hers, pulling her in closer as I wrapped my arms around her shoulders. I wanted to kiss her, badly, but wasn't sure if she was ready for that. Or, honestly, if I was. I didn't want it to gloss over all the work we had ahead of us.

But she's your wife.

Moving my hands to her face, I pulled her into a hard, fierce kiss. I didn't let go of her lips until she relaxed in the kiss and it felt like she was kissing me back.

"I'm a shit," I said, pulling away, both of us slightly breathless. "You deserve better than whatever the fuck quarter-or-mid-or-whatever-life crisis I'm in right now, if that's even a thing."

My hands stayed on her face as I spoke. She brought her hands to my wrist and perched them there, not pulling back or pushing me away.

"I deserve you." Her eyes moved wildly across my face, wide and vulnerable. "And you deserve me."

"We've got so much shit to talk about." I sighed, resting my forehead against hers.

She nodded, keeping her hands on my wrists as mine stayed on her face. "We've got to trust each other again. Figure out what we want. Decide if we're all in …"

"I want to be all in," I admitted in a gravelly whisper, anguished at even the thought of losing her. I decided I'd have ten million kids tomorrow if that's what it was going to take to get her to stay with me. That she was worth whatever compromises I'd have to make.

But, as we sat silent, pressed into each other like we were weathering more than just an emotional storm, something deep inside me told me we wouldn't be in that position. That the vows we spoke to each other in Cape Cod three years ago were being put to their first, of what would likely be many, tests. For better or worse.

Georgia pulled back, pinching my chin between her thumb and forefinger. Her eyes were tired and glassy, but she smiled as she spoke. "I'm all in, too. Always."

CHAPTER TWENTY-NINE

CJ

ORD WAS REGAN wasn't coming back to the tour at all. I hadn't spoken to him or Georgia since Minneapolis, but I told everyone that I'd believe it when I saw it. The day Regan left, Nessa told me he'd gone to California to patch things up with Georgia. I wanted to check in with them, but I was pissed about the broken nose that left me with two black eyes that were now fading to a god-awful green. Clearly Regan needed a timeout if he was going to start swinging at me.

Still, I had a job to do. We were in Chicago, without Regan, and with no real plan. Yardley had tucked me into a few songs with The Brewers, and some of the guys and me had a little drumline thing, but I was feeling a lot like extra baggage by the time we rolled into the Windy City.

"I've got an idea." Nessa plunked down next to me in the bar at the hotel the night before our first show.

I gave her a sideways glance. "Talking to me now?"

For the past several days, she tried to make it my fault that Regan had taken off, which left a couple of acts high and dry. I didn't even respond to the bullshit and, it seemed, she'd finally calmed down.

"You wanna hear my idea or not?" Her tone was a lot shorter than I'd expect for someone who's fault it actually was that Regan wasn't here. Even if that was an unfair assessment.

I shrugged, taking a sip of my beer. "Shoot."

"I'm playing with Moniker tonight. Just before your act with Regan normally takes place. Why don't you and I do a few songs together?"

I laughed with a mouth full of beer, which burned as hoppy bubbles pushed their way through my nose. "Yeah, okay. You've been a giant scardey-cat, or whatever, with that violin till now but, sure, why don't you go ahead and try to fill Regan's shoes."

She recoiled like I'd slapped her, her cheeks turning pink as she swallowed and looked away. Without another word, she stood to leave.

I grumbled, grabbing her arm and turning her around. "Sorry."

"You're an asshole," she replied, quiet.

I nodded. "Yeah, I am. Sit and have a drink. Let's try this again."

Five minutes later, Nessa was halfway through a dirty martini.

"Easy there ..." I eyed the toxic concoction. "That shit'll kill ya."

"Hmm," she hummed, taking another sip. "And your steady diet of beer and cigarettes is superior?"

Grinning, I clinked my bottle against her glass. "Point for Nessa."

"Why'd you send Georgia that video?" she asked, sliding an olive into her mouth, chewing it slowly.

"Why'd you dance with my married cousin?" I shrugged.

"We were just dancing, for fuck's sake."

I sighed. "For you, it was just dancing. For Regan ..." I trailed off, still not really wanting to get involved.

"Are you saying he wanted me, or something?"

I rolled my eyes. "Please. Sure, you're hot as hell and know how to give men a run for their money, but Regan's game is monogamy." Shrugging again, I sighed. "I don't know if it would have gone there, but …"

"You didn't want him to find out," she answered.

"I believe you're the kind of girl he'd have fallen for if he were single." It was honest, and not something I'd admitted to Georgia or Regan. "But he hasn't been single for a long time and isn't that guy anymore."

She huffed. "Shouldn't you let people run their own love lives? Given what I hear about yours?"

An irritated grin formed across my mouth. "You're awfully bitchy for someone who came to me for a favor."

"A favor for you," she shot back.

"Look," I sighed, rolling my head back, "yeah I believe people should run their own love lives. But I also know sometimes we get so bogged down in our own shit that we can't see what's right in front of us."

She opened her mouth, but I cut her off. "As for my love life? Yeah, it's fucked. For now."

When Frankie and I last spoke, we just agreed that she'd come to Chicago. We hadn't talked since, and I didn't know her plans. It was a real bitch to give her the space she needed, when I needed her. I was scheduled to be here for a week so, in theory, I knew she could come at any time. She had the itinerary and show schedule—the rest was in her hands.

"So," I continued with a dismissive eye roll. "What? You wanna play a set together? That'd be cozy."

"I wanted to," she started, bitingly. "But I don't think so anymore."

I squinted at her. "Oh please … because I hurt your feelings? Because we had a grown-up conversation? Get a grip, grab your violin, and meet me in my room in ten minutes." I stood, tossing a twenty on the bar, more than enough to cover both of our drinks.

She stared at me blankly for a few seconds, chewing the inside of her cheek. "You're lucky I'm buzzed enough to ignore your personality for a while."

"I think I'm the lucky one, buttercup. If you're this fucking pleasant to work with when you're buzzed, I can't wait to see what you're like sober."

***

Nessa was fine to work with, if just a little nervous at first. Yardley didn't need much convincing to slide us into the lineup, and I think she and I were both relieved when Nessa nailed her songs with Moniker without a hitch. I never got the full story on what the holdup with her playing those songs was, but it didn't matter. She nailed them, was as natural on the stage with her violin as she was with her vocals, and it was pretty easy to play with her.

She was a little less polished than Regan was, but I doubted that was anything the audience could pinpoint without coaching. She flew through solos and complicated flows with me with ease. We only did a few numbers, easy ones for her that didn't need a lot of review—Turkey in the Straw, Cotton-eyed Joe, and a piece of Devil Went Down to Georgia she was familiar with, and we only had to run through five or six times in rehearsal.

Nessa seemed to settle into her natural state on stage, a lot like Regan, actually. She played the crowd with energetic movements and fast, complicated solos, which they always loved. I did end up feeling a little bad for being a dick the night before, but it was what it was and I'd said what I needed to say.

It was a short set with Nessa, but I was happy to get a little more stage time to keep my mind off when Frankie was going to show up, if she didn't change her mind.

There was an unusually high-end after party waiting for us in the more uppity of the two bars in the hotel we were crashing at. Word was, Yardley organized it with friends of hers who were still, miraculously, in the newspaper business. I didn't think there was any young blood in newsprint any more. Either way it was more media coverage, and none of us were dumb enough to turn that down.

After patting my friends on the back and engaging in small talk and elbow-rubbing for a half hour, I found myself a quiet stool at the end of the bar and ordered a beer. A side benefit of a cross-country tour like this was the opportunity to try out the local beers at each stop. Coming from New England, I was spoiled with what seemed like hundreds of local microbreweries that were all on top of their game. Turns out, the rest of the country seemed to be coming along nicely, too. So far, Seattle was tops, but Chicago was in a close second with what the bartender told me was Half Acre Daisy Cutter Pale Ale.

Scanning the crowd as I enjoyed my beer, I watched as everyone schmoozed, or pretended to schmooze, but I was so far away in my head that I couldn't even pretend tonight. For days I'd been tossing around what to do about my dad. I still couldn't believe he'd look me up, let alone track me down at Frankie's. With a heavy sigh, I ordered another drink from the bartender who looked about my age.

"Something stronger," I said, sliding my empty pint toward him.

"Stronger beer or just stronger?"

"Just stronger."

He set a bottle of Jack Daniels in front of me. "You a whisky guy?"

I nodded. "Yep. Johnnie Walker if you have it. Straight up."

Seeming to pick up that I was in no mood for small talk, he poured me a glass of Blue Label and set it in front of me before moving onto other thirsty patrons.

I sipped it slowly, pretending I liked it. Because I'd need my dad's old standby swimming in my stomach to do what I knew had to be done. I thought about asking for one more. Instead, I left my empty glass on the table and headed for the noisy streets of the Financial District.

Picking up my phone, I dialed the number from memory. It was a ten-year-old cellphone number, and I'd be lying if I said I wasn't hoping it belonged to someone else. After one ring, someone picked up.

"CJ?"

He wasn't the only one with the same cell phone number for over a decade. His voice hit me like a two-by-four in the back of the head. I wanted to sit, but needed to move through the adrenaline, so I walked fast, angry steps down the sidewalk.

"CJ?" he asked again, his voice sounding light and hopeful like he wasn't a piece of shit. I wanted to hang up. "You there?"

"Yeah." The first words I spoke to my father in over ten years. "If you had my number, why didn't you just call me instead of showing up at my girlfriend's house?"

That Frankie was still technically my ex-girlfriend wasn't a detail he needed to know.

His tone was softer now. A little hesitant. "I didn't think you'd pick up."

"I wouldn't have." I huffed, stopping to lean against a light post and light a cigarette.

It was a few seconds before he said anything. "So why'd you call me?"

After a long drag, I answered. "Because I couldn't get you to stay when I was a kid, but I can tell you to stay the hell out of my life now."

Words I'd wanted to say almost my whole life didn't feel as good as I thought they would. Because it didn't change any of the facts of who he was or how I grew up.

"Listen. Don't hang up," he added quickly.

I sucked on my cigarette like it was the only thing holding me together, because maybe it was. I was doing this thing by myself. No friends, family, or Frankie by my side. No one to coach me through it or hold my hand. I had to face him alone, the way he left me. Even if it wasn't face-to-face, it was the best I could do, and the most I was willing to do at the moment.

"What?" I snapped. "Are you dying, or something, and smoked me out to try to make everything right?"

"No," he answered.

To my confusion, I felt a twinge of relief. I chalked that up to being a non-sociopathic human, rather than actually wanting him to live.

"Then what?" I demanded for a second time, making my way back to the hotel to avoid the shady alleys that awaited me if I continued forward.

He sighed and went quiet for a while. "I was hoping we could do this face-to-face. Maybe I could come to one of your show—"

"No," I cut him off. "Don't come anywhere I am. Got it? Now, tell me what you tracked me down for or I'll hang up and change my number and make damn sure you never find me again." My anger was hot and loud, crashing into my brain like hurricane waves against the boardwalk at home.

I reached the hotel before he spoke, so I continued walking. I was afraid if I stood in one place for too long I'd punch something.

Finally, words came through the phone and stopped me in my tracks.

"I'm sorry, CJ. For everything."

Dizzy with rage, I lit another cigarette.

The fucking nerve of this guy.

"Oh that's rich," I seethed. I didn't even know what to say next. "What brought on this moment of bullshit clarity?"

"My ten-year-old son," he answered flatly.

I'd known for years that he had kids. I never knew how many, their ages, or anything else. Rendered speechless, I grabbed a seat on the nearest bench and leaned forward, holding my head together.

"I found out Miriam was having a boy a week before your high school graduation," he started.

"Shut up," I growled, but left the phone to my ear.

"I'd thought about you each time the girls were born, of course," he continued, telling me I had half-sisters, too. "But when we found out there was a boy … I just … I couldn't—"

"Deal with what you'd done?"

"Yeah," he sighed his answer.

"Sucks, doesn't it?"

"And now he's turning into this young man and showing me all this stuff I missed with you, and he's into music and I—"

"Stop," I growled, standing, needing to end this conversation as soon as possible. "I don't care that some kid you had with your mistress suddenly implanted a conscience in that empty space you call a chest. I don't care if he plays the drums or the fucking flute or a goddamn trombone. I don't give a shit," my voice cracked, "if you've got daughters who think the sun shines out of your ass. Because I know it doesn't. And I'll never forgive you. Leave me the fuck alone."

I ended the call, wishing there was a phone to hang up and throw against the wall that wouldn't cost me six hundred dollars. I navigated my way back to the hotel with clouded vision and a pounding head from holding back tears I'd gone over twenty years without shedding.

All I needed to do was feel my way to my hotel room, and try to sleep away these feelings before tomorrow's show.

CHAPTER THIRTY

CJ

I SLEPT HARD. THAT much I knew when I woke to repeated knocking on my door. My head was pounding and my eyes were so heavy I thought I'd have to pry them open. To my dismay when looking at the clock, I realized I hadn't slept the day away like I'd wanted. It was only eight in the morning. Sure, ten hours of sleep was exponentially greater than anything I was used to on the road, but it wasn't enough to make up for last night.

To make up for him blasting into my life in the same way he left—like a tornado. The seismic pressure of last night's emotions set my muscles rigid and on edge, vibrating as if waiting for the next blow so they could react. My head felt like it had been slammed against a brick wall and left there. Walking to the door took extra effort. I scanned the itinerary in my head before reaching it, knowing for certain I had no responsibilities today. Glaring at the white wood, I was annoyed that the Do Not Disturb sign was currently in a state of flagrant uselessness on the inside door handle.

"Who is it?" I forced out through a hoarse voice that only served to remind me how much I'd screamed last night—long after the phone call with Daddy Dearest ended, and into the pillow before collapsing into sleep.

"It's me," she said in a cool, confident tone. Needing only her voice to identify herself.

Frankie.

I cleared my throat. "Just a sec."

I wanted to swing the door open, swoop her into my arms, and set her on the bed with the deepest kiss I could. That was reason enough to pause. What I needed to do was splash cold water on my face to regain my sense of appropriate behavior with my ex-girlfriend, and to try to wipe the war-torn look from my eyes.

No luck on the second endeavor—my eyes were swollen like I'd smoked all the weed in Chicago last night by myself.

Shit. Oh well …

I'd slept in my jeans, apparently, but no shirt. Grabbing the plain white T-shirt from the floor, I threw it over my head before setting my hand on the door handle with the deepest breath I'd taken in weeks.

"You're here," I said with the best smile I could produce when I finally got around to opening the door.

Frankie stood grinning softly in the doorway, all five foot eight and sexy size twelve of her. A brown messenger bag hung over her shoulder while a small purple suitcase was perched on the floor next to her sandaled feet and bright yellow-painted toenails. "And one hell of a sight for sore eyes."

Her smile faded slightly as her eyebrows pulled in a little. "Sore eyes—I guess," she said, reaching for my face. Her soft, lilac-scented skin cupped my cheek as she grazed her thumb under my eye.

I swallowed hard, frozen in the doorway unsure what to do. Seeming to catch her breath in ex-boyfriend boundaries—boundaries she'd set—she dropped her hand, tilting her head to the side. "What happened?"

Stepping back, I pulled the door open, gesturing for her to walk in. She wore a teal sundress that swayed like petals just below her knees. Spaghetti straps criss-crossed in the back, showing off pink skin from what was probably only a short sun-screen-free stint in the sun. Her long, deep-brown hair was in a French braid that tapered off a few inches below her broad shoulder blades. My eyes fell to her slim, tight waist and curvy, God-help-me hips. I breathed in the floral scent of her wake, closing my eyes and demanding my brain commit it to memory if today didn't go the way I wanted it to.

Truth be told, I wished that once she was in, I could barricade both of us in that hotel room until we were ready to reemerge as a couple. I chuckled at the budding romantic in the back of my brain, closing the door behind her. All the evidence from the last couple of weeks suggested she would fly all the way here only to finalize our break and set the ultimate no-contact boundaries my behavior deserved. Not to reconcile.

"Let me take that for you." I slid the handle of her suitcase from her hand and wheeled it to the corner of the room by the window—far away from the door. "I wish I'd known you were coming. I'd have tried to not look so—"

"Run over?" Her eyes worked me over with such tender concern that I had to look down out of fear I'd forget the reason for this visit and act like a desperate puppy, only pushing her further away. "It was a last minute decision. I wasn't sure if I could ... you know ... go through with it. Once I landed I called you, but it just rang and rang until it hit your voicemail. Long night last night?"

Looking at the bedside table where my phone lay, I noticed a few missed calls. Giving a quick scroll, I saw two from Frankie, and one from my mom—complete with a voicemail I'd listen to later. Somehow, I'd never gotten around to calling my mother after last night. She rarely left voicemails, so I had a good guess as to what was contained in that forty-five second message, regardless of how she found out. To my knowledge, she hadn't spoken to my dad in about as long as I had.

Setting the phone down, I slouched onto the bed, hunching my shoulders and rubbing my hands over my face. "Yeah … a long night."

The conversation with my dad only lasted ten minutes, tops. But in reality it had been going on for more than ten tense, silent years. Looking up at Frankie, who situated herself on the queen bed across from me, crossing her ankles in front of her, I realized I could keep pushing her away, scorching any hope of her seeing the reformation I'd been working on or—more terrifyingly—I could be honest.

Leaving my hand perched over my mouth as if to filter the words as they poured out, I spoke. "I called my dad."

"You did?" she gasped. The pale blush of her cheeks deepened as her eyes took me in, wide and concerned. She swallowed hard, taking a deep breath.

I nodded, removing the hand from my face and lacing my fingers together in front of me as I sat with my elbows on my knees, still hunched over. I didn't know how long it would take for me to bounce back physically from the toll last night had taken.

"Wh—what'd you say?" She fidgeted, working the hem of her skirt between her thumb and forefinger.

"To leave you alone," I started with the easy stuff. Honest, but easy, and far away from the hole in my chest he'd carved out long ago.

She nodded, her eyes—brown like mine—darting around the room like she was grasping for the right thing to say. She wouldn't find it here, and through no fault of her own. There was no right thing to say.

"It was this whole thing," I continued, shaky as the disorganized flashes of last night forced their way into order in my brain. "He wanted to see me … knew I'd avoid his phone calls

… there was a lot of yelling." I pointed to my throat as an explanation of the persistent crackle in my voice.

Frankie shook her head slowly, fixing her eyes on me. I couldn't make eye contact, but from my periphery I saw her sit on her hands before speaking. "What was it about? Why did he want to track you down after all this time?" She shrugged, searching for an answer.

I wished I could tell her he was dying. That the doctors had given up hope and he had three months to live before the tumors strangled his insides. But, I couldn't. This was worse. Lingering. Permanent.

Bowing my head, I thought of the boy at the root of the phone call. Not just me—the one he'd left—but the one probably sitting in blissful ignorance in the spacious Long Island home Callum Kane had built for the family he chose. The boy who maybe had dirty blond hair like his mother. The boy I'd never seen, and never met, who haunted my dreams last night. The innocent kid, with a prick of a father, that I threw out with the bathwater of last night's conversation. The kid I disregarded.

"CJ?" Frankie's voice rose in panic before I realized I'd been lost in thought and had tears running over my cheeks. In a second she was by my side, her hand breaking mine free from each other as she laced her fingers between mine. "What?" she whispered, giving my hand a squeeze. "What happened?"

"I've got a ten-year-old brother," I forced out before my voice cracked into a sob I couldn't restrain.

It was all I could say for a long while. Minutes flowed one into another as I left my head in one hand, crying, as if it was something I'd always done. Frankie gripped the living daylights out of the other hand. She was silent, taking her free hand to rub the tense space between my shoulder blades.

In the middle of the agony, a thought swirled into my head. It wasn't just that I couldn't remember the last person I'd cried in front of—I'd never done it in front of Frankie, for sure—but I couldn't remember, no matter how long I searched my memory, the last time I'd cried at all.

The only thing that came to mind was a package that came via UPS a million years ago. A brand new baseball and glove that smelled of fresh leather. There was a small, square notecard that completed the deal. Have fun, slugger. I miss you. Dad. My mom watched helplessly as I rearranged the glove with a pair of kitchen shears, and said nothing when I hurled the ball over the neighbor's fence to let their Yellow Lab eat it for lunch.

It was my tenth birthday.

"I fucking hate baseball!" I growled, pulling my hand away from Frankie and scraping both hands through my hair, trying to hold my brains in. "I've always hated it!"

"Um … I …" Frankie whispered, pressing her hand firm against my back. "I know," she said, unaware of the memory in my head.

But she knew I hated baseball. She learned that the day she excitedly waved Red Sox tickets in my face like they were unicorn eggs. I had to gently reveal my loathing for the game—an atrocity worthy of excommunication from the State of Massachusetts, but one I rarely hid.

Still, she knew. And he didn't.

I yelled garbled combinations of consonants and vowels, cursing my father and the bullshit move of dumping a brother in my lap. A brother I couldn't ignore. Information I couldn't un-hear. A kid with a heap of shit for a father who was "into music," whatever that meant.

"Shh …" I heard her gentle whisper through my unrelenting noise as her hand stroked back and forth across my back like the soothing needle of a metronome.

"I don't know what to do ..." I managed a full sentence, lifting my head to find her in the same position she'd been for several minutes—next to me, stroking my back, with one leg tucked underneath her as she pored over me with empathetic eyes.

This wasn't how I'd planned my first face-to-face with Frankie since our breakup. I figured there'd be a few tears one way or another, but this wasn't quite the scene I'd pictured. With a long, shuddering breath, I forced the tears dry—which took more effort than expected, and wiped my hands across my face.

"Sorry," I said in a sigh. "I didn't plan for ... this." I ground my teeth together, pushing back a fresh wave of despair.

Reaching for my phone, I pressed the home button, grimacing that it had only been a half hour since Frankie arrived at the hotel. By the same token, it had been the longest I'd cried in well over a decade—combined. My head was pounding and I felt emptier than I did the night I was on the phone with Frankie when she found out about Clara. With tired eyes, I forced my gaze to Frankie's face. Her eyes were glassy, and she seemed to be holding her breath as if exhaling would break the dam in her eyes.

"Don't be sorry," she finally forced out, running a hand across the top of my shoulder and down my arm. She set her hand on my forearm, giving it a gentle squeeze. "Don't be sorry at all."

I glanced out the window, running the heel of my hands under my ever-swelling eyes. I figured it would be a miracle if I could see at all by sundown. "I'm a real fucking mess right now, Frankie. I didn't mean for you to fly all this way just for ... this."

Her hand moved to my face as she nudged my attention back to her. "For you. Not the you you want me to see, or pretend to be. I came all this way to see you, and … You're giving me you. All of it." So help me God, her thumb ran across my bottom lip and I stopped breathing.

Reaching up, I grabbed hold of her wrist, turning my face with eyes closed to inhale the garden scent she always sprayed there. I let my lips rest against the silky skin of her arm while I breathed her in. She was as still as could be. Finally, I opened my eyes, and caught her staring directly at me with her lips parted.

"Frankie," I started, setting her hand down between us, but keeping mine in place on hers, "I had this whole speech prepared … all the things I regretted, and was and wasn't sorry for, and ways I have changed or am going to change. But … I can't … I'm kind of beat up right now. I'm empty, and I can't—"

My macho show didn't last long as a few more tears announced their presence, betraying my speech. I cleared my throat, determined to at least get through this.

"Just bear with me?" I begged in the form of a question. "I just need a couple days to—"

Frankie grinned, cutting me off. "This is going to take more than a few days."

"I don't want to waste your trip out here. I don't want to blow this, Frankie."

Shifting her leg out from underneath her, Frankie sat cross-legged in front of me, moving the folds of fabric from her dress around her. She looked kind of like a cupcake in that moment—bright teal with yellow sprinkles from her painted fingernails, which matched her toes. In that instant, I not only missed everything about her that had been gone from my life for the last couple of months, but I missed Georgia and Regan, too. I felt desperately raw and alone and, for the first time in my life, I needed someone. And acknowledged it.

"CJ you haven't wasted anything. I meant what I said. I only ever wanted you—not the bizarro you from the stage. We had a lot of good times together—a lot. But, I've never felt—" A choked sob cut her off. She cleared her throat before continuing, seeming to ignore the delicate tears trickling down her cheeks. "I've never felt more connected to you than right now."

I managed a grin. "All I had to do was bawl like a baby?"

She chuckled. A light sound that warmed my chest. Shrugging, she grinned back. "Guess so."

"So what are you saying?" I hesitated to ask, not wanting to push this in a direction she wasn't willing to go. My heart raced, despite my eyelids protesting being awake. Being so open is exhausting.

Frankie took a deep breath, gently wiping under her eyes with her pinkies, assessing the damage to her makeup by the amount of black mascara on her fingertips. I reached for the box of tissues behind me, handing them to her while she seemed to mull over her answer.

"You're killin' me here," I admitted after what seemed like forever.

She smiled, staring at her black-streaked tissue as if it held the answer. "I'm saying ..." she trailed off.

I puffed out my cheeks, exhaling heavy.

"I'm saying," she continued with renewed resolve in her voice, "that I want to start over."

The words seemed too much for both of us as she broke into a full sob and I couldn't help the silent tears escaping my eyes. This was totally off the charts for me, and I didn't know what to do. I lurched forward, pulling her toward me and holding the back of her head as she sobbed into my shoulder. I let my tears stream off my chin and drip on her back.

"I want that more than anything," I said, resting my chin just off her shoulder, squeezing her tighter. "I am so sorry,

Frankie. For everything. Just … fucking everything. God, I was such an asshole."

Her head shook side to side before she pulled back. "You weren't always an asshole. Don't do that to yourself."

"Why would you forgive me? That's what you're doing, right?" I couldn't remember ever having being forgiven before by anyone besides family. And even then it was often accompanied with a frustrated smack upside the head or a resigned eye-roll. But not here, and not now. She was forgiving me with tears. And love.

Frankie sniffed, roping me into her gaze. "Sometimes that's all you can do before the anger eats you alive. I didn't know the depth of what you'd been through with your dad, or that you were willing to be like this in front of me." She gestured to me, chuckling and shaking her head some more, as if trying to prove to herself that this wasn't a dream.

"I was so pissed, CJ," she continued. "But seeing you like this …"

I hesitated to press on the point, but I was so tired and confused, baffled that this woman used the word forgiveness in an affirming way with me. "You forgive me because I cried in front of you?"

She shrugged. "Because you are being open with me. Raw. And you didn't plan it. It wasn't staged or orchestrated. It wasn't a gimmick or a gesture. You just helplessly offered yourself to me. Why are you questioning me?" she asked with a comical eyebrow arch. "Are you trying to talk me out of it?"

"God no!" I answered quickly, causing her to laugh. "No. I just … I'm trying to understand why you would forgive me for all my bullshit."

"Knowing you, it'll take a long while for you to forgive yourself. So, someone has to show you how. You did screw up, in a lot of ways. And forgiveness doesn't come with automatic trust, CJ—"

"I know," I cut in, reaching for her hand. "I know it doesn't. That's a time thing …"

"It is. But I'm willing to try if you are." She wiped away the last of the mascara from her cheeks.

I nodded, pulling her to me once more, so overcome by emotion that I could hardly stand it. "Please," was all I could say before the tears fell again.

"I'm so fuckin' tired," I said, trying to cover up the tears. I couldn't go from never crying to a puddle of mess in the span of a day. It was bullshit and overwhelming—probably as much for Frankie as it was for me.

She yawned almost instantly, her shoulders sinking. "So am I. I had to leave so early this morning."

I turned around, eyeing the pillows over my shoulder. Looking back at Frankie, the only desire I had was to hold her and never let go.

"Nap?" I asked with a shrug and the only grin I had left in me.

She nodded, slipping her sandals off. "Please."

At nine-thirty in the morning, my not-so-ex-girlfriend slid under the covers and backed into me where she fit like a glove, our bodies curving together. I draped my arm around her waist, pulling her in as close as I could get her. The last thing I remembered before falling to sleep was kissing her shoulder and telling her I loved her.

I wasn't awake long enough to hear her response, but it almost didn't matter. I wasn't saying it for reciprocity. I was saying it so she knew. Because I did and I'd try my best for her, always.

CHAPTER THIRTY-ONE
REGAN

GEORGIA AND I were in Dr. Weeber's office for the third time since I'd been home. Our first session was the Monday after I got back, which only gave us a day and a half of awkward tangos around our home before spilling everything to our therapist. As we hadn't seen her in quite some time, there was a lot to catch up on, and the reminder that regular checking in, both with each other and her, if needed, was vital in "watering the tree of our marriage." Those were her actual words. Despite the cheesy turn of phrase, not even Georgia rolled her eyes at the sentiment, which was more powerful on its own than the words uttered by our licensed marriage repair specialist.

Dr. Weeber listened in the first two sessions about the busyness that had become our lives, the various ways we were, or were not, supporting each other through the transitions, and, more specifically, the detailed events over the past couple of months that landed us in a heaping mess in her office. The tour, the trying to conceive, Nessa, and all of our unmet expectations.

"It can often be the case," Dr. Weeber opened our third session by reviewing what we'd discussed previously, "that unstated expectations are pre-planned resentments.

I winced internally at the sentiment. And, perhaps, a bit externally. Taking in the words, I sat silent for a moment, giving myself three inhales and exhales before responding, as Dr. Weeber herself had suggested Georgia and I practice with each other.

"No," Georgia answered quickly. She was still practicing the breathing response thing. "I don't want to resent Regan."

Her fingers interlaced with mine, she gave my hand a squeeze. Despite the pregnant pauses and downcast glances that highlighted our existence over the last two weeks, we'd spent more time in physical contact with each other than we had in ages. We hadn't had sex—not since the night after I got home and we were so wracked with anger, guilt, and sadness that we sought solace in each other. The next morning, though, it was glaringly apparent that the sex hadn't done anything to change the root of our discord. We didn't fight—hadn't since the night I came home—but we were both so raw that we agreed we should focus on our emotional relationship for a while.

Inexplicably, we'd become closer. Of course there were tough days in there when I wanted nothing more than to strip her clothes off, but I'd been able to redirect that. So had she, it seemed. Handholding resurfaced—like it had been at the beginning of our relationship, and we sought each other out for a stroke of the lower back, a kiss on the cheek, or an arm around the waist or shoulders.

It's like we were trying to trust each other again in ways we hadn't realized we'd lost it. We were trying to find each other again.

"I don't want to resent Georgia, either," I echoed.

Dr. Weeber nodded slowly, her sweet-and-sorry smile almost saying, you fools. "Relationships are, quite stereotypically, tangled webs," she started. "Patterns of behavior are learned over time, to the point that it can be tough to remember the motivation. Sometimes what can happen with couples, is they learn how to breed guilt in the other as a means to cry out for and receive the affection they're desperately seeking, but have lost the vocabulary to assert for themselves."

Georgia and I sat silent, staring—almost gawking—at our doctor.

"I do that," Georgia answered softly with a pinched, tear-laden voice. "Jesus Christ, I do that. And I don't know why. Regan's never withheld affection from me—not ever—but I still sometimes play games with him. I don't mean to—"

"Hey," I cut in with a whisper, turning my head to her. "It's okay. I know you don't mean to."

"Regan," Dr. Weeber interrupted with a warning tone. "Is it okay? Do you mean that? Or are you acting in the overburdened role of relationship martyr, wanting to avoid conflict to the point of preventing growth for you and Georgia?"

I swallowed hard. Dr. Weeber didn't mince words. It's one of the things I loved to hate about her. And the reason she was the perfect choice for me and Georgia. I sighed. She was right.

"You're right." I sighed again. "I mean, I know she doesn't mean to do it, so I just let it roll off my back most of the time. I don't want it to turn into a whole thing and have her feel beat up for something that's hard for her to change."

"I can't change it if you don't make me," Georgia said.

"Make you?" Dr. Weeber questioned. "Explain."

Georgia took a deep breath. "I mean, if there are no consequences for the behavior, what need would I have to change it? No, I don't do it intentionally to Regan. It's … habits. Old, old habits of, of …" she trailed off, reaching for a tissue.

"Receiving affection," the doctor suggested softly.

Georgia nodded, dabbing under her eyes.

"Both your parents responded well to the guilt … because that's what they had taught you. Right? You felt like you deserved love when you fixed something you felt guilty about and, in turn, you learned that things like the silent treatment and guilt were surefire ways to get people to crawl back to you, so to speak."

Georgia nodded again, sniffing before she spoke. "Yeah. And we've even talked about it here a million times, but it's hard."

"Because that's how you're wired," Dr. Weeber confirmed before turning to me. "And, Regan, you're a longstanding peacekeeper. Don't rock the boat and everyone stays safe and happy. Because as long as there's no fighting, you're good, right?"

I sighed, thinking back to the early days after CJ's dad left.

"Yeah," I answered. "That's right."

CJ had stayed at our house for what seemed like months back when I was in second grade, but it was probably a couple of weeks, while his mom nearly gutted the inside of the house. Not with construction, just lots of new furniture. And, I think a mild emotional breakdown. I'm sure from a psychological standpoint it probably wasn't the greatest idea for CJ to lose his dad and the entire contents of his house, except for his bedroom, in the span of a few weeks. That's probably why he spent so much time in his bedroom from an early age.

While I didn't understand what was going on, except for knowing Uncle Callum wouldn't be living with CJ and Aunt Christine anymore, I knew CJ was angry and upset. He hit me a lot when he didn't get his way. At first, I'd hit back, and we'd fight like little snot-nosed kids. Until my parents pulled me aside one day and said that CJ was going through a hard time, and we needed to be extra kind to him.

Which was true. We did. He was a hurting little kid and I was, for all intents and purposes, the older-brother figure.

"With CJ when we were kids," I started, "I saw how it was like a switch—when I just let him freak out but I didn't freak out back at him … he calmed down faster than if I engaged with him. That was my introduction to pacifism." I chuckled.

Dr. Weeber grinned. "The world needs pacifists," she assured. "So do marriages, from time to time. But it's not healthy to be locked into roles, because this isn't a play, this is your life."

I nodded. "Yeah." I had to stop, swallowing a few times in an effort to get ahold of myself as I leaned forward, afraid the tears would start.

Georgia's hand found the space between my shoulder blades where I often held tension. I relaxed the muscles immediately, but still held my breath.

"What is it?" she asked softly, as if we were in the privacy of our own living room.

I shook my head, sitting up with a great sigh. "I just couldn't … I couldn't …"

I took another deep breath, allowing some of the tears to drip like an annoyingly slow leaky faucet. "I couldn't keep him from hurting," I said of CJ. "I tried, I really did. We played sports and climbed trees and I brought out all my action figures and board games, but … he wasn't ever the same."

"Did you think you could fix it?" Georgia asked.

I shrugged. "I was in second grade. What did I know? He was just so damn sad all the time. Then he got angry. And he's stayed angry. I just thought if I'd tried harder, I could have made him feel better."

"Do you still think that?" Dr. Weeber was silent as Georgia and I talked.

"I haven't in years," I admitted. "But I try to stay out of his business—you know that. If he's angry I don't push him. If he's sad, or something that resembles sad, I don't leave his side, but I don't say anything."

At this, Dr. Weeber interrupted. "Regan, what are some negative outcomes for you when shouldering the emotional onslaughts with the grin-and-bear-it attitude?"

Looking at Georgia, I almost regretted what I was about to say, but figured since we were in the safety offered by our therapists spacious, white and seaside blue office, it was now or never.

"I feel a lot of the time like I'm either putting out fires or waiting for the next one."

Georgia visibly recoiled from my words, but didn't let go of my hand. I continued.

"I'm not on edge all the time, but that gets worse as time goes on—the anxiety. Like we'll have a long stretch of calm waters, and I let my guard down a little bit, then when the other shoe drops, big or small, I'm knocked off balance and it's sort of like that proves to me that I need to be on guard all the time."

"Expect the worst and you're never disappointed," Georgia offered.

I sighed again. "Yeah. But it's not like that all the time—"

"Regan," the doctor entered, but I waved her off.

"I need to get this off my chest."

She grinned. "Go ahead."

I turned toward Georgia, running a hand over my hair. "I love you. That I have some fucked up need to keep everything honky-dory all the time is not your fault. Yes, it's our problem together, but it didn't originate with you. Just like with your guilt stuff. I know I didn't cause it, but I have to live with it. We have to live with it. I think maybe we have an opportunity here to accept each other as we are and always work to be better. I don't want to exploit your weaknesses, Georgia."

She shook her head, looking down for a moment. "I don't want to do that, either. I feel like we've kind of been acting like high schoolers for a while …"

Dr. Weeber sighed contentedly. With a smile on her face, she gave us her plan of action. "We'll spend some time rewiring your language. Both of you. It's important to be able to state what you need, but even more dire that you two realize you'll never be one hundred percent of what each other needs. Humans were meant to live in communities. Friends, co-workers, and family are important aspects in life. Neither of you can or should shoulder everything the other is dealing with."

"Will you have a problem with me having female friends? I've got Ember, and—"

"I have a problem with you being friends with Nessa." Georgia put up her hand, her lips forming a thin line of repressed rage. It was as calm a voice as she seemed to be able to manage, though it still stung.

My face fell. I wasn't even attracted to Nessa, but my actions had provided no proof of that. "Okay," I answered, nodding.

"Do you mean that?" Dr. Weeber shot me a sideways glance as she asked.

I eyed her, then Georgia, then settled on gazing out the window for a few seconds. "I mean … we're part of the same tour, but she's not with our label, so it's not like she's a co-worker, or anything. She's become a friend—"

"Yeah," Georgia cut in, "I'll say."

Dr. Weeber motioned to Georgia to let me finish, but I turned to my wife, fighting rage and choosing rationality.

"I fucked up, Georgia. And I'm sorry. It was inappropriate, the way I handled my friendship with Nessa, but I wasn't even fully aware of what was happening. And that's never happened with me before, not just since I've been with you, but ever."

Georgia squeezed her eyes shut, crinkling her nose like she'd just stubbed her toe, or something. "I'm sorry."

My mouth dropped. "What?"

"It wasn't ever about Nessa. Not for you and not for me. It was about us all along, wasn't it?"

My heart raced at the possibility that we might actually have a real conversation about this. I nodded, agreeing, but wanting her to continue.

"I can't keep punishing you for my father's mistakes. Or my mother's, or any of the assholes that strolled in before you came along and showed me what it's like to be loved."

I took both her hands and, smiling, I kissed the tops of her knuckles.

"You're human," she said with sweet sarcasm. "And I have to deal with that."

I laughed. "I really am. And I have to deal with that too. And …" I continued, hesitating for a moment. "You're a grown woman, in a marriage with me. You might have a wounded child inside you but you aren't that hurt kid. I can trust you with my feelings. For better or worse."

Georgia brought one of my hands to her lips, kissing softly. "For better or worse."

I can't explain what happened in the moment her lips touched my skin, but it felt like some heavy shackles had been cut off my ankles, and all I had to do was take a step forward to be free of the chains.

Staring into the eyes of my wife, for the first time I had no doubt that she'd take that step with me, and we had the chance to be free of the weight of the past—together.

***

It was a wobbly few days after the session with our therapist. We'd uncovered a shitload of deep-as-hell issues, and were trying to figure out how to deal with them. We were the same people we were before, but now we were treating each other like those people, and not the little kids behind the masks. It felt a lot like walking around in the sun after ripping off thirty

Band-Aids. Raw, confusing, and a little painful. But, we didn't need the bandages anymore anyway.

I'd kept in regular contact with Yardley, assuring her that I didn't plan on bailing completely, but that I needed to talk things over with Georgia before I recommitted. I was cautiously optimistic that I'd be back in the fold by the NYC show, but if not, I'd really make a case for Massachusetts, if Georgia and I hadn't hashed out the details by then.

One Saturday night, while the tour was continuing on in Ohio, Georgia and I walked our dinner down to the beach across from our apartment. I'd finally received some text messages from CJ after the Chicago leg of the tour. He sent some videos of various acts and, in the most recent set of pictures he'd sent from the tour bus, there was a familiar face.

"Look at this." I grinned, facing my phone to Georgia once we set the blanket close to the shore. Low tide gave us some more space.

Georgia took the phone, and immediately her eyes lit up at the sight of a selfie CJ and Frankie had taken together. Sitting next to each other on his bed on the tour bus, their faces were screwed up in goofy smiles with their cheeks pressed together.

"Did you know?" Georgia asked, handing me back my phone.

I shook my head. "I haven't talked to him since the fight."

This was his way of apologizing for his role, though most of the blame was on my shoulders. I'd have felt bad for not reaching out first, but I had other things to deal with, and I knew he'd understand the need to be selfish in this instance.

"I still can't believe you punched him." Georgia folded onto the blanket, stretching out her legs and crossing them at the ankles as she leaned back on her hands.

I sat next to her, mimicking her pose. "I'm not real proud of myself there," I admitted glumly.

"Give me your phone for a sec." Georgia held out her hand. She was notoriously often without her phone. Whether down in the bakery with it up in the apartment or vice versa, at the grocery store, or sometimes out of town. She was tethered to so very few things in this world, and the cell phone was definitely not on the list.

Georgia held the phone out in front of both of us, poised to take a picture. I smiled, and I could feel by the rise in Georgia's cheeks that she was smiling, too. Just before she pushed the button, she turned and planted a warm red-stained kiss on my cheek.

"There." She handed the phone back and dug through our picnic basket, pulling out the bottle of white wine and a corkscrew.

While she busied herself opening and pouring us glasses of chilled riesling, I tapped a message to CJ.

Me: That's awesome :)

After sending the text, I sent the picture in a second message.

CJ: No. THAT'S awesome.

Me: Look ... I'm sorry about wrecking your face.

I winced, thinking about the broken nose that left him with black eyes almost immediately.

CJ: You blind, man? I'm lookin' fine. All healed.

Me: Coulda fooled me ;)

CJ: Let's just forget about it, okay? We were both kind of out of our minds, huh? Things okay on the West Coast?

Me: So far. We're working through it.

CJ: You coming back to us, or …

Me: Yeah. Don't know when yet.

CJ: Don't be gone too long or they'll find someone to replace your sorry ass.

I laughed, setting the phone down and focusing on the way the late summer sunset formed an orange glow around Georgia's form.

"You're stunning."

She grinned, handing me a glass of wine and raising hers. "You're not so bad yourself. To us …"

"To us," I echoed, clinking our glasses together.

Although the spot we were sitting on was directly across from our apartment, our specific location that evening was bringing back some very specific memories. Among them was when I knew without a doubt that I was in love with Georgia. Staring ahead and to the left was the beat up dock on which we'd had kind of a joint meltdown. An old, unopened letter from my deceased ex-girlfriend, Rae, had surfaced, and despite the falling in love with Georgia I'd already been doing, Rae's handwriting was like a blow to the center of my chest. I wanted to be over her without forgetting her, and I wanted to give Georgia the attention she deserved, and it all came together in a fury right there on that dock when she saved me from drowning inside myself.

"Where'd you go?" Georgia asked softly, tilting her head to line her gaze up with mine.

She'd always been a woman of strength, courage, and determination. She proved that early on.

I tilted my chin forward, echoing the thoughts swirling in my head. "That dock. Where you saved me."

"Oh, I don't know … I think we did a little saving of each other that summer, don't you?"

I grinned, leaning into her arm. "We did. Listen, I want to talk about something—a few somethings—just the two of us."

In the short time I'd been home, we'd agreed to save our first few big discussions for the sturdy walls of our therapist's office. We'd been so off-balanced and poorly communicating that we knew we couldn't tackle those early conversations alone. But now we had our feet under us a bit, I felt comfortable talking to my wife without an expensive—albeit sometimes necessary—chaperone.

She inhaled audibly. Slow and deep as she set her eyes on the skyline, squinting as the sunset turned her face red and orange. "You go first."

Leaning forward, I swallowed the rest of my wine and set the glass back in the wicker basket. I practiced breathing for a few seconds, committing the act to memory, because the pending conversation was shooting up plumes of anxiety through my chest. I needed to trust her here, in this moment, with my thoughts, feelings, and my heart.

The way I had out on that worn-down dock not far from us all those years ago. But this time, she was my wife, and there was much more on the line than a summer fling. This was our marriage, and our future. It was my life.

CHAPTER THIRTY-TWO
GEORGIA

H E THOUGHT FOR a long time. Looking down as the colors from the ocean sunset took a cue from his rich, copper-colored hair and shone across his furrowed brow. I chewed on my tongue until it hurt to avoid hurrying him along, as was customary.

Get the first blow over with so we can get on to the meat of the fight.

I hated that I was such a fighter. I'd spent so much of my life fighting for myself and with myself, that dissent was my first reaction to everything. Even a simple question like, "Wanna get some breakfast?" could fetch a biting remark from me like, "It's a little early, isn't it?" or, "Now? It's almost lunchtime, which you'd know if you hadn't slept half the day away." Both were unfair, but the last one was horrifying as he wouldn't have to sleep past noon if he didn't work so late, which was part of his job—just like waking up before dawn came with the territory of owning my own bakery. That I'd eaten lunch while he was still dreaming was no one's fault.

Who knew eggs could be so divisive?

Through the crashing waves breaking over the rocky shore, Regan's chuckle filled my ears.

"Sorry," he said. "I got lost there for a second," he seemed to explain away his extended silence.

"It's okay," I encouraged, squeezing the top of his leg. "Go ahead."

He sighed, untying and retying his hair back in a messy ponytail/bun thing that looked sexy only on him. This was one nervous habit I never wanted him to stop—it was too adorable watching him fiddle with his hair in a way typically attributed to women.

"I'm not saying I never want children," he opened with, causing my stomach to turn over, forming a million miniature knots through my insides. "I think everything just got out of hand so quickly. We jumped in, then the tour took over and, honestly, I knew it was going to be six months, but that seemed shorter in our pre-baby world. We've gone through extended tours before—but none that involved any discussion of ovulation."

I laughed, relieved and nervous. Then, the tears I'd begged for days to stay back pressed on, squeezing themselves through my tightly-closed eyes. I forced out a few more chuckles before my breath caught in my throat and I looked at Regan, who was staring at me in regretful horror.

"No …" I shook my head, waving him on. "I'll explain in a minute … I'm fine, just please go ahead."

The pain in my chest was unrelenting, begging me to throw up every feeling and thought right that second. But I was practicing not doing that anymore. I was not a child for whom tantrums had to be extinguished on the spot. I was a grown woman with emotions that could survive for a few breaths while another person shared their insides.

I could wait my turn.

I could listen to my husband, without whom I wouldn't have even known I was capable of feeling such deep feelings. For better or worse.

Regan's wild hazel eyes studied me for a moment, and I did my best to beg through my intent gaze and simple nod that it really was okay for him to continue. It seemed he believed me.

"You're the most amazing woman I know, Georgia. Kind and fierce, compassionate and brave. What kind of man wouldn't want you to be the mother of their children?"

The kind who doesn't want kids?

The kind who doesn't want a mental case as the mother of their children?

I pressed my lips together, repeating a million affirmations in my head that I'd learned over the years in an effort to not sabotage this conversation. Ones about my uniqueness, my kindness, my ability to love. All of them. I set them on loop to keep my mouth shut.

The wind picked up and seagulls butted into our conversation as they wandered the beach—the hobos they are—begging for scraps of our uneaten dinner. With my eyes fixed on Regan, I leaned forward and closed the lid of the picnic basket, shooing away a few fat birds with a flick of my foot.

He grinned at my bird-wrangling in the middle of an otherwise intense moment, and kept on. "I just think you and I didn't really talk about it, you know? We just figured it was the next thing to do. Shower, get dressed, go to work, fall in love, get married, have children."

I crossed my legs in front of me, nodding as I replayed the similar conversation I'd had with my mom just before Regan showed up in our home, unexpectedly abandoning the tour.

In his silence, I allowed myself to speak. "So where are you now?"

He swallowed, eyeing me through wisps of hair that were blown free by the gusting wind. "I love you," he said quietly. "And I want to talk about it. I think maybe I wanted to prove to myself and you that nothing would have to change about our lives if we did have a baby. Even though I planned on scaling back my tour schedule when you got pregnant."

I gasped at this seemingly unanticipated turn of events. "You did? Why didn't you say anything?"

"Because I didn't want you to fight me on it. Then once the tour started, I remembered all the things I savor about touring, aside from the sidesplitting pain of missing you every second. And I kind of panicked about the resolution, even though it was only to myself."

The tears I'd successfully stowed away returned with a vengeance. "Oh God," I said through streaming tears. "We need to fucking talk some more."

Regan tilted his head, focusing on my face as he brushed my tears away with his thumb. "Yes," he said almost comically. "That much is clear."

"I'm not ready yet, either," I finally admitted, my chest clenching around the idea. "I'm ready to talk about it, but when we stated it like it was fact, while you were planning to prove to me nothing would have to change, I was busy trying to prove to you that it would. Beating you over the head with my ovulation calendar and starting all kinds of fights with you that I haven't started in years? Jesus … It was an old pattern I haven't been in for years, and I'm sorry …"

I looked down, playing with my hands as they sat in my lap. "I think we both just really fucked up here, huh?"

"Yeah," Regan agreed as the wind finally died down. "I guess so. So …" he hesitated, wincing as he seemed to grapple with his next words.

"So?" I asked softly, my heart racing.

"Could we, um … Can we just talk about this again—for real—when the tour's over? I want to finish this thing and then—" he started to ramble, his hands moving the way they do only when he's nervous. He doesn't talk with his hands like I do. When his hands start flying around, I know it's time for me to step in.

"Yes," I cut in. "I think that's a fantastic idea." My tears had dried without me noticing, and suddenly it was just me and my husband having an adult conversation on the beach.

"What?" he asked with a grin matching the one that had slowly taken over my mouth.

"I think it's probably time for us to get back to work. Mom and Jennifer have handled most of the work at the bakery for the last week, and, you know, you've gotta get back on tour," I said with my throat closing up a little before I forced out a light laugh. "I can't believe you bailed on it."

Regan didn't laugh. He didn't smile. Instead, he leaned forward and took my face in his hands, kissing me on the tip of my nose before he spoke. "I kind of bailed on us before that. I have no idea how to fix that, or make it up to you."

I smiled broader, pinching his chin between my thumb and forefinger. "We just move forward. I'm no innocent party here," I admitted of my tantrums and subtle mind games.

He looked down. "You weren't dancing in a club with some guy."

I sighed. "Yeah, well, after you help me hide Nessa's body we can have a clean slate."

I tried to sound serious and nonchalant, but when Regan's eyes met mine with a comical concern, I broke into laughter. "Look, I'm not saying I'm going to forget that any time soon—maybe ever—but I think I can forgive it. Just, maybe, don't have her hang out in your hotel room?"

In truth, the stubborn, jealous girl inside me was clawing at me to beg him to never see her ever again, to have her thrown off the tour, and maybe toss her violin in the nearest river for good measure. But the reality was, Regan had a long track record of fidelity. One hundred percent, unless you were the kind of person to count dancing as cheating. And, I was ready to be the kind of person that didn't.

There was only a sliver of sun visible over the horizon of the ocean, so we had less than an hour of decent dusky light left in which to eat our dinner on the beach. I got up on my knees and reached for the picnic basket, but Regan stopped me with a rough grab of my wrist.

"What?" I asked, alarmed.

He rose to his knees, then sat back on his heels so our height difference wasn't so profound.

"I'm damn lucky to have you, Georgia," he said with a seriousness that took my breath away.

My chin quivered once before I cleared my throat, inching my way toward Regan until I was wrapped in his warm arms. "We're lucky," I corrected, breathing in salt and wind and Regan.

"But, Regan?" I asked, sitting back on my heels and sniffing away a few lingering tears.

"Yeah?" he asked, full of concern as he studied my face.

"Can we eat?" I grinned. "I'm really fucking hungry."

Regan threw his head back, letting out a laugh I hadn't heard in weeks—longer, maybe. "Yes. Food, please."

We chased the last dregs of daylight with Brie, prosciutto, a baguette, and a renewed commitment to each other. After cleaning up our space on the empty beach, we trekked to the bakery where we feasted on cupcakes I'd over baked from a wedding order.

And I even joined him as he sat on the counter.

***

Regan had missed the rest of Minneapolis, and all of the Chicago and Ohio shows, but was scheduled to rejoin the tour in time for their New York City shows. Saying goodbye to him this time was harder than it had ever been.

This time, though, we had a much more defined plan. I was going to fly out to Massachusetts, meeting him there at his parents' house for the entire duration of his set there, and the break following. This would allow us to spend some much-needed quality time with his family, as well as time for us to spend with our friends, Bo and Ember, in New Hampshire.

Before Regan left, CJ called us to fill us in on all that had gone on with his dad and Frankie while Regan was MIA. As shocking as it all was, I was proud of CJ for handling it on his own—meaning dealing with it at all—and coming out the other side relatively okay. Frankie had traveled with the band through Chicago and Ohio, and was planning to stay on the road through the tour's arrival in Massachusetts.

I was a bit rabid with envy at Frankie's profession when I'd heard that, one that gave her time off during my busiest season. I'd never particularly had a desire to travel the road with Regan and some of the musical behemoths he runs with, but seeing the fun Frankie and CJ seemed to be having—not to mention the quality time they were able to rack up—left me wanting.

I sat with the thought for a couple of days, wanting to make sure it was a true desire rather than a moment of fancy, before texting Regan about it.

Me: How's NY treating you?

Regan: Good. It's so weird seeing CJ and Frankie together. I mean, we saw them together for years—but not like this. Something's definitely different. In a good way.

I smiled, a warm feeling enveloping my chest at the thought of CJ and Frankie finally finding the happiness they both deserved—and with each other, to boot. I sighed, steeling my resolve as I decided to jump in.

Me: I want to do that sometime—join you on tour. I couldn't do it for, like, months, but … I want to. Sometime. If you'll have me.

I stared with panicked anticipation at the three blinking dots on my screen indicating he was typing back his response. The wait was short lived.

Regan: Are you serious? I'd love that.

I let out a breath of relief, smiling as I leaned against the counter inside the bakery while a bride and groom pored over my portfolio in a booth by the front window.

Me: You would? Is it weird? Do people give Frankie and CJ shit?

Regan: Tons of shit, it's not weird to me, and I would love it. ;)

Me: Let me look at my schedule coming up. Maybe I can lose my mind and shut down for September—or at least put Jen and Mom on part time for basic stuff—and join you for a few stops after Massachusetts?

The dots blinked for a little longer this time, and I wondered if I'd overplayed my hand. I ushered those thoughts from my mind when I reminded myself this was my husband I was talking to—not some new boyfriend and I was worried about seeming too needy. Because this was Regan. I needed to need him, and he needed me to need him, sometimes. But, more than that, I needed to offer the gift of time to him. Something that can't be bought and sold, but runs through our fingers faster than money ever could.

The blinking stopped without a message coming through, which admittedly deflated my sails. But, the phone rang and Regan's name appeared on the screen.

"Hello?" I was breathless with nerves.

"Are you serious?" Regan's voice was an excited whisper. Airy and soft, and a little hesitant. Restrained hope.

I grinned, biting my lip as heat spread to my cheeks. "Yes."

"Jesus …"

"Good or bad?" I asked, peeking at the future bride and groom who were still peering through my cake pictures.

He let out a sigh inside a laugh. "Good. So good. I love you."

"And I love you. See you in Massachusetts?"

Regan's voice dropped, now producing a low moan. "That's so far away."

"It's like a week, champ. I think we can manage," I answered with a chuckle.

"Tonight," he whispered. "Can we … you know?"

I set my eyes on the newlyweds in my shop, making sure they were out of earshot, before I whispered back, "Sext or phone?"

"Phone," he replied without a second thought.

"Eight my time?"

"Oooooh fine," he answered with a comical sigh. "I guess I can manage."

The blond, suntanned couple in my front-and-center booth signaled me with matching waves and pearly white smiles that they were ready to discuss their options.

"Gotta go. Business to conduct. Be amazing tonight."

"You, too, Babe. Oh, wait—" he stopped himself with a bright question in his voice. "You're sending cupcakes, right? Cookies, too?"

A lump formed in my throat at his eagerness. Despite the standard sweets-delivery protocol we'd had for all his other tours, this was the first package I'd be sending out for this one.

He hadn't asked.

I hadn't done it.

We'd fallen apart on the most basic levels in ways that were no more evident than when missing things turned up. Requests for phone sex, cupcakes, and cross-country rendezvous among them.

"Yes," I answered after a lost-in-thought pause. "Of course. I love you."

"I love you."

CHAPTER THIRTY-THREE
REGAN

AND FINALLY, WE were in Massachusetts.

It felt like it took forever to get there, and even then I had to face the fact that we were only half-way through with the tour. I was able to meet back up with the tour in NYC, and I was glad for that because it was a trip watching CJ play for a huge crowd in Central Park.

Moreover, seeing him and Frankie together was reassuring somehow. For him, them, and all of us, maybe. If they could make it—and it seemed like they just might—then there were few excuses left for the rest of us.

We'd already played our shows in Barnstable and Wellfleet, and were scheduled to start a three-day stint at a wild arts and music festival in Provincetown before being granted a nearly two-week break. During that time, most members of the tour would scatter back to their home bases—mostly in California— or take vacations before we headed out for the second half of our tour. Georgia and I were looking forward to downtime spent between my parents' here on the cape and Bo and Ember's in New Hampshire.

I picked Georgia up from the airport first thing in the morn- ing—she'd taken the redeye—and as we wandered the grounds of the festival hand-in-hand, I couldn't help but steal a thousand and one glances at her.

"You're freakin' me out," she chuckled, squeezing my hand. "Why d'you keep staring at me?" She'd only been back on East

Coast soil for a few hours, but her accent was thickening by the second.

I grinned. "I still can't believe you're here."

"We planned for me to come out here months ago," she reminded me of our original plans when this tour first sprang into our lives.

Untangling my hand from hers, I wrapped my arm around her shoulders and pulled her close to my side as we walked over the grassy sand toward the far end of the festival. I kissed the top of her head and she let out a satisfied sigh that left me wishing we were walking toward our bedroom. Anywhere but where we were headed.

"You know what I mean," I whispered as if we were in a crowded room.

"I know," she whispered back.

The fact was, as recent as a few weeks before this moment, I wouldn't have been able to tell you that we would be hand-in-hand on this beach, or that she'd be joining us for the next month—our two-week break, plus the following two weeks on the road. I couldn't have told you that we'd even be on speaking terms, never mind anything else.

Georgia stopped, turning to face me as she placed her hand under my chin, eyeing me carefully. "I love you, Regan. I'm so happy we're here. Not just here," she gestured with her other hand to the land around us, "but here." She moved her hand to point between the two of us. "We got a little off-track there, huh?"

I nodded solemnly. "We did. But, not for long when you really look at it. And, you know what? We got through it to-gether, and back on track together. The same track even." I gave her a wink, then rejoiced in her yelp when I scooped her off her feet, spinning her around once with my lips locked onto hers before setting her back down.

"Sure you're ready for this?" I asked as we resumed our walk, a few paces from our intended destination.

She shrugged, but I caught the deep breath she took underneath her raised shoulders. "It's just a building, right? Some salt-worn wood and cement."

Her hard swallow highlighted the glaring lie.

I gave her a smile and grabbed a hold of her hand again. "Yeah. Just a building," I said softly.

Dunes was the beachside townie bar Georgia's father had owned and operated for decades. Long before Georgia was born, all through her childhood, and right up to his death, by which time Georgia had been living with her mother in California for years. It looked like a glorified shack that could blow away with a low-grade hurricane wind, but the emotional weight pulled heavy at the corners of my wife's eyes.

Aside from the years Georgia spent tending bar and cleaning up after her father's messes inside the tattered walls of the place, Dunes had held the complete setting for her father's rise and fall as a father and a man. It wasn't even the bar itself, or the alcoholism it let him poorly conceal for years. It was what it stood for—the choices he'd always made ahead of his only child.

While Georgia had returned to Massachusetts several times in the fifteen years since she left the dank, one-bedroom apartment on the second floor of the bar, she'd never once reentered Dunes.

I'd been there as a late teenager, watching CJ play with various incarnations of garage bands, and sometimes playing myself, but never when Georgia was there that I know of. I'd met the owner of the place a time or two—Georgia's dad I found out later—but there's not much to tell there. He was your standard rundown drunk with a charming smile and a quick deal to turn around every corner. But, I hadn't been back here since then. I learned early on how painful this pitiful little section of Provincetown was for her, and did my best to respect that.

"Here we are," she said with flat intention, like she'd reached the edge of a thirty-foot-high diving board and hadn't yet looked down. "Ready?"

I nodded as if she needed my permission—or my readiness—to enter. "Are you?"

She looked away from me for a moment, furrowing her brow. After chewing her answer over her bottom lip for a while, she answered. "I have to let go of this place if the back of my brain is ever going to let me stop waiting for you to treat me like he did."

Her honesty was straightforward, resolute, and firm. A new leaf she'd promised in our counseling sessions to turn over—facing demons with honesty and conviction. To acknowledge their existence which, in theory, would immediately cut their power off at the knees. Then head forward to begin the work of dismantling the rest of them.

"Well then, let's do this," I said in an effort to remind her that, while this was her past she was facing, she wasn't doing it alone.

She arched an eyebrow and set her hand on the door.

We stood in the breezy quiet outside the bar, only a few inches of wood separating us from the drunken noise on the other side. While it was traditionally a townie bar, the arts and music crowd drew ironic hipsters through the door who looked like they sort of fit in, but didn't, if you asked me. But no one asked, and money was money, so I'm sure Dunes was more than happy for any extra business that came its way.

The joyfully raucous noise of stereotypically drunken Irish pub music swarmed into our ears as we pushed the door open. Not long after came the stench of beer, sweat, and sand—a heady combination that oceanside bars specialize in.

During the steep decline of his health before he passed away, Georgia's father had handed operation of the bar over to an old friend and part-time manager of the bar—a man Georgia called Creature, without any further explanation. As if that were his name.

On the mission of a lifetime, Georgia pushed toward the bar, never letting go of my hand as she tugged me behind her to handle all the "excuse me's" necessary when my pint-sized stunner of a wife hip-checked her way through the thick crowd.

"Here we are." She stood up on her toes to speak in my ear as we reached the broad, pine, horseshoe-shaped bar.

I nodded, waiting for her to make her next move. Normally when a guy wants to peek into his girl's past they'll go to her high school reunion, or something. Not us. Never mind the fact that Provincetown High School only existed as a K-8 building now—their doors closed as a high school in 2013 when their final graduating class of eight students gathered their diplomas. Teenagers in P-town had to go to nearby public or technical high schools now. That aside, Georgia isn't the smiley reunion type.

She's the kind of girl who grips the edge of the bar and hollers, "Creature!" nearly out of nowhere.

But the broad-backed guy she yelled to, who stood about my height, turned around. And, finally, the name was explained. His jet-black hair was wrapped into thick, corded dreadlocks held back from his face with a moss green bandana. He had the weathered skin you'd find on lifelong fishermen in these parts—ruddy and wind-beaten, ashen around the eyes. Those deep brown eyes of his lit up in utter disbelief as he seemed to question his sanity, assessing who stood before him. And, somewhere behind a thick, full-faced dark beard, he smiled.

"Georgia fucking Hall?!" he hollered back with a deep, bar-reled voice. Thick and gritty, much like the character of the bar he ran.

Georgia held up her left hand. "Kane to you, sir. I'm spoken for."

Creature slapped the bar as he moved towards us. "You've gotta be shittin' me!"

Without yet acknowledging the man holding her right hand, Creature grabbed hold of her left and closely inspected Georgia's ring finger. Despite the crowded bustling of the bar, Georgia and Creature's interaction garnered the attention.

"Is that Billy's kid?" I heard from someone who looked about a hundred and two, but was probably in his late sixties.

Georgia almost never used her father's name, so hearing it always took me by surprise. This intense, anti-heroic character from her past had a name. And a face, and presumably a smile, though I know Georgia saw less and less of that as time went on. He was a real person before his liver turned to stone.

"You're a sight for sore eyes, kid," Creature said with what seemed to be uncharacteristic gentleness in his voice. Given my few-minute assessment of the man who went by the title Creature. "How's San Diego treatin' ya?"

I eyed Georgia carefully during the entire interaction as she answered questions of varying degrees of intimacy. She seemed surprised that Creature knew which questions to ask.

"You've kept close tabs on me," she said with mild accusation as two bartenders flitted around Creature, who remained fixed against the bar, leaning over it to talk up my wife.

He shrugged. "That cocky drummer friend of yours stops in to play once in a while. Kind of a closed book when it comes to you, though—gotta give him that. Took me two years to get out of him where you ran off to. How long you been married?" Creature finally acknowledged my presence.

Georgia smiled. "Three years. This is Regan—cousin to the cocky drummer friend."

His eyes met mine, and I saw the faintest glimmer of familiarity pass through them. "Say if it isn't," he said slowly as he extended his hand to shake mine. "You … you've been here before."

I shook his hand, nodding. "Like a hundred years ago. Used to play with CJ from time to time."

Georgia knew all this, but often forgot that we may have crossed paths in our youth without even knowing it.

Creature nodded knowingly. "Fiddler," he stated, not asked. "That's me."

He tilted his head toward Georgia, dropping his hand from mine. "You taking care of her?"

"Yes sir," I answered as if I were speaking to her father. This was the most fatherly conversation I'd ever been in regarding Georgia, so I figured I ought to take it seriously.

"You bettah," he replied, his eyes boring into me uncomfortably. "If not, I've got guys—"

"I'm sure you do." I held up my hands in mock defense. But I knew he likely wasn't kidding, and I wasn't interested in hearing about the creative ways they'd separate my insides from my outsides if they got word that I'd somehow hurt Georgia.

Georgia cleared her throat. "This is going to sound weird, but, who's living upstairs?"

Creature shook his head. "No one. Just used for storage now."

She swallowed. "Mind if I take a look? And in the office, too?"

He shrugged, pulling his tree-trunk arms back from the bar, appearing to get back to work. "This place is more yours than mine, doll. Have at it."

She winked, leaning all the way across the bar to kiss Creature on the cheek before pulling me across the floor to the tiny office that was down a short, narrow hallway near the bathroom.

Georgia didn't say a word as she opened the heavy, steel door. The office was no bigger than a glorified broom closet, holding a metal desk, a rolling chair with a tattered cushion, and a small filing cabinet. There was barely room for the furniture, let alone two people, so I stood in the doorway and watched her.

Her back was to me for a moment as she stood still in the center of the space and took a deep breath. I imagined that her eyes were closed, as they often were when she inhaled the scent of things. "So you can smell them all the way," she always said.

She ran her hands slowly across the top of the desk, as if searching for memory-Braille. With smooth, calm movements, Georgia squared herself in front of the shoulder-height filing cabinet, crouching in front of the bottom drawer, opening it, and reaching into the set of folders in the very back.

"Um," I broke my own vow of silence, "what?"

Unruffled by my vague accusation of theft, Georgia slid a yellowed sheet of paper from the farthest back folder. Soft with age, it didn't produce a noise when she folded it and tucked it in the back pocket of her jean shorts.

"Want to come with me upstairs?" she asked, eyeing me with a hopeful, non-criminal look.

I looked between the filing cabinet and her three times before answering, "Of course. But, maybe tell me about the little klepto-action there?"

She smiled, laughing once before grabbing my hand. "Creature was right," she said as she led me up a set of stairs down the same narrow hallway as the office. "This place is more mine than his. My dad owned the building outright. When he died, it naturally went to me, as his only living kin."

I stopped midway up the dusty staircase. "Seriously? And you were going to tell me … when?"

She shrugged. "It hardly mattered. This happened before I met you, and Creature has a lifelong lease on the place, assuming all responsibilities for taxes and whatever. Unless he fails to pay them, I guess."

"Then you'd be on the hook?" I asked with what I considered an appropriate amount of concern regarding the hefty taxes on this kind of location.

Georgia rolled her eyes and continued up the stairs. "He'd sooner sell his soul to the devil than fuck me over."

"I saw that tattoo on his neck," I mumbled before pinching her butt, deciding to let it go and trust her judgment.

"Anyway," she said as we reached the top of the stairs, "I'm transferring the deed to him. Or selling the place to him for a dollar, or whatever."

"Does he know this?"

She shook her head. "No. We've never talked about it since he signed the lease."

"This is a hefty piece of real estate." I peered out a porthole window on the stairwell, which overlooked the ocean.

Georgia's voice softened. "Emotionally, too. It's been like this vestigial organ-thing hanging off me for fifteen years, or whatever, and I just don't want it anymore." Her words spilled out faster as she talked, like she was trying to prove something, which I hadn't intended—not intentionally, anyway.

Wrapping my arms around her waist, I pulled her close and kissed her nose. "I know. I support whatever you want to do. As long as you let me take you and all your other organs home."

She smiled, then put her hands on my shoulders, pushing me back slightly. "So, listen. I haven't been back up here since I moved out. And my dad lived here until he died, and I'm not sure what condition it's in or anything like that ..." She swallowed hard and took a deep breath.

Wrapping my hands over her wrists, I gave her a soft kiss on the lips. "Take as much time as you need. I'll just wait ... right here." I took a seat on the stair below her and waved her on.

Georgia leaned forward and kissed me on the top of the head. "Thank you," she whispered.

Turning for the door, she tried the knob and it clicked—locked. I was anxious for her, but evidently I was the only one, because a second later, she reached into a rusted old watering can on the floor and produced a key that allowed her entry.

"I'll call when I'm ready," she said before disappearing behind the dusty old door.

I was dying to know what it was like in there. While Georgia had spent most of her young childhood in a modest house she shared with both parents, when her mother left, she and her father moved up here—he couldn't afford the house and the bar. But, while I wanted to satisfy my own curiosity and hold the hand of my wife as she undertook such an emotional overhaul, I was practicing treating her like the adult she was, rather than a figurine destined to break at any second.

She could do this.

I thought about reaching for my phone to pass time, but decided against it. I wanted to be as present in this moment as I could—ready for Georgia if she needed me, and just comfortable in the discomfort that sometimes comes with life. A lot of the breakdown that occurred between me and Georgia had to do with reluctance on both our parts to be present—to face reality. Sure, sitting there on a narrow staircase in the back of a bar might not seem like a huge deal to anyone from the outside, but I needed to be patient here. For Georgia. I could sit here and wait for my wife.

Not more than a few minutes had passed before the door creaked open behind me. I stood to face Georgia. Her eyes were red, fighting tears. Her jaw was relaxed, though, and it seemed she was just letting the emotions work their way through her.

"Are you okay?" I asked quietly, climbing the two stairs that separated us.

She nodded, blinking slowly once. "Want to see? There's a bunch of boxes around but, honestly, not a lot's changed."

My pulse raced at the thought of being in the space that hosted some of the worst damage that Georgia faced. She stepped back, holding the door open.

While I'd planned to take a slow look around, giving attention to one space before moving on, the place kind of swallowed me all at once. It looked like the fisherman apartments I'd seen in movies like The Perfect Storm. Wide open spaces, a galley kitchen with a broad window overlooking the ocean, and a tattered couch and recliner facing an old tube television.

Sliding my hands in my pockets, I paced carefully through the place while Georgia stood by the door. The floors creaked beneath each step, and muffled, thunderous noise bellowed up from below.

"Was it always this loud?" I ask, facing her, checking on her. She seemed okay.

Georgia shrugged. "I guess it had to be, but I don't remember it like this. I was probably just used to it."

I pointed to a small framed-out room near the back, which looked like it hung right above the bar itself. "Bedroom?"

She nodded, taking a slow step toward me, her arms crossed over her chest. "I haven't gone in there yet. It was mine. He mostly slept on the couch if he slept at all. I think he felt all kinds of bad for making me move out of our house—served him right," she added under her breath.

"Can I?"

"I'll go with you," she answered nervously. "I just didn't think I could bear it alone. I mean, it's just four walls, right? I don't know if I even left anything, and whatever I did is probably—"

Georgia's words ceased with the flicker of the light illuminating the room. The walls were painted a pale blue, and in one corner was a twin bed, unmade. The walls were bare, save for old pieces of tape that looked like they used to hold posters, given their squared-off arrangement.

But, on the table next to the bed was the reason for my wife's sudden speechlessness. A picture. Three-by-five, in a tarnished silver frame.

"I have this … at home … right?" she questioned to herself in a whisper.

Sitting on the bed next to her, I held one edge of the frame as she held the other. "Yeah," I agreed. "We have this."

It was a picture of Georgia and her parents on the day they brought her home from the hospital—all hopes, dreams, and smiles.

Georgia swallowed hard, bringing a hand to her mouth as tears spilled from her eyes. "He must have … he must have moved in here when I left and just … put this up. I—I didn't know he had one."

I put an arm around her shoulders, pulling her in to kiss her temple. "He loved you."

She nodded, swallowing through a rush of tears. "He tried. I really believe he did. He just … it wasn't enough."

"I know," I whispered, pulling her as close as she'd go. "Sometimes …"

I trailed off, not knowing what else to say. In truth, Georgia had some great memories from her dad, and half of who she is—challenging and wonderful—came from him and the time she lived with him here in this emotional anchor of an apartment.

We sat in silence for a long time while Georgia ran her thumb over a picture we saw every day in our own apartment three thousand miles away. Because this one was different in every emotionally possible way.

"Let's go," she finally said, rising to her feet with the picture still in her hands.

"Are you sure?"

She nodded and a faint smile pulled at the corners of her mouth. "I can come back here any time I want—I've had enough for today."

I stood, kissing her once before leading the way out of the room. "I'm proud of you."

"Thank you for coming in here with me." She paid little attention to the rest of the apartment before turning off the light and shutting the door behind us.

Once back on the staircase, Georgia locked the door and dropped the key back into the watering can. With a deep cleansing breath, she looked me in the eyes. Looking back at her, I saw a storm of resolve, along with a calm wisdom I swear hadn't been there before.

"It didn't kill me," she said, almost to herself. "I faced the big ugly thing, and it didn't kill me."

"No," I grinned, "it didn't. What are you gonna do with that?" I gestured to the picture still in her hands.

She descended the stairs ahead of me, answering over her shoulder. "I don't know yet. But are you heading over to the stage?"

"Yeah," I replied, checking the time on my phone. "It's about that time."

"K. I'll meet you there. I'm going to go put this with my stuff at your parents' house so I don't forget it. Leave me here, though," she said as we prepared to enter the cacophony of the bar. "I need to talk to Creature."

"You sure?" I leaned forward, searching her eyes for hesitation. I found strength there instead.

Georgia rose up on her toes, kissing my nose. "I am. I really am. Up there? That was really four walls. But this?" She held the picture between us. "This is ... more than I could have imagined." Her eyes welled with tears and I lifted her chin with my index finger.

"Are you sure you're okay?"

She smiled through the tears. "You know, I don't think I ever told you this, but I didn't cry when my dad died."

I swallowed, unsurprised given all I knew about their relationship—and Georgia's reluctance to tears—but I was floored by her honesty. "You never told me that."

"Because I couldn't grieve the man I lost—a shell of the father I knew." She held up the picture again. "But this man? This is the father I lost and ... I think I'm going to need some time—to cry a lot."

I pulled her into a tight hug. "I'll be here. Whatever you need."

As quick as the emotion came on, she pulled out of it, backing away and drying under her eyes. "Gah," she mumbled to herself. "Stop making me cry, I've got a business transaction to attend to," she said, pulling the deed to the building out of her back pocket.

I laughed, kissing her once more before facing the maze of sweat that lay before us. "See you at the show?"

She smiled up at me with raw openness. "I wouldn't miss it for the world."

CHAPTER THIRTY-FOUR

REGAN

A COUPLE OF WEEKS later, we were playing the closing number of our afternoon set at the P-Town festival, and I was on cloud nine. Yardley had arranged a banjo to play "Dueling Banjos" with me. For the rest of the tour, Nessa and I were scheduled to do this piece together, but she'd been absent since I rejoined the tour—her brother had major surgery and she flew home to be with her family. She was scheduled to return after our break was over.

I'd originally feared that playing with Nessa again would be awkward—for me and her and, of course, Georgia. But those fears were lessening as time went on. Georgia and I had a long talk about it before I returned to the show—both alone and in the company of our therapist—and Georgia agreed that it was a part of my job, and I agreed that if it became a problem for me emotionally that I would pull back.

I'd been working on rehearsing boundaries that I hadn't re-alized had been so messy before. Nessa and I would practice and perform together, and socialize in the company of other musi-cians, but that was it. I did not intend to socialize one-on-one with her anymore. I was one hundred percent committed to my wife, but I didn't need to go looking for trouble.

I was soaked with sweat while Ben from The Brewers scratched away on his banjo in the blazing heat. We were in the zone. Near the end of our song, members from the tour came on stage in kind of an impromptu jam session. We were joined by guitars, tambourines, a keyboard, and several drummers. CJ had seemed distracted earlier in the day. Over what I had no idea, but he was able to leave that all behind—like the rest of us—and kill it on stage.

My eyes scanned the crowd until I found my gorgeous, loud wife, front and center in a group that would have swallowed her if she weren't so damn scrappy. Holding her own on a two-by-two section of trampled grass, Georgia jumped and shook her hips and cheered along to every song. I did all I could to stop myself from leaping off the stage toward her, but as the energy of the crowd surged, I couldn't hold back any longer.

With a quick wink in her direction, and a nod to Ben, which had come to mean "keep playing," I leapt from the stage with my violin in my hands, earning a chorus of cheers. Georgia stared at me with a seductively wicked grin as I played my way toward her. I couldn't grab her and pull her to me while I played, but I could lean in with some skill to kiss her on the round apple of her cheek. With a small circle encasing us, Georgia danced around me, clapping her hands to the rapid beat, and encouraging the crowd to do the same as sweat dripped from my forehead.

God, it was just like it was when we first met at that tiny bar in San Diego. She'd liked the music right away, but it took her longer to get on board with me—well, a relationship with me, anyway. As the nights wound down, Georgia would spend more time on or around the stage, dancing to our beat, and sometimes her own. She had also been known to hop up and dance with me on stage between waiting on tables. It annoyed her manager at first, until he saw how the customers loved it.

There on the grass in Provincetown that day … that was us. Lost in the music and each other. And, even though it had been two weeks since she'd set foot in Sweet Forty-two, I swear she still smelled like butter and brown sugar.

"I love you!" I shouted over the music, meeting her eyes, and her eyes alone.

Her smile broadened and she yelled back, "And I love you!"

At the conclusion of the song, the crowd erupted into cheers and I was greeted with high-fives and backslapping, but I had only one focus—Georgia.

I picked her up, swinging her around in a tight hug. "You're hot," I whispered.

"You're sweaty," she teased back, planting a heavy kiss on my lips.

I quickly made my way back to the stage, hopping up with a helpful hand from CJ while the rest of the members from the tour, including Yardley, joined us on stage for a final bow. We'd have to do this all again at sunset, and even though I was more than ready for our two-week break to start, this crowd was particularly invigorating.

Georgia leaned up on her tiptoes toward the stage as I crouched down to meet her.

"I'm going to go check out all the vendors." She hitched her thumb back toward the tents and tables scattered through the boundaries of the festival.

I nodded, kissing the tip of her nose. "I'll catch up with you once we're all cleaned up here."

She shot me a quick wink before strutting off in her platform sandals.

"Well … look who it is!" a scratchy old voice hollered.

I whipped around, disbelieving my ears. But, in a second, I spotted the man who made my whole life possible.

"Ernie?!" My mouth swung open at the sight of my first violin instructor, and it stayed there as he made his way slowly up the stairs to the stage.

I shot a glance into the crowd for Georgia, but she was long gone.

Ernie had lost some of his height in the seven or eight years it had been since I'd seen him, and now walked with a long, knotted and twisted cane that made him look like a wizard— but it was him. His long hair was pulled back with an elastic, and what was once salt-and-pepper was now snow-white. His long beard seemed even more over the top now that it was as white as his hair and blew in the ocean breeze.

I walked over to him, grabbing his hand to help him up the last step. "You're here?" I asked, feeling like I was in a bit of a twilight zone.

"Damn right. You think I'd miss this?" Despite the cane and the slow pace, he wasn't out of breath or otherwise elderly sounding when he reached me. And he still had the twinkle in his greying eyes. The twinkle that taught me music was magic.

He stuck out his hand, and when I shook it he tugged me in for a hug. He stood just a few inches shorter than me, and had far more strength than it looked like he should.

"I'm proud of you, kid. Real proud of you."

Backing away, I grinned and gestured my hands to my sides as if presenting the stage to him. "Because of you, sir."

He lightly whacked the back of my calf with his cane. "Because of you. And, no need for that sir nonsense."

I set my hands on my hips as the last of the crew disappeared, and the two of us were left alone on the suddenly grand-feeling stage. "What are you doing here?"

He looked at me like I'd sprouted another head. "I've got a booth, fool. Or have you forgotten?"

I blushed, laughing at the same time. "I could never forget. I just didn't realize you still did this."

He shrugged. "Not dead yet."

"Fair enough. I really want you to meet my wife, Georgia."

He grinned. "Was she the little firecracker dancing around you in that last song?"

I only blushed deeper. Ernie met me when I was five. It was weird talking about my wife with him now. "That was her."

"Good on you, Kane. And that cousin of yours with the wild streak—seems he's got himself together a little bit. All he needed was a little organization to really be something with those sticks."

I moved my head side-to-side, considering. "He can be organized," I chuckled. "Or a damn mess."

"Drummers," Ernie mumbled, shaking his head. "Anyway, I gotta get back to the booth. The kids' corner thing is starting in a few. Care to swing by and share some of yourself?"

My chest burst with excitement. "Yes. Absolutely. I'll bring Georgia by, too. Are you free for dinner tonight? My mom's cooking."

Without hesitation Ernie answered, "I wouldn't miss that woman's food for the world. See you in a few." He turned and made his way for the stairs.

"Need some help?" I jogged behind him, cupping his elbow.

Once again, Ernie hit me with his cane. "I've got help. Go get your wife and come impart some wisdom to the youth who can barely tell a fiddle from an iPhone."

He made his way down the stairs, mumbling about technology and the death of the arts.

While I shared his angst on the subject, I needed to track down Georgia. I hopped off the stage and weaved through the thick crowd, nearly obtaining a contact high while I searched for a short, sexy blonde.

"Regan!" Georgia's urgent voice called to me through the noise, then two more times.

Finally, I spotted her and walked over to the white tent she was in front of. Massachusetts Adoption Resource Exchange was printed across a blue banner with white lettering. It was an information tent—as many local and regional organizations used the festival to promote their causes—and a long white table was filled with brochures, charts, and stuffed envelopes of some sort.

"What's up? Ernie's here! You'll finally get to meet him, and—what's wrong?" I tapered the end of my excited speech as my wife's eyes shined glassy as if she was holding back tears.

"Look at this. Did you know this existed?" She gestured to the table, pointing to a couple of trifold poster boards that held the faces and information of at least a dozen children aged six months to sixteen.

… Would do well in a home by herself or with other children.

… Needs one-on-one attention. Best with a single mother.

… Sibling group. Looking for someone who can take all four children.

I swallowed the rocky lump forming in my throat.

"What …" I looked at Georgia, clearing my throat. "What is this?"

Her voice lowered to just above a whisper. "None of those kids have homes. There are more than six hundred kids just in this state that are waiting to be adopted. They—they don't have anyone, Regan." Her panicked eyes met mine and she was breathing heavy.

I put my hand on her shoulder and pulled her close to me as we looked at the boards in front of us. I stayed quiet for a long time, an unfamiliar and overwhelming emotion surging through my chest.

I thought of Ernie, working with young musicians through-out his whole life, filling the need for positive adult role models that all children have. This was deeper. These were children who had no stable home, no consistent caregiver. Based on the information in front of us, most of the children came from abusive or neglectful situations. Many of them had some sort of developmental and/or social delays.

My vision blurred behind powerless tears. I looked at my wife, and she looked back up at me.

"Do you think they have something like this in California?" she asked, sounding broken and resolved at the same time.

I nodded, taking a step closer to the table. "I'm sure they do."

"Can I answer any questions for you?" A bubbly, college-aged looking woman asked us.

I cleared my throat. "We're visiting from California," I started, my voice shaking like I was riding a jackhammer. "And we were wondering if there were any organizations like this out there?"

Stacey, as her name tag stated, tapped away on the computer in front of her. After a minute, she produced a printed list of websites and phone numbers.

"Here are the groups in California we've worked with in the past. Certainly there are more, but we can recommend these as having good practices. Are you two considering fostering? Adopting? Both?"

Dropping my hand to my side, I grabbed Georgia's sweaty palm and squeezed it in mine. I looked down at her as she, again, looked up at me with a wide-eyed mix of pain and hope.

This ... thing passed between us. Our story. Our love. I don't know what it was, but it felt like the time I stuck my tongue in a D battery when I was eight. Only this surged through my whole body as I stared at the woman who made my life exponentially more amazing than I thought it could ever be.

Turning our attention back to Stacey, Georgia and I squeezed each other's hands once more, and answered in unison.

"Yes."

"Wait a second. Can we have a second?" Georgia asked, politely as she ushered me a few feet back from the booth. Stacey seemed unconcerned as she gathered sheets of paper and brochures into a manila envelope.

"What is it?"

Georgia's eyes moved from me to the table and back again, I could see a million starts to a million sentences running through her eyes. "We just went through this whole ... baby thing."

I nodded, swallowing hard. "Yeah we did. But this feels ... different somehow."

She placed her hands on her hips. "This kind of came out of nowhere."

Setting my hands over hers with a wave of calm washing over me, I kissed the top of her head. "Some of the best people do."

I grinned, watching the woman who fell backwards into my life when I was least expecting it.

"We didn't handle the baby stuff well before."

"But we know it was about more than the baby stuff," I reminded her. We'd been through a lot of therapy, teasing apart our fears, anxiety and expectations.

Georgia nodded, chewing her bottom lip.

I sighed, smiling. "Maybe ... maybe there's a kid out there, already born, who needs us. Us."

She nodded, and a small weep escaped her throat as she pressed her forehead into my chest. "I think you're right, Regan."

I swallowed my tears back, feeling emotional and calm at the same time. A feeling that told me to hang onto my wife, no matter what. Gently rubbing the back of her head, I spoke softly. "I think when we get home we call these numbers, get some information, and take it from there. And talk with Dr. Weeber. And each other. A lot with each other."

Georgia's voice quivered. "There were kids in high school, too. I mean, Jesus."

"I know," I sighed, "I saw."

She took a step back, expertly wiping mascara-stained tears way from her face. "Would you want a baby?"

I hesitated for a moment, not knowing how to answer such a huge question. "I think ... I think I want the child who needs us most. Whoever they think could put up with us," I joked to lighten the mood a little.

Georgia's face lit up with a smile I'd missed in the last year. One that had only returned in the last month, or so. She looked up to the sky, holding out her hands as if she were caught off guard. I think we both were. "Oh my God."

I laughed. "Yeah. Are you ready?" I took her hand and tilted my head back to the table where Stacey was waiting expectantly.

With a deep breath, Georgia's smiled morphed to an assured, soft grin. "I am. Are you?"

Giving her hand a small squeeze, I nodded. "I am. Let's do this."

It was, of course, just an envelope filled with names, numbers, facts about fostering and adoption, and brochure upon brochure that created more questions than answers, but it was a start. Georgia and I knew the road would be a long one as we pored over all the information in front of us, but it was a road we were willing to walk together. As we sat on a rocky ledge, taking a few minutes to gather ourselves before heading to Ernie's tent, I took a quiet moment to think.

I knew there would be sacrifices and tears and heartache along the way, but as I stared at one of the strongest women I knew—one I was lucky enough to call my wife—I knew deep down that we would be okay. We were Regan and Georgia Kane, for God's sake. A quirky couple who had already fought their way through a thousand thorny mazes filled with trapdoors in the name of our love for one another.

We had an opportunity to build something great on the foundation we forged through years and hard work. A family. One as unlikely as the two of us were. One as unique and in love as we were with each other.

"What are you thinking about?" Georgia asked quietly, sliding the last of the paperwork into the envelope, folding the brass fasteners to seal it.

Standing, I held my hand out, helping her to her feet. "I was thinking … I was thinking that there has never been a man as happy and in love as I am this moment."

"Not even you on our wedding day?" Georgia challenged sardonically.

I shook my head, arresting her with a serious glance. Her face froze as she seemed to hold her breath, waiting for my next words.

"That day doesn't hold a candle to this one. That was just the beginning. This?" I wrapped her into a warm hug as the cutting ocean wind broke over us. "This is where it gets good."

CHAPTER THIRTY-FIVE

CJ

"JESUS I'M NERVOUS," I said out loud for the first time in my entire fucking life.

My palms were sweaty and I'd already had to change my shirt—thank God my mom lived close by so I didn't look like a complete Neanderthal.

Frankie shifted on the rocks next to me and put her arm around my shoulders as we stared into the Atlantic. "You're doing the right thing, CJ."

She sounded brave enough for the both of us.

It had been one hell of a ride having Frankie finish out this half of the tour with us—on the bus with me, at all the concerts, everything—but it hadn't been completely carefree. Something changed between Frankie and me that night in Chicago when I spilled my guts in front of her in my hotel room, revealing more to her about my dad than I'd ever told anyone in my entire life.

Not to mention all the crying I did. Jesus.

"What time is it?"

Frankie looked at her watch—she was the only person under forty in my life that I knew wore one. "Ten of."

"Shit …" I huffed, standing. I needed to pace away this nervous energy. Ten minutes was a long time when the previous ten years hadn't exactly been a picnic. "I wish there was a way I could just, you know, meet him without having to see him."

Frankie winced sympathetically, standing to follow my erratic wanderings. "Yeah, but Provincetown during festival time isn't really the place to just leave a ten-year-old boy."

I hadn't been able to push the thoughts of my half brother out of my mind from the moment my dad spilled the beans about his existence. As pissed as I was about how this kid got to have the life I'd always felt was mine—one in the big beach house with married parents and annoying siblings—I felt a strange pull to this faceless, nameless boy.

Frankie listened. And listened, and listened, and listened as I tortured myself over this kid. What did he look like? What was his name? Was he really into music, or was that a ploy by my dad designed to tear open guilt? I didn't know the answer to any of those questions, but I did know one important fact about him—he had an asshole for a father.

Maybe my old man had changed. I mean, he'd already been married to his new wife longer than he was to my mom— maybe it was time to stop calling her new. I had my doubts, though. It takes a special kind of monster to walk away from an otherwise happy family. I'd talked about it a lot over the years with Regan and Georgia and as we got older we realized no one ever really knows what goes on deep inside a marriage. But, I knew it wasn't bad enough to warrant abandonment. Not after watching the way my mother fell apart for a couple of years afterward.

"You forgave me," I said to Frankie, stopping to light a cigarette. I was working on quitting again, but today was not the fucking day. "I don't know if I can forgive him … ever."

Frankie sighed. A long, soft, slow sigh signaling an adult life-lesson was on its way. "You know … Forgiveness isn't about the other person. I wanted to stop resenting you. I wanted to stop the knots in my stomach and the anger and the awfulness that I was carrying around in my chest. I'd decided to forgive you long before I went to Chicago."

She'd told me this before, when we'd talked until sunrise her first day in Chicago. She explained that all of that forgiveness stuff, but said she was caught off guard when she saw I'd clearly become a changed person—clearly was her word, not mine. In that moment, she told me, she was able to completely forgive me and begin to imagine a life with me again.

"Yeah …" I didn't know why I was clinging to the hate in my chest like a life preserver. I'm sure any psychologist worth their weight would say it was pulling me under more than keeping me afloat.

Frankie grabbed my hand, lacing her fingers between mine. "At the very least, what you're doing right now is not transferring the hate you have for your dad onto a kid who didn't ask to be born in the first place."

I squeezed her hand, taking one last drag of my cigarette before burying it in the sand. "He doesn't deserve that," I agreed. "He didn't do anything wrong and, you know, he might need me someday. Like if our dad turns out to be the same guy he always was and leaves him, too."

I used to think I wanted that. I wanted my dad to abandon another family as punishment to them for taking him away, as if he wasn't the one who packed his own damn suitcase. I didn't think I thought that anymore, though I couldn't be sure. Revenge is a tricky, slippery thing.

Frankie sighed again, but soft enough to make me think she was trying to hide it. "And even if he doesn't leave this family …" she prodded.

"A kid can never have too many adults on their side," I admitted. "Even if we're playing fast and loose with the term adult." I laughed at myself, releasing Frankie's hand to wipe my palms on the back of my jeans.

"And I'm not saying you ever need to befriend your dad, CJ. I want to make sure you know I'm not suggesting that. What he did was emotionally abusive, traumatizing—"

"I know," I cut in, facing her as time ticked slowly. The wind blew long wisps of brown hair across her face that she kept trying to tuck behind her ears. Lifting her chin with my index finger, I gave her a soft kiss on the lips. "And that might be where I'm headed with him … I don't know."

Setting up the meeting with my little brother—a term that was still hard to come to terms with—happened through a series of awkward texts and tense phone calls. I texted as much as I could, avoiding phone communication at all costs until my dad insisted on vocal communication. He said he wanted to ensure his son would be safe. I had to refrain from asking which one he meant.

We agreed to meet at a pier near the festival, and I could go off with the kid for a couple of hours—if we both lasted that long. I was clear from the outset that I didn't want to have a big father-son day with him and, if that's what he was hoping for, we'd scrap the idea entirely—I told myself I didn't need to meet my brother that badly.

But I think I did, even if I couldn't articulate why.

Still, my dad agreed and said his wife did, too. They seemed overeager, in fact. I didn't doubt that my dad was hoping this would somehow open a port of communication between the two of us. In the interim it did—as we had to coordinate this meeting—but I always felt sick at the end of our interactions— ill from pushing rage and tears down my throat.

"What are you guys gonna do?" Frankie asked, tugging me back to the present.

Now it was my turn to sigh. "I don't have a fucking clue."

Frankie's breath caught in her throat as she gasped, looking over my shoulder. "Better think fast," she whispered. "They're coming."

My stomach sank and my heart pole-vaulted into my throat in perfect time with each other, leaving me wanting to throw up and pass out at the same time.

"Stay for a second," I blurted out, throwing our plans for her to dart away immediately right out the window. I hadn't wanted to bear the stilted introductions and awkward pauses that would certainly follow when we were all face-to-face.

Her eyes widened for a split second before she reached out and grabbed my hand. I was oddly calmed by the fact that her palms were sticky with sweat. "You got it. Ready?"

I let out a hard chuckle, looking down. "Nope. Let's do this."

I turned around and, sure enough, my dad was walking toward us with a boy who was clearly his son by his side. I had no idea what average ten-year-olds were supposed to look like, but I had to suppress a grin at the fact that this was no average soon-to-be fifth grader. He shared my DNA through and through. While he did have sandy hair like his mom, he was built like I was at ten: tall and lean, moving with an awkward gate that I remember came with rapid growth. I couldn't tell from as far back as they were, but he was easily over five feet, which I did know to be tall for a boy of that age, because I was. He was dressed in standard kid-jock wear: black Nike shorts that went to his knees, a sleeveless neon yellow shirt that also sported the Nike swoosh and, yes, black Nike basketball shoes—even though we were on a beach.

I was dressed more like my dad—almost exactly like him, actually—but my black shirt was sleeveless. I wore tattered old Teva flip-flops that had served me well for longer than he did.

I had to swallow back a rush of emotions, as they got close enough for me to make out their faces. My dad had aged, but well. Fine crows feet framed his eyes, but his skin was holding up well otherwise. Salt-and-pepper scruff dusted his chin and jaw, but his hair was as black as I always remembered. I was used to seeing him in suits, so the casual khaki shorts and black T-shirt threw me for a loop, but only briefly. He was smiling, but I was glad to see he looked a little nervous, as the smile didn't quite reach his hopeful eyes.

Frankie gave my hand a squeeze as my dad extended his.

"CJ," he opened with, a little breathless that was likely more from nerves than athletic ability—he looked remarkably fit, especially for a guy nearing fifty. "It's good to see you."

"Hey," I answered after an attempted swallow through my cotton-dry mouth. I shook his hand—we all had sweaty palms, it seemed. "Uh, this is Frankie, my girlfriend."

She smiled, shaking his hand. "It's nice to officially meet you."

My dad smiled sheepishly. "Callum," he said, nodding once. "It's nice to meet you, too. Sorry about showing up—"

Frankie waved her hand, gracefully sweeping the stumbling apology aside. "It's no trouble. I'm glad we could meet."

"Hey," the boy cut in without an ounce of nerves, it seemed. He even held out his hand toward me. "I'm Danny."

I cleared my throat, hoping that would cover up the involuntary quiver of my chin. It helped a little. Simultaneously, Frankie and my dad stepped back, giving Danny and I some space.

"Hey," I replied, looking into the hazel eyes of a younger me. "I'm CJ, it's nice to meet you."

His handshake was firm and sure, and it left me wondering how much he knew about what it took to get to this point—since the three adults standing around certainly hadn't assumed it would ever happen.

"Good to meet you. Dad talks about you all the time—says I might even get to try out your drums?"

"Danny," our dad cut in with a cautionary tone.

I laughed to beg the tears away, stuffing my hands in my pockets. "I think I might be able to arrange that."

Dad talks about you all the time …

I looked at my dad, Callum, Sr., whose eyes volleyed between his two sons expectantly, and wondered what he talked so much about in regards to me. I had flashes of guilt and anger vying for attention inside me, quickly reasoning now was not the time for such a discussion with dear old dad.

"Callum," Frankie said, socially aware enough to realize we needed help toward the next step, "would you like to come grab lunch with me while the boys do their thing? There's a hell of a clam stand—sorry," she corrected herself, blushing, "heck. There's a heck of a clam stand on the festival grounds."

Dad laughed, firmly patting Danny on the shoulder. "He's said worse in church before."

Danny rolled his eyes, looking a little sheepish underneath tween angst.

"That'd be great," my dad continued. "We'll meet you guys back here in, what? An hour, hour and a half?"

I nodded and shrugged at the same time, a move Frankie said is specific for decision-disabled men. "Sounds good."

He smiled, patting my shoulder this time. It didn't hurt like I thought it would, but I couldn't look him in the eyes. "Text or call if you need anything. Either of you."

Danny and I nodded and watched Frankie and our dad walk away for a few seconds before I realized another human being was under my care—God help us all.

"Welp," I started, turning toward Danny and gesturing in the direction he'd just walked from, "ya hungry?"

I didn't know what to say, but figured food was a good place to start.

He shrugged, "Sure."

I chuckled. "You're probably always hungry, huh?"

He mimicked my laugh, following me as I led the way down the worn-down boardwalk. "Yeah. You look like you're always hungry too." He seemed to try to hide the grin that took over his face.

"Slay!" I hooted, earning a shocked look of respect from him at my correct use of current slang—thanks to Frankie's tutelage. "So, you play sports or just dress like you do?"

He huffed out a chuckle. "I play. I'm good, too."

"Basketball?"

He nodded. "Lacrosse, too."

"Ever considered football?"

He shot me an annoyed look from the corner of his eye. "Of course, but my mom thinks it's too dangerous."

"What does your—er—what does Dad say?"

"He's all for it—said you were really good, too."

That punched feeling returned to my diaphragm. "So he really talks about me, huh?"

I knew the question was inappropriate as soon as I asked, but I didn't care that much.

Danny nodded. "Talia and Grace, my—our—whatever—sisters, say you're a jerk who wants nothing to do with us."

The truth—or a variation of it, anyway—stung. "How old are they?"

"Talia's twenty and Grace is fifteen."

I swallowed hard. Talia was born two years after my dad left. It seemed he wasted no time …

"Is that true?" Danny asked, stopping my train of thought.

"What? That I'm a jerk?" I tried for the joke, but neither of us laughed. I sighed instead.

I stopped a little ways back from the crowds ahead of us and leaned against a worn split-rail fence. Danny put his hands in the pockets of his shorts and hung his head a little. He looked so sad with his downcast eyes and slight frown that I could hardly bear it.

"Hey," I started, "listen. Families are really complicated, okay? I don't even know what I'm doing right now. I haven't seen Dad in forever, and, yeah, I never thought I'd talk to him again—"

"Why?" Danny chewed the inside of his cheek as he waited for my answer, a habit I was known to exhibit under emotional stress.

"I don't really know what to say, Danny. I mean … he left me and my mom when I was five. I was mad. Then I got pissed. And stayed that way. Jesus …" I ran my hand over my face, leaving it across my mouth for a second before I spoke again. "You're ten. I don't even know what the hell I'm supposed to say or not say."

Danny grinned. "I've got older sisters. I've heard a lot."

He seemed like an emotionally put-together kid—especially for a ten year old. I had to give him that.

"Why do they think I'm a jerk? Did Dad tell them that?" I resumed our walk forward. Fried food would fix this, somehow.

He shook his head. "No. I think they just figured since we never heard from you or see you, or whatever … and Dad always said he invited you to Christmas—"

"He said that?"

Danny nodded. "Didn't he?"

I was stuck between a rock and a hard place. He had. Every year by phone or card. Then I stopped answering his calls and opening his mail.

"He did. I was just—"

"Pissed," Danny cut in.

"You probably shouldn't use that word," I half-heartedly cautioned. "I'd hate to bring you back to your—our—dad with a filthy mouth."

Danny laughed. "My sisters swear all the time."

"But, yeah. I was pissed. I guess … I don't know … I guess I'm trying to kind of fix that, or something, now."

Danny looked up at me, wide-eyed. "So can you come to Christmas this year, then?"

I winced, then bit the inside of my cheek. "I'll think about it, okay?"

"Okay," he answered, growing quiet.

He didn't believe me. There was no reason for him to.

Instinctively, I put my arm around his shoulders. To my surprise, he didn't pull back, and we walked for a few steps like that, until we were in front of my favorite P-town food truck. Fried Everything. That's really what it was called, because they fried everything from potatoes and chicken to pickles and Oreos. It was a grand thing.

"Fried Everything?" Danny questioned, laughing. "Awesome. I want everything!"

I laughed, pulling out my wallet. "Let's do our best, then …"

***

An hour later, I'd learned that Danny was as passionate about sports as I was about music, and his interest in music was close behind. I promised I'd let him try his hand behind my drum set before our evening show. He was beaming.

I learned his oldest sister, Talia, was a junior at UConn, studying political science, while Grace was just starting her sophomore year in high school.

"She's so loud," Danny said, shaking his head. "And she and my mom yell at each other all the time. Dad says it's just hormones, or something."

I chuckled. "That sounds about right."

"Did you and your mom fight a lot when you were a teenager?"

I shoved the last deep-fried Oreo into my mouth. "Not a ton, but not never. It was just the two of us, you know? But teenagers are teenagers, so I gave her a hard time when she wouldn't let me do whatever I wanted."

"You spent a lot of time with Dad's brother, too, right? Uncle Ronan?"

To avoid choking, I washed the Oreo down with what was left of my soda. "You know Uncle Ronan?"

Danny shrugged. "I met him a couple times—he's come over before. Dad told me that he's the one who took good care of you when he moved to Long Island."

I sighed. What a picture must have been painted for Danny. I didn't want to ask the details, because I knew they'd just piss me off—and that wouldn't be fair to him.

"Yeah. You'll meet Regan, too—wait. Have you met Regan?"

He shook his head. "No, but I've heard of him."

I grinned. "He's a great guy."

Just as we were about to get up from the picnic table and walk back down the beach, I spotted Frankie and Dad walking toward us.

"Look who found us." I motioned ahead.

Frankie grinned as she approached. "I knew we'd find you here at the health food stand."

Danny laughed, and so did I. "Pretend you don't love it," I teased.

"Oh no, I do," she said with wide eyes, placing her hands on her hips. "Can't keep this figure without a deep-fried pickle once or twice a week."

Dad sat across from me and Danny at the table, gesturing to Danny's half-eaten plate of fried clams and scallops, and French fries. "Save any for me?"

Danny pulled his plate closer. "Get your own."

The seriousness in his tone made the rest of us laugh.

"Dad, guess what?" Danny's tone suddenly shifted to excitement. "CJ says I can play on his drums tonight before his show. Can we stay? Please? Please?"

I'd assumed their plan was to stay for the show, so his question took me off guard. My dad shifted in his seat before shooting me a quick glance.

"If it's all right with CJ, I don't have a problem with it."

I waved my hand. "No, it's good. I'd like that." Then, I kept talking. "Dad, uh, can we talk for a second, like … alone?"

I eyed Frankie for assistance, and she understood, ushering in to ask Danny to walk her through the Fried Everything menu while my dad and I slipped away.

I led us around the backside of the food truck and down the grassy sand a few yards so we were out of view from Danny and most everyone else.

"He's a great kid," I started, not wanting to simmer in awkward silence. "Smart and, I gotta say, kind of a smart ass."

Dad laughed, running a hand through his hair. "Yeah, I think we'll keep him." He stopped in his tracks and went grey. "CJ, that's not what I meant, I—"

I held up my hands, sparing him from what, admittedly, would have been an interesting backpedal to watch. "It's fine. I know what you meant. Look, um …" I looked down, kicking the sand. "I stopped opening your mail years ago."

His face fell, but knowingly. "I'm not all that surprised. Why bring that up?"

I sighed, heavy, and looked to the sky. "Danny wants to know if I want to come for Christmas. But I know your girls don't think very much of me—"

"They're just hurt. In ways Danny doesn't understand yet because he's still young enough not to read between all the tense lines."

I tilted my head. "I think he picks up on more than you think he does."

Dad sighed and grinned simultaneously. "I was afraid of that."

"Your wife … what's she like?" I'd avoided asking Danny any questions of his mom, and, thankfully, the conversation never forced us there.

He swallowed hard. "Patient. Lovely."

"Sounds like Mom," I mumbled.

"CJ …" he trailed off, looking out onto the water.

I shook my head. "No, I'm sorry. I am. That was … Jesus … I'm actually sorry."

Because this time, I was talking to Danny's dad. A man he clearly adored. It wasn't just about me anymore.

"God," I continued. "What the fuck do we do now?"

He shrugged, stuffing his hands into his pockets. "Take it from here? Do you … do you want to come for Christmas? Thanksgiving, maybe?"

I worked on swallowing what felt like a boulder while I thought. "Do you guys do anything for Halloween? I feel like that's a low-pressure, no-expectations kind of holiday."

He laughed, sniffing like he'd been holding back tears. "We could start something … together."

I growled, looking down to hide my own traitorous tears. "Why'd you keep coming after me?" I asked, unable to meet his eyes. "Even after I made it clear I wanted nothing to do with you."

There was a long pause. Long enough for me to look up and find my dad staring at me with confusion. "Because I love you, CJ. And when you love someone the way I love you … you keep trying."

"Ugh …" I wiped under my eyes. "I'm still so pissed at you."

"I'm angry with myself, too. I should have tried harder when you were younger, maybe … I don't know." He looked down. This was all too much.

I cleared my throat, wanting nothing more than to get this over with. "Maybe we just needed Danny," I offered.

As his eyes met mine, he was smiling. "Maybe you're right."

"Can we be done now?" I asked, laughing.

"Yep," he answered, then seemed to hesitate, chewing on something to say, maybe.

"What?" I asked, taking a step toward him as I started my way back to Frankie and Danny.

He stared at me in intense silence for a few seconds more, his eyes working over my face like he was being tortured from the inside.

"Wh—"I started to ask again what he wanted, but I didn't get to finish my question.

My dad took one large step forward and wrapped his arms around me, squeezing as tight as I bet he could. It nearly knocked the wind out of me—emotionally more than physically. My first reaction was to push him away, but I couldn't—not without hurting him anyway. And, for the first time in years, I didn't want to hurt him. I kept seeing Danny when I closed my eyes and, eventually, inexplicably, I hugged him back.

My voice cracked and a muffled cry clawed its way out of my throat as I gripped the back of his shirt, holding on for what felt like dear life. He made a similar noise, holding me just as tightly.

I didn't know what it meant or what it would mean for the future. All I knew was I was hugging my dad for the first time since I was younger than Danny. And maybe, if I got out of my own way long enough, something good could come of all this.

EPILOGUE
REGAN.

I T TOOK ME a good couple of years to get used to spending Christmas on the West Coast. Growing up in Massachusetts allowed me to enjoy the delightful stereotypes of the holiday season and take them for granted. Here in La Jolla there were no snow-capped evergreens, no risk of frostbite, and the only snow gear was found in stores filled with people traveling to ski resorts in other states. We had an inflatable snowman in front of the bakery, but that was as close to Frosty as we'd get living out here. But what we lacked in icy precipitation, we made up for in sunshine, and Christmas on the ocean without the risk of pneumonia looming over our heads.

The tour was over, ending with an incredible show at Red Rocks in Colorado. Yardley worked for well over a year to make that show happen, and I'm sure it will go down as one of the greatest experiences of my career, just behind the Grammy win.

Immediately following the conclusion of the six-month tour, CJ flew back to Massachusetts and was settling in with Frankie on a more permanent basis. I think he still had his apartment in Barnstable, but was slowly emptying it and his old life.

Sitting in my favorite oversized armchair in our home, I stared at a lit Christmas tree in the corner of our living room, and the Pacific Ocean out the window. All in the same frame. I breathed in a chest full of gratitude at the hope springing up around me.

"Here you go." Georgia handed me a mug of steaming hot chocolate with a borderline-obscene amount of whipped cream on top.

"Thanks, babe. I talked to CJ today."

"Yeah? How is he? You know …"

I sipped the sinfully delicious drink. Georgia once told me what kind of fancy, shaved chocolate she used to make the drink, but I forgot it all as the heavenly ribbons of rich cocoa swirled over my tongue.

"He says he's going to his dad's," I answered, my voice sounding as encouraged as it was surprised.

"For Christmas Day?" Georgia looked nervous.

I shook my head. "Day after. Halloween went well, but this is much more …"

"Real," she filled in.

"Yeah."

Georgia curled up next to me on the arm of the chair. I shifted to the side enough for her to slide into the corner while I wrapped my free arm around her.

"I think they'll do okay," I continued. "He talks and texts with Danny a lot. He met his dad's wife—"

"His stepmom," Georgia corrected.

I chuckled. "Yeah, that. Old habits … Anyway, I guess things went well with her and the girls. The older one is still a little weird around him, but I'm sure CJ's just as awkward."

"Can you even believe we're having this conversation?" Georgia's voice carried the awed weight of history. One she and I knew all too well. All the anger CJ had. The pain, the frustration, all of it.

"He's really turned himself around. And inside out. I mean … It's really incredible."

Georgia kissed my temple. "Things have certainly changed, haven't they?"

I looked down at my wife, and a glow came from deep within her that was brighter than the tree in front of us.

"Yeah," I grinned, "they certainly have."

During the last three months I was on tour, Georgia and I did a lot of research on adoption. A lot. We tracked down information sessions in La Jolla for her, and in cities where I'd be traveling. If she happened to be with me at a certain stop, we'd go together. Either way, we talked, texted, and emailed constantly about the sessions we'd been to—comparing notes and thoughts and fears. We Skyped a few therapy sessions with Dr. Weeber, and resumed seeing her once a week once the tour ended.

As Georgia and I gazed at the white glow of the Christmas tree, we were in a state of hopeful limbo. We'd filled out the official—and incredibly lengthy—adoption application, and had completed the first of a few interviews earlier in the week. Up next would be more interviews, letters of recommendation, and home visits from a social worker.

We were planning our family.

From what we'd been told at information sessions and from families we met who had been through adoption, the whole application-interview-home visit process would take roughly six months. If everything went through and we were approved for adoption, the agency told us it could take a year or two before we received our child.

We were ready to see it through. To be patient. We did hear a story of a family who received their six-month-old daughter three weeks after they were approved, and while we didn't anticipate this would be the case for us, it did remind us of the uncertainty that can come with adoption. With parenting. Building a family was going to be full of trials, joys, and surprises no matter how we went about it.

"I love you," I said to Georgia. I'd been watching the soft glow of Christmas and impending motherhood radiate from her face for a couple of minutes. She was stunning. And mine.

She gazed up at me softly, and from the white-painted brick fireplace in the living room, an old clock chimed with the notice of midnight.

"Merry Christmas, Regan." Georgia kissed me with a chocolate and whipped cream-flavored kiss. "I love you, too."

"Merry Christmas," I whispered back. "You have no idea how happy I am to be home."

She grinned. "I'm happier to have you home." Georgia nuzzled into my side as we sat in the quiet of the first minutes of Christmas Day. A new beginning.

As of January first, I was slated to draw up a new contract with Grounded Sound. One that would keep me at home for more than ninety percent of the year, and focusing on local outreach. Dates and responsibilities would shift when our child arrived. I'd still be writing and recording, of course, but I'd be doing it from La Jolla, and not all over the continental U.S.

Whether we received the next piece of our family puzzle in the next several months or the next couple of years, it didn't matter. Life was good when I slowed down long enough to realize what had been right in front of me the whole time. And it was only from that point that Georgia and I could focus on the future. Together. As we always had been, and always would be.